WINGED VICTORY

WINGED VICTORY

V. M. YEATES

GRUB STREET · LONDON

First published in 1934 by Jonathan Cape

This edition first published in 2004 by Grub Street Publishing,
4 Rainham Close, London SW11 6SS

Copyright this edition © 2004 Grub Street, London

Reprinted 2005, 2007

Copyright text © V. M. Yeates / Guy Yeates

British Library Cataloguing in Publication Data
Yeates, V. M. (Victor M.), 1897-1934
    Winged victory
    1. World War, 1914-1918 – Aerial operations – Fiction
    2. War stories
    I. Title
    823.9'12[F]

ISDN 978-1-904010-65-4

Cover design by Hugh Adams, AB3 Design

Printed and bound in Great Britain by
MPG Books Ltd, Bodmin, Cornwall

PHASE ONE

'WHAT makes you think you think with your head?' inquired Cundall, alluding to a remark of Williamson's. 'If ever you get a bullet in your seat, I'm sure you'll find it very disturbing to thought. How could that be, if you think with your head only? You might as well say that all business is done in London because that is the seat of government. What about the solar plexus, or Birmingham; the liver, or Manchester? What the liver thinks to-day, the brain thinks to-morrow. After all, the brain is only part of the body, and cerebration is only part of thinking. Haven't you noticed that a fat man never thinks in the same way as a thin man?'

The woman brought their eggs and chips and coffee and two bottles of wine, a Muscat and a claret, for their choice.

'One bottle'll be enough, won't it?' suggested Williamson.

'To start with anyhow. Let's have the Muscat,' said Allen.

Cundall addressed the woman. 'Nous voulons le Muscat si'l vous plait madame.' Madame was the proprietress of the tiny estaminet in the tiny village of Izel-le-Hameau. It was a mile or so from the aerodrome by the path through the fields.

Two gunner subalterns came in for a quick drink. 'Hullo Flying Corps,' said one, 'how's life?'

'Pretty quiet just now. The Huns have got wind up,' Williamson replied.

'Heard about this big push the Huns are supposed to be going to make any minute?'

'Heard about it!' exclaimed Tom Cundall, 'my God, we hear of nothing else. We're not particularly looking forward to it as we've got to go down and shoot it up when it does come.'

'Don't worry,' said the other gunner. 'Personally I don't believe Jerry'll dare come over at all, but if he does all the Flying Corps'll have to do will be to count the corpses.'

'H.Q. seems windy about it,' Williamson commented. 'Sending round reams of bumf.'

'Don't you believe it. They want everyone keyed up, that's all.

They know damn well Jerry can't come over against field artillery and machine guns without getting shot to pieces. By God, I wish the old Hun would come over. We've got every yard zoned and he'll never get as far as our wire. It'll be the biggest shoot-up ever. They haven't even got any tanks.'

'They've got some guns though,' Tom remarked.

'Our front is stiff with them, too; and ammunition, I don't mind telling you.'

The gunners swallowed their drink. 'Well, we must be off. Cheerio.'

'Cheerio.'

'They seem confident enough,' said Allen when the gunners had gone.

'The wish is father to the thought,' answered Williamson. 'You get like that, all blooded up and longing to smash the fellow across the way. It's a different life from ours.'

'Thank God for that,' said Cundall. 'I took up flying with that hope. PBI certainly didn't suit me.'

'I wish I'd had the experience.' Allen was very young, and out for the first time.

'You should have mine if it were transferable,' offered Williamson.

'Marvellous how these Frenchwomen can cook,' Cundall remarked. 'Even a meal of fried eggs and potatoes has style about it. The French have always been attentive to the practical needs of life. In England we've been worrying our heads about political things and theories for a thousand years and neglecting the basis of living. Look how we are, or were, fed. Anyone can make a fortune in England by advertising a remedy for indigestion.'

'Let's have another bottle of wine.' Allen liked to get Cundall talking. He was young enough to admire his flow of verbiage, even if it was sometimes faintly professorial.

Williamson commented on what Cundall had been saying. 'Doesn't that show Englishwomen have failed in comparison with Englishmen? Englishmen have built up what men ought to build up. Look what they have done in science and literature. Yet their womenfolk can't even feed them properly. They are a worthless lot.'

12

'Hear, hear,' Cundall agreed: but Allen revolted. 'Women have been what men have let them be. What chance have they had in a man-ruled world?'

'Plenty of chance to learn cooking,' Cundall replied. 'I agree with Bill. Women are inferior creatures, mentally, physically, morally.' He had had the misfortune a few months previously to be in love with a married woman who used him to make her husband jealous, and then dismissed him. He had got over it, but it left him with a tendency to amuse himself with misogynistic talk; especially when Allen was listening.

'Morally?' Allen was almost indignant. 'Don't talk rot. Everyone knows they are better than men are.'

'Good God,' exclaimed Cundall. 'Pass the wine, Bill. Isn't England the paradise of the enthusiastic amateur, who has almost got official recognition as part of the war? Aren't there already enough war babies to supply a division to the B.E.F. in a few years? And look at the way they gloat over the war.

But Allen interrupted indignantly 'Gloat, you say. My God, d'you think a mother likes to hear of her sons being killed?'

'Not usually, though they like the importance it lends them. They have to pay for their luxuries sometimes.'

'Rot,' said Allen; 'you know you're talking nonsense. It's rotten for women. It's worse to wait at home than go and get on with the war.'

'You don't seem to have convinced the lad, Tom,' said Williamson. 'It's no use telling the truth to the very young. The bitter, old, and wrinkled truth. They won't believe it. They have to find it out for themselves.'

'Lot's of them never do. I doubt whether Allen will ever grow up mentally, even if he lives to be seventy-seven. He will go on thinking women are angels, however much they cheat him sexually and upset his digestion.'

'Oh shut up, Cundall. You talk like some old bird who's been unhappily married for twenty years. Let's have another bottle of wine. Cheer you up.'

'You'll get blotto, drinking at this rate, and in your love for all the sex you'll probably assault the woman here.'

'Not me. There's only one I'm interested in.'

13

'Then you ought to be ashamed of yourself,' said Williamson. 'You're neglecting a lot of deserving young women, I'm sure. An intrepid young birdman like you; tall, good-looking, plenty of money, in pink breeches and trench boots. You must have dozens of them running after you.'

'Dry up, Bill. You and Cundall do nothing but rot. I like you, and all that, but I wish you'd talk sense sometimes. I've got the only girl that matters to me, and what do I care about the others?'

'You'll find out when you've been married a year or two,' replied Cundall.

'Rot, you arid cynic.' Allen pulled a case from his pocket and tenderly took a photograph from it. He handed it to Cundall, who saw the representation of a passable young woman very like a million other passable young women. He glanced up at Allen, and, perceiving how he felt about it, said 'Allen, my son, I congratulate you. Many happy years.' He lifted his glass, and he and Williamson drank the toast.

Allen could hardly speak, being near to tears of alcoholic emotion. 'Thanks,' he said after a little, and then, 'This bloody war'.

'Hullo!' exclaimed Williamson, 'who wants cheering up now? You wait till it's over and we go home conquering heroes. We won't half have a time.'

'Until our blood money's spent, and then there'll be hell to pay.'

'Why?'

'They'll expect us to settle down to three hundred a year jobs while the profiteers have the good time. You'll see.'

'My God, we're not going to put up with that!' Allen said indignantly. 'We're doing the fighting and we're going to have a say in things when it's over. The first people who'll have to be considered will be the fellows who've done the fighting. The profiteers will have to fork out or by God we'll shoot 'em.'

'I hope we shall. Meanwhile we've got the Huns to practise on. You ought to have been with us this morning, Allen, and seen that two-seater go down.'

'Good work,' said Allen. 'I shall be glad when I've got a Hun.'

'Bloodthirsty young scoundrel. How can you be so unfriendly? Pity the poor Hun.'

'Shoot first and pity afterwards. You've got six haven't you, Bill?'

'Counting all the odd quarters and fifteenths when the credit has been divided.'

'Six is damn good. You're a stout fellow, Bill. I wish I'd got six!'

'Huns or bottles of wine?' Tom asked.

A girl came into the room as Tom was speaking, followed at once by madame. She was short and fat and pleased to see the *aviateurs anglais*. She said a great deal they did not clearly understand about *Boches* and *avions*, while her mother smiled in the background. Cundall secured one of her hands, and Williamson the other. Allen, however, would have nothing at all to do with the girl, being heart-bound. Cundall used his French to advantage and was able to establish understanding. They discussed the amenities of Izel in war time very pleasantly. Then he said 'Je serais tout à fait heureux si vous voudriez me donner un tout petit baiser, belle mademoiselle.'

Belle mademoiselle laughed and looked round to smiling madame, who agreed that the brave aviators deserved kissing. She would charge another three francs.

So mademoiselle kissed Cundall and Williamson, and would have done so to Allen, but he blushed and avoided.

'No, I mean non. I say, Cundall, for goodness sake tell her not to.'

They all laughed. 'Monsieur n'aime pas les baisers, hein?' said mademoiselle with great good humour.

'Il aime une demoiselle anglaise avec tout son coeur,' explained Cundall. Soon afterwards they left and walked along the miry footpath to the aerodrome. Williamson remarked that French footpaths always had double tracks, and English only single ones, which showed what unsociable pigs the English were.

'You two seem sociable enough for anyone,' said Allen; 'what the devil you wanted to kiss that fat little French female for beats me. Do you kiss the servants when you're at home?'

'The very young Anglo-Saxon in love,' Cundall commented.

'I think we'd better strangle him, Tom, and bury the body here. No one will know. We will cut off his left ear and send it to his girl with the legend "Faithful unto Death" written in blood on the box.'

It was a cloudy blowy evening with occasional drizzle and an obscured gibbous moon. They were twenty miles behind the lines, and the only indication of war was the everlasting rumble and the distant flashes.

'Looks as though to-morrow might be a washout,' said Williamson.

'Not at dawn, I bet. We've got the dawn show. You're coming, aren't you, Allen?'

'Yes, I start my war to-morrow.'

Cundall and Allen were in C flight, and Williamson was in B flight. Allen was new to the squadron, only having been in France three weeks, which had been spent in practising flying and shooting and bombing. The squadron flew Sopwith Camels, single-seater scouts with rotary engines.

'My engine's been rotten since I over-revved it when we chased a Halberstater that got away.'

'Mine's a peach. It's a genuine Le Rhone Le Rhone.'

'The French are damn good at making engines. . . .'

They arrived at the squadron mess, and Williamson joined in a game of slippery Sam. Allen went to the hut to write letters, as usual. Cundall joined the group sitting round the fire. Desultory talk about the war in the air was going on. Thomson was there, A flight commander, and Bulmer, commander of B flight, and Robinson, who called everybody 'old bean' or 'old tin of fruit', these phrases being brand new (in fact, he was the originator of them). And Franklin, vast and sleepy, who was utterly unaffected by the chances of war. He got into frightful scrapes, and would come home with his machine full of bullet holes and tears. Not content with the usual two shows a day, he often went out alone to look for something to shoot at; but unlike most sportsmen he appeared to enjoy being shot at also. To Tom Cundall he was a mystery. Did he think? Had life any value or meaning for him? He was completely good-natured and good-tempered, and did not appear to dislike anyone or anything; certainly not Germans. To him war seemed a not-too-exciting big game hunt, Tom imagined.

And MacAndrews, C flight commander, who already had a bag of twenty-six Huns, and had been given a flight after only three months in France. He was Canadian, a dangerous man, a born fighter. His efficiency was tremendous, and he was a first-rate leader. He saw everything in the sky within ten miles, never led his flight into a bad position, and he was very successful at surprising unsuspecting Huns, often miles and miles over Hunland. He would drop on them out of the clouds or out of the sun, put an efficacious burst into his selected victim at point blank range, and away. It was too risky to stop and fight perhaps fifteen miles over the lines; one dive and away was the plan. Dog-fighting was an amusement for rather nearer home. Mac usually got his man when he could engineer one of these surprises, a thing which was not easy; and if it was a formation they attacked, the rest of the flight bagged one or two between them as a rule.

He was playing poker with some more of the Canadians of the squadron. At about ten o'clock he strolled over to the fire.

'I guess I'll turn in now. Don't forget we've got the dawn show, Cundall. Bombs.'

'Right you are, Mac. Are you taking Allen?'

'Ay. He's going to be a good lad. He's keen.'

Tom wondered whether the last sentence was a hit at him. He was never quite sure how to take Mac.

11

TOM CUNDALL awoke unwillingly. 'Half-past five, sir. Leave the ground at half-past six,' the batman said. He grunted and turned over. 'Six o'clock, sir,' the batman said.

Tom sat up. His lamp was alight. Allen was washing himself. Williamson and Seddon were asleep in their corners.

'What the hell are you washing for?'

'Because I'm not a dirty pig like you,' retorted Allen. 'Get up, and don't be so lazy and dirty.'

It was cold. Tom put on some clothes and brushed his teeth and his hair. Then he put on his sidcot suit and walked across to the mess with Allen for tea and eggs. The stars were fading, and the sky was clear. It seemed as if it would be one of those brilliant mornings before a dull or rainy day. He seized Allen's arm and declaimed:

> Full many a glorious morning have I seen
>> Flatter the mountain tops with sovereign eye,
> Kissing with golden face the meadows green,
>> Gilding pale streams with heavenly alchemy.

Allen did not interrupt him; then he said: 'You're a weird bloke, Cundall. As a rule you're perfectly foul-minded, but I've never known anyone wallow in poetry like you do.'

'Mind you,' replied Tom, 'the poet is not describing anything he ever saw. It is pure fake. No morning ever was so glorious as those lines, which are a showing forth of the poet's glorious mind.'

'I hope your egg's hard boiled,' Allen retorted. 'Better buck up. They're running engines.'

Mac and Debenham were already in the mess, and Miller, a compatriot of Mac's, came in soon after. Mac gave out instructions.

'Before we do O Pip we're to reconnoitre the ground and look for something to drop bombs on and shoot up. The big push is due any time now and they want reports of all movements. So keep your eyes skinned for anything moving.'

Tom went back to the hut and donned overshoes, flying helmet, and gloves. He put his automatic pistol in his pocket. It might possibly be useful if he had to land on the wrong side of the lines. But he could hardly fight the whole German army with it. It might be better to leave it behind. After hesitation he pocketed it, and then walked to the hangars. It was almost half-past six, and light enough to take off. He climbed into his waiting Camel, which was marked W. Mac, in V, was already running his engine. Tom settled in his seat, and a mechanic called out 'Switch off, petrol on'. Tom answered with the same words, and pumped up pressure, fastened his safety belt, waggled the joystick, kicked the rudder bar, and pulled up the CC gear piston handle, while they turned the engine backwards to suck in gas. He gave his goggles a rub up with his handkerchief. 'Contact' shouted the mechanic, and Tom switched on and answered 'Contact'. The engine started at the first swing. He eased the throttle back and adjusted the petrol flow until it was ticking over. His goggles were misty and he gave them another rub. They would clear after a little. Looking round he saw Mac taxiing out to take off. Miller was following. Tom opened out with a roar, looked at the rev counter, throttled down, and waved his hand. The mechanics pulled away the chocks from the wheels of the under-carriage, and ran round to the rear of the planes to hold the rear struts in order to help him turn.

He swung round and opened out at once. The effell, as the thing was called that showed wind direction, was hanging limp; so he could take off in any direction that gave a clear run.

The grey morning air was as still as cream, and the dizzy ground fled by, leaving him in utter stillness except for engine vibration. He held the Camel's nose down to gain speed, and then pushed the stick over to the left as he let it zoom, doing a steep left-hand climbing turn, his wing-tip almost brushing the ground, and it leapt up with glorious release over the trees that surrounded the mess.

He flattened out, and then put up its nose to climb until the whole machine was shuddering with the strain. He knew what it could do, and kept it there until the aerodrome had become a little lawn and Izel a village in Lilliput.

They were to pick up formation at three thousand feet; but where was everyone? There were four other aeroplanes somewhere quite near him, yet the sky seemed empty. He turned and saw three of them above his right top plane. He flew up to them and took position on Mac's left hand. Debenham was behind and outside him, and Miller on Mac's right. Allen should be behind and outside Miller, but he was not there. Probably he could not find them. Then sud-denly he appeared.

Aeroplanes had this way of appearing and disappearing. Huns loomed up out of nowhere and were gone again as quickly. Many people got shot down without knowing anything about it. But Tom had been out there two months now, and ought to be less surprisable. Seeing in the air was a matter of getting used to the conditions of seeing, knowing what to look for. Inexperienced pilots were shot down easily because they did not see approaching danger; the first weeks over the lines were quite the most dangerous.

In a few minutes they were over Arras, recognizably a town, if a battered one. The sun thrust a glowing shoulder dimly through the eastward murk, but the earth below was still twilit.

It was difficult to make out the features of the ground in front of them. Even the Arras-Bapaume road merged quickly into the undifferentiated greyness. A few clouds, the forerunners of an army, were coming up below them from the south-west on a freshening wind. The bitter desert of the lines passed beneath them.

Mac began zig-zagging about, gradually losing height while he looked for anything interesting that might be visible. About three miles within Hunland they had worked down to two thousand five hundred feet, keeping beyond range of machine-gun fire from the ground. Tom was startled by a pop-pop-pop behind him, and as by reflex he went into a vertical turn; but it was only Debenham trying his guns. He reversed bank and took up position again. He dived and got what might once have been a farmhouse into his Aldis and pressed the trigger on the triangular top piece of the joystick. The two machine guns rattled. He zoomed into formation once more.

The brains, thought Tom, of the Johnnies who made the weapons of war! They invented an engine to drive a two-bladed air-screw at twelve hundred r.p.m. They invented a machine gun that would fire six hundred rounds in a minute, and when the inconvenience was felt of the propeller's masking the fire of the guns, a beneficial genius known as Constantinesco arose and made a gear that synchronized miraculously the absence of a blade with the presence of a bullet. It worked by oil pressure, and having taken a course, he was supposed to know all about it; but the fervid ingenuities of lethal genius were too much for his unmechanized brain. Within the past year, having never before approached nearer to mechanical operations than to clean a rifle, rewasher a tap, or maintain a push bicycle, he was supposed to have mastered the workings of several aero-engines, the Vickers gun and the Lewis gun, photography, the Morse code, aero-dynamics, bombs, the structure and rigging of sundry aeroplanes, and the Constantinesco gear. He was also learning how to fly and how not to get shot down. But why didn't inventors confine their talents to inventing pleasant things? Anyone revising the Inferno would have to make up a new worse-than-any circle for machine gun makers.

A loud double cough made his heart jump. It was Archie taking notice of them, and his first shots were always startling if you weren't thinking about him. The black bursts were right in front, and he flew through them and then turned outwards. Mac circled. It was no use trying to keep strict formation, and the only thing was to keep somewhere near him. Archie put up a lot more stuff to distract them and break up their formation. It was not easy to watch both the heavens and earth closely and keep formation when Archie was coughing with black hate all the while. His sudden spectral appearances were more surprising than dangerous, but it was not advisable to go on flying straight for long when he was active.

Tom wished Mac would go down and drop bombs on some trenches and get it over. It was uncomfortable to be floating over Hunland below three thousand feet, a prey to all the Huns that might care to dive on them, loaded with eighty pounds of bombs. An extra eighty pounds made a lot of difference to a Camel; gave it a water-logged feeling.

He pushed his goggles up and scrutinized the sky anxiously. If they were going to be attacked he was going to drop his bombs. But the sky was clear. The Hun pilots must be sitting a long time over their breakfast sausages. A burst of Archie appeared right over his head. It seemed extraordinary that it had got there without hitting him on the way. Mac was waggling his wings; the 'enemy seen' signal. Tom looked round again, but could not see any enemy. What the hell? Then Mac put his nose down and dived and the rest flopped after him. There was something on a road, difficult to make out. By jove, it was a half a dozen motor lorries, probably with camouflaged tops. They were not moving, hoping to remain unseen; but Mac saw everything. Tracer bullets came streaking up from the ground. Hunland was full of machine guns. You couldn't often see them and didn't know who was shooting or where the next lot was coming from. It was a matter of luck whether you were hit or not.

Tom slewed outwards so as to take the road fore-and-aft, got his sight on to the convoy and released his bombs hurriedly and pulled out of the dive into a climbing turn. His engine spluttered, and he had to push the stick forwards to keep from falling into a spin. What had happened? He was less than four hundred feet up. The pressure gauge had blown. What a racket there was going on when the engine didn't drown it! The proper thing to do was to switch

21

over to the gravity tank. He was losing height quickly. His hand fumbled the switch. Get over, damn you. It went over. Nothing happened. Two hundred feet. He would have to land. What a din of machine guns. Bullets were coming too near. He went into a side-slip. He would have to land near the people they were bombing. Would they kill him? The engine started up with a roar. He zig-zagged about, relief bubbling up from his stomach. Where was he going? He must get home out of this. Home was in the west. My little grey home in the west. Where was the west? He dared not fly straight for a moment. Hunland was full of machine guns. But the more he turned and side-slipped, the faster his compass spun. Where the devil was he? The sun, of course! The sun was in the east. He was flying towards it. He would soon be at Berlin. There was a frightful crack in front of him that made him jerk nearly into a flat spin. Was a field gun taking a shot at him? Guns ought to mind their own business. He put his nose down and loosed off at the puff. There was another terrific crack that seemed to lift him about fifty feet and drop him again, leaving his entrails in the sky. He was frightened to death but damned annoyed and dived and fired again at the puffs, this time from the side. He couldn't see any guns. They seemed to be firing from nowhere, but he felt he had got his own back, and he made off all out with his tail towards the sun. It was best not to climb, but to keep his nose down and trust to speed. It would be difficult for a machine gun Hun to know he was coming if he kept well down on the horizon, and by the time the Hun had got his Parabellum or whatever he called it working, he would be half a mile away. And he was less likely to be noticed from above than if he climbed. The great thing was to get home before the gravity tank was empty.

It took him about two minutes to reach the front line. He kept on turning slightly without banking, so that he was always side-slipping and never going quite the way his nose was pointing. Machine gun fire from the ground was the very devil. This low work was the last occupation on earth for longevity. The German trenches seemed deserted except for an occasional sentry. The others were all asleep in their dugouts dreaming of their sisters-in-law at home. No doubt they were nice lads. It was a shame to shoot at them. He had an instant glimpse of a grey figure raising a rifle at him. He waved and passed on over the barbed wire, but not yet into safety, for a machine gun sent a final dose of hate after him. He heard its rattle, but nothing came of it, and it quickly faded out. Thank God to see khaki again and feel safe.

Not that there had been so much to worry about. He had been upset by his engine spluttering out like that, but if nothing worse than that ever happened to him he wouldn't have much to grumble about. Nevertheless, it was wrong the way pressure gauges blew in a dive: this was not the first time it had happened to him. He tried to pump up pressure with the hand pump, but without success, and floated gently homewards and landed a little after half-past seven. The sergeant fitter came out to see what the matter was. Tom cursed the pressure gauge and got out and took an inventory. There were a few bullet holes dotted about. One was in the side of the cockpit, and he couldn't make out how the bullet had missed him. He shook himself, but no bullet dropped out. A lump of shrapnel was buried in the leading edge of the left-hand top plane.

He went to the hut, where Williamson and Seddon were still asleep. It was no use going up to the office to report, so he got into bed and slept too, until Allen came crashing in.

'Get up, Cundall. Mac wants you up at the office to report. By George, I was glad to see your bus here when we got back. I thought you'd been shot down.'

'Enjoy yourself?' asked Tom, getting out of bed.

'Rather. Good fun diving on that transport. Mac says we cleaned 'em up nicely. Nothing much else happened. We climbed to twelve thousand and did a patrol. The others say we were dived on by some Pfalz scouts. Mac says seven, but Miller swears there were nine. I didn't see any. All I knew was that we were splitarsing around like wet hens for a time. I wondered what it was all about. Anyway, it seems they cleared off after having a look at us. They must have been queer blokes.'

'Huns are queer blokes.'

'They are.' Williamson was awake. 'They won't fight before breakfast. It puts their digestion out for the whole day. Evidently the ones you met were a before-breakfast patrol.'

Allen threw Tom's pillow at him, and they went to the office, where the major was taking the report.

'What happened to you, Cundall?' asked Mac.

Tom told him.

'Can you give me pinpoints for that battery you shot at?' the major wanted to know. Tom did his best.

'The next time anything like that happens to you,' said Mac, 'keep with the flight and give the dud engine signal, and we'll see you back across the lines. You've got a longeron split by a bullet, and it doesn't look safe. You'll have to have Y this afternoon. You'd better take it up after breakfast and see if it's all right.'

III

TOM had a good breakfast, lit his pipe, and went up to the latrines. The morning latrine was quite a social affair. The squadron had an excellent five-compartment house with canvas walls, very convenient for conversation.

'We shall learn one thing from this 'ere war,' said Tom to an unseen audience, 'and that is the social value of the latrine. Visceral activity is undoubtedly stimulating to thought. Besides eating parties we shall have excretory parties, and the *Daily Telegraph* will print glowing burbles about the interior decoration of Mayfair cabinettes.'

This idea was approved, and an interesting quarter of an hour's conversation followed, in connection with which Robinson told a fantastic story about a man who broke into Buckingham Palace in the reign of Queen Victoria.

Der-DER shouted the klaxon in its blaring gurgle, and again der-DER. It was time for A flight to prepare to go up. The klaxon was the major's pet. If he was in the office a little before the time at which a flight was due to go up he morsed A, B, or C with a switch key controlling the klaxon, a powerful instrument attached to a tree in front of the mess. If he was not in the office, the adjutant was supposed to sound it. If nobody was there and the horn was not sounded, the flight went up just the same. Its chief effect was to make people with ragged nerves curse at it.

24

Apart from his klaxon the major did not bother them unduly. He was a shy, ineffective man who made efforts to be convivial on binge nights and did not care for flying Camels. The only flying he did was going up to see if the weather was dud, and his average flying time was about ten minutes a week.

Flying Camels was not everyone's work. They were by far the most difficult of service machines to handle. Many pilots killed themselves by crashing in a right hand spin when they were learning to fly them. A Camel hated an inexperienced hand, and flopped into a frantic spin at the least opportunity. They were unlike ordinary aeroplanes, being quite unstable, immoderately tail-heavy, so light on the controls that the slightest jerk or inaccuracy would hurl them all over the sky, difficult to land, deadly to crash: a list of vices to emasculate the stoutest courage, and the first flight on a Camel was always a terrible ordeal. They were bringing out a two-seater training Camel for dual work, in the hope of reducing that thirty per cent of crashes on first solo flights.

Tom very well remembered his own first effort. Baker, his instructor, had given him a preliminary lecture.

'I suppose you haven't run a Clerget engine before.' (It was a Clerget Camel.) 'You'll find it just like a Le Rhone; you've taken up the Le Rhone Pup, haven't you? You'll find it a bit fierce to start with: you've got another forty horse-power and plenty more revs. You'll soon get to like that. Be careful with your fine adjustment, they're a bit tricky on that. Ease it back as much as you can as soon as you're off the ground, and the higher you get the less juice you'll find she wants. I expect you've heard all about flying them. Be careful of your rudder. You may find it a bit difficult to keep straight at first. Keep just a shade of left rudder on to counteract the twist to the right; when you're on anything like full throttle you can feel the engine pulling to the right all the time. Remember to use the rudder as little as possible, you hardly want any when you turn. But don't be afraid of putting on plenty of bank. A Camel's an aeroplane, not a house with wings, and you can put 'em over vertical and back again quicker than you can say it. I expect you'll find three-quarter throttle or so best for getting used to it. Keep her between eighty and ninety at first. Don't get wind up, and you'll be quite happy.

25

Now this is what I want you to do. Take your time in running the engine on the ground, so as to get used to it, then go straight up to five thousand all out. You'll be up there in no time. You're not to turn or do anything except ease the fine adjustment back below five thousand. Climb at eighty-five. Then you can try turning to the left, all out or throttled down, just as you like. Don't be afraid of spinning. If you do spin, you know how to get out: pull off the petrol and give her plenty of opposite rudder and stick. Have the stick well forward, but don't keep it too far forward when she's coming out, or you'll dive like hell and lose a lot of height and jerk yourself about and lord knows what.'

Tom had got in and run the engine. There wasn't any difficulty about that. He taxied out and turned round. The wind being easterly he had to take off over the hangars. He opened the throttle and the engine roared. Then it spluttered. Hell! He caught a glimpse of people jumping about with excitement. Too much petrol. His hand went to the fine adjustment. By the time he had got the engine running properly he was almost into a hangar with his tail hardly off the ground. He pulled the stick back and staggered into the air just clearing the roof: if the engine gave one more splutter he would stall and crash. But the engine continued to roar uniformly. His heart, having missed several beats, thumped away to make up for them, and he felt emulsified; but he was flying.

The engine was pulling like a chained typhoon. He seemed to be going straight up. Two thousand feet, and he had only just staggered above the hangars! It was difficult to hold the thing down at all; the slightest relaxation of forward pressure on the stick would point it at the very zenith. The day was excellent for flying, there being no wind or bumps. A grey mist was still weakly investing the world, limiting the field of vision, wrapping the horizon in obscurity. At his back the south-westerly sun was touching the greyness and transmuting it into a haze of golden light, blinding to peer into; in front the mist hung like a solid but unattainable wall, ending abruptly in a straight line at some three or four thousand feet, and on it stood the base of the pale grey-blue vault of sky, seeming only a degree less solid.

He soon became aware that he was not flying straight. At first the sensation peculiar to side-slipping had been lost in the major sensation of flying a strange machine, but when his senses were less bewildered by the strangeness of it he became aware of a side-wind, of a secondary vibration within the normal vibration of the engine, of the particular feeling of wrongness that is associated with side-slipping. He had seen beginners doing this sort of thing. A few days previously someone had taken off on a Camel and gone across the aerodrome almost like a flying crab, while everybody held their breath and waited for the side-slip to become a spin and the pilot a corpse; but he had got away with it. Tom had been scornful at the time, but here he was doing much the same sort of thing; he had no idea why. He could fly any ordinary aeroplane straight enough. He experimented with the rudder, but soon came to the conclusion that side-slipping was an ineluctable vice of Camels; at any rate of this one. It would not fly straight for more than a second at a time.

At five thousand feet he put the machine on a level keel in order to try to turn, but flying level brought such an increase of speed and fierceness that he was constrained to throttle down the engine considerably before he could bring himself to put on bank. Then, very carefully, he pressed the stick towards the left and the rudder gently the same way. What happened was that all tension went out of the controls, there was an instant of steep side-slip, and the earth whizzed round in front of him. A spin! At once his hand went to the fine adjustment to shut off the petrol. Full forward opposite stick and rudder stopped the spinning, but he found himself diving vertically and side-slipping badly at the same time. He had fallen from the seat and was hanging in the belt. He pulled himself back into the seat by means of the joystick and set about getting out of the dive. Gradually he brought the nose up to the horizon, or to where it was hidden in the mist, and restarted the engine which roared away furiously.

Looking at the pitot he found the speed was a hundred and twenty, so he eased the stick back and climbed. For some minutes he didn't care to do anything but fly as straight as he could, and it cost him an effort of will to decide to try again to turn. This time he was ready for a spin, and as soon as he felt the controls going soft he came out of the turn. By this means he succeeded in turning through a few degrees without actually spinning, and after a few more such turns he let his strong desire to get back to earth have its way. He made out that he was some way east of Croydon, and it was necessary to turn west. To do this he shut off the engine and brought the machine round in a long sweeping glide. The thing would turn on the glide without spinning, anyhow: that was something. He flew towards the sun until he judged the aerodrome must be close ahead, though it was invisible in the golden haze, and stopped the engine again and soon found himself gliding over the aerodrome at a thousand feet. He started the engine, throttled right down, and buzzed the engine on the thumb switch. To get into the aerodrome he had to perform another complete half-turn, which he did on the glide, not without some qualms about the nearness of the ground. He wouldn't have stopped up any longer for the wealth of all Jewry. He would never make a Camel pilot. He would give up flying and go back to the PBI. He drifted on downwards to land, approaching the aerodrome correctly from leeward, but rather fast, being afraid of stalling and spinning into the ground. He floated across the aerodrome. He suddenly realized he would never get in. His wheels touched the ground and he bounced like a kangaroo. Desperately he opened the throttle. The engine spluttered. He was heading for that same hangar again. He would hit it this time. He moved the fine adjustment and the engine roared. He pulled up and once more staggered over the roof, having caught a glimpse of Baker shaking a fist at him. He held on his way shakily up to three thousand feet, and then shut off the engine and glided back.

This time he hardly reached the aerodrome at all, and opened the throttle, but the engine wouldn't pick up. He just floated over the boundary hedge and pancaked on to the rough ground at the edge of the aerodrome. Luckily the undercarriage stood it. His prop stopped, and he sat there waiting for mechanics to come and swing it: safe, profoundly glad to be back on earth, but feeling a perfect fool.

It took the mechanics a long time to reach him, and that gave Baker time to cool down. All he said was 'Well, how d'you like it?'

'Oh, not too bad,' Tom lied. 'I spun turning.'

'You'll soon get over that, but for the love of heaven don't do that comic taking-off act of yours any more, or you'll smash the only

Camel I've got left, and we shall have to scrape you off with a knife.'

But that was long ago: four months in fact. Or was it four years? Camels were wonderful fliers when you had got used to them, which took about three months of hard flying. At the end of that time you were either dead, a nervous wreck, or the hell of a pilot and a terror to Huns, who were more unwilling to attack Camels than any other sort of machine except perhaps Bristol Fighters. But then Bristol Fighters weren't fair. They combined the advantages of a scout with those of a two-seater. Huns preferred fighting SEs which were stationary engined scouts more like themselves, for the Germans were not using rotary engines except for their exotic triplanes, and the standard Hun scout was the very orthodox Albatros. They knew where they were with SEs, which obeyed the laws of flight and did as properly stabilized aeroplanes ought to do. If you shot at one, allowing correctly for its speed, you would hit it: it would be going the way it looked as if it were going, following its nose. But not so a Camel. A Camel might be going sideways or flat-spinning, or going in any direction except straight backwards. A Camel in danger would do the most queer things, you never knew what next, especially if the pilot was Tom Cundall. And in the more legitimate matter of vertical turns, nothing in the skies could follow in so tight a circle, so that, theoretically speaking, all you had to do when caught miles from home by dozens of Huns was to go into a vertical bank and keep on turning to the right until the Huns got hungry and went down to their black bread and sauerkraut, or it got dark: the difficulty was that you might run out of petrol and have to shoot them all down on the reserve tank, so that it might be as well to shoot them all down at once, as recommended in patriotic circles.

The same with the half-roll. Nothing would half-roll like a Camel. A twitch of the stick and flick of the rudder and you were on your back. The nose dropped at once and you pulled out having made a complete reversal of direction in the least possible time. The half-roll was quite a new invention. Tom had never heard of it before he reached France; but after one of his practice flights, when he had been just throwing the bus about, Jenkins, whom he had known at Croydon, made a remark to him about his half-rolls. Tom accepted the compliment and made inquiries in other directions as to what a half-roll actually was. Thomson, the squadron stunt expert, told him it was just the first half of a roll followed by the second half of a loop; the only stunt useful in fighting. If you were going the wrong way it was the quickest known method of returning in your slipstream.

The roll of course he knew. It was newish, but familiar at Croydon. He had seen George kill himself there by pulling the wings off a Pup with too much rolling. And young Fleming, who had a flair for Camel flying and took to them like an Arab right from his first flight, used to roll a Camel just over the hangars and scare everybody stiff . . . and then one day he broke his neck making a careless bumpy landing; such being life.

And the loop was positively prehistoric. The ancient animated bird-cages that used to flap precariously about just over the chimney-pots with the mistaken notion that they were being aeroplanes, even they on occasion looped the loop, and contemporary newspapers published diagrams with dotted lines and arrows showing how the marvel was accomplished. But the man who first conceived the idea and had the heart to carry it out in one of those flimsy museum pieces must have been a hero of purest descent. Tom did not, however, enjoy looping a Camel, and as there was really no point in doing so, he very seldom did. A stable machine, an SE5 for instance (you could set the adjustable tail-plane, calculate speed and distance, wind up the alarm clock, and go to sleep with the sober certainty of waking up right over your destination), would loop so that you didn't know anything about it except that first it was all sky and no earth, and then all earth and no sky and you must throttle down until things were normal again. But a Camel had to be flown carefully round with exactly the right amount of left rudder, or else it would rear and buck and hang upside down and flop and spin. There was a fellow at Fairlop who spun five thousand feet with the engine full on from a loop. Probably he was not strapped in very tightly and was jerked out of his seat when he fell into the spin and hung with his head above the centre section, unable to pull himself back into the seat because of centrifugality. He must have watched the ground whirling up to hit him for a good half-minute before the light went out: unless, as was remotely possible, he had banged his head on something before he spun. There wasn't enough left to guide the guessing.

That was the worst of being in the flying service: you were always in the front line, even in England.

But it was just this instability that gave Camels their good qualities of quickness in manœuvre. A stable machine had a predilection for normal flying positions, and this had to be overcome every time you wanted to do anything, whereas a Camel had to be held in flying position all the time, and was out of it in a flash. It was nose light, having a rotary engine weighing next to nothing per horse power, and was rigged tail heavy so that you had to be holding her down all the time. Take your hand off the stick and it would rear right up with a terrific jerk and stand on its tail. Moreover, only having dihedral on the bottom plane gave a Camel a very characteristic elevation. You could tell one five miles off, so that Huns had plenty of time to think twice before attacking.

With these unorthodox features, a Camel was a wonderful machine in a scrap. If only it had been fifty per cent faster! There was the rub. A Camel could neither catch anything except by surprise, nor hurry away from an awkward situation, and seldom had the option of accepting or declining combat. But what of it? You couldn't have everything.

Unfortunately they were good machines for ground-strafing. They could dive straight down on anything, and when a few feet off the ground, go straight up again. They practised this on the aerodrome, having a target marked out on the ground. Tom sometimes dived so close to it that he ran into dollops of earth that his bullets kicked up. Once two pieces had hit his head, one after the other, in exactly the same place. This was curious, and made a bruise. Ground-strafing was interesting, but not safe. It was, indeed, the great casualty maker. No one minded much about scrapping with air Huns. There was some risk, certainly, but nearly all the risk was run by the Huns. Except for a few big circuses they were not formidable, and seemed to do their best to lead a quiet life. Their average pilots were very middling indeed in 1918, and they seemed to concentrate all their good men in the circuses. But ground-strafing was another matter. You could do very little to avoid machine-gun fire from the ground. The most cunning and experienced pilot was liable to be brought down, though he might feel perfectly safe upstairs, and cheerfully war against odds. Experience and cunning were everything there, and the war in the air was not too worrying once you were properly acclimatized; but machine-gun fire from the ground no one could get used to.

When Tom had arrived in France for flying duty, not feeling at all sure of his ability to fly a Camel even moderately well, his ears feverish with rumours of enormous casualties among Camel pilots, he was sure his life wasn't worth two sous. Bold, bad, terrific Huns would pounce on him like hawks on a sparrow. But when he got to his squadron he was surprised to find everyone as happy as cats in a dairy. There was no wind up about Camels at all. They seemed to be liked. There were no horrific tales of crashes, such as he had been used to hearing, and as for Huns, anyone listening to Bulmer or Thomson or Robinson might have thought Huns were just queer birds that flapped about the sky to be shot at, and had amusing tricks that added to the gaiety of nations.

He was relieved to find that in quiet times casualties were rare; and it was very quiet then; the depth of winter and the lull after Cambrai. He would not have to go near the line for a month, during which time he would practise flying and shooting and bombing; ferry new machines from the park at Candas; and do orderly dog once a week.

The war in the air wasn't such a bad war, after all.

I V

HAVING finished his pipe, Tom strolled up to the hangars to see about Y. The fruit trees were just beginning to show awareness of the possibility that even in 1918 there would be spring. The orchard would look very pretty in another six weeks, and he hoped he would still be there to see nature's annual tricking out for the pageant of summer. It was soothing to behold the complete indifference of the rest of natural things and processes to the tumults and thuddings and trumpetings of men; a devastating comment or no-comment

32

upon the church-and-press war clamour. And men returned the same frankly by being blindly indifferent to everything except the system erected to meet their passioned interests of the moment.

The squadron occupied for its officers' mess one side of a square farm building which enclosed a yard full of animals and dung. It was quite picturesque, the low stone façade roofed above with old red-brown tiles. There was a plain doorway in the centre, and on each side two windows, giving light to the dining-room and the ante-room. They were comfortable quarters. There was a huge fireplace in each room and a supply of toasting forks. Of course there was a bar, and it was usually well stocked.

In the barns which formed two sides of the courtyard there were kept three ridable horses that had got used to the row of aeroplanes, and would trot about the countryside. Tom, who had no sort of seat, was out on one of these beasts one afternoon, and some silly ass, flying low overhead, let off his machine guns, attacking the target at a ridiculous angle that would send bullets ricocheting all over France. The nag could not put up with it, and bolted for home. Tom hung on, expecting each heavenward lurch to end the partnership, seeing himself with one foot caught in the stirrup having his brains bashed out on the ground. But somehow he was still in the saddle when the horse stopped with a jerk in front of his stable door. He could not but admire the animal's sound instinct in bolting for home on hearing machine-gun fire, but decided he would keep to safer than equestrian amusements; flying, for instance.

The pigs were indistinguishable from English pigs, except for a greater pungency of odour, which was not their own fault. The cows, however, were less ladylike than English cows. Tom missed that air of placid and spinsterish chastity that make English cows and women so irritating to bulls and men. The chickens, too, had not been hatched in the protestant tradition, and lacked moral grandeur. Nevertheless farming seemed to pay in France.

Having read the first hundred and twenty-four pages of *La Terre*, Tom thought he knew something about French peasants, and was always hoping to catch some glimpses of delightful Zolaesque sordidness. So far he had failed. They seemed quiet, hard-working, orderly, polite. On week-days they worked from dawn till dusk, the

C

women in the fields with what men there were. Unlike Gray's friends they did not drive their team afield jocund, but wrapped in impassable blankness. No tricks of aviation could amaze them. Even the near whizz of bullets left them unmoved as they worked within a hundred yards of the ground target. At the most they gazed with monumental stolidity; so they would gaze at an angel sounding the trump of doom on a week-day. Their massive continental plough-horses were very like them.

Y looked all right. They pulled her out and ran the engine. The guns were ready for loading, and when Tom pulled up the CC gear handle it stopped up. There was a little sideways play on the stick to be taken up. The seat was comfortable, the timepiece functioned, the engine gave its revs. Tom dressed and took it up. The sky had clouded over and there was quite a wind blowing from west of south-west. At ten thousand feet there would be a strong west wind; the sort that took one over Cambrai in a few seconds and made the return journey seem like half-an-hour, with Archie taking full advantage of one's difficulties and turning the sky black. It probably cost about five hundred thousand pounds for Archie to bring down a two thousand pound aeroplane; but that did not matter; it was das Krieg.

It climbed well, and in a minute reached the cloud layer, which was at fifteen hundred feet. After a few preliminary obscurings he was involved in the grey deleting mist. The world had gone; dissolved into intangible chaos. Nothing had form except the aeroplane and himself and perhaps that queer circular ghost of a rainbow that sat in the blankness in front. Every motion had ceased, for all the roaring of the engine. Nevertheless, he knew by experience that in this no-world it was necessary to keep the pitot at eighty or more, and the joystick and rudder central, or bad sensations as of dizzy flopping would follow. The mist grew darker. He put his head in the office and flew by the instruments. He kept the speed right but he could feel that all was not well, without being able to tell what might be wrong. The mist brightened. He came suddenly into sunshine. A cloudless blue vault of sky arched over a gleaming floor of ivory rocks. It was all around him in the twinkling of an eye, and the grey chaos away in another universe, a million light years or a few feet distant. The two spheres were as close together and as far apart as life and death. He saw that he was flying with unintentional bank.

The bright glare of uncontaminated space and the cold purity of the air had their usual exhilarating effect. He performed several rolls and contorted in nameless rudder-kicking spasms that spun the sky and cloud-floor jerkily about; and, satisfied that Y was not likely to fall to pieces, he dropped to the floor and contour-chased over its shining hillocks and among its celestial ravines. This was not the majesty of cumulus, with its immitigable towering heights and golden threatening; its soul of fire and shadow; pile on pile of magically suspended gleaming dream-stuff; glory of vision and splendour of reality; shapeless splendour of form; empty solidity; fantastic, mutable, illusory as life itself. This was the level-floating rain-cloud, a layer only a few hundred feet thick, that makes the earth so dull a place when it eclipses the sky, and, concentrating all dullness there, leaves the region above it stainless, and very like conventional heaven. On those refulgent rocks should angels sit; like them insubstantial, glowing like them. Music should they make with golden wires, unheard; hymning the evident godhead of the sun, from whom the radiance flowed of those immaculable spaces: wings faintly shimmering with faint changing colour, and unbeholding eyes. In that passionless bright void joy abode, interfused among cold atoms of the air. Breath there was keen delight, all earthly grossness purged.

He raced over the craggy plain, now dropping into glens, now zooming up slopes, leaping over ridges, wheeling round tors. Sometimes he could not avoid a sudden escarpment, and hurtled against the solid-seeming wall that menaced him with destruction: he would hit it with a shockless crash that expunged the wide universe; but in a flash it was re-created after a second of engulfing greyness. And when he had played long enough in the skiey gardens, he would land on a suitable cloud. He throttled down and glided into the wind along the cloud surface, pulling the stick back to hold off and get his tail down. He settled down on the surface that looked solid enough to support him, but it engulfed him as he stalled, and the nose dropped with a lurch into the darkness and almost at once he was looking at the collied world of fields and trees and roads. It was like a bowl coming up round him. He pulled out of the dive and

35

looked about in the dimness to discover where he was. He recognized a railway and the railhead of Achiet-le-Grand. He headed north-west.

The disadvantage of coming out of the clouds in a vertical dive was that there might be someone flying just below one's point of emergence, and in that case disaster would be complete. The chance was nearly infinitesimal perhaps, but Tom thought his life too precious to be subjected to blind risks. He had been exhilarated beyond his usual caution. If he must land on clouds, he would have to pull out of the stall dive at once, and come gently and circum-spectly into the real world.

He soon found the aerodrome and saw two people contour-chasing over the countryside towards Avesnes. He went to join them: there was often good hunting in that direction, some of the roads being unprotected by trees or telegraph wires. He dived on the aerodrome in passing, intending to put the wind up someone, and suddenly near the ground an RE8 appeared in front of him. With a jerk of the joystick he turned somehow away, missing it by a foot. It was annoying nearly to run into anything, but a confounded Harry Tate! What business had a Harry Tate around their aerodrome? He hoped he had put the wind up its inhabitants, anyhow.

It was bumpy. He chased across the fields towards Avesnes, jumping over obstacles, until he came to a suitably unprotected road. He followed it with wheels two feet off the road, taking its slight curves as accurately as he could with the slight degree of bank he could use. Fortunately the French character, less fantastic than the English, had made their roads fairly straight. He overtook a motor lorry going in the same direction; a covered four tonner empty and open at the back, with a Tommy lounging there like a Carter Paterson's boy. The fellow gazed at the approaching aeroplane with a gape of astonishment and amazement; and seeing that it was about to fly right into the van with him, he turned and leapt to the front end. Tom skipped over the lorry at the last differential instant, a little sad at the failure of British phlegm. Possibly the fellow had yelled as he ran; his mouth had been open. Tom would see if the driver was made of sterner stuff. He pulled up and turned and went back to meet the lorry head on. The driver saw him coming and stopped, and moved as though to jump out. To teach him a lesson Tom turned away without going near him, hoping he would appreciate the snub. Then he went in search of worthier prey. The first thing he met was a Camel marked M. That should be Hudson. He had a scrap with him over the tree-tops, in the course of which he got in Hudson's slipstream and nearly crashed with the jolt it gave him. He regained control just in time to avoid the ground, but was so scared that he flew straight up to a thousand feet, where he began to get into the clouds. They were getting lower, and rain would probably soon set in for the day and the afternoon's job would be washed out. This cheered him up and his heart recovered its normal beat and he went down again. There was no fun in flying comparable with the sport of contour-chasing. As soon as you got up a few hundred feet all the sensation of speed was lost. It was induced by the sight of objects whizzing by, and by this only, and the nearer they were, the more dizzy the feeling of speed. There was really no sensation at all in pure speed. Blindfold, you couldn't tell two miles an hour from two hundred miles an hour. It was the vertiginous back-rush of the world that was efficacious; and this was the one new sensation made possible by science. All the rest were known of old. Even the violent sensations of sudden acceleration and change of direction, such as were abundantly produced by stunting, were only intensifications of the antique pleasures of the swings and roundabouts, and they were too violent to be in themselves pleasurable, and stunts only gratified vanity. Everyone stunted and pretended to enjoy it, and it was a good way of working off surplus nervous energy. But Tom was sure in his own mind that no one really enjoyed stunting for its own sake; admittedly no one liked being taken up in a two-seater and stunted by someone else, in which case the vanity motive was absent. Ninety per cent of stunting was mere vanity and emulation. Intrepid birdmen, said the newspapers; fearless aviators. The young men jeered, but did their best to live up to it.

But contour-chasing was pure joy, charging across country at a hundred miles an hour, flashing past villages where nervous old women swooned as you roared by their bedroom windows, jumping trees and telegraph wires, scattering troops on the march, diving at

37

brass-hats in their expensive cars; in fact being a great nuisance with complete immunity from reprisal. Occasionally a brass-hat would put in a complaint, but it was never possible to track the offending pilot, and as a rule it was all taken in good part, for there was still a certain glamour surrounding the R.F.C. and most people seemed to feel slightly honoured by its snook-cocking. To non-flying folk there was something marvellous about flying, and the aviators who came thundering about their ears were more wonderful than irritating. The newspapers called them knights errant of the air, or possibly knight errants.

Tom saw two choice brass-hats being driven along a tree-bordered road; the red in their hats was visible from far off. Soon they would come to a gap where the road was unprotected by trees for perhaps half a mile. He swooped to meet them there, attacking from the front. The driver stopped the car. Tom hopped, missing the windscreen by a few inches, and went into a turn at once in order to keep the car in sight. The brass-hats were waving their arms; whether in admiration or rage he could not tell. He kept on turning and succeeded in rounding on them in vertical bank, and threatening them with his nether wing-tip. This must surely put the wind up them if alarm could invade brass. It was impossible that they should feel at all confident that an aeroplane right over on its side could be relied on to keep its menacing wing-tip out of their car. As soon as he had passed, the driver started up and scuttled along as fast as he could go to the shelter of the trees. Tom turned again, gaining a little height for a final dive. It was just possible. He dropped on to them as they were reaching shelter, and forced them to crouch, but he had to pull vertically up out of his dive, and his undercarriage swished through the top branches of a tree.

Tom was well satisfied. He had shown those brass-hats plainly that the earth did not belong to them exclusively, and so ministered to the prejudice against brass that all right-minded people had. Moreover there was always the chance that they might be generals, and it was a virtuous act to pay back a tiny bit of the trouble that these real, pukka, regular, Aldershot chiefs heaped on the wretched cannon fodder, enlisted for the duration, in pursuance of their policy of making duration eternal for as many as possible. Into their barrack-square heads, Tom was certain, the doubt never entered whether, when you had killed off all the available fit young men, the residue of the nation was worth fighting for: the weak hearts, the elderly business men making the profits, patriots with urgent jobs at home. There was reason in strafing brass-hats.

The clouds were lowering rapidly, and he returned to the aerodrome, tried his guns on the target, and landed. He told the sergeant rigger he wanted Y a shade more tail heavy. There was an RE8 outside the next hangar.

'I wonder if that's the Harry Tate I nearly hit,' Tom remarked.

'That's the one, sir. It's General Mitchell's. He's here. I believe you rather put the wind up him.'

Tom kept out of the way till lunch, but the general did not go, and had lunch in the mess. Afterwards he harangued them about the great German push that was expected to start at any moment. A great deal would depend on their efforts, both in keeping command of the air and in bombing and shooting the attacking troops. It would also be their job to report the exact position of the front line. All this would entail difficult and dangerous work, but he had every confidence in them. Then he let his monocle hang by its cord, detached his pilot from the bar, and set off in his Harry Tate through the rain back to his château.

The major spoke to Tom about it. 'That was you that dove on General Mitchell, wasn't it?'

'Yes, major. I'd no idea it was he. I hope he wasn't annoyed about it.'

'He wasn't very pleased. He said you only cleared him by inches. Then he said it was remarkable flying and he hoped that was how you attacked the enemy.'

'He evidently wants me shot down,' replied Tom; but the incident had turned out quite well.

v

Tom Cundall was blaming the Victorian Age. 'We've still got some left-overs from it, and at this moment some of them are sitting at home writing sentimental poetry about the war. That they know

39

nothing about it makes no difference: they are professional poets, and can sentimentalize anything. They learn in others' suffering what they teach in slop.'

'Wonderful,' said Williamson. 'This is the life for me. We sit here for hours discoursing like elderly professors on a walking tour. Think how we'd be cursing the Huns if we were in the lines among the lice and rats and mud and h.e.'

'And in England,' said Seddon, 'we'd be irritated with propagandists and patriots and wind-up merchants.'

'And women,' added Tom.

'Whereas in this blessed R.F.C.,' Williamson continued, 'we live cleanly and fight cleanly. We are the only sane and reasonable people left in Europe or America.'

Here Allen came in with a rush out of the rain. 'What a perfectly bloodstained day. The French climate is as bad as the English.'

'My God,' exclaimed Williamson, 'here's a man complaining about a dud day! Is the war over, Allen?'

It was so long since he had heard anyone do anything about the rain except bless it, that Tom felt unduly irritated with Allen.

'You know, Allen, you're too pure and good for this world. I believe you believe all the church and the press and the other recruiting people tell you about fighting for your king and country.'

'Don't you take any notice of them, Allen,' said Seddon; 'they're a pair of juiceless cynics, especially Tom. Preserve your charming naivety. It's akin to genius.'

'I'm certainly not a genius, and I thought it was an infinite cap—'

'Shut up, for God's sake,' shouted Tom. 'What a ghastly place the world would be if genius were the virtues of mercantile pettifoggers.'

'The world is a ghastly place,' remarked Seddon.

'What you lack,' said Tom, 'is philosophic detachment'.

'Well I'm damned,' said Williamson. 'You're a nice one to talk about philosophic detachment. And you wait till you come back from a job with your hand shaking so that you spill your drink, and then try some philosophic detachment.'

'But I don't think it will shake; not because of the war anyhow.

And I don't remember having seen you blokes spill any drink except through being tight, either.'

'Hear, hear,' Allen broke in. 'Quite right, Cundall. I believe Williamson's got wind up.'

Tom turned on him. 'Allen, you've got the makings of a first-class prig. And if you can't talk sense, for Christ's sake don't butt in.'

'Good Lord,' said Allen, astonished, 'can't you put up with a joke? I shouldn't have said it if I had thought it was true.'

'Tom, you're getting nervy,' said Seddon. 'Irritability is a sure sign.'

'No. I've always been irritable. My chief vice. Allen, I'm sorry.'

'What a confession for a philosopher!' laughed Williamson.

'Bill, you are without true politeness. The *preux chevalier* never takes advantage of a confession.'

'*Preux chevalier!*' Seddon mocked. 'There aren't any in wartime. He may have put in an appearance rarely at jousts, but never in battle. Battle always goes in favour of the blackguards, who, for instance, dive on an unsuspecting enemy out of the sun. Who beat the Trojans? Not Achilles, but Odysseus. . . .'

'But Achilles was a blackguard,' Williamson objected.

'Not by Greek standards, whereas Odysseus was a blackguard by any standards. It's always the same. Fighting is essentially a blackguard's job. And look at the gang we're fighting for.' Seddon walked over to the stove, opened it, and spat.

'I say, what's the idea?' Allen protested. 'England's not so bad as all that.'

'England!' Seddon exclaimed, 'do you think we're fighting for England? In private life I'm a ruddy bank clerk, and it's some of those big bank balances we're fighting for. They're not England: they're what gangs of financiers, Jew and Gentile, get out of England. It's too damn funny the way the people think England belongs to them because they've nearly all got a vote, whereas it is parcelled out among a lot of blasted tradesmen who run it as a business for their own profit.'

Allen was puzzled. 'Do you think that's true? I've never heard anything like it before.'

'No,' said Tom, 'it's not true. Nothing is true except what you read in the papers.'

Allen laughed. 'You three are a queer bunch of birds. I like to hear you talk. It makes up a bit for not going to Oxford.'

'Is that all you think of our conversation? Undergraduate stuff?'

'Anyway, now we're all here, what about some bridge?' said Tom. It wasn't a bad life, four in a hut. They got on pretty well together and liked bridge, but not too much bridge.

'There's a tender going into Avesnes at six o'clock,' said Allen. 'What about going?'

They agreed to make the outing, and settled down at the home-made table with the comfortable prospect of three hours' bridge and a French-cooked meal. The table was rickety, but it served. Tom would never have believed what a trouble it was to make a table that would stand evenly on its four legs, but that he had the experience of doing it. The table had cost him and Williamson and Seddon and Johnson (now deceased) a great deal of trouble, but there it was, a veritable, usable table, covered with a green cloth that Tom had purchased in Doullens for 14 francs 50 centimes, which was about four times its value. He had walked into a suitable looking shop and demanded a *couverture pour table*. Never having used the phrase before, he accented the *cou*, and the woman failed to understand him. He repeated it. Why the devil couldn't she understand? These low-class Frenchwomen were so confoundedly dense. After several repetitions, light came to her. 'Ah, couveRture,' she cried with that mouthing of the word that seems such bad taste to Anglo-Saxons, and produced table-cloths. He chose a green one, paid the price she asked, and went in search of carpet, but first had café-cognac at an estaminet. In estaminets they were more intelligent, or more used to the English. After a few drinks he sometimes had entrancing conversations with the natives; on that day he got talking to a savant Frenchman who told him that women should never drink café au lait, as it produced irregularities. He bought a mirror, a square of carpet, a lamp, some writing paper, a bottle of mouth wash, and one of eau de cologne, and a block of alum.

The hut was heated by a large tortoise stove. There was a door at each end of the hut, and four small windows. It was apt to get stuffy.

Tom had impressed on the hut his taste in pictures by sending for a supply of prints of such familiar spectacles as The Avenue at Middleharnis, The Haywain, The Mill on Mousehold Heath.

In this abode they dwelt in peace, far from womanly interference. Batmen did the work with a devoted assiduity which was so disinterested as to deserve the name of virtue; whereas women always demanded appreciation of what they did.

And yet there was young Allen, who had several things still to learn about bridge, aching for contact with some young woman from whose web he ought to be joyful to escape. And even Seddon, Tom feared, was not entirely free from desire for his wife's governance; she had the hold over him that two young children give. But Seddon was decently reticent about his domestic desires, and it was not easy to detect the taint. But there the taint was. Williamson and himself were quite free from it.

'If you spent less time thinking about your girl, Allen, and more in mastering the art of bridge, you might know that the jack should be led from king, jack, ten. . . .'

'I don't see that,' Allen interrupted.

'. . . and that when a man discards high he wants that suit led,' Cundall finished.

'Oh, leave Allen alone and come and have some tea. Life's too short for post mortems,' said Williamson.

There was a good toasting fire, and both gentleman's relish and paté de foie gras, besides some jam of indeterminate composition and slab cake of sturdy British manufacture. After tea Seddon and Allen exercised themselves with a bout of ping-pong, for which game Seddon had a gift, being able to smash with wonderful accuracy from quite ordinary bounces, and when he had defeated Allen twice they went back to the hut and continued the bridge until it was time to embark in the tender for Avesnes.

At the Poisson Rouge Lucie *cher-amied* them and stroked their heads and chattered and demanded the news. She was not beautiful, but she was easy; she admittedly had a figure; and she was as vivacious as a sparrow. It was all that Allen could do to maintain the distance he thought proper. She brought vermouth, and they arranged to have soup, lobster salad, roast veal with peas and potatoes, and

Camembert cheese. Tom took advantage of his superior knowledge of French to discuss Allen with Lucie. The poor boy was of a melancholy nature. He needed to rejoice. It was a pity that one so young, who might be killed any day, should not be more happy.

They had some good St. Julien, and talked shop when Lucie was not fluttering around. The coming German push was an inevitable subject. The decisive struggle that would really end the war seemed to be approaching, and according to the verbiage of brigadiers and colonels the Camel squadrons would be expected to stop the German advance by ground-strafing: a gloomy prospect, but one that could be discussed with becoming levity when they were fortified with such a dinner as they were having. The chance of surviving continuous low work for, say, a fortnight was not great. To do so meant being missed by several million machine-gun bullets aimed particularly and personally at one. But a few bottles of St. Julien lessened the probable duration of the Hun offensive considerably. It might well be smashed within a few days. And then for Berlin.

Camels weren't the only air people involved. There was a rumour that Nines were being fitted with pom-poms firing a one-inch shell. Were DH9s going to be used for ground-strafing? It would be difficult for the Hun emma gees to miss them. They would be sending blimps next. Presumably the SEs would have to look after things upstairs on their own for the time being. They didn't have to do much low work, lucky devils. While the Camels were winning the war on the floor, they would merely have to scare away the Albatros and Pfalz, and eat any two-seaters that got within reach. And when an SE pilot wanted a rest it was so easy for him to make a bad landing and write off his bus. There was an SE squadron just round the corner, more or less on the same aerodrome, and every day there was an undercarriage smashed, sometimes a complete turn-over. It seemed quite the expected thing. They said SEs didn't like the ground.

No, but the SE blokes put their backs into it sometimes. Most of the big Hun getters flew SEs. Being twice as fast as Camels, nearly, they could catch Huns. They went miles and miles into Hunland and dogfought like blazes. They had more pitched battles than Camels and their entertainment and that of Bristol Fighters kept the Huns busy doing defensive patrols a bowshot from their bower-eaves. Altogether the Huns had been having a bad time of it in the air lately, and were definitely on the defensive, and it was reckoned that five of their machines were knocked down for one British, in spite of their enormous expenditure on Archie. They were trying all sorts of new scouts. There was the Fokker triplane that was fearsome to look at and climbed straight up like a lark, but had a way of falling to pieces in the heat of battle. And a Fokker biplane that might be a little better than an Albatros but nothing to bother about. Someone had sworn to having shot at a scout with two tail-planes, and reports of other strange scouts were rife, but it was easier, as with miracles, to believe that the reporters were seeing imaginatively. Of course there were dangerous Huns about, circuses like Richthofen's, but they weren't met frequently on that front, and the German habit of draining their best pilots away into circuses left the ordinary people very ordinary.

Allen became more human under the influence of the feast, and lost starch in the flow of Lucie's chirruping admiration of her brave aviators. His nerves would not keep perfectly quiet with her caressing hand on his shoulder; his heart refused to be unaware. But he was only eighteen, and Anglo-Saxon, so he knew Right from Wrong. Alcohol acted on his moral nerve as it might on an aching tooth; it dulled the throb but left an awareness. The final result was that when they left he followed the example of the others and kissed Lucie good night.

It had cleared up, and they set out to walk the four miles back to the aerodrome. Tom and Williamson argued about poetry, with occasional comments from Seddon, but Allen was pensive.

When they were settling down for the night, Allen was looking very gloomy. After some urging he confessed what was troubling him.

'I kissed that girl.'

'That's nothing to be sorry for,' said Tom.

'Are you worrying about the girl at home?' asked Williamson. 'If so, remember that she doesn't know anything about it, and as kissing's no crime, don't bother your head any more.'

Allen shook his head.

'Look here,' said Seddon. 'I appreciate your scruples, but as you are penitent and she doesn't know, it's over and done with.'

'She will know,' said Allen. 'I shall write and tell her.'

'No, don't,' urged Williamson. 'It's fantastic.'

'I must. I should never be able to face her unless. I shall feel rotten until she forgives me.'

'Good God,' they said; 'Good God.'

V I

TOM was awakened in the morning by Williamson coming back from the early job.

'Hullo Bill. What sort of a job?'

'Oh pretty bloody! I came back with two bombs on. The plug wire's getting stretched. I hate not being able to get rid of all my bombs. What the devil happens when a bullet hits one? Muir hasn't come back.'

'Shot down?'

'I expect so. We were machine-gunned like hell from the ground. He just vanished. Nobody saw him go.'

'I hope the Huns are giving him a good breakfast if he's not coming back; or a good burial. Did you see anything to bomb?'

'No. It was so quiet you'd think all the Huns were dead, except Archie, and he wasn't much good this morning. But when we went down and bombed some trenches there seemed to be hundreds of machine guns waiting for us. I don't think we did much damage. We climbed and did a patrol four strong. A bunch of Albatri dived on us. They loosed off a few bursts at long range, but didn't do any damage. They kept too high for us to get a shot at them. We had a climbing match, but when we got to fifteen thousand feet they cleared off. I expect they felt the cold. It was bitter up there this morning. I'm afraid of frostbite. Anyhow, we didn't see any more of them.'

Tom was only due for one job that day, C flight having a Close Offensive Patrol at half-past ten. Low bombing was only the order for the dawn job. The Germans made all their movements as far

46

as possible under cover of night, but early birds might occasionally catch a worm of some sort, and movements might be seen that would give information about the scope of the coming attack. But the later jobs were devoted to patrolling the heights, far from the gloomy war-bitten earth. Up there machine guns were attached to aeroplanes and you knew who and what was shooting at you, and Archie was merely entertaining after the rigours of ground-strafing. He made flying interesting, and only occasionally came too close. What a fervent and consistent hater he was, and what a lot he spent on his black hating with little result! Tom sometimes wished the Germans would offer him the price of the shells Archie fired at him in a month, to retire from the war.

Archie had his uses apart from the actual shooting down of aeroplanes, or even German war chiefs might have noticed his inadequacy. He was a useful adjunct to their defensive strategy because he made it difficult to surprise Huns. Archie bursts were very much plainer to see in the sky than aeroplanes, and by giving British machines an accompaniment of black smudges he advertised their presence to all the world. He protected his two-seaters doing shoots admirably. At the approach of an enemy formation he would put up a burst near his two-seater as if to say 'look out', and follow it up with a row of bursts pointing to the enemy. At this the two-seater sent down a signal to his battery meaning *auf wiedersehen* and put his nose down and went away out of it. Indeed, the observer could get on with his spotting quite comfortably when there weren't many clouds near, knowing that Archie would tell him anything he ought to know.

The British Archie, white bursting, high explosive, did what he could in the way of warning, but as the war was always over Hunland, his job was not so easy. Nevertheless he occasionally gave warning of invisible Huns high up in the sun, and it was always pleasant to be greeted by a friend in the wastes of sky. He was useful, too, for confirming doubtful victims. It was his business to see everything that happened aloft within range of his telescopes, and he was on the telephone, and you could ring him up, give him time and pinpoints, and he could usually tell you all about your scrap, and whether the Hun that spun away really crashed. Of course, if you were miles away over Hunland, or dodging among clouds, he couldn't help, but otherwise he did what he could to justify his pleasant existence. It was said that once he brought down an Enemy Aircraft, but the story was apocryphal.

Mac had a great thought at breakfast. They would take off in formation. That meant that they could head straight for the lines instead of wasting time wandering round the aerodrome picking up formation in the air, and so save ten minutes. They carried enough petrol for a two hours' flight, and a small reserve supply in the gravity tank. Allowing ten minutes to pick up formation, fifteen minutes to reach the lines and fifteen minutes to return, this meant an hour and twenty minutes of actual warfare in each patrol. Mac's idea of bringing this up to an hour and a half did not seem to Tom a particularly good one. Unpleasant things might happen in that ten minutes.

The whole squadron turned out to see them off. The personnel of the flight was altered from that of the previous day by Taylor's taking Debenham's place, as it was Debenham's day off. Mac taxied out, and they followed into their positions, spacing at twenty yards intervals. When Mac saw that they were ready he waved his hand, and they all opened out and took off in perfect order. It was all very simple, and it seemed absurd that no one had thought of it before. And as far as the actual manœuvre was concerned, it was agreeable. Five machines taking off together in pattern gave an air to the business. Never again could the straggling one-by-one take-off be tolerated. It was immediately superseded, ridiculous, amateurish. Here was style; here was efficiency; here was the way to win the war. All scouts would have to take off like it. It was a new departure in war flying. What with Robinson's invention of a phrase like 'old bean' and Mac's invention of taking off in formation, the squadron certainly was leading the world.

They went over Arras at about eight thousand feet. There was a belt of cloud and mist five or six thousand feet below, giving a definite horizon, and obscuring the floor completely except for a pear-shaped patch directly underneath tapering away from the south-eastern sun. The sky was clear but of whitish blue.

They flew unhurriyingly as far south as Bapaume, which was the extent of their front. Everything was calm and peaceful. Archie barked occasionally when he judged they had forgotten about him, but he was pleasantly inaccurate probably owing to bad visibility. The war was a thousand miles away. There were some Dolphins dotting the empyrean at an enormous height away out of reach of all mundane things but Archie's loftiest flights. They saw a bunch of nine Bristol Fighters coming from an Archie barrage in the far east. But it seemed to be a Hun's holiday.

Mac suddenly dived away just to lose height. Tom wished he wouldn't do it so unnecessarily. The quickly changing air pressure made his ear drums crackle and from time to time cease to function. Mac dropped some four thousand feet, floated about a little, and then went down below the clouds to see if there were any two-seaters to chase. They met a couple of Harry Tates and an Ak-W buzzing about industriously on their business of shoots or reconnaissance, and kept near them each in turn for a while to cheer them up. The observers would be able to watch the ground more intently while they were confident of protection; without which the sky was apt to be more interesting to them than the floor, especially when there was some cloud just overhead. It was no joke for a Harry Tate to be surprised by scouts. They were slow, old-maidish buses, very suitable for conveying elderly generals on tours of visits. The daring pilot who put on more than about forty-five degrees of bank might find himself in a spin, and as it was said to take five minutes and a special incantation to get an RE8 out of a spin, the result was often fatal. To go on active service in such an ark was an occupation for heroes, although the people who flew them did not appear to think themselves so heroic as unfortunate. Inexplicably, most of them seemed to come from the Midlands; and heroism in England, Tom noticed, only prevailed north of Dee and Humber and south of Thames. He was not going by statistics, but by conversation.

They returned with an entirely negative report after a pleasant outing. Possibly this was the lull before the storm. If so, the Germans were camouflaging their preparations well. They were keeping their troops away out of sight, perhaps, and would march them up at the last moment straight to the attack. It must be known soon, for the attack could not be put off much longer. Every day brought more citizens of the United States of America to Europe to be destroyed in the interests of civilization. There were already many there, both terrestrial and aerial, but only a few of the latter had passed the training stage. These flying Yanks Tom thought were extraordinarily nice fellows. Apart from their unusually vivid use of English and money, they settled down as typical hard-drinking but modest members of the R.F.C.

An American canteen had been established near Izel, and Tom had gone into it one day to see if there was anything interesting to buy there, but at the moment the stock consisted of tobacco, chewing gum, safety razors, and ink. They were quite pleased to see him; in fact the sergeant or whatever he was that was in charge, called him buddy, which sounded like a term of affection. They must have a deep affection for something, he thought, to come so far from home for the doubtful pleasure of fighting a war everyone else was sick to death of. Why had they come into it? He would ask Seddon. Seddon was sure to have a theory. He bought some cigarettes called Camel.

Certainly the storm must come soon. The American invasion meant certain defeat for the Associated Powers later in the year, unless, bringing their victorious troops from the east, they could smash the Allies on the western front within the next month. The advance would be ruthless and there should be plenty of ground targets. Perhaps the greatest factor in favour of the Allies was British air supremacy. In early 1918 it was as complete as the supremacy at sea. Tom's own notion was that the Canadians were very much to be thanked for this, and, much as he disliked their national expletive, he was very glad he was on their side when it came to a scrap. They seemed to have all the qualities of a scout pilot that Tom had been told at Turnberry (where he had spent a fortnight playing bridge and catching chills while supposed to be taking a course of aerial gunnery) he ought to have; and the Turnberry virtues included everything a committee of brass-hats could wish in their eldest sons except that polish that gives such lustre to brass but is irrelevant to piloting. But however obtained, this supremacy was to be exploited to the height to check the German attack.

In the afternoon A flight had a job at two o'clock. Moss smashed his prop taking off and Chapman soon returned with his engine missing on most cylinders, so it sounded, and Thomson only had Seddon and Maitland with him.

'These cursed rotaries,' Chapman grumbled. 'They do nothing but throw oil and foul plugs. I wish to God I could get on SEs.' He was always neat and elegant, and hated castor oil.

A lorry arrived at the aerodrome with some Guards machine gunners and a couple of camera guns with ring sights. Tom and some others went up to fly for them, doing imitation trench-strafing while the Guards took pictures with their camera guns to see if they were getting the right deflection. The British were beginning to take seriously the possibility of operating against low-flying aeroplanes by ground machine guns. The Germans already knew all about it; they had so much more practice.

By the time Tom had finished trying to overcome guardee imperturbability, A flight had landed and B flight had taken off. A large consignment of bombs and ammunition had arrived, which gave Chadwick, the armament officer, something to see to, and he felt he had earned his tea. There was honey. Chadwick had crashed badly and disarranged his profile a little and upset his nerves for flying. In consideration of these disabilities and his service in the infantry, a comfortable job had been found for him and he had become a penguin, as those were called that had wings but did not fly. As he was hard-minded, smooth-mannered, and amorous, he had great success among French women in spite of the slight derangement of his features. Casanova, Tom called him when he wanted to please him.

A flight had got a Hun, Seddon told him. They had found seven Pfalz scouts worrying an unfortunate RE8. Tommy had shot down one of them out of control and the rest had cleared off. Pfalz seldom stopped to fight. If they had a big advantage of height they would dive and zoom, but without this advantage they would never dogfight Camels. They were safety first, long range merchants. The Pfalz was a very pretty aeroplane, and quite fast, but it looked too frail to stand the sort of pulling about an aeroplane got in the heat of battle. They were very slight where the fuselage tapered into the

51

tail-plane. It seemed that people who had to fly them had wind up tremendously. One had landed, new and silver-glittering, on a neighbouring aerodrome, its pilot being weary of the war. He considered it murder to be put on Pfalz; but he obviously could not be accepted as a typical case.

After tea the Guards departed, and a parcel arrived for the mess president. It was from the *Daily Express*, and contained games: ludo and halma. They were greeted with hoots and derision, but soon some enterprising people found out that you could have quite a good gamble at ludo. Every time you were pipped you paid a franc to the pipper, and drew a franc all round for each counter home. There was a twelve-franc pool for the winner. Soon there was a great demand for the two ludo sets, and shouts of agony and exultation shook the mess as chasings and pippings proceeded. It took the R.F.C. to discover how exciting ludo might be.

Then a Royal Fusilier band arrived to play in the ante-room during dinner. The wing colonel was expected, and no less a person than McCudden, who was doing a tour of encouragement before returning to England. In view of the special occasion, James, the adjutant and P.M.C., had secured a few oysters. There were five each for ordinary people and probably a few extra at the top of the table. Otherwise the meal was the usual joint and two vegetables affair with an inferior champagne. Some port was consumed in toasts, but a real binge did not develop as the occasion was more or less official and McCudden was quiet and not disposed to riotousness. Tom found him a fount of information, about two-seaters particularly. He knew all their habits and weaknesses and liked to tackle them single-handed. He would sit about high up alone on a favourable day and wait for a two-seater to appear. He did not attract much attention high up alone, and was often able to drop out of the sun or a cloud and shoot the Hun unawares. Or if the Hun had warning and made off, he got into position under its tail and waited till he couldn't miss. If you sat properly under its tail-plane, the Hun couldn't touch you. Of course, you had to keep there; that was a matter of flying, and a scout ought always to outfly a two-seater. Then, when the Hun flew straight for a quarter of a second, you put in a burst. One burst should always be enough. Good gunnery was the key to

Hun-getting. The finest pilot on earth was little use unless he had the nerve to shoot from point blank range.

McCudden flew an SE5, and it was all very well for SE merchants to sit under two-seaters' tails and wait for them to pose for a photograph (which anyhow wasn't so easy as it sounded when these supermen with rows of ribbons gave recipes). SE5s had water-cooled stationary engines; Hispano Viper engines that you could rev to blazes. But it was different with Camels. Their air-cooled Le Rhones would melt and drip at 1,500 r.p.m. You had to dive and shoot, or the two-seater would walk away and apply for a pair of Iron Crosses for having outwitted a lot of horrid Camels.

At least two Camels should work together against a two-seater; while the observer was firing at one the other killed him. The same might be said of any other scout, for it took a great man like McCudden to work alone. Tom tried to put this to him, but his view was that any really determined man who would practise shooting could do as much as he had done.

The band departed at nine o'clock. Chadwick struck up a tune on his mandoline and Hudson accompanied him on the piano. Hudson could play quite well. He had an accommodating disposition, and made any sort of noise that was in demand. But Chadwick attacked his mandoline with a real and assiduous liking for the unsophisticated tunes he was able to produce. Singing began to take the place of talking shop. James and Thomson, or Jimmy and Tommy, did a dance that was quite funny. Jimmy was large and fat. He had a worried expression, and it was universally agreed that he was absolutely priceless when he was tight. He said the most priceless things. Tom could never remember any of them afterwards, except his usual oath 'God spare my teeth', but at the time they certainly sounded priceless. Tommy was short and slight, so much so that his flight complained that he climbed away from them, his bus having so little to carry. He had M.C. and Bar and was recommended for D.S.O. He was one of those people that seem incapable of coming to any sort of harm. He had never crashed and bullets refused to go near him. There never was a nicer fellow. He had shot down about two dozen Huns, and a day or two previously had tackled single-handed six Albatri that were attacking a Harry Tate and had driven

53

them off. He was easy-going, and a great man for a sing-song or a rag. He was due to go on Home Establishment, and would be leaving any day.

The evening did not develop well. Tom became bored and went to the hut. Allen had been there since dinner composing one of his tremendous letters. Williamson was also there, reading. Tom wrote a letter home to say that his leave, which was due in a month, would probably be interfered with by the expected German push. He hated writing letters.

VII

SEDDON came in towards ten o'clock looking pleased with himself.

'Feeling good to-night?' inquired Tom.

'You're a lot of weary willies,' said Seddon, 'all creeping back here instead of helping the troops to rejoice.'

'Aren't you on the early job, Seddon?' Williamson demanded.

'No, darling. It's my day off. But what the hell would that matter anyway?'

'Look,' said Tom. 'I want to ask you a serious question, so pull yourself together and hearken.'

'Now what's bothering your baby mind?'

'Tell me, for I'm sure you know, why did America come into this war?'

Seddon was delighted. 'Inevitable sooner or later. The immediate cause was the Russian collapse putting the Allies in danger of defeat. You see, this war is being financed for the Allies by an international gang that works London, Paris, and New York. It was getting hold of Berlin as well. It dominated St. Petersburg completely, pensioning the government. Roughly it ruled the roost in the whole of so-called western civilization and its dependencies, except the central European block against which we are fighting. It was getting a grip on these, and that is the fundamental cause of the war. For there's one thing financiers cannot or will not see. They have visions of a frontierless world in which their operations will proceed without hindrance and make all human activities dependent on them; but their world state is impossible because finance is sterile, and a state living by finance must always have neighbours from which to suck blood, or it is like a dog eating its own tail. And as the financiers widen their influence it is the ever-lessening group of nations to which they are fastening tentacles that bears the ever-increasing brunt. In a sense, then, this war is a Germanic revolt against the international Jew. In another sense it is a clash of financial despotism with industrial despotism. In another it is a conflict of incompatible imperialisms. In another, a struggle for land for national expansion. But the side on which America has been brought in is the side of international finance. Enormous sums have been invested in this war, and an Allied victory is essential to preserve them as capital. You must understand that all this money that is being lavished on war supplies is not wiped out as it is spent; not a bit of it; it's mounting up as national debt, huge blocks of which are held by members and nominees of the gang. When the Associated Powers have been defeated at the cost of a few million more lives, including ours, and peace has been dictated to them, the gang will own a further hold over the Allies in the form of millions of pounds of gilt-edge security. And you may be sure Germany will be held down in the mud and kicked. There'll be a famous orgy of money snatching over our bones.

'To return to America, the danger of an Allied defeat, that is to say, of the collapse of all that gilt-edge security, had to be averted. Those awful Russians! They let down their masters as much as their masters let them down. So the American politicians were told to be ready for a change of popular feeling, and an intense war-fever inoculation was carried out by the press. It took rather less than three months, I believe, to make the popular demand for war irresistible. That is the reason for the entry of America into our wonderful war. You asked me.'

A silence followed Seddon's unexpected oration. Allen looked so overcome with astonishment that Tom burst out laughing, and the others joined in.

'No,' remonstrated Allen, 'don't laugh about it. Do you mean all that, Seddon?'

'Of course I mean it. D'you think I could make up all that as I went along?'

'That's not the only way of looking at it,' said Tom. 'Seddon mentioned a few other ways, but I dare say what Seddon says is about right. As a rule the worst way of looking at things is the truest, and the loftier the feelings the baser the real motive, and there's been a lot of lofty feelings connected with this war. The only thing is, I don't expect his gang is either so definite or so powerful as he suggests, and mass movements of peoples are not quite so much under their control as he gives the impression. It is not easy to find entirely trustworthy partners in crime, and no doubt financiers don't hang together. . . .'

'They ought to,' Seddon interposed.

'. . . in uninterrupted amity. And I don't suppose they are so intelligent as all that. They have found out that money can be made by various immoral manipulations, and they work on rule of thumb. But you won't persuade me that the ordinary run of money-grubbers understands the remoter effects of their actions. Sir Felix Goldberg is not the *felix qui potuit rerum cognoscere causas*. The causes of war are blinder than Seddon thinks. I don't believe that mass human movements are ever directed by intelligent control. Wars may be the outcome of greed, and of dirtier greed than even Seddon can tell us, but greed isn't aware of anything beyond its object and the technics of getting it. Seddon thinks that financiers like war because they can make more out of one year of war than ten of peace. But that is a new discovery, and one that nobody suspected. Why, there was a financial panic when the war broke out. Don't you remember the moratorium to save the bankers' businesses? The remarkable thing to me is that America developed war fever so suddenly. In Europe years and years of well-kindled suspicion and armament competition had heated the pot, but America had nothing to fear from European aggression and had a Monroe doctrine as a corner-stone of foreign policy. Moreover Americans were making unprecedented fortunes as neutrals. I expect the fear of losing all the billions of dollars that had been invested in the Allies was the sufficient inducement for the American government to come in, but how did the government secure the popular support that enabled it to declare war? Even Americans aren't gullible enough to be stirred up by a three months press campaign to do something so drastic as declare war on sentimental grounds, unless the war feeling was already subconsciously there. It seems to me that human nature is inverterately quarrelsome, and, in spite of the outlet of family life, it is constantly accumulating bad feelings of which war is a fine and righteous purge. But the curious thing is that it is not so much the people with bad feelings who do the fighting as their victims. To take American examples, Maitland and Selby haven't bad feelings about anything on earth. . . .'

'Except bully beef,' said Williamson.

'. . . except bully beef and American brass-hats. They are here because their country is in it. The people with bad feelings work them off vicariously like good Christians and by activities on the home front. Doubtless Maitland and Selby would accumulate bad feelings in time, but I expect the quantity would not become dangerously great until they were over military age. Of course I don't deny that there is quite a number of soldiers with bad feelings, and they're very good soldiers. They have the right spirit, the blood lust and hate that military training is intended to instill, or rather to draw out and sanctify, instead of leaving dormant and ashamed.'

'I don't like that damned depressing old doctrine of the wickedness of human nature,' said Williamson. 'You admit it isn't in younger people who actually volunteer to fight. . . .'

'And if they didn't they would have to, patriotism being an enforceable sentiment, like matrimonial devotion.'

'Do let a man speak. You admit it isn't in the young, so that it can't be innate. I think it grows in people as they grow older, through too much competition. Competition in itself isn't bad, but we've made a god of it, and too much irritates people against each other. People individually are fairly sensible, and get over their irritations, especially as there is always a policeman near at hand to stop breaches of the peace. But people in the mass, crowds, aren't sensible. In fact they are damn silly: look at our yellow twins, electioneering and advertising. Crowds are very irritable, and don't get over it without blood-letting. They get worked up by the wickedness of foreigners. The big industrial blokes who are always being

57

knocked by foreign competition, and their dear pals in parliament, naturally get very worked up about wicked foreigners and unfair competition. By the way, what is fair competition? And the more they get worked up the more they compete and the more they compete the more they get worked up. The excitement is very catching, for it affects everybody's livelihood, and it spreads over the whole nation. The wicked foreigner is a very handy scapegoat when it comes to explaining low wages and unemployment. No wonder we wanted to fight the Germans. Their wickedness was enormous.'

Tom took up the theme. 'There isn't so much difference between individuals and crowds. Crowd behaviour is individual behaviour intensified by induction, to speak electrically. The individual doesn't get over his irritation without active expression any more than the nation does. It's individual bad temper multiplied by mutual induction (if that's the right phrase) that makes war possible. Young people are irritable, but they are usually happy, and happiness is the world's great disinfectant. What we need to stop war is a way of keeping people happy.'

'Perhaps people are only happy when they are fighting,' suggested Williamson.

'They're certainly not happy at this sort of fighting. An attraction of war is that it gives some relief from the deadliness of industrial life and morality. We have only to provide them with other ways of escape and no one will bother to fight.'

'Gin, whores, and Saturnalia?' Seddon inquired.

'Possibly. The first thing is Chairs of Hedonistics at all universities. The subject must be investigated and a science or art founded. Compensate thwarted lives. Relieve the unhappily married. Away with protracted virginity. Instead of some people having a Good Time all the time, and others none of the time, ration Good Time so that everyone can have a spot now and then. All that sort of thing.'

'Very nice, Tom,' said Seddon. 'We'll see about that after the war. . . .'

'I thought we were all going to be dead?' Williamson interrupted.

'Not for this argument. I was going to say that competition is deeper and more deadly than Tom seems to realize, and some of the

58

fiercest is for what he calls Good Time. How the blazes is it to be rationed then?'

'I don't know. But food is rationed, and that is more important still.'

'It's nice to hear Tom talk nonsense,' said Williamson, 'he's so good at it. But let's have a little sense. Grab is fundamental, however much we paint it over, and war is the only possible outcome when two equally strong sets of grabbers are after the same booty. War is fundamental, and it only stops for a while when one super-grabber has grabbed everything grabbable. Witness Rome. England has been less successful.'

'Now who's being depressing about human nature?' Tom retorted. 'And there's no need for grab. It can only exist because of poverty and lack of education. Bring up people in comfort and security, and grab goes and with it war. Grab is barbarous, and we are breeding barbarians by frightening people with poverty and insecurity and treating education as a training to compete instead of to live. That can easily be altered.'

'You're a resourceful debater, Tom,' Seddon put in, 'but unfortunately your proposal to do away with poverty, for that's what it comes to, isn't practicable, and you must know it. Competition in the labour market must keep wages uncomfortably low, and if you push them up by legislation you kill the export trade. As competition can't be stopped without stopping everything, poverty must continue and war must continue. In fact there is a number of powerful people who want it to continue.'

'Seddon, you are a profound pessimist. It has been for three thousand years a philosophic truism that nature is a flux, and every second the world is new. And yet you say in a voice like an axiom that competition cannot be stopped. I expect you are drawing conclusions from a mere century and a half of glorious industrialism. Competition in the extra-human world is pure anthropomorphism; I mean in the sense of members of a species fighting among themselves. In human affairs it is purely a nineteenth-century notion. It was invented by pig-minded industrialists who made fortunes through sweated labour and justified themselves by calling themselves successful competitors, competition being part of Somehow

Good, a divine ordinance greatly respected by whiskery prelates and statesmen, every one of whom had some sort of interest in sweated labour. The nineteenth is the hideous century of all English centuries. All its monuments show it was diseased. Think of frock-coats, Mr. Gladstone, slums, Balfe, the death of young Dombey, and any other of the horrors that may come into mind. And don't sling Victorian stuff at me. There need be no competition to live. Read Ruskin. He was horribly Victorian, but he saw the swindle and it sent him mad.'

'But you can't eliminate pressure of population, and, after all, that is at the bottom of competition,' Williamson argued.

'Unless there is scarcity, population doesn't press very hard, and there seems enough to go round at present. Moreover, we can or shall be able to control population; it's a matter of education. But I expect population will control itself. The outburst that started at the end of the eighteenth century is just beginning to slow down. The idea that population increased because of the industrial revolution is all rot: you might as well put it down to the romantic movement in literature which began at the same time. All three were due to one of those human eruptions that have so often occurred in history: Hyksos, Assyrians, Mongols, Turks, Huns, Goths. These peoples had no industrial revolution, but they multiplied suddenly and became a damned nuisance. These surgings of humanity seize whatever means of life are at hand; the nineteenth century gave to its own wave steam power and protestantism. But the wave is breaking, and with luck we may have a period of glittering soullessness in which to be happy for a while. Then we shall abolish the causes of war. Back to Mozart.'

'We shan't,' Seddon contradicted. 'Say what you will, Tom, industry can't function unless it makes a profit, and nations either have to make a profit or borrow, and all the nations are trying to make a profit out of each other; which is absurd. We are up against an economic impasse.'

'Hullo, there's the FEs,' said Williamson, who was getting bored. 'I didn't think it would be fine enough for them to lay eggs to-night.'

Several engines started up across the aerodrome, where there was a squadron of night bombers of the Independant Air Force, and soon an FE took off.

While this was going on Allen said, 'This is all frightfully interesting. You are the three wisest birds flying.' Allen was a splendid audience. He listened with the most flattering attention. 'But I thought we were in this jolly old war because of the violation of Belgian neutrality, or whatever it was, and our alliance with France, which the Huns attacked and it was up to us to do the honourable thing. Yet you chaps have been yarning away for hours and haven't so much as mentioned all that. What about America and the Lusi—' The remarks of Allen were cut short by a crash. 'That must be a bomb not far away.' The klaxon gave tongue, shouting the air-raid warning.

'Hullo, the major's got wind up,' said Tom.

'Let's put the lamps out and go and have a look,' said Williamson, and they did.

'I'm not going down that beastly dugout,' declared Allen.

Taylor, who was orderly dog for the day, dashed past them. It was his job to see that the machine guns were manned: though what use machine guns were likely to be against an invisible night raider was not clear. The major's voice flapped about among the trees, ordering this and that. Chadwick bumped into Tom. He was in pyjamas and British warm. Here was something for him to see to, machine guns being his care. Everything except the major was quiet. He could be heard telling people to go down the dugout, and calling for Taylor, telling him to stand by the machine guns and listen for engine noises and direct the firing.

There were three machine-gun pits on the aerodrome. It amused Tom to stroll round and watch the crews preparing for action. They would show the invaders just where to drop bombs if they fired. Everything, even the major, soon calmed down. James' vinous voice floated from the distance 'I believe the priceless old Hun has gone down to sit on his egg wherever he laid it.' It was a very quiet night. The rumble of the guns was faint and downwind and the flashes infrequent. But there was no sound of aeroplanes, and Tom returned towards the hut. Someone bumped into him among the trees.

61

ho's that?' It was the major's voice. 'You ought to be down the
_ ut.'

'Right, major,' said Tom, and went on to the hut. By inquiring
in the darkness he found that Seddon and Williamson were already
there. He undressed without a light, which was a bother and made
him feel uncharitable towards the Germans. The klaxon sounded
again, possibly to indicate that the raid was to be considered officially
over. Allen came in and struck a light.

'You fellows all in bed? Sleepy lot you are. They say one of the
FEs dropped that bomb by accident.'

Nobody bothered to reply.

VIII

THE next morning was peaceful, as the clouds were too low for the
early show. A great stillness involved the officers' quarters until a
few early hungry ones emerged at about nine o'clock and sought
breakfast. B flight had a job at eleven, C at two, and A had the
dusk patrol. But after breakfast, when Tom was enjoying the
sweetness of the day's first pipe, the rich tang of nicotine on a palate
suitably prepared with bacon and coffee and marmalade, the quietness
of a satisfied and eupeptic belly, and visceral anticipation of the
delicate delights of the latrine, the klaxon horn shouted DER-der-
DER-der.

What the hell? Of C flight Miller, Debenham, and Taylor, as well
as Tom, were in the mess, and they hurried to the office to see what
had happened. It appeared that there had been a call from wing to
requisition a flight to escort a big Ak-W which was to photograph an
area towards Cambrai as soon as possible. As the major considered
that C flight with Mac leading was the best possible protection for a
lonely Ak-W he had klaxoned accordingly. They were to leave the
ground in half an hour and fly over to the Ak-W people and make
further arrangements there. A flight would take over the two o'clock
O-Pip, and C the dusk job. Mac was annoyed. It had certainly
cleared a little, but what on earth was the good of trying to take
photographs on a day like that? Wing must be loopy.

They went up six strong. Allen had the uncomfortable position in the middle at the back, where it was necessary to keep above the three front machines so as not to get in their slipstreams. He took off on the extreme right, since a slipstream bump near the ground might cause a crash. They reached the Ak-W squadron in a few minutes and landed and reported to the C.O. He was surprised to see them. Photographs on a day like that? They had better go and make themselves comfortable in the mess for the present, and see if it cleared up. So they went to the mess and talked shop and compared news with the Ak-W people, while the gramophone played the familiar songs: 'Any Time's Kissing Time'; 'Three Hundred and Sixty-Five Days'; 'The Bells are Ringing'; 'I've Always got the Time to Talk to You'; and the rest. Tom would never in his life hear (if he survived) any of those tunes without being transported to a R.F.C. mess among the ghosts of dead time.

He was absorbed into a bridge four. Allen listened thirstily to the stories of the Ak-W pilots and observers. They seemed to have some fairly hectic scraps and found some of the new Fokker triplanes and biplanes rather trying. They were so confoundedly splitarse.

One of them took Mac up for a joy-ride. Mac said afterwards it was like flying a floating steam-roller, and God preserve the poor devils. What a lot of heroes these two-seater blokes were! Excepting Bristol Fighters, safest of all aeroplanes. There had been a rumour a few days ago that four Bristol Fighters away miles and miles over Hunland, had been attacked by a circus of sixteen Albatros scouts. They had shot down nine of them and the rest remembered other appointments. Archie was so mad about it that he put up a £50,000 barrage between the BFs and home, but they dived under it and, rumour had it, they looped in formation just to show Archie what they thought of him. This was probably an exaggeration; how could they arrange the stunt? And it wasn't wise to stunt after a fight, as you never knew what had been shot through and wouldn't stand the strain. But BFs would be BFs.

The Ak-W squadron gave them lunch, and then they returned home, the job having been washed out by Wing, which had decided that it already had enough photos on its grand piano, or else had happened to look out of the window and see the impenetrable weather. They took off in formation, and then Mac turned back and they dived right down on the Ak-W merchants just to learn 'em. He went home along the ground, zooming over houses and fences and trees and people that wouldn't lie down. Formation flying at a height of two feet – most joyous of joys. You are in the midst of the world, yet not of it, a supernal being thunderous with speed and leaping flight. And not alone (in which state carpers might think you a mere nuisance), but in formal company with others of your winged kind, forming together a terror vast, shattering, and majestic, as much beyond the futile comment of crawling humanity as an earthquake is. To the pleasure of formidable foolishness is added the pride of style and strength of comradeship. But beware of telegraph wires and horses. Brass-hats and troops at drill were fair game, and Chinese labourers that perched on long poles.

There were sardines for tea. A flight had had a perfectly quiet job among the clouds. They had played hide-and-seek with a few Albatri, but the Albatri didn't seem serious about it, and nothing happened. It was Thomson's last job, as he was posted to Home Establishment, and his D.S.O. had come through. He was to leave the squadron on the next day, and James was very busy gathering materials for a first-class binge that evening. Nothing less than Veuve Cliquot would do for the sad occasion.

It was a little clearer when C flight took off for their job at quarter to five, but there were still great masses of cloud between two thousand and five thousand feet, and visibility was bad generally. Miller was not on this job, so Debenham was flying the deputy leader's streamer. No sooner had they taken off than Debenham went down again. Apparently his engine had cut right out. Tom saw him floating down towards a field and then lost sight of him. And Taylor didn't seem able to keep up, and when they started to go through clouds they lost him altogether. Allen came up on Mac's right. Mac took them through a good deal of cloud. It was difficult not to do so, but Mac seemed to be doing some of it for amusement. Flying in formation through cloud was not what Tom considered amusing. It was too nerve-racking, this flying blind, knowing that someone was possibly only a few yards away. What was the actual range of visibility in a cloud he had very little idea, never having seen any external object while he was enclouded. His own wing-tips were quite plain to see. He thought the average cloud was certainly less dense than a good pea-soup fog, but he had never been in one of those black terrifying solidities that looked as though they might be too dense for one to see one's eyelashes.

They succeeded in keeping company well enough until they were in the clear above. The sun was in the west, his chin but fifteen degrees above the cloud horizon, his countenance aurate and misted, glaring upon the cloudy slopes and juts, declaring his radiance beyond shadowed sheers, flinging the scarf of evening towards the dusking east. Even a burst of Archie was lovely in the vesperal fires . . . Archie? It was bursting white; their own Archie. Tom anxiously looked for Huns. This was no time for dreams. Other bursts appeared in line below. Evidently Archie had seen them through a gap in the clouds and was calling them down. Mac waggled his wings and went down in a steep dive through a chasm, where it seemed possible to slip between clouds down to their lowest level without much risk of being seen from below. They worked down to three thousand feet, dodging sailing masses of cloud, and came into clearer regions below. Mac waggled his wings again and put his nose down, going north-west all out; for there was a grey-looking Hun two-seater a little below them, and it was just possible to get between the Hun and his home. Black Archie opened on them, woof-woof-woof-woof, but in half a minute they were right over the Hun, who was making for home as hard as he could go, but too late. It was a brilliant surprise by Mac. He disappeared, going vertically down on his prey, and Tom and Allen fell after him. It was a difficult shot for the observer, three scouts dropping almost vertically on him, six machine guns firing at him. Mac went straight on to him, and looked as though he would dive right through him. Tom came in at an angle, doing about a hundred and fifty. The observer had no time to shoot at him, being occupied with Mac. Tom kicked at the rudder bar, jerking about until the Hun was in his Aldis. Then he pressed the control lever and his guns set up their rattle and his tracers streaked at the Hun, apparently going into him. As the Hun went from underneath him, he necessarily eased out of his dive to keep his sights on the mark. After a two seconds' burst of perhaps fifty rounds he had

E

to pull up and turn outwards to avoid hitting the Hun in his dive. The observer was certainly shot. Mac was unable to pull out and went on down behind the Hun's tail and zoomed up at him. Then Allen got in a burst, and as he did so the Hun zoomed up, standing on its tail. Then it fell over on its right side and went down in a jerking spin, smoking. It was the death plunge. Flames leapt along the fuselage, making a hideous comet. The pilot and observer were dead and not suffering the last fiery agony. They could see it going away down and down. Would it never hit the ground? Archie was bombarding them furiously. They zig-zagged into the west.

What was the reality of it? Tom felt that his mind glided off actuality, touching it at too oblique an angle either to be smashed on it or to pierce into it. The scene was an elaborate staging of an uncomprehended drama. It was a dream, it was a presentation, it was a prefiguring of remote inspirations that compelled the action of some fundamental extraneous imagination. The directing shell bursts, significant amid the empty pageantry of evening; the swoop through chasms of tremendous cloud; the sudden sight of prey; the final sheer drop and staccato of guns; the ghastly falling pyre; these things were the play of fantasy, and he sat there, incredibly perched in air, playing an automatic part, yet out of it all, unaffected, immune. These things did not happen; they were fantastic images of whirling specks thrown stereoscopically on the untextured screen of blank space by whatever lamp lights the sun and sets dust on fire with life. Behind the screen lay unending meadows where the bovine Absolute endlessly ruminates, chewing the perfect cud.

Somewhere below in the German lines there was a smouldering scatter of wreckage spattered with red protoplasm and smashed splinters of bone. A black trail of smoke still stained the air. They climbed among the clouds, Archie sending a few parting bursts after them out of sight. Archie above all was unreal; a silly ghost bursting out of utter nothing with a bark. But in process of this bright ridiculous whirl of coloured shadows two men had been killed. It made little difference to those that had played the part of killers. Mac was no doubt pleased about it, Tom was excited, Allen happy at getting his first share of a Hun. Yet the experience was a fleeting one, that would merge and blend with others similar, the sharp

66

contours fading under the abrasion of flowing hours. But to the killed — what was it to them? Did it really abolish all their universe as though it had never been? That would be a strange dichotomy of experience, extending the ancient habitual cleft between me and thee to the limits of life and death. It seemed wrong that an event of passing and of no great importance for one should be ultimate and catastrophic for another through a mere accident in the course of one bullet rather than another. It would be an intolerable duality in nature. Somehow the whole affair must be illusory; but the illusion was so real that it was the only possible reality for human minds. The formless structures of shadowed golden clouds, aeroplanes, shell bursts, death; these absurd overwhelming things were real. But Tom, sustained by the substanceless air, felt himself a million million miles away, in that moment immortal.

Mac led them round about the clouds, up and down, in and out. It was the very evening for surprising two-seaters, the westering sun dazzling them, the clouds giving cover for approaching them. But they saw nothing else except a bunch of scouts too numerous and too far away in Hunland to be attacked. They were mere dots in the sky, and it took an experienced eye to see them at all; but they were Huns doing defensive patrols.

From time to time they met British machines, which were always plentiful on a fine evening. There were Nines doing, possibly, reconnaissances in the midst of black clouds of Archie. There were stray Camels frisking among the clouds, a flight of SEs solemnly protecting a Harry Tate that was doing something important and must not be disturbed. But in the vast cubicity of the sky above the front from Arras to Bapaume these were no more than a dance of midges; they were swallowed in the immensity and lost, and the heavens were lonely, a desolation of clouds marching endlessly from nowhere to nowhere.

At length Mac turned homewards. It was darkening rapidly on earth, though cloudland was still bright. They had to go at full throttle to the aerodrome to reach it while twilight lasted, and as they approached they were guided by rockets and flares and Very lights that were being let off, possibly as a prelude to the festivities of the evening, but ostensibly to guide the belated patrol. The only adequate response was to dive on the pyrotechnicians, and they dived. A rocket fizzed up in front of Tom, narrowly missing him. That was dangerous; if the thing had hit him it might have brought him down in flames. He pulled out of his dive and completed the circuit soberly. It was so dark that he tried to land about two feet up in the air, and pan-caked, but without doing any damage. Taylor had returned with an oily plug, and Debenham had got down safely in a field about a mile away.

They were already famous. Archie had been so pleased with the dashing response to his signal, and so pleased with himself for being so clever, that he had telephoned Wing about it, and Wing had traced squadron and expressed august pleasure. The question was, whose Hun? Mac said they had all had a shot, and were entitled to a third each. Tom said he thought Mac had done the damage. He had certainly shot the observer. He thought Allen was firing when the Hun actually went out of control. Allen said he thought Mac and Cundall had settled the Hun before he fired. As soon as he shot, the Hun stalled. Probably the pilot had died or fainted then.

After further altruistic argument, the major said it seemed to be a case of a third each, and flamers were the stuff to give 'em, and they must get the report done or they would keep dinner waiting. With the help of James they put it into official language '. . . after falling out of control some distance the LVG was seen to burst into flames. The patrol encountered no other EA.'

'He was no good,' said Mac. 'The durn fool just put his nose down and flew straight. He was cold meat.'

Allen and Tom went to their hut to change for dinner.

'Do you close one eye when you look through your Aldis?' Allen inquired.

'No damn fear. I want to see what I'm likely to run in to.'

'That's the first time I've shot at a Hun, you know.'

'And,' said Tom, 'you are pardonably proud of the happy result. May you always be the one to come home to dinner and rejoice in the downfall of the wicked.'

'There's no need for your sarcasm, Cundall. I've never called the Huns wicked. I'm sorry that we kill each other, but . . . .'

'Oh, don't let's discuss the ethics of war. There aren't any. We've

68

every excuse and no excuse. I hope to God there's a good feed for us and some decent fizz. I feel like throwing a drunk to-night.'

Dinner was shown to be a binge by the traditional addition of lobster mayonnaise and champagne, in this instance Veuve Cliquot. Tom was too late for preliminary gins and vermouths, but got in some sherry with the soup. Corks started popping when the lobster appeared, and talk soon became noisy and the funny side of the war predominated. There was a plentiful supply of drink, and the more the corks popped the funnier the war became. The squadron humorists, James and Tommy and Robinson, were surrounded by rotating rings of varying laughter. What funny things happened. Franklin coming in with a bullet hole in every square foot of his bus that didn't matter, how priceless! Or Moss claiming two Huns that had collided when they were both firing at him. Or Robinson dropping his bombs on a two-seater when his guns had jammed. Or Bulmer keeping B flight out so long when his watch stopped that they all ran out of petrol. Or Maitland having a scrap with a Dolphin the first time he saw one, under the impression that it was a Hun. There had been a bit of a strafe about it, and Maitland had a grievance against the English for making kites that looked like Boche. Maitland and the Dolphin was the greatest of all jokes; even Maitland was beginning to think it funny.

Dinner became vague when the champagne soaked in. Possibly roast beef and something with it and then something and they were bringing coffee and you had to finish off the bubbly if there was any in your bottle. You passed cigarettes. Everybody was trying to pass cigarettes. Fellows were shouting a bit. Someone threw bread. That wasn't done. Wonderful how good gaspers were in wartime. The world might perish but the yellow peril improved. Tom had just had a huge consignment of a strange brand from home, and was giving them away as fast as he could. What was that Jimmy had said? God knows, but he looked funny.

The old Hun was paralysed with fright, Tom said. All he did was put his nose down to go home. Couldn't have had any training. Damn bad luck on the observer, such a mutt of a pilot. Didn't have much time to do anything, though. Mac was on him like a hawk. Hardly got in a shot. Poor old bean. Must have filled him with lead. Heaviest corpse ever known. Till the lead melted and ran out. Funny if two blokes shot at each other and their bullets met head on. The port. Now for the talking. The King. Bloody awful port. Shame to pour it on the Cliquot. The major was talking about Tommy. Fine fellow. One of the best flight commanders in France. D.S.O. Twenty-four Huns. Sportsman. Made you thirsty listening to the major. The port was coming round very regularly. Pour and pass. Then Mac. A flight commander's job was to get seven times as many Huns as casualties and Tommy did it and more. Without worrying about it. No one would ever think Tommy had a care in the world beyond wondering what his banking account and his girl were up to. That was pretty good for Mac. Everyone laughed and cheered, and Bulmer got up to speak and started: 'Talking about old Tommy,' and he began to laugh and couldn't go on. They all laughed like hell. It was killing, old Bully standing there grinning and couldn't get a word out. Then he managed to say 'Old Tommy' and stuck again and they nearly died of laughing. Bully was priceless when he was blotto. He drank some port and had another shot. 'What I mean is . . .' There were shouts of 'Go on Bully!' 'Ole Tommy . . .' People were getting hysterical with laughter. 'Gobblessim,' and Bulmer collapsed. Everybody yelled. The mess rocked with the noise. One of the most successful of speeches ever made.

Robinson, Tommy's deputy leader, got up, comparatively articulate. Tommy had discovered two new methods of fighting Huns. One was to drive them so far from home they didn't know the way back, and the other to shoot them down with Very lights.

These two allusions were uproariously appreciated. On one occasion when his guns had jammed Tommy had fired a Very light at a Hun just for amusement. On another occasion A flight had attacked a two-seater when it was flying west. It was fast and they did not get near enough to shoot it down, but they chased it so far into France that the pilot gave up all hope of getting home again and landed.

Robinson admitted that Tommy had brought down a few of his Huns by orthodox means, and mentioned some of his exploits, such as his single-handed rescue of the two Harry Tates. He brought up the old complaint that he could outclimb the rest of the flight because of his lightness, but although one of the smallest aviators in France he was one of the greatest. And he did it all on one lung, the whole of his left side being taken up with heart.

Robinson was in form. They swayed about, laughing, and banged the table. Tommy's health. Tommy! For he's a jolly good fellow. Waves of affection broke against him. He stood up to say his good-bye. Not so much row. Poor old Tommy; could hardly speak. Tight as . . . Damn sorry to leave them, he said. Finest lot of blokes ever let out of quod to win the war. Good old Tommy! Parting advice was, be kind to Huns. Put 'em out of their misery quick. They'd got complete wind up. Wasser use o' living with wind up? Most of the Huns he'd met seemed delighted to be shot down. It was worse sometimes for those that didn't want to be shot down. Fancy feeling like that and having Mac or Bully on your tail. It wasn't fair the way Mac had been bagging them lately. They ought to send him home before he shot down all the Huns there were and did everyone else out of their jobs. Or put him on Harry Tates.

Mac driving an RE8! An overwhelming tumult of cheers and laughter, and Tommy braced his half-drowned rational soul to sentiment. He would always remember them. His period with the squadron was certain to be the outstanding time of his life, however long or short it might be. And in a way a very happy time. He wasn't the sort of fellow that liked war as war, but there was the comradeship of it, and who could help being happy working and fighting together for a common end with such a fine crowd as the squadron was, none finer? This binge to-night, looking round on all their inebriated countenances, would always stay fixed in his memory. In saying good-bye he wished them with all his heart plenty of revs, good luck, and a safe return home.

At that moment, how they loved Tommy! The major got up and they flowed into the ante-room, surging round Tommy, everyone having something to say to him. The waiters were handing round drinks as fast as they could get them from the bar, where Hancock was emptying bottle after bottle. Selby and Maitland, the Americans, were getting him to mix strange potions. A final sing-song started. The mess was beginning to get unsteady, and there were obstacles one knocked against and people weren't quite where they looked as though they were. 'Thanks,' said Tom, taking a drink. What the hell! Then he sang:

> The parson came home drunk one night
> As drunk as he could be.
> He saw a hat right on the peg
> Where his hat ought to be.
> 'My wife, my wife, my darling wife,
> What is this hat I see?
> This hat I see right on the peg
> Where my hat ought to be?'

On and on. Hell of a lot of it. Tune was 'Shepherds Watch Their Flocks'. Never noticed that before.

> 'I've travelled east, I've travelled west,
> Ten thousand miles or more,
> But rolling pins with —— on
> I've never seen before.'

Wonderful song. Go on singing all night. God, he was blotto. Could hardly stand. Could sing though.

> 'When shall I see you?'
> Said the shy young maiden.
> 'Never no more you bloody old 'ore,'
> Said —— Bill the Sailor.

Funniest song of the lot. Laugh like hell. Laugh. Laugh. Where was Tommy, dear ole Tommy? Everything was going funny. Place was dark. Hut. Allen. Thanks Allen. A terrific crash. Shook everything. Things hit him on the head. Where was he? Perhaps he was dead. Then it was daylight. What a hell of a thirst. He got out of bed. His shaving gear was strewn on the bed, and stuff fell on the floor with a clatter and disturbed Williamson who sat up.

'Hullo,' he said, 'so you've come to. I was pretty tight last night, but you were absolutely paralytic. Even that bomb in the night didn't rouse you.'

'Bomb? I seemed to remember something. What happened?'

'Only that a Hun dropped a bomb just outside at half past two this morning. There's a big hole. Luckily there was a tree in the way, or we'd have caught it. And for the Lord's sake pass over the water.'

'Here you are. God, what a morning after.' Tom put his hand to his forehead. 'Hullo, I'm wounded. My stuff fell off the shelf when that bomb banged, and I've a bruise on the forehead. D'you think I can wangle home on the strength of it?'

'You were funny last night,' said Williamson when he had had a drink. 'You were staggering round the mess saying "Wherezh Tommy? Want to kiss him good-bye," and you tried to kiss half a dozen fellows, including the major, before you found Tommy. He was as sozzled as you were, and you both fell over and couldn't get up again. You'd never have got to bed if Allen hadn't kept fairly sober and given you a hand.'

'I don't remember a thing about it. I feel fine now though, except for a head. I'd better try to sleep it off.'

I X

A FEW mornings later, the twenty-first of March, the batman called Tom and Allen for C flight's dawn job, and for once Tom did not go to sleep again. There was a tremendous racket going on; every kind of artillery seemed to be in action. It was certainly the prelude to the big German push. Thank God he was away from that rain of high explosive. Even to hear the distant tumult made his belly unhappy. Allen sat up.

'What a row! I suppose it's started.'

Seddon awoke. Williamson awoke. They sat up in their camp beds, listening.

'Good Lord! It must be on a fifty mile front,' said Williamson.

'Anyhow, it brings the end nearer.'

Outside the sky must be bubbling with flame, but the light of the lamps prevented their seeing more of it than small alterations in the tone of the windows' blankness as the tree-filtered glare varied.

'I expect we shall find it quite interesting watching the big push

73

from above, and I dare say we shan't get machine-gunned so much as in peace-time. They'll be busier with other targets.'

'You're a great optimist, Bill,' Tom replied. 'All the same, I wouldn't mind an armour plated seat.'

'Why not a seat at the War Office while you're wishing? All among the patriots. Haven't you any influence?' Seddon inquired.

'If you only disliked Germans as much as you dislike patriots, in two months you would be known to the press as Captain Seddon, Terror of the Huns.'

'Put in a V.C. if you can spare me one.'

'V.C., R.I.P., Defender of the Faith.'

'Against Tom Cundall.'

'Stop it, you back-chat comedians,' Williamson demanded. 'You're painful. I'm going to sleep again.'

'Sleep no more, Macbill. The push has started.' Tom got out of bed. 'What about it, Allen? Shall we try to capture our eggs before they're hard boiled?'

'Right. I'm with you.' Allen sprang out of bed.

'It's the greatest achievement of the Huns so far, getting Cundall up twenty minutes earlier than necessary,' declared Seddon.

The eggs, nevertheless, were boiled hard; but they had time for a comfortable smoke before going up, and Allen fortified himself by re-reading a letter from his girl.

It was a fine morning, but misty. To the west the mist lay in dense patches, but it was clearer towards the lines. There the ground was thickly dotted with appearing and dissolving smoke of shell bursts. Tom's engine started to miss, and would not pick up, so he gave the 'dud engine' signal and turned back to the aerodrome. As it was only a matter of a plug, the trouble was soon put right. Then Tom wondered whether he should stop at home or go out again and try to find the flight, which was not due back for an hour. He wasn't particularly likely to run across them, but perhaps the attempt should be made. He need not go far over the lines alone if it looked dangerous, and it seemed out of proportion to miss nearly a whole job just for a dirty plug. So he took off again and made for the lines. The ground mist was increasing; better not stay out long. He turned south when he reached the lines, watching the eastern sky carefully for Huns; but he seemed quite alone in the sky. Looking westwards, there was little to be seen but the white carpet of mist. He made a quick dash over Hunland, dropped his bombs from six thousand feet, and dived away westwards. It seemed to take an hour to get down to a thousand feet, with the mist all the time increasing until it covered everything except for here and there breaks. Soon he was flying over an apparently limitless sea of shining white cloud; and his engine started missing again. He flew north to where Arras had been a few minutes ago, but Arras was quite obliterated. All he could see through occasional rifts was the infinite desolation of an old battlefield; water-filled shell-holes and disused trench-systems.

He must remember that the wind was from the west, and would drift him towards Hunland. He turned west to look for a gap in the fog where he could land: the sooner he found one the better, or there might not be any gaps left to find. He soon came to a dark patch in the whiteness, and went down to investigate it. Circling, he made out a road with all sorts of motor traffic passing along it. He was on the right side of the lines, but there were too many shell-holes about for him to attempt landing there, and he wandered farther west.

Gaps were very scarce. He had been a fool to set out again. In consequence of an exaggerated sense of duty, seemingly brought on by the big push, he ran a considerable risk of being wiped out in a stupid crash trying to land in a fog. But if he got away with it this time, he would always listen to the still small voice of discretion.

He made calculations. Probably he could keep on another forty minutes. There was no chance of the mist clearing in that time. He had to find a gap or crash.

He flew and flew. A dark line showed ahead. As he approached, it broadened into a long gap in which lay part of a village and a strip of fields. He circled and glided down into the nearest field; but he found when he tried to land that it was impossible; he was floating down the side of a hill, and he had to open out and climb through the mist. Probably the gap was along a ridge of high ground. He flew over the end of the village and went down to have a look at a field visible there. This seemed flat enough, but it was ploughed land. He zoomed out of the mist, but quickly decided he must take the chance of trying to land on furrows. He might not find another

75

gap. He circled to get in position. He had never come down on furrows before, but he knew that the correct thing was to land with them and not across them. Luckily they seemed to run more or less with the direction in which the wind would be blowing, if there still was any wind; there had been a little when he took off. Landing, you had to hold off as long as possible so as to pancake, and touch ground with as little forward motion as might be.

Having got the theory of it clear in his mind, Tom glided down, side-slipping to lose speed. Then he straightened out and floated along the furrows into the mist. He got his tail well down and pancaked a little way in good style, but the ground was so soft that the wheels dug in dead, and up went the tail till the Camel was standing on its nose; then gently over on its back, with Tom hanging upside down in the cockpit.

He put one hand on the ground and undid the belt with the other and wriggled out of the wreck, a little muddy and feeling foolish. There was nothing to be seen but a small area of ploughland in the enclosing mist; but he could hear again, and the dominant sound was the thunder of unceasing bombardment: it was very distant.

He lighted a cigarette and inspected the aeroplane. It had settled down gently and did not seem damaged beyond the broken prop and crumpled rudder upon which the tail was resting. It would have to be stripped to be taken away, and that would be a muddy job for somebody. Well, he must do something, and the correct thing was to find a guard for the aeroplane and then telephone the squadron. The village was probably half a kilometre away, but where was the road to it? He certainly could not explore in the mud and fog with nothing to guide him. So he sat down on the tail plane and listened for any sounds that might indicate the direction of the nearest road. For a long ten minutes nothing happened. Then he heard a motor approaching. He got off his perch and went forwards a few yards and came to the edge of a bank which had lain just beyond the range of vision and would have caused a more interesting crash if the aeroplane had drifted a very little farther. A few feet below him lay a road. He scrambled down the bank, and the motor, an A.S.C. lorry, loomed through the mist.

The driver said that the next village (they were almost there) was

'Arkeeves', but he didn't think there was anything there; he was bound for the railhead about two miles beyond. There would be a telephone at the railhead. There were two men beside the driver on the lorry. They both wanted to see the crash.

'I shall want one of you to guard the aeroplane while I go along to the railhead and telephone. The lorry can pick up the guard on its return.'

'It's a mercy you weren't killed, sir,' said the guard, when he saw with wonder the upside-down wreck.

'I could do that a dozen times without getting hurt. Now your job is to see that nobody so much as lays a finger on it, and that no matches are struck near it.'

Tom returned to the lorry and they set out for the railhead. They soon ran out of the mist and through the village of Arquèves and down a hill into the mist again, but it was beginning to clear. In ten minutes they reached the railhead, and Tom went to the telephone room and asked the operator to get the squadron for him; but the operator said he couldn't get Arras area, the line had been broken somewhere by shell fire. Perhaps if he tried again in an hour or two it might have been repaired. The operator was a difficult man to talk to, being permanently engaged, apparently, in six different but simultaneous conversations. So Tom went out of the telephone room with the immediate idea of looking for food. It was half past nine. A tender emerged from the fog, and he was pleased to see that the driver was in R.F.C. uniform. He waved a beckoning arm, and the tender pulled up by him. The driver, who was alone, got out and saluted.

He was from a local Aircraft Park, about ten miles away. Tom told him what had happened, and he said he thought his people would send over and collect the crash right away. He would get them on the telephone. He was an elderly man, and inclined to father Tom.

'I'll get you some breakfast, sir, if you like. I dare say you could do with it. If you wouldn't mind eating it in the tender. I'll get it a lot quicker than if you went to the R.T.O. I know my way about here, sir.'

'Thanks,' said Tom, 'I wish you would. But we'd better ring through to your people first and make arrangements.'

So they went to the telephone room and talked to the A.P. which said it would send along transport to deal with the crash at once, and the Ak Emma[1] went off in search of food. He returned in a few minutes with a tray containing plenty of bacon and eggs, bread, butter, marmalade, and coffee.

'That's fine,' said Tom; 'you're a friend in need.'

'That's all right, sir. If you'll excuse me, I'll go and have a snack myself.'

Tom ate his breakfast with appetite. It was these wallahs with stationary jobs away in the rear who did themselves well, he reflected. They had means of tapping supplies before they got through to the mere cannon fodder in the trenches. A railhead must be a particularly good spot. Who would be a hero? 'Not me,' said Tom to himself. The distant gunfire rumbled and rattled: heroes were being blown to pieces while other people ate bacon and eggs in comfort. Who would belong to the death or glory group if he could join the bacon-and-eggs party? There was no point in being blown to pieces, and as for glory, it might some day help to keep a first offender out of jail, and that was about all that could be said for it. And anyhow, what was it all about, this fighting? It certainly wasn't Tom Cundall's affair. Let the property owners fight their own battles. He would have bacon and eggs if he could get them.

The Ak Emma returned later with an air of serenity. 'Had enough, sir?'

'Yes thanks. Good feed. I gather you manage to do yourselves pretty well in these parts.'

'Grub's none too good at the A.P., sir. But there's usually plenty doing 'ere if you know the cook.'

'Well, have you anything more to do here? We'd better be getting along to the crash in case your people turn up.'

'I've got a few things to pick up. Won't take me long, sir.'

'Right. Will you tell the driver of the A.S.C. lorry I don't want him to do anything else except pick up his man.'

Before he left the railhead Tom inquired again at the telephone room. The line to Arras was still out of order.

The mist had cleared at the scene of the crash, and the news of it

[1] Air Mechanic.

had spread. A dozen people of various races were looking at the aeroplane, and the guard appeared to be having an argument with some of the khaki element who possibly did not take his authority very seriously. However, the argument ceased at Tom's approach, and some saluting was done.

'Anything to report?'

'No, sir. All correct.'

'Your lorry will be along soon. You are relieved now.'

The guard saluted and dismissed himself for a smoke. Tom had nothing to do but wait. He leaned against the fuselage and listened while his new friend the Ak Emma told him about his wife and family at Camberwell. He had a girl of seventeen and a boy of fifteen, besides smaller children. But it was the two eldest that were troubling him. The boy swore he would join up the day he was sixteen. And as for the girl, the missis said there was no holding her.

By half past ten the Ak Emma had become restless, and suggested he had better go and find out why help had not come. Tom was bored with him and agreed. He was in no hurry. Doubtless he would be able to get lunch in Arquèves. He sat on the fuselage and waited.

The number of sightseers remained fairly constant, but the individuals kept coming and going. No officer, however, appeared among them for some time after the Ak Emma's departure, and then Tom saw the approach of a captain's badges and a clerical collar. He slid to earth.

'Good morning, padre.'

'Good morning. Are you all right?'

'Quite, thanks.'

'That's good. I heard there had been a crash here, and I came over to see if anyone was hurt. Is your machine damaged?'

'Not a great deal. But I shan't be able to fly it away.'

'Won't you? Oh, it's upside down. I see now.' The padre laughed with remarkable heartiness, and then checked himself. 'You're lucky to be alive, I suppose.'

'Not on account of this little crash. I only turned over landing on this soft ground. I might do it a dozen times without hurting myself.'

79

'Indeed. And what are you going to do now?'

Tom gave him an account of the then state of affairs, and the conversation became discursive. After a time Dulwich for some reason entered into it, and they discovered that they had both been born there. That two natives of so sequestered a hamlet as nineteenth-century Dulwich should meet for the first time beside an overturned aeroplane in a field near Arquèves was too queer an event to be disregarded. There must be some Purpose in it, if only to secure Tom a luncheon. It appeared that the padre lived at a Corps School, which had its locus in a valley some fifteen minutes walk away.

'School?' inquired Tom. 'What do you teach?'

'Oh, gas and bombs and such things.'

Tom glanced at the padre, but saw no doubt in his face. The man of God and the men of gas; by a supreme act of tolerance, was it, that they fraternized? Not so. Neither of them really meant what they taught. Their real selves were compartmented from their professions; they were all good fellows together steering by Current Usage. Not exactly hypocrites, Tom thought, for *fingent simul creduntque*, they believed in their own simulations.

The padre was a charming man to talk to. The time passed quickly, and it was half past twelve.

'Come back with me and have some lunch. We can send a guard for your aeroplane, and you can telephone your squadron from there, and wait in some comfort.'

'Thanks very much. I'd like to. But I must get one of these men to do guard until you can send a proper guard.'

That done, they set off. A little way along the road they met an R.F.C. tender, which stopped when the driver saw Tom.

'Do you know where an aeroplane has landed near here, sir?'

'I landed a little way along the road.'

'Oh well, sir, we're from 72 Squadron. The Aircraft Park rang up and asked us to send someone along to start you up.'

'They're crazy. I turned over. I told them it was a crash. You can wash out.'

Tom held on his way lunchwards indignantly. These non-combatant R.F.C. people must be quite mad.

'Never mind,' said the padre, 'worse things happen in wartime.'
The immense reverberations of gunfire supported his statement.

X

THE Corps School was a restful place, undisturbed by hurly-burlies
and war, except for noises incidental to courses in bombing. And the
staff mess was the most peaceful spot in the happy valley. The C.O.
was a colonel and his adjutant a major. Besides the padre, there were
two captains and two lieutenants in charge of courses of instruction.
The actual instructing was done by sergeant-instructors, so that they
had little to do but put in an occasional modest appearance in the
background of a class, and fill in a few daily returns. The adjutant
also prepared daily returns, or supervised their preparation by the
orderly sergeant, and the colonel signed them. The colonel also
took part occasionally in instructing a class, probably with the object
of infusing the right atmosphere of kindliness. He was very well
seconded in the kindliness department by the padre, who was in
himself a tower of good will. It was impossible to be in his presence
and not receive the illusion of the fundamental goodness of things,
let the guns rumble in the distance how they might. Such, Tom
thought, was the triumphant power of professional training allied
with good natural ability.

Being introduced into this mess was, to one used to the R.F.C.
atmosphere, something like finding oneself in the holy calm of a
Pall Mall club miraculously endowed with faint but persistent Moral
Purpose, after a New Year hullaballo in a Regent Street bar. Conversation was leisurely, prolonged, and decorous, and alcohol was used
only in such small quantities as stimulated the larynx to this sort of
talk. No one swore or discussed women. The profound purity of the
mature English gentleman away from his womenfolk reigned.

They were pleased to have a flying man to talk to, being all quite
ignorant of flying and having the impression that there was something
specially daring and heroic about it. At luncheon, Tom, being plied
with questions, yarned away about the war in the air; how whacked
(the word was tolerated) the Huns were, and how the R.F.C. was

F   81

keeping them whacked. Then he was taken to the office to telephone, and was able to get through to the squadron and had a rather indistinct conversation with James. If he was comfortable he might as well stay where he was, and transport would be sent for him as soon as possible, but it would not be till to-morrow. The rest of the flight had got back before the mist covered the aerodrome. Glad he was all right. . . .

Tom felt very foolish; if only someone else as well as he had been caught by the fog so would he have been kept in countenance. But to be caught by the fog foolishly and unnecessarily, and then to crash his bus forty miles from home just at the time when it was most needed, that was not the sort of thing to do whether the war was his concern or not. It was a failure, and it hurt his pride to fail ridiculously. He had taken on a job that offically assumed that he possessed all sorts of fine qualities of head and heart, and even if it was pure bluff, he hated his bluff to be seen through. Nothing hurts pride, he reflected, like being found out. But was he 'found out'? Suppose someone else, Williamson for instance, had done what he had done, what would he have thought of him? None the worse; he would have congratulated him on getting away with it unharmed. There was nothing extraordinary in turning over landing on soft ploughed stuff, rather it was to be expected; Camels were notorious for that sort of thing. And he would probably have congratulated him for having got a day's rest from the war by the crash.

While this debate was going on inside him, he had reported the substance of his conversation to the adjutant, who at once placed a cubicle at his disposal for the night and put him in charge of his own batman. The batman borrowed pyjamas and toilet apparatus for him and told him the history of everyone in the mess; they were all gentlemen, if ever there were gentlemen, he said. The batman also talked about himself. He was by trade a dental mechanic, and he strongly advised Tom to have all his teeth out at the earliest opportunity, as it would save him a lot of bother in the long run, and false teeth were far easier to keep properly clean. Tom thanked him and went to sleep for two hours and the batman brought him a cup of tea and some cake. The colonel thought he might prefer tea in his room, as he must be tired after his adventures. Dinner would be at seven, and would he care to borrow a pair of slacks? Tom would, and some note-paper too. He had found the right spot for a forced landing.

At dinner the subject of conversation was flying. The usual questions were asked: why had he taken it up? what did he feel like the first time he went up? had he ever looped the loop? had he shot down any Huns? did he know McCudden or Micky Mannock or the Mad Major?

Tom told them that he had transferred to the R.F.C. because he needed a change from the infantry. He had been assured at the time that the average life of a pilot was six weeks. That was ten months ago. He was very glad he had made the change, for it meant a great deal to live in comfort and cleanliness all the time. And in winter the life was not so very trying, days being short and the weather often too bad for flying. Sometimes it was impossible to leave the ground for three or four days at a time. No doubt with summer coming on life would be a great deal harder, but the war might be over quite soon now, didn't they think?

This suggestion split the conversation up. The balance of opinion was against the probability of an early finish. The summer campaigns would have to work themselves out, and if nothing decisive happened, such as the capture of Paris and the Channel Ports, or on the other hand a German reverse ending in demoralization, then the war might be prolonged into next year. The colonel did not think the war would be won in the field at all, as a real break through had been proved impossible. It was a matter of which population was starved to breaking point first. One of the junior officers suggested that the American invasion must lead eventually to victory on the western front, but the colonel smiled. For him there were only two real nations on earth, English and French. And even the French had their faults, being pig-headed and rather too French.

Then they got back to flying, and Tom told them the first time he went up was in a Rumpty, that was to say, a Maurice Farman Shorthorn, a queer sort of bus like an assemblage of birdcages. You climbed with great difficulty through a network of wires into the nacelle, and sat perked up there, adorned with a crash helmet, very much exposed to the wondering gaze of men. There did not seem to be any *a priori* reason why this structure should leave the ground, but after dashing across the aerodrome at forty miles an hour for some time the thing did imperceptibly and gradually climb into the air. It was very like a ride on top of an omnibus. A Rumpty was no aeroplane for stunting. The flight was a quiet trip up to three hundred feet and down again. A few daring spirits who had tried stunting were dead. The C.O. of that squadron, a pompous and bossy penguin, Major Beak, maintained that Rumpties were good buses when you knew how to fly them. He had been on active service on them, in Mesopotamia, where he had contended valiantly with the heat bumps engendered by the fierce sun until the heat made him so bad tempered that he was invalided home to get rid of him. On the home front he was sufficiently senior to be able to avoid flying, and work off his bad temper on junior people who did fly. According to him Rumpties were fine, and it was only damned junior stupidity that jeered at them. They had to be used, for hundreds of them existed, a big order having been placed; and as they were of no use for any practical purpose, the only thing to do with them was to use them for training. The trainees would have to unlearn later all that they learnt then, but young pilots must begin at the beginning, and a Rumpty certainly was only just beginning to be an aeroplane. Flying with their antiquated controls was a mixture of playing a harmonium, working the village pump, and sculling a boat.

However, Tom became habituated to staggering through the atmosphere in these soaring cats'-cradles, and in the fullness of time he took one up by himself, and stayed up for an hour and a half, reaching in this time the eagle-baffling height of three thousand feet, whence he gazed down on the still sleeping western suburbs of London and felt himself to be a pilot. This flight was so successful that after breakfast he was sent up again in another machine.

By this time a fairly strong breeze was blowing from the south-west, and there was a ceiling of cloud at about seven hundred feet; not the weather in which a novice in a Rumpty was likely to enjoy himself. He flew round and round the aerodrome at five hundred feet, being bumped about irksomely by the choppy air. It was a great change from the still clear atmosphere of dawn . . . but an

84

hour passed, and he might soon land. Then the engine spluttered and stopped. Tom knew one thing, that he must not stall, and immediately put the nose down into gliding position to maintain speed. The engine did not pick up. This was a forced landing, and by the time he realized the alarming truth he did not seem to have enough height to glide on to the aerodrome so as to land into the wind. There was a field in front that he must make for. The engine gave a splutter but subsided again. The field was rushing up at him. He was going down much too steeply. He was almost in the field. He was doing seventy; he would never get in. Trees were in front. The engine spluttered again. He had left the throttle open. He looked down and pulled it off, and then there was a shock and he was out of the aeroplane, lying on the ground a dozen yards from the remains of it. He had been thrown on his head, but the crash helmet had saved him. He must have flown into the ground; he didn't really know exactly what had happened; he found himself on the ground and the Rumpty smashed. He might have been unconscious for a little while. The nacelle was upside down on the ground with a pile of wreckage on it. He had been strapped in, but the safety belt had given; otherwise his neck must have been broken. But what a mess the old Rumpty was! One more write off. It was an achievement to smash up a Rumpty like that and not be hurt. He shook himself. Yes, he was quite uninjured; one shoe was missing, and the ankle felt a little bit wrenched. He walked over to the wreck and found his shoe wedged upside down under the nacelle with the toe projecting. He pulled at it, but it was fixed firmly. He got both hands to it and tugged and wriggled it, and suddenly it came away and he rolled over on his back.

Someone flew overhead as he was putting on his shoe, leaning over to look at him. He walked round the wreck, his own wreck. It was a good one. He ought to be dead. Was he, by the way? He couldn't see his dead body about, but it might be under the nacelle. The motor ambulance came jolting over the field towards him, and it was a relief when the orderly spoke to him, and he knew he was not a spirit. The matter ended with a fortnight's sick leave and a few words with Major Beak about his incompetence.

Since then he had had a number of minor crashes, mere landing accidents, but nothing to compare with that destruction of the Rumpty. Probably he had done the right thing in keeping straight on when his engine had conked. It was very easy for an inexperienced pilot to stall when he was doing turns with his engine off to try to reach a landing place, and that meant a dive or spin into the ground, which killed in nine cases out of ten. On a Rumpty, with the engine behind you, there was no hope at all. It would pulp you. How many fellows, some that could fly too, had been killed through trying to turn back to the aerodrome when their engine had cut out after taking off! Engines had a way of cutting out just then, and the instinct was to turn back, when really there wasn't room to do it, and the pilot inevitably held the nose up too much in trying to keep height and in a jiffy he was spinning with no chance whatever of getting out of it, and that was the end of him. Tom had only seen one case where the fellow got away with it. He had spun a Camel from a hundred and fifty feet right into the arms of a sturdy oak which caught him. He climbed down to earth none the worse and went into a pub across the road and celebrated his escape with an admiring audience which stood him so much whisky that he had to go back on the ambulance after all.

Tom yarned away. After Rumpties he had gone on to Avros which really were aeroplanes, and quite different to fly. A number of people were killed on their first solos through doing a flat turn after taking off, and getting into a spin near the ground; but there was no hope for flat turn merchants. They just hadn't flying sense, and might as well kill themselves quickly.

Apart from flat turns an Avro would do anything you wanted, and when it had got used to you would even do a flat turn just for fun if you kicked the rudder with decision. Touch was the thing in flying; though not so much in war flying, in which the heavy-handed pilot was more likely to survive, because he yanked his bus about and sideslipped so much that he was a difficult target. On the other hand, the fine pilot gained more height on turns, and perhaps turned in less radius. But Tom put his faith in sideslipping for getting out of trouble. No sights could allow for movement sideways.

You soon got used to doing steep turns and spins on Avros. To do a vertical turn you just pushed the stick hard over and then pulled it back and held it like that for as long as you wanted to go on turning. There was not much sensation about it unless you hung over the side and watched the earth. You were sitting parallel to, as it were, an earth that was swinging round like a huge wheel that was painted as a large scale map. A spin was much better, and more difficult to get used to. Some Avros were so stable that it was difficult to make them spin. You shut off the engine and pulled her nose up until she stalled. As she fell into a vertical dive you kicked on full rudder and held the stick as far back as it would come on the same side, and you should spin. But sometimes, especially if you tried to spin to the left, you fell into a steep spiral, which gave a very different sensation. In a spiral you were on the inside of the turn, with centrifugal force pressing you into your seat, whereas, with the machine rotating about its longitudinal axis in a spin, its tendency was rather to throw you out. A spinning machine was really out of control, but you could quickly regain control by pushing the joystick forwards, when the spin changed into a dive. Once he had been spun when doing dual with Baker, before he was used to aerobatics. Instructors as a rule had no time for anything but circuits and landings and a few turns; everything else the pupil had to find out for himself. But once Baker had wanted to get down from three thousand feet in a hurry. The engine stopped, the nose went nearly vertically upwards and the Avro hung like that for a second and then fell over to the right. He clung to the sides of the cockpit as he was thrown out of the seat on to the loose safety belt. The earth vanished and there was nothing but dizzying sky until the sheer catastrophic flop brought the world leaping at him, rushing to swallow up the sky, and there was no heaven but only the titubating earth. He had never been able to recapture the breathless horror of that first spin, when he had clung terrified to a bucking aeroplane that seemed trying to throw him, and the world had jerked past as though a giant were spinning it with a whip. It was always the first time that was memorable: moreover it was more shocking to be stunted than to stunt, just as one couldn't tickle one's own ribs effectively.

But he had never been looped and didn't know quite what to expect when he made his first attempt. It was on a day of westerly wind and patches of nimbus clouds between fifteen hundred and two thousand feet that he took off with his mind made up that he was going to loop. He had had to screw his courage to the sticking place before he had been able to make the resolution. It was always an effort for him to do a new stunt; he was nervous. He flew steadily up through a space in the clouds into the bright upper air, from where, looking down, the patches and rifts between the clouds were dark and sombre, and it was difficult to distinguish features of the dun world of shadowed fields and pale roads against the brilliant cloud-floor.

He flew until he was some five hundred feet above the clouds and had a definite horizon to steer by. He was invigorated by the pure sparkling air above the cloud belt, and happy enough to try anything. He held the joystick forwards to put his nose down for speed. There was nothing dangerous about looping at that height, but there was a certain blind physical repugnance and timidity of earth-bound habit to be overcome. The pitot soon showed a speed of eighty miles an hour, then eighty-five, and as soon as it touched ninety he brought the joystick slightly back. The cloud-horizon dropped away at once, and he was heading into blank space. He felt himself pressed tightly and more tightly into his seat as he shot upwards, till it seemed he would be forced through it. He was doing a bad loop. He had jerked the stick ever so slightly and pulled the aeroplane upwards too abruptly, creating excessive centrifugal pressure. For perhaps two seconds he felt crushed against the seat and then the pressure suddenly ceased and he was hanging uncomfortably in the belt. Petrol spurted in his face from the pressure gauge, the engine spluttered, and the whole aeroplane shook. The controls were limp. He pulled the stick further back with the intention of getting over the top of the loop, but the machine would not respond, and fell out of its stall with a great lurch. The clouds leapt from beyond the limits of vision and occupied the whole of space. He realized that he was diving vertically, and quickly shut off petrol from the spluttering engine and let the stick go forwards until he could ease out of the dive; and when he was in a normal glide, he pumped up pressure in the petrol tank vigorously and relieved his feelings by shouting. He had stalled on top of the loop because friction against the air had caused loss of speed, had hung upside down, and fallen out sideways; a thoroughly unsatisfactory attempt. He must do better than that.

He flew steadily for a minute to regain lost height, and then got up speed again. This time he let the stick come back as it were of its own accord. The horizon dropped away, and he continued upwards drawing the stick towards him with only the minimum of pressure that would make it continue to come back. There was no unpleasant feeling either of pressure or falling and he was sitting quite comfortably when the opposite horizon appeared from behind him, and he knew he was successfully over the top. He shut off the petrol and let the stick go slowly forwards while the cloud-floor swung past and the horizon he had originally been facing reappeared. A perfect loop ending in a normal glide.

Tom went on talking until he thought they might have heard enough of his voice for one evening, and then he forbore. The air was still shaking with the unceasing gunfire. They played bridge. Tom was out of luck; kings were in the wrong place, distribution upset his attempts to establish: but what did it matter at a franc a hundred? He was like a generalissimo sending his forces to do battle; if they were slaughtered it mattered very little to him. The game, the battle was the thing. How ever many more clubs had the fellow got? Where ever did they get all the explosives from to keep up this interminable tattoo? It was very trying when an opponent established a long suit and you had to throw away a lot of good cards; but it was all in the game. Re-deal and play a fresh hand. He wondered how the new American troops were liking the war. A useful hand this time if his partner could support him a little better than last time. The Americans would be more effective allies than the Russians. . . .

In the morning, after family breakfast at eight o'clock, all the staff except the padre went off to attend to duties. The padre was good company and the morning passed pleasantly enough. The battle still raged and there were rumours of a big German break-through. The padre said that the death-roll was not terrible to a believer in personal immortality; how could it be? It had never occurred to Tom before that this queer belief could be practically efficacious;

and could it, indeed, to a combatant? To old-style Mohammedans and such, yes; but to civilized Christians? If it could, here was another pernicious effect of religion, to encourage war by removing dislike of death. At every turn, it seemed to him, the religious, with their preposterous insistence on the unimportance of the world (except as a snare, the barbarians!) hindered mankind from making the world comfortable. They did not believe their own doctrine after they were thirty, but it was part of their mental habit then, and so very useful for keeping young people in order and swindling them into fighting their elders' wars. God, what a wicked crew!

'Apart, for the moment, from revelation,' he said to the padre, 'do you think there is any logical reason for believing that one is immortal?'

The padre thought it was one of those subjects where the reasons pro and contra balanced, and it was impossible to know anything about it except by revelation. The Christian Revelation established the fact but left the mode quite uncertain, as he read the scriptures. That did not matter; the fact was sufficient.

How the deuce could an otherwise reasonable man of the twentieth century talk comfortably about the Christian revelation? It was one of those extraordinary failures of human intelligence that Tom could see no accounting for. Why did some people refuse to use common sense about certain fragments of their experience when they used it about all the rest? The subject ought to be studied. Was it merely the power of vested interest?

After lunch he telephoned to the squadron to inquire about his transport. It would be there that day some time. The squadron was busy.

XI

TOM eventually got back to the squadron after midnight. He went quietly into the hut and lighted his lamp. The stove was still hot. Williamson and Seddon were asleep in their corners, but where was Allen? His bed was empty. Tom felt inclined to wake up one of the sleepers, but refrained. He got into bed and was soon asleep himself. When he awoke, Williamson was shaving.

'Hullo Bill,' he said.

'Hullo Tom. What time of night did you get back?'

'Towards one o'clock. How have you been getting on? Where's the others?'

'Seddon was on the early job and hasn't shown up yet. Allen has been missing since yesterday morning. Selby is missing too. He was seen to go down, but no one knows what has happened to Allen. I gather that the flight got split up ground-strafing somewhere towards Bapaume, and Allen just vanished.'

'I'm sorry.'

'So am I. Damned sorry. By the way, you've got a new flight commander. For some reason Mac has taken over A flight in Tommy's place, and you have the benefit of the new blood. If the idea was to give you a rest it's a mistaken one. They say he's a proper hell-fire merchant, and when he goes out on low work he spends all his time at fifty feet. No wonder the flight splits up. You'll have to look out for yourself, Tom. There won't be any C flight left in a few days. There's a most terrific offensive on, and the earth and air are full of Huns. God knows where they've all come from. Anyhow, have you had a good holiday?'

'Damn fine. Been living in peace, comfort, and respectability at the staff mess of a Corps School, if you know what a Corps School is. It's a sort of home for the war-weary. They treated me like an officer and a gentleman and an intrepid aviator. I feel spoiled for this sort of life. I'm sorry to find Allen gone. I don't suppose there's any hope for him if he's been missing since yesterday morning.'

'None at all, except that he may be a prisoner.'

'What have you been doing? All low work?'

'Pretty well. It's the devil of a game. We have to find out where the front line is by going and looking at the trenches to see who's in them. All ground communications seem to have gone to pot. The Huns seem to have pushed about ten miles in the last two days. There's a bulge in the line south of Arras, and it goes on down to Albert and the Somme. The earth is just lousy with Huns in some places. You can see them lying about, dead and alive, piles of them. Sort of mass formation affair. God knows what their casualties must be. And ours. In the air they are having a go at us, too. Richthofen's gang is all over the place, the SE people say.'

'All this is remarkably cheering. I'd better get up and report myself to someone.'

Tom went to the office in suitable négligé; slacks and slippers were *de rigeur*, by way of demonstrating that the squadron was not there to manufacture hot air. The major advised him not to go flying in fogs any more, and told him to see his new flight commander, Captain Beal. Him Tom found in the mess; a nice-looking young man without any of the warlike earnestness Williamson had led him to expect. He had been out before on FEs, and when he had first taken up flying had actually flown the legendary Bloater.

There was a shortage of aeroplanes in C flight, and Tom would not be on the next job. Skinner and Orr had gone over to Candas to fetch two new ones, and when they arrived Tom could pick one of them and get it shipshape for his permanent use. Skinner would have to come on jobs now that Allen had gone, so he could give the other bus a trial and Tom could take him for a tour of the lines.

That was a very pleasant programme for the day, Tom thought. Seddon came in to breakfast and sat by him.

'Hullo Tom! Fancy seeing you back so soon. I hear you've been having a good time.'

'Fine. But as soon as I'm not here to look after him, Allen gets himself shot down.'

'Yes. I'm sorry about him. I think he was a bit too keen on winning the war quickly to last long. If these young knights of the air would only go slow, they might develop into useful pilots.'

'Like you and me. But what sort of job have you had this morning? How do you like Mac as leader?'

'He's good. He seems very safe . . .'

'Oh does he? He must be breaking you in gently.'

'Well, he was very safe this morning, anyhow. There were lots of Huns about, and we didn't cross for some time. When the air was clear we made a dash and bombed some trenches and cleared off back and climbed into the clouds and spent a lot of time fiddling about trying to get into position to attack some of the Huns that were cloud-creeping. We suddenly came right on top of a dozen Albatros scouts, whether by accident or through Mac's cunning I really don't know. I suppose it was five miles over as the line is now. We dove and shot at them. Mac and Robinson got one each and they made off and so did we. If that isn't safe, what is?'

'Sounds all right. Especially if it was judgment and not luck that put you on top.'

'Then we went down on a two-seater and got it in a nasty-looking spin, but we couldn't follow as a whole skyful of scouts came and chased us off.'

'That doesn't sound so safe.'

'No, but they'd got no guts. They kept above us, and as long as we edged off westwards they seemed content. We crossed and worked up to fourteen thousand feet and went back to look for them, but didn't see any more of them.'

'Three Huns before breakfast, what? That's the sort of thing that happens with Mac in charge. Between you and me, I don't think he's so very interested in ground-strafing, but he has a gift for bagging Huns. After all, you don't get much thanks for dropping bombs, and you don't often see anything to shoot at on the ground that makes a good story in *Comic Cuts*. But if you come back from nearly every job saying "Lo, I have shot down a Hun" you are soon on the path of glory.'

> 'The paths of glory lead but to the grave,
> So little Eric shouldn't be too brave.'

'This little Eric seems to have another day off. I've got to take over a new bus from Candas when it arrives and get it ready for action. Then I take Skinner on a personally conducted tour of the lines to get him ready for action. How's that for peace in war?'

'Very nice. Don't go too near the lines. Look after Skinner's skin.'

The fellows from Candas landed at about half past ten, and after the new Camels had been inspected and entered in the account books, Tom took up D6080 because he liked the number. It was a good bus, and the engine, though rather noisy, gave more than its revs and pulled well. He found himself over the aerodrome which No. 5 squadron, that flew RE8s, inhabited, and he went down and roared along a few inches over their mess to say good morning to Briggs whom he knew there, if he was still alive. Some of the fellows came out to look at him. He climbed away and threw a couple of rolls with his engine off, coming out of the second into a dive at the watchers. He probably looked out of control, for they scattered for their lives. That was fine, and Tom went home as pleased with his bus as a king with a new crown. He took it on the range and got Chadwick to help him with the guns. They obtained a group right in the middle of the sight at thirty yards; a reasonable range, but a trifle longer than the official distance.

C flight had come back with some bullet holes and a good deal to discuss among themselves, but no actual damage. Tom obtained an account of the job from Taylor, a youth with an expression of dark craftiness which did not seem to be a good index of his character, but gave him a certain piquancy. He was not too pleased with life. Beal had taken them straight along the Arras-Cambrai road at five hundred feet; whoever heard of such a thing? 'Giving the Huns machine-gun practice. We went on until he spotted some troops in a shallow or battered communication trench and went down on them. It's a bit awkward five people strafing one trench, so I went on a bit but couldn't see much so came back to where the others were buzzing round and laid my eggs. Only just in time, because a mixed bunch of Huns came down on us and there was the hell of a scrap. Luckily a whole squadron of SEs had spotted the Huns and they came on the scene unexpectedly, otherwise we'd have been for it. I was splitarsing round wondering what the hell to do about a couple of Huns that were trying to sit on my tail when I saw one of them go streaking down with an SE after him. The next minute there was an awful mix up; us and fifteen SEs and somewhere between ten and twenty mixed Huns, Albatri, Pfalz, tripehounds. Of course the Huns got wiped out. Beal opened his bag with a tripe and a Pfalz. Miller and Debenham got an Albatros each. I don't know if I got a tripe or an SE did. The SEs got four on their own, they say. That's nine, and one SE got shot down. I saw the poor devil go. I suppose the rest of the Huns got away. You never saw such a mix up, right down on the floor. The place was strewn with crashes. Ghastly sight. It turned out all very nice, but it was damn lucky those SEs came down when they did.'

'I certainly seem to have missed something,' said Tom. 'What do you think of the Fokker triplanes?'

94

'Marvellous. They climb like lifts.'

It sounded as though life was going to be exciting with Beal in charge. Perhaps he was one of those people who liked fighting, even when it consisted in being shot at by unseen machine guns from the ground. But such a state of mind seemed to Tom absurd. No one could possibly enjoy ground-strafing. He must be suffering from an inflamed sense of duty, resulting from his appointment as flight commander on active service. Doubtless the inflammation would die down in a few days. If those SEs hadn't come down there might have been sufficient casualties to have removed it that day.

After lunch he found Skinner and they went to the office to mark the latest version of the front line on their maps. Before they took off he gave Skinner a lecture. Skinner was a sandy young Scot, and should be amenable to common sense.

'We're going to have a look at the lines without crossing into Hunland,' he said as they walked across the aerodrome from the office to C flight hangar, 'so you need not bother about anything but not running into me and map reading. I expect we'll have plenty of trouble to-morrow, so we'll do our best to keep clear of it to-day. And if I were you, Skinner, I'd be very careful for the first month you're on jobs. That's the dangerous time. Look at Selby and Allen, for instance. Selby had done eight jobs, I think, and Allen five. You'll find that eighty per cent of casualties are fellows who've done less than, say, twenty jobs. War flying is a trade you've got to learn, and however much you may fancy yourself as a pilot, remember that that's only a part of the trade. The great thing is to see things, and, believe me, until you've had a month's practice over the lines, there'll be the deuce of a lot going on that you ought to know about but won't. Many a fresh pilot is shot down before he even knows there is a Hun within miles. Push your goggles up when you're over the lines if your eyes will stand it and practise looking round you so that you study every square foot of the earth and sky every two minutes. Watch the region round the sun specially; it's not a bad idea to put up your thumb against the disc of the sun. You've got to know exactly what to look for; what an aeroplane looks like against the sky above you and below against the ground, and they look a bit different against every variation of background. Remember

95

eroplanes approach each other at four miles a minute, and con-
ate at first on seeing in time. Never mind about shooting down
Huns; if one gets in your way, shoot at it, but make quite sure first
that no other Hun is getting into position to put in a burst at you.
You'll get your Huns later, and do a lot better than if you rushed
into the war all heroic. Drop your bombs where the leader drops his,
and keep close to him all the time; it's his job to look after you.
And when you've got to the stage of seeing everything and keeping
your head in a scrap and knowing when to fight and when to clear
out, if you ever do get to that stage, then you can begin to take an
active part in the war, and do some fighting if you feel inclined.
But give yourself a chance. Anyone can shoot you down if you don't
see him coming, but it takes a wonderfully good Hun to bag a
Camel if the pilot is expecting him.'

Skinner listened with attention, and when Tom had finished he
said 'I'm much obliged for your screed, Cundall. I've hairrd a good
many since I joined the Flying Corps, but they've all been how not to
give the Hun a chance. This is the fairrst I've hairrd about giving
yourself a chance, a subject which seems to me desairrving of con-
seederation. I've noticed that it's the experienced pilots who get
the Huns, and where's the experienced pilots coming from unless
the inexperienced ones take care of themselves? And, speaking for
myself, I've no desire whatever to be shot down. It would be a
waste of a good Camel and a good Scot.'

Tom was pleased with Skinner's response, but was at the same time
faintly aware that he preferred Skinner with a little whisky in him;
it had a mellowing effect.

They had to keep fairly low because of the clouds. In front of
Albert Tom climbed to ten thousand, but there was so little of the
earth to be seen that he went down to one thousand again. The big
retreat was going on, and the roads a mile or two back were full of
traffic. What a target for low-flying aeroplanes! If the Germans had
had the nerve for low flying they could have played hell. God, what
a target.

When they got back, B flight had just arrived without Jenkins,
and C and A had just taken off. B had been in a couple of dog fights.
Bulmer, Williamson, and Jenkins had got a Hun each, and Franklin

two. Unfortunately Jenkins had been shot down while he was watching his Hun go.

Tom found the job of clearing up Allen's belongings awaiting him, which kept him occupied, with some help from Williamson, till the return of the last patrol. There was nothing in his possessions that needed suppressing as unfit for the scrutiny of his next of kin. As a rule the relics of heroes were not all fit to be seen by their nearest and dearest, but in Allen's case this did not appear. There was, however, a bundle of letters in his beloved's handwriting, and these Tom tied up separately with the intention of getting whoever went on leave next to forward them to her. He also kept out a few objects of intrinsic value which were unlikely to reach their destination, as the habit of scrounging could be indulged safely on the kit of the wounded and dead. Then he strapped up the bundle, and that was all that was left of Allen and his fine young passion. He wrote a cheerful note to the girl, saying he would let her have her letters as soon as leave started again, and he hoped there would soon be some good news about Allen.

A and C flights came back in triumph from a massacre. They had surprised two lots of Huns, one over Quéant and one near Mossyface Wood. Mac had taken full advantage of the western sun and the clouds, and the Huns had seemed to know nothing about the attacks until they were being shot down, and then they ran for cover. Perhaps they were new pilots out for practice; the Huns seemed to choose the evening to send their worst pilots out, or perhaps their vespertine incompetence was the effect of dazzle. Anyhow, eight of them had been shot down. Mac had two, Beal one, Robinson two, and Miller, Moss, and Seddon one each.

Altogether the squadron had shot down twenty Huns and dropped a hundred and twenty bombs that day, which was easily a record, and dinner was a binge.

XII

TOM was not in the mood for getting drunk and raising a shindy, especially as he had taken no part in the day's triumphs, so he returned early to the hut, where he found a new-comer named Smith and the

G   97

batman getting the corner that had been Allen's into order. His speech betrayed Smith as a Yorkshireman. He was one of those plain, decent fellows that people like at once. Tom soon found out that he was newly married, hated war, had no very good opinion of himself as a Camel pilot, but was a hundred break man at billiards.

'Do you play bridge?' Tom inquired. 'We're four in here you see.'

'I have played a little, but I'm not much good. I like solo better.'

'Like solo better! You can't be serious.'

'Well, I'm more used to it, but I don't mind trying to play bridge if you want me to.'

Seddon came in. 'Devil of a row in the mess.' Tom introduced Smith, and in a few minutes they were cursing away at the war, as married men, well and heartily. Tom laughed at them.

'It's all very well for Seddon to shout about the wickedness of killing,' he said, 'but he managed to bag a Hun to-day, and it's not the first time either. To tell the truth, he's a hell of a pilot and going to do well.'

'Thanks for the unnecessary bouquet, but what's a fellow to do? In general, it's a case of kill or be killed. We've got to keep the upper hand, and I freely admit that in war I'd rather kill than be killed. The Hun to-day just sat still for me to shoot. I don't think he saw me.'

'Not only do you slay Huns, but you admittedly slay them by pouncing on them from ambush. You don't perform your trudications openly in fair fight, but by stratagems and, literally, stabbing them in the back. Bah!'

'You're quite right,' said Seddon soberly. 'We're just a gang of tricky murderers like all war merchants. And the papers still call us knights errant. I dare say they are right, and that the methods even of those painful warriors wouldn't bear scrutiny.'

'Now you're raising a side-issue and maligning the Tennysonian heroes of the mahogany dining-table at the court of King Albert . . .'

Here Williamson entered.

'Ha Bill, meet our new co-hutter, Mr. Smith of Huddersfield. We were just explaining to him how wicked it is to shoot down the gentle Hun. Smith, this is Williamson, and he is another of the wretches that have this day slain Huns.'

98

'For heaven's sake don't let Seddon and Cundall corrupt you. They would talk the innocence out of a cherub.'

Smith smiled it all off. 'This seems to be a wonderful squadron. Fancy getting twenty Huns in one day! And for only one casualty. I didn't know such things were possible.'

'Nor did anyone else,' said Tom, 'but you never know what you can do till you try. And don't be so pleased about the one casualty. If you work out what one casualty a day mounts up to, you will notice that we shall all be casualties within a month. It's daily vigesimation.'

'I don't know what that is,' said Williamson, 'but the pace is too hot to last. At the present rate all available German pilots, machines, and morale on this front would be smashed in a few days. They'll have to give up fighting us in the air and go back to their defensive tactics. Perhaps they'll send Richthofen's circus here to have a go at us. Things obviously can't go on as they are.'

Things did not go on as they were, for on the next day, the Sunday before Easter, only three Huns were bagged, all by A flight in the morning, Mac and Robinson getting an Albatros scout each, and the whole flight shooting a two-seater. There were a good many Huns in the distance, but no one else got into contact with them. In the air, German agressiveness was on the wane, but on the ground their advance was going on invincibly.

Tom was on a job in the middle of the morning. Beal seemed not to be feeling so fond of machine-gun fire as he had been on the day before, and took them along the Arras-Bapaume road, over which the enemy had rolled, at eighteen hundred feet; but not being able to see well enough from there, went down to a thousand, where Tom felt far from comfortable. What was three hundred yards to a machine gun? Archie shelled them, but they were too low for him to be very accurate. Beal disregarded the shelling entirely, and held straight on, which Tom thought silly of him. There was no need to help Archie even when he wasn't shooting very well. Then Beal spotted some troops in shell holes, and circled round losing height. He dived away from his objective to four hundred feet, and then turned sharply back to the attack. Tom hated it; he could see German soldiers crouching in shell holes, and he was supposed to go down on them in cold blood and kill as many as he could.

99

It had to be done, and done as effectively as possible, for every German killed meant, directly or indirectly, that the life of one of their own men was saved. At any rate, that was the theory. It would have been useful to be able to regard all Germans, or any other enemies, as a particularly foul and dangerous sort of vermin that should be exterminated when you could get at them, male and female and young. But Tom could not feel like that, and had to remain aware that it was an affair between human beings of close relationship.

There was, however, about his particular method of murder a strangeness and unreality which relieved the horror of butchery. He pulled a wire and released a bomb. There was nothing dreadful about pulling a wire. If you put your head over the side and dropped a wing you might see the bomb drop away, but you weren't as a rule able to follow its fall to the ground. You saw some bursts, whitish-grey puffs, but it was not possible to tell if they did damage to troops already prostrate. You got rid of the four bombs with alacrity (if they all dropped), very glad to lighten the aeroplane. Then with twice the life in the bus, you dived and zoomed and dived and zoomed, loosing off bursts at the wretched troops, keeping an anxious look-out for machine guns, and then cleared off and picked up formation to do a patrol. Fortunately you couldn't do very much shooting as there would be no use patrolling without ammunition, and the two machine guns could shoot off all their ammunition in less than a minute's continuous firing. Two seconds' bursts were the thing, which each gave a group of about forty bullets, and ought to be enough for the immediate purpose.

Again, you couldn't tell what sort of effect your shooting was having on a target of that sort; it must be doing damage, but the damage was remote and not a direct consequence of your actions. You pointed your aeroplane towards the ground and pressed a lever on the joystick for a second or two, that was all. It wasn't like going up to a man and sticking a bayonet into his neck or guts and giving it a twist; nothing like that: you pressed a lever.

Nevertheless, Tom hated it; kill, kill, kill: why? In the interests of usury, Seddon would say, and that was as likely to be true as the recruiting-poster reasons: the Honour of Britain, Remember Belgium, and Lord Kitchener; though why Lord Kitchener should ever have been held up as a reason for anything but despair, goodness only knew. Not that Tom attributed his dislike of ground-strafing to humanitarianism primarily; the primary reason was its unavoidable danger, unavoidable in the sense that you never knew whence you were being shot at. He was more concerned about his own skin than that of such Germans as he happened to blow up or shoot up, and machine-gun fire from the ground was the very devil. Still, there it was; it would have been a vile job even if he had been able to perform it in safety.

In the present instance everything went off well for them, as they did not seem to be within range of many active machine guns, but it was difficult to know when they were being shot at, for engine noise drowned the rattle of a machine gun more than a hundred yards away, and tracer bullets were not always used. They gave the ground Huns a bad five minutes and then went away upstairs, where Archie expended a great deal of ammunition on them, and Beal condescended to dodge about.

They climbed up beyond the cloud region to twelve thousand feet, where it was very peaceful but cold, and as there was nothing to do up there Beal took them down again to two thousand, where Archie could see and entertain them. Then he went down to where there seemed to be a particularly bad spot on the ground near Achiet-le-Petit. German artillery was very active; they went so low to investigate that the concussion rocked them. The British seemed to be falling back on Beaumont Hamel and Hébuterne. The Germans were pushing them, and it looked as though they might be driving in a wedge where all the hate was going on. Beal went down to take a crack at Jerry, but Jerry was well supplied with machine guns and bullets flew thick. It was not at all easy to make out the front line; in fact there didn't seem to be any front line. Things looked bad.

They went home and made their report. Beal was full of information and corrections of the front line, which was not so much a line as a movement. Tom made a point of the trouble near Achiet. The major informed them of a new development. Patrols were washed out, and they were to spend all their time at low work. They would stand by all day and go up when needed and make for a certain objective, do their stuff, and hurry back to report on what they had seen. It was special service. The SEs and Dolphins and BFs could look after the upper air. Another thing was, they would probably have to evacuate the aerodrome in a hurry soon, for they might be within range of back area shelling at any time, especially if the expected attack on Arras should be successful; so they must keep their stuff packed as far as possible.

What a life! They sat in the mess playing any sort of game that made a gamble, waiting for the shout of the klaxon. The weather was almost bad enough for a washout, there being a layer of cloud at fifteen hundred feet, but in the present crisis when the word came through from Wing for a certain job to be done, they would have to go out and try to do it, and if the Hun machine gunners didn't have a good bag it would be through poor shooting and not through lack of opportunity.

C flight went out at three o'clock to visit the district south of Bapaume where the retreat was going on at the rate of a mile an hour, and something had to be done. There was a strong west wind driving a blanket of low misty cloud; it was worse than ever. All the time they were bumped to blazes, couldn't get up even to a thousand feet, and couldn't see anything that wasn't almost directly under-neath. What a day for stopping in bed! However, there certainly wouldn't be any Huns about in the air to trouble them. Even Beal seemed less enthusiastic; he took them down to Albert without going within shot of the lines. Tom shouted and sang to cheer himself up: he could at any rate make any amount of noise without being over-heard, and shout out loud in the greatest possible privacy.

> If I had the wings of an Avro
> Far, far away would I roam.
> I'd fly to my friends way in Holland,
> And never no more come back home.

God! he would clear out of this; get lost and land in Holland, or anywhere a long way behind the German lines. If he didn't reach Holland, no doubt the Germans would be pleased to see him. He might even land by mistake on one of their aerodromes and make kind inquiries as to how they were enjoying the war in the air. A pity he couldn't talk German; it would give him more confidence.

They turned east and were soon over the desolate country of the 1916 Somme battlefield, which had taken four months to capture and half a million casualties, and was being lost in as many days, possibly with as many casualties. The ground was dotted with grey wool of shell bursts that quickly streamed away in the wind. They went down to two hundred feet over a line of bursting shrapnel perhaps near Longueval but it was difficult to be certain where they were so low over the uniform desert.

There were swarms of Huns in shell holes or in the open. They pullulated. It was mass attack. Bombs could hardly fail to do a lot of damage. Tom used up all his ammunition, and thought he didn't waste it. When he had finished, none of the rest of the flight was in sight. He climbed away in the direction that must be west, but as soon as he got away from the battle it was impossible to tell which way he was going; his compass was spinning after all the turning and skidding. He flew just under the clouds and waited for it to settle down. He was over strange country and found at length that he was heading south-west; of course he should have known he was going directly against the wind, but hadn't thought of it. He turned through a right angle and put his nose down and contour-chased. He didn't care a damn where he was. The job was over and done, well done this time, and he was alive, and nothing mattered. He followed a road, skimming over lorries and skipping over a village that appeared suddenly without his seeing a *ralentir* notice. A little farther on there was an aerodrome near the road, and he pulled up, circled, and landed. It was a DH9 squadron and they were surprised to see him on such a dud afternoon. He only stopped to get a map reading, and set off north for home, and in ten minutes was on familiar ground. He landed just behind someone else whom he recognized as Debenham. A few minutes later Beal, Miller, and Skinner appeared, which left only Taylor to come. They went to the office and gave the latest pin-points of the front line where they had been: 57D, 27, a4 to b6, and told their story, and Beal signed all the documents that a job gave birth to. After all that, Taylor was still out.

Tom went to the hut and threw his map, his automatic pistol, his leather gloves, his woollen gloves, his silk gloves, his sidcot, his helmet, and his goggles on the bed, kicked his overshoes under it, and went to the mess for tea. He toasted himself some bread at the fire, and heard that Marsden of A flight, a snub-nosed Midlander, had had his left arm damaged by a bullet and had gone to hospital very pleased with himself for having picked out of the dip the ideal Blighty. Two new pilots had arrived, both Canadians. One was Jones, and Tom thought he must have a horse among his ancestors. The other was a French Canadian, looking as melancholy as cold mutton, and Tom got talking to him, hoping he might feel better for some quiet but cheerful conversation. His name was Dubois and he came from a place called Trois Rivières, where, Tom gathered, there were two rivers, one being the St. Lawrence, a river that Tom had heard of. The thought of his beautiful river made Dubois horribly nostalgic. He hoped, however, to have an opportunity of seeing Paris, the home of his ancestors, before returning, or not returning, to his beautiful river. He had a wife. . . .

Married men, thought Tom, really ought not to go to war until they had got tired of their wives, and then they ought, divorce laws being what they were. Those that were still happy were the most unenthusiastic, and those that weren't the most reckless, of warriors. Why not form a Married but Marred brigade? It would be the very thing for ground-strafing, balloon sinking, and aerodrome raiding.

The klaxon sounded, producing an instant hush in the mess. DER-der-der-der it shouted, and again DER-der-der-der. 'Hard luck, Bill,' Tom called out to Williamson. Bulmer hurried off to the office for instructions, and other members of B swore and swallowed their tea. The blasted war wouldn't even let them have tea in peace.

Dubois wanted to have a look round, so Tom walked up to the hangars with him. He found that three bullet holes in the main planes of his machine were being patched.

'That's the worst of this confounded low work,' he remarked to Dubois. 'You're being shot at all the time, and don't know it. By the time you're on jobs,' he added, 'I expect this spell will be over. It can't go on much longer. We've had more casualties this last four days than for a month previously. There's one missing and one wounded to-day. I hope we'll soon be upstairs again among the Albatri. It's not such a bad life up there.'

They were still pottering about when B flight landed, having dropped their bombs in front of Albert, where the enemy was still advancing, and was within three miles of the town. Once again Albert was being shelled.

But who cared about Albert? It was too late for any more jobs, and there was whisky in the bar. Also it was Sunday and the padre would perform a short service in the church hut. Taylor was definitely missing. After dinner the FEs set out night-flying, the weather having cleared sufficiently. Later, night-flying Huns began to buzz around and give Archie some shooting. Occasional crashes were dropped bombs. Heavy artillery was banging away. At about ten Beal entered the hut, which was already enriched by the presence of Chadwick, Burkett, Miller, and Sawyer. Poker was in progress. Tom, having lost the money he set out to lose, had dropped out. He hadn't a poker face, and anyhow nobody could thrive at poker against Canadians, whose national sport it was, though some seemed willing to lose a lot of money in the attempt.

'Here's three of you,' Beal said, indicating Miller and Sawyer and Tom. '6.15 in the morning.'

'What's the job?' asked Miller.

'Usual. See if the line's altered between Arras and Bapaume.'

'Sounds nice,' said Tom.

'Come on, jackpots.' Chadwick was not interested in the war. After three years of it he had retired from active service to a comfortable job where he could indulge his passion for gambling, revelry, and women, safe from his wife. In these pursuits he was tireless.

XIII

TOM put out the light and went out into the grey dusk of the quiet morning. Through the leafless trees he could see in the east a single cloud very faintly rosy. It was the sort of dawn, he knew, that promised a fair day. The weather had been far too good lately, and there was still no sign of respite.

Beal and Miller and Debenham were in the mess eating their eggs and going over their maps to make sure they had got the latest version of the front line, according to Beal, marked correctly.

'Morning Cundall,' said Beal cheerfully, 'got your map?'

'I'll get it,' said Tom, and going for it met Sawyer, who looked like a sleepy boy hurrying to early school. 'Better get your map. Beal's worried about whether we know where the front line is.'

When they had settled where the line really was or ought to be, Beal said they would fly along it down to the Albert-Bapaume road and look for any variations. Tom shuddered as he ate probably his last hard-boiled egg. Twenty miles of machine guns at least, and another twenty back if Beal felt that he hadn't seen enough. What a lovely war it would be if there weren't any machine guns! Or if only he had taken up aviation as a lad, and come out in 1914 on some pre-cambrian flying machine and exchanged pistol shots with a gallant foe once a week. By now he would be a colonel snoring gently at some wing, awaking later and ringing up his favourite squadron, commanding it to send out a few Camels to find out what fuel the Huns at such and such pin-points were using to cook their breakfast sausages. Or even a plump general with a château, a monocle, and a private Harry Tate.

As soon as they got over the lines Beal went down to five hundred feet, and Tom tried to get rid of his bombs on some trenches. He saw one go, but no more, and the machine still felt loaded. He found it intensely depressing to be a target for dozens of machine guns while loaded with a half-hundredweight of undroppable high explosive. He lost interest in the whereabouts of the front line. His mouth got dry and foul. He must go to the American canteen and get some chewing gum. There did not seem to be any movement on the floor; just shelling. The sun was rising behind the eastern mists, gilding a few high clouds. Archie was busy with something miles above, possibly a patrol of SEs. How very nice for them, only to have Archie to bother about. Beal was darting about a lot, which made it difficult to keep any sort of formation; it was impossible to watch the floor while following a zig-zagging leader. Sawyer was being a nuisance. He kept getting in everybody's way. If there was one thing a pilot ought to be able to do properly, it was to formate. A fellow who barged about as Sawyer sometimes did was as danger-ous as a dozen Huns; or, say, half a dozen. Some tracer streaked up between him and Beal, and Tom sideslipped outwards. How the devil could anyone do reconnaissance while being shot at and keeping formation? There didn't seem to be much point in keeping formation so near the lines; they could always skedaddle across if they were attacked, and pick up formation in safety on their own side; for Huns seldom ventured out of Hunland. But Beal liked to have them all near him. His methods were different from anyone else's. Whoever except him would take a flight along twenty miles of front at five hundred feet? At Serre he evidently saw something, for he dived and fired in the direction of the ruins. Tom dutifully followed and loosed off a few rounds without seeing anything in particular to fire at. He pulled out, and saw that one member of the flight was making off westwards. It must be Sawyer. Tom picked up formation again towards Thiepval, and in another two minutes they were over the Albert-Bapaume Road. He hoped that Beal had seen enough of what was to be seen, and would be satisfied with having run the gauntlet once. Beal turned westwards and flew over Albert, and then went away north-west, evidently making for home. Tom settled down to enjoy the trip. Another job done, and still alive. He crept up to Beal and put his wing-tip in the angle between Beal's tail and main planes, and Miller did the same on the other side, while Debenham flew with his nose a little above and behind Beal's tail; and thus compact they arrived over the aerodrome at ten minutes past seven. Sawyer was not there; probably he had had a forced landing somewhere.

They reported on the front line. Beal had one or two deviations to note, and said that the enemy seemed massed near Serre.

Tom was sure of a peaceful shave and breakfast, and then the waiting for the next job would begin. How life had changed in the last four days! Before then, jobs were gentlemanly affairs at stated times, with regular days off and plenty of dud weather. A two hours' patrol was a pleasant memory: a brush with a bunch of Albatri, a two-seater chased, Archie coughing away, a stable sweep of line from Arras to Bapaume with Cambrai ten miles in Hunland, a visitable distance: dear memories of a dead past when deep brumal peace brooded on earth and in the circumadjacent air. That was all far away; and now the flowering of the cavalry and cricket mind of the professional soldier was being seen. They had never been able to regard trench warfare as real war; where were the horses and the lances? Victory was a matter of getting the foe running and chasing him on horses and sticking him in the back; every school-soldier knew that. So they were careful not to encourage digging in, not at any rate to the extent those filthy rotters the Germans had done, for trenches were only places to wait in during preparations for glorious attacks, which would have won the war long ago if the Germans had played the game. But they didn't; they had Hindenberg lines and no traditions; why, there weren't any Germans before 1870. They ought to follow the lead of older and better nations, full of tradition: Crécy, Agincourt, Blenheim, Fontenoy, Waterloo . . . .

'Bakerloo, Peterloo, Clapham Junction, Spion Kop,' added Seddon, to whom Tom had been expressing disgust, 'and wha. do you think the French said at Crécy, when the English archers planted stakes and shot down the Flower of French Chivalry from a great distance?'

'Of course they said *quels barbares! c'est magnifique mais ce n'est pas la guerre. Ce n'est pas bien-élèvé, ça.*'

'Precisely. And at Agincourt they said something about a nook shotten isle of Albion, which sounds even worse. *Plus ça change plus c'est la même chose.* But what were you saying?'

'Oh, I was only grumbling about being the Light Camel Brigade and doing a Balaclava dash twice daily. And the worst part of it all, or a heavy additional burden, is going to be this waiting about for the bloody klaxon.'

'If it lasts long,' said Seddon, 'I shall go gibbering barmy. And I shall never hear a klaxon horn again without my blood changing colour. I should think this is the War's Worst Job.'

'No, the PBI gets that every time,' said Tom, 'but it's hard enough, especially in C flight.'

The klaxon called for A at ten o'clock and for B at eleven. Tom waited. A flight came back safe, reporting a big war on the Somme as usual. Tom waited. B flight came back safe. The Huns were within a mile of Albert. Tom waited, and had a whisky and soda before lunch. He had won nearly forty francs, he thought, during the morning, at one thing and another, and that was a lot for him. He wasn't often lucky that way. What trouble was waiting for him to balance things? Lunch came along at one o'clock, and, having discussed with Hudson the relative merits of being shot down in flames and dying of cancer, he went to the hut to fill his tobacco pouch. But as he was passing the tree where the klazon nested, the confounded thing shouted and made him jump out of his skin. DER-der-DER-der. He cursed it, and it answered DER-der-DER-der in gurgling iron command. Perhaps the start this blaring voice of fate had given him was the offset to those forty francs. It was worth quite that. Beal came hurrying out of the mess.

He couldn't make Beal out. No one was freer from officiousness, hot air, and martial bearing, yet he seemed almost to like doing jobs, and he did his best to have them done properly. He must be one of those unnatural people without fear. Personal risk hardly affected him. It was part of the job, and only had to be considered because to be shot down was bad for the job. As for a casualty a day, that was nothing. Tom had heard him say in the mess he remembered six going west in one day, and twenty in a week. Tom thought these figures must include pilots and observers. If Camels had been two-seaters they might have reached twenty casualties that week.

They were to go south of Albert towards Bray on the Somme, where Third Army's right wing was in trouble. Beal flew straight down to Albert without crossing the lines. They could see the hell of a war on just in front of Albert and towards Beaumont Hamel. Then Beal went right down over the roofs of Albert, out of which all sorts of transport was pouring along the Amiens and Doullens roads. In a few seconds he was shooting up a wave of advancing Huns. Tom followed him closely. Bursting shells bumped him about. The air must be thick with bullets. He saw holes in his planes. There were thousands and thousands of Huns; piles of dead and masses of living. He dropped bombs that could not miss, and dipped and fired, and pulled up and dipped again. South of Albert the line no longer swung away east, but seemed to go straight south: a tremendous advance must have been made by the Germans. Suddenly his engine cut clean out. Something vital had been hit. He turned west, and as he was doing a hundred and thirty he could glide some way even from a hundred feet. He was across the lines in a moment. Machine guns were rattling at him, and then he was over a ridge and out of range. He glided down the declivity. God, it was a marvel they hadn't got him, gliding straight across their front like that. Thank the Lord the west wind was very light that afternoon, or he would never have got away. But he still had to make a landing on ground that was rough and pitted. He pancaked, bounced, and flopped upside down into a shell hole, cracking his head on the back of the machine guns. He was hanging in the belt, and then he was scrambling out of the hole. 'Put that away,' someone said, 'you're among friends.' He was waving his automatic about. He was telling some troops what had happened. He walked off in the direction everyone else was making. They were Scots. Machine guns were clattering damnably beyond the ridge, and once again he heard the shriek of shells. There was an occasional burst of shrapnel overhead, and now and again the earthy mess of high explosive, and 'posturing giants dissolved in drifts of smoke'. Sometimes the shriek ended in a plop. Duds or gas? He had no tin hat and he had left his gas mask in the aeroplane, which he ought to have set on fire as it would soon be in advancing Hunland. But the remains of one more Camel wouldn't be of much interest to the enemy. He trudged on and on.

'What are you?' demanded a Scots voice. It was a corporal in charge of some troops digging in. Tom started to explain himself, which was a mistake, but he was not in a condition to reflect that he need not be challenged by a corporal.

'Where's your aeroplane?' interrupted the corporal.

'In a shell hole over there,' replied Tom waving an arm warwards. He had not much idea where it was. It seemed a long time since he had crashed.

'I've seen no aeroplane come down. You're a bleedin' German spy.' The corporal drew his revolver and covered Tom.

This was as dangerous as it was absurd. The man looked quite capable of shooting him. The war had upset his nerves. No apposite reply came to Tom. There ought to be something to say that would demolish the absurdity. He opened his sidcot to show his uniform and wings.

'I am an officer of the Royal Flying Corps,' he said, 'and don't point that blasted thing at me.'

'Ye're a German spy,' insisted the corporal, keeping Tom covered. 'There's a lot of 'em aboot. The uniform's naething to go by. Ye'll be shot.'

'Take me to your officer,' ordered Tom angrily, 'and don't talk such bloody nonsense.'

The corporal glowered at him, but agreed. 'Ay. I'll tak ye to the officer, and we'll see if it's nonsense. Walk in front of me and put your hands up.'

'There's no need to put my hands up.'

'Ye'll put yer hands up at once or I shoot.' There was nothing to be done but comply. It was damned ridiculous, but it would have been more ridiculous to be shot for so slight a matter. This was no time to boggle at trifles; the world was hysterical, and absurdity was normal.

Directed by the corporal, Tom came to a sort of small ravine that a number of men were making defensible. He was commanded to halt. Some of the men stopped work to look. One of them in private's uniform scrambled out and stood in front of Tom, looking at him perplexedly. The corporal stood beside Tom still keeping him covered with his revolver. Nobody spoke.

'Are you the officer in charge?' Tom asked at length. The man nodded. Tom lowered his arms.

'I'm an officer of the Royal Flying Corps. I've been shot down, and your corporal has arrested me as a German spy.'

'Well, aren't you?'

'Hell, no!' Tom displayed his badges of rank and wings. 'I'm a R.F.C. pilot and I've been shot down. Will you please put an end to this farce and let me go.'

'Just a minute.' He turned to the corporal. 'Why do you think he's a spy?'

'There's been no aeroplane come doon near here, sir.'

The officer spoke to Tom again. 'Where's your aeroplane?'

'In a shell hole over there.' He indicated the east. 'You can't see it from here. I just got over the ridge.'

The officer looked troubled. 'We've been warned about spies,' he said, and remained thoughtful. After a little he spoke to the corporal. 'Take him to brigade headquarters.'

'Look here,' Tom remonstrated, 'You can't do that. I'm an officer, and if I'm under arrest, I am entitled to be escorted by an officer. I have no objection to going to brigade if you think it necessary, but I'll go properly escorted, and not at the point of a pistol.'

The officer nodded and considered. Then he said, 'I'll go with you. Wait there a minute.'

He gave some orders to a sergeant, had a look round, and returned. Meanwhile the corporal was still covering Tom, who took no further notice of him.

They walked in silence, the corporal behind, towards some higher ground to the south. After ten or fifteen minutes they came to head-quarters, which consisted of a worried brigadier studying the eastern horizon with a pair of glasses, his brigade major, staff captain and other officers, also worried, grouped behind him. Tom's escort told him to wait, and went and conferred with one of the staff, who took him up to the brigadier and waited to be noticed, which did not happen for some minutes. There was a brief colloquy, and then Tom was taken to the brigadier. He saluted.

'What's your squadron?' asked the brass-hat quickly, and Tom told him.

'Where is it stationed?'

'Izel-le-Hameau, behind Arras.'

'The name of your commanding officer?'

An utter blank possessed Tom's mind so far as the major's name was concerned. What was the damned man's name? He could see his ugly face. Oh, what the devil was his name? Good God, how maddening. The name would not come. He would be shot for a silly lapse of memory.

The brigadier studied the east, and then spoke to one of his staff. The name came to Tom. He was agonizing with the effort to recollect, but it slipped back into place, as it were, quite independently of his mental tenesmus. The brigadier glanced at him.

'Major Barlow, sir.'

'Why didn't you answer at once?'

'My mind went blank. I have just crashed and I'm still rather dazed.'

'Get back to your squadron,' said the brigadier, and examined the horizon again. Tom was not sure whether the interview was over, and stood still. Someone touched him on the elbow. It was a lieutenant member of the staff whom Tom realized he had already subconsciously noticed because he had a permanent expression of slight surprise.

'You'd better get along,' said the lieutenant; 'it's that way.' He pointed west. 'Try and find transport going towards your aerodrome.' Tom was vaguely surprised by this kindly, almost fatherly advice. He thanked the giver, saluted brigade headquarters, and set off down the slope, taking no notice of his late captors; not because he still disliked them, but because he had forgotten them. The crash had dazed him, and the Alice-in-Wonderland atmosphere that pervaded happenings on the ground had induced a sort of enchantment. He wandered on through the glamorous afternoon, away from the noise of battle and German shells. It was hot walking in flying kit. He unclasped his overshoes, kicked them off, and left them. The automatic pistol had gone from the pocket of his sidcot, but a map was there. What had happened to the pistol? He had had it. The map was useful. The village near which he had come down was Morlancourt, and if he went straight ahead he would come to Mericourt after about three miles, where he could cross the Ancre. Seeing that he had a map and knew where he was going, various lost, leaderless, hopeless soldiers followed him, and he was soon at the head of a small troop marching to Mericourt. They climbed a slope, veering off from a battery that was blazing away over the crest, and descended on the other side. The going was rough, but not very bad. The ground had not actually been fought over, but there were shell holes and trenches. It had been out of cultivation a long time and was covered with coarse grass. Tom felt queer and light headed. What was the matter with him? Had there been a trace of gas in the shell hole in which he had landed? His legs, however, kept on walking. They seemed all right, and if he left them alone would go on for miles and miles. The edges of things were bright and blurred.

Uphill again, and then he was looking over the valley of the Ancre, with Mericourt half a mile away down the hill. His watch showed quarter to five; they would be having tea in the mess. On the higher ground beyond the Ancre lay the Amiens road, and at one point he thought he could see a moving line of transport on the horizon. His troop of followers had melted away. Had they been real? The corporal, the brigadier, had they been real? Would he soon meet the White Rabbit and the Duchess and the Queen? His legs went on and on, past deserted cottages, over a railway, past a cemetery, up hill, on to the main road. There was a canteen tent, but nothing to be had there but a bottle of soda water. They were packing stuff on lorries. The traffic-congested road would make a good target for low-flying aeroplanes. It was a fine enough afternoon, too, and it only wanted some further torment of this sort to drive everyone mad and turn the retreat into a rout. But all the aeroplanes in the sky were British. It was fortunate, too, that the enemy was not able to get his heavy guns up over the battle-broken ground to follow up his tremendous advance, or he could have blown the road to blazes.

Tom did not want to go towards Amiens, as he was longing for the comforts of home, but it was the only thing to do. He stopped a tender, and climbed in the back. There was a wounded officer and some baggage on the floor, and a R.A.M.C. orderly with his legs up on the seat that ran along one side. Tom occupied the other side.

'Come down, sir?' inquired the orderly.

'Shot down.'

'Are you hurt?'

'No. I'm all right. Hungry.'

The man on the floor groaned occasionally. He was in a hopeless state. Evidently a machine gun had got him. Red round patches showed through his torn bloodstained clothing. Tom imagined black cloths of darkness smothering him.

Tom crawled up to the front and asked the driver if he knew of an inhabited aerodrome on the way to Amiens. The driver said there was one about a mile off the main road, some fifteen or twenty kilometres ahead.

He sat and dozed. The tender went slowly along in the procession towards Amiens. The officer on the floor died. The sun set, and dusk closed down.

XIV

TOM was roused from his lethargy by the driver who called out to him 'Nearly there now. Next turning on the right.' He scrambled to the back and looked out. They were crawling along in the darkness through a wood. The driver shouted again. 'Will you jump off when I tell you? I don't want to stop in case we get bumped.' They emerged from the wood and the driver's voice came again. 'Here you are. Mile up there.' Tom got on to the step and dropped off when he saw the road. 'Right you are, thanks,' he shouted, and set off on what he strongly hoped would be his last spell of walking that day.

The road went slightly uphill: God, he could do with a drink. And if he didn't soon have a feed he would faint. What a day! The luminous hands of his watch showed half past seven. It was over five hours since he had been shot down, and still he was friendless and far from home. It was very unlikely that he would get home that day, but no doubt the people at the aerodrome he was looking for would have a spare bed; vacant beds were very plentiful just then. The wood stretched across the road ahead. He came to it and plunged into deeper darkness, in the heart of which he heard a familiar noise, the voice of a gramophone playing one of the regulation tunes from 'Chu Chin Chow'. He found a pathway leading towards the noise, and soon came among huts. A door opened, showing a patch of light in the end of a big hut, and the music became louder. Someone went in and shut the door. Tom made straight towards it, but tripped over something and swore and followed the path. He reached the door, opened it, and walked in. It was a Flying Corps mess right enough; thank the lord.

Naturally, the first thing they did when he said he had been shot down that morning and had just got back was to pour half a tumbler of whisky into him, and as he was weary and empty as a blimp his mind whirled. He talked a lot, probably about himself. He was talking to a major. He tried to take off his sidcot but found he had already taken it off. The notion emerged and became dominant that he must telephone to home. He followed the major. He hoped to

God he didn't look as tight as he felt. He bumped into the doorpost; drink on an empty stomach. He sat down. The major talked on the telephone. They were in a squadron office. The major beckoned Tom to the telephone. Hullo. James' voice. Damn glad, he said. 'Major, here's Cundall on the line,' he heard him say, then 'are you all right?'

'Quite,' Tom answered. 'Tight as a prince. They've filled me with juice when I was starving.'

'Good. That's the stuff. Have some more. I'll send transport as soon as I can. First thing in the morning. Very pleased you're alive.'

Tom staggered in the major's wake. Someone conducted him to a wash bowl. Then back to the mess for food. God, he was tired. Half asleep. He had been on the dawn show that morning; no wonder he was sleepy. What had happened on the dawn job? He could hardly remember, it was so long ago. Young Sawyer had vanished. Had he got away with it, too? More whisky. The squadron whose guest he was flew Camels. They had fellows going west every day. They were all packed to move back to an aerodrome behind Amiens and were off in the morning. He couldn't talk, couldn't keep his eyes open. He was blotto and dead to the wide world. Bed. He was fast asleep before he got into it. There was a light when he felt he had been asleep a long time, and a face he had seen somewhere before. Oh, go away and let a man sleep.

They woke him up in the morning at eight as they were waiting to pack his bed. He felt fine; there was nothing like a dead-drunk sleep to pull a man together. They were running engines on the aerodrome. At breakfast he was told they were just off on a squadron show, and would land at the new aerodrome.

'I suppose you know,' someone said, 'that your C.O. sent his car for you last night and you wouldn't go.'

'No, I don't know anything about it. Did I? He'll be mad. I'd better telephone.'

'Well, finish your breakfast first.'

Then Tom remembered the face in the night. Of course, the major's chauffeur! Why the devil hadn't the b.f. roused him thoroughly? If he knew the major, he would take this rebuff to his kindness as a personal insult and have it up against him for some time to come. It had certainly been decent of him to send the car. He wished he'd known it was coming. The only thing to do was to apologize prostrately and say he had been left alone with a case of whisky.

He went to the office to telephone immediately after breakfast, and the major answered. When he heard that it was Cundall he wanted to know what the hell. Did Cundall think he'd nothing else to do but . . . Tom kissed the rod and pleaded the whisky. People were making a row taking off and the line was crackly and he couldn't hear half the major said, which was perhaps as well. He gathered that something was coming to fetch him at once. It would not be the squadron car this time.

They were packing the office records, and when he had finished talking, they disconnected the line. All the aeroplanes, gear, and furniture had gone. The last lorry was being loaded. Only the adjutant and ordnance officer remained to see the place clear. They left at half past ten, and Tom remained monarch of the deserted aerodrome, with a packet of chocolate, some biscuits and a bottle of beer. He had not even his pipe, and had to be satisfied with cigarettes, which were much less consoling in times of real distress. He calculated that whatever vehicle was coming to fetch him would arrive at about midday, and soon after eleven he sat down by the side of the approach road to consume his provisions to the music of not far distant heavy guns. The breeze was cold and he was glad of his sidcot. But before he had finished his beer, a motor cycle combination came chugging along the road. Home was within reach at last. A settled home was a great comfort; except when you could land near a Corps School.

'Everybody thought you was killed, sir,' said the driver.

'Disappointment for them. By the way, have you heard what happened to Mr. Sawyer?'

'Lieutenant Sawyer was killed, sir. They say 'e was wounded in the air and crashed and killed 'isself.'

Tom nodded and finished his beer. He had had a good deal of practice, one way and another, at drinking out of bottles, and he could pour from a distance and swallow, like a Spaniard. He looked at his watch.

'It's nearly half past eleven. Can't possibly get back to lunch.'

'Might do, sir.'

'No, don't go fast. I get nervous in those things. Go back through Doullens, or anywhere where there's food and a barber.'

They reached home at three. James was in the office alone when Tom reported.

'Hullo Cundall,' he said, 'welcome back from the field of battle. Have you lost any limbs? Recount your startling adventures.'

Tom told him briefly what had happened. Damn the man and his heavy-humorous verbosity. It wasn't funny really, but it sounded funny in his juicy voice.

'God spare my belly and teeth,' he exclaimed when Tom told him of being taken for a spy, 'you should have been spared that with your elaborately British cast of countenance.'

'Is the major still upset about his car coming back empty?'

'No. I think he's got over that. He trampled the ground at first, but he realizes that you were, and rightly, impenetrably blotto.'

Tom found Smith in the hut, and yarned with him for a time, and they went then across to the hut for tea. Nearly everyone was there, and to Tom's surprise he was greeted with a yell of laughter and cheering, led by the major, who appeared to be in one of his clamorous moods, and to have decided that Tom's escapade was a good joke. Then Tom was questioned and cross-questioned, and he gave them the whole story, which was getting into shape in his mind with telling. It was much more real in a formal dress of words.

'When your engine cut out, did you switch over to gravity?' asked Bulmer.

'No,' Tom answered.

Bulmer looked significantly at Beal, but did not say anything else. Tom realized that he had made a mistake, at first by not switching over to the gravity-feed tank on chance that the engine would pick up, and then by admitting it. The truth was that he hadn't thought about it. Why not? It was a thing that should have come into his mind at once. The obvious answer was wind up. He could still justify himself by saying that pressure was still up, so that there wouldn't be any point in trying the other tank. This would imply that he had looked at the pressure gauge, as, in fact, or to the best of his recollection, he had not. Why not? Wind up. He was on the point of making the pressure defence, but he thought of another one, that his engine had cut clean out (this was true), whereas if pressure had gone it would have spluttered. It was probably the ignition that had ceased functioning. But this was not a sound defence, as he still ought to have tried the gravity feed, that being his only chance. And if he said that he was too low for the engine to have time to pick up, which was doubtful, there was the reply that he should not have taken this for granted.

By the time he had thought of all that, the original question was too far past to be answered further, and it was better to let it go than to recall it and debate the point. No doubt it would be forgotten quickly enough by everybody but himself.

Nevertheless, that glance spoilt Tom's homecoming. It was one thing to admit funk to oneself, or to confess it spontaneously to a friend, but it was damnable to be caught and indicted publicly. He hated being found out.

In the night Tom woke up with a pain in his stomach. It grumbled on through the dark hours, keeping him uncomfortably between sleep and waking. What, he wondered dimly, had he eaten that was poisonous? He wished he had some liver pills. . . .

He seemed to be at Victoria Station carrying a small leather hand-case that was full of grass-cuttings from a lawn-mower, and there was a small flat thing in it too. He put it down in a corner of a sort of waiting-room with a parquet floor where there were many other people and bags. He went to look for her. She was sitting on a seat. He looked up into her face. She was wearing a long pointed blue and red hat on the back of her head. They were very intimate, and went together to get the bag, but could not find it. He wanted to go to the lost property office and went along and asked a porter who was an old woman who was a nurse: she said 'it's best not to take any pills the doctor doesn't give you.'

There was a light. The batman was calling Williamson for the early job. Tom thought he wouldn't be fit for jobs with that pain in his belly. He dozed interminably. Williamson came back from the war. Tom heard him tell Seddon they had dropped bombs some-where and come straight home, as it was windy and cloudy and they couldn't see anything. Tom reflected that if it had been C flight with Beal in charge they would have been dashing about in formation at fifty feet for the hell of a time; whereas he could imagine Bulmer taking B flight over out of range of machine guns (and who cared about Archie?) and then they would go down and do their work, and pick up formation again and get out of range. Time, four minutes: quite sufficient for five or six persons. Even in that time, Tom calculated, each aeroplane had to be missed by three thousand bullets.

Then Tom began to consider what he ought to do. The pain was still in his stomach, and he hardly felt fit to fly. But if he went sick it might be thought he had wind up. In a way it was true; he had got wind up. The thought of ground-strafing made him feel like a jelly that would not set. He lived in a state of utter funk, and the only carefree time was the journey home from a job. The evenings weren't so bad, but they were drawing out disgustingly, and the thought of the next day and the day after was always lurking in the shadows of the mind when one was on the ground; but in the air there were no shadows, and nothing mattered but the present moment. Why this was so Tom could not find a satisfactory reason, but there was no doubt of it. The finest way to forget war flying was to do some peace flying. But, to get back to the problem, he hadn't the sort of wind up that made a fellow sham sick, and he didn't want to give anyone the impression that he had. There was his forced landing on the twenty-first; once the idea of wind up was started, might not that event be ascribed to it? It had certainly been convenient for him. He began to feel bothered. He'd better get up and go and drink a cup of tea and appear ready for work. Seddon was dressing, but not feeling sociable Tom went on shamming sleep until he had gone. Smith had got up early for some reason; probably to go to Candas. Seddon went to breakfast soon after nine and Tom stretched himself and thought about getting up. He did not feel any inclination to do so apart from the urge of duty, and went on thinking for some time, and the door was opened by Beal.

'Good morning, Cundall.' He came to the bed.

'Good morning, Beal.'

'How are you feeling this morning?'

'All right, except for a belly ache that's been keeping me awake.'
Then he wondered if that sounded feeble.

'You look tired. There seems to have been something wrong with
the food yesterday. One or two others are off breakfast to-day.
Anyhow, you needn't get up as I shan't want you to-day. Shall I
tell them to bring you some tea and toast?'

'Thanks, but I say, I expect I shall be all right soon.'

'I hope you will,' said Beal going, 'but I shan't need you for jobs.'

The only thing to do was to take it that Beal was being damned
nice, Tom thought, and have as pleasant a day in bed as he could with
that foul stomach. But who would take his place? Surely they would
not take Smith over the lines yet, he had only been out there three
days. It would be murder. If he was to have time off at Smith's
expense, he would have to — to what? There was nothing he could
do. If he was told not to fly, that was the end of it. Meanwhile
Smith had gone to Candas, and C flight would have to go out again
four strong. Tom drank the tea that the batman brought him and
settled down to read Williamson's *Boswell* and disregard luxuriously
the ululations of the klaxon. *Boswell* was the only book in the world
likely to triumph over a queasy stomach.

'Hullo, Tom,' said Williamson, who came in after breakfast, 'day
in bed?'

'I've got a belly ache, and Beal commanded me to stop in bed.
I don't like it though. We're under strength already. I hope they
won't take Smith over yet.

'Well, it's no use your trying to fly if you're not fit, is it? As for
Smith, I don't suppose he'll have to go over until he's done some
more shooting and bombing practice, but he shapes well, and he'll
have to go over in a few days anyhow. He's gone to Candas this
morning, so you needn't worry about him for the present. Besides,
you're the wild man of the squadron at present. No one else has
been shot down and got away with it. It's lucky you're back at all,
and you can certainly take a day off with a clear conscience.'

'It sounds all right as you put it,' said Tom, 'and it will be no end
of a luxury to lounge about and listen to the klaxon without getting
the jumps about it.'

He had a whisky and soda for lunch and tea and toast for tea, and, feeling a little better towards evening, dressed for dinner and ate soup, potatoes with butter, and apricots. The artillery was banging away. The squadron had been doing jobs in front of Arras for a change, where trouble was expected.

X V

AFTER dinner Tom brightened himself up with a few drinks and lost a few francs at the latest diversion, roulette. Before going to bed he asked Beal if he knew what the jobs for the next day were.

'Not yet, but we're not on the early show. I suppose we'll be going up about nine. We stand by then. But I don't know that you ought to come.'

'Why on earth not?'

'The major thinks you look a bit groggy. It's no use trying to fly if you're not fit. The wing doctor will be here some time soon, and he can have a look at you.'

'But, good Lord, I'm all right. I can't hang about indefinitely doing nothing with the flight under strength. I'd much rather work. I shall be perfectly fit in the morning.'

'Well, if you're quite sure you're fit. . . .'

'Quite sure.'

'And if you are all right in the morning. . . .'

'I'll be all right and I'll be ready by nine.'

'All right, then. If the major should have anything to say I'll let you know.'

Beal was a nice fellow, Tom thought. A pity he was so very keen on winning the war all by himself, or with the assistance of C flight. He would be killed, and he was the sort of young man that ought to be kept alive to . . . what? In peace time, what on earth did people do? They went to offices, they tried to make money, they bought and sold, they did a little gardening or played a little lawn tennis at week ends. They got married and lived for fifty years with one person, and told lies to their children, and died and their children told lies about them. It was very queer what, when you came to think of it, people did in peace time. They worked in factories, they slaved in shops, they dwelt ignorantly in carcerous back-streets. Peace was mean and dirty and genteel. There were no fine qualities that were fit for times of peace. Perhaps after all it was best to fight and be killed, if one could fight cleanly and fearlessly, maintaining one's self-respect. Beal could do this, Tom thought, but he himself could not. There was a weak fibre of fear in him. He was weak-nerved and could not withstand the shock of danger serenely. He was not fit for war; only for peace, when cowards and weaklings ruled the roost and sat secure behind their police-protected suburban walls, living the long lie of the respectable citizen. He was not fit for war, and his anger against it came ultimately from his sense of unfitness.

And yet, even greater than his fear of . . . but what was he afraid of? He loathed death because it was the end of life, but he could hardly think that he feared it. Was it, after all, fear that troubled him, or was it love of life? It was difficult to decide, and all the time, no doubt, pride was trying to persuade him that he was no coward; love of life was much more admissible than fright. There was some old Johnny who used to say *timor mortis conturbat me*, but no doubt he was rightly afraid of hell. But Tom was not concerned with hell, and saw no more reason to be afraid of dying than of going to sleep. Yet fear persisted, and could not be reasoned out of existence. Perhaps it was fear, not of death, but of being killed. That was more likely, but almost as ridiculous. So very many people have been killed and were none the worse for it; compared, that was, with people who had merely died; and unfortunately one had to do one or the other some time; why not while life was still good? According to most accounts life had a way of losing its sweetness . . . but no, not for Tom Cundall; life could never lose its attractiveness for him while he was not in physical pain. His nerves were not weak in that way. He was supremely confident of ability to endure life with all its wear and tear and minute exacerbations. The chances of continual pain or starvation were not great, and all the stuff about the heartache and the thousand natural shocks was so much romantic nonsense, a morbid cult of suffering and insufficiency. So long as there was warmth in the belly, so long was life worth living; the delicious central glow of base animal life in the cunning belly.

No doubt it was this old visceral Adam that made all the fuss about being killed, and turned one stiff and cold with fright and got hold of nerves and pulled them taut. It was no use reasoning with Adam; you might as well tell a scared baby to stop its yelling. You had to soothe him, cajole him, get him interested in something else. You could say 'don't be frightened, we won't go too near the silly old Huns; we know all the tricks, and we won't be caught'. Then you might try 'look, nobody else is frightened. You be a brave little Adam like them, and don't let them see you crying'. And again, 'be a good Adam and daddy will give you lots of nice things' and you took him up for joy-rides in your aeroplane and chivvied people on the ground, which made him laugh: you poured alcohol on him that made him wildly excited till he fell asleep: you found girls for him to play with: Adam's delights were easy to get for him in war time; had they not been, millions of Adams would have been yelling day and night, driving their owners mad, and that would have been bad for the war.

The old Adam that inhabited him, Tom thought, was especially susceptible to the persuasion 'don't let them see you crying'. He was terribly frightened of being jeered at, and that seemed to be how he could be kept in some control; one fear must be set against another, and a delicate Gothic balance obtained. Perhaps, also, Tom ought to give him more delights; pour more alcohol on him and find some frisky harlots for him to sport withal. He would see; and meanwhile go to bed and sleep as well as the artillery and night-flying people would let him. On a fine night one squadron of night-flyers would drop six or seven hundred bombs, and this sort of thing was so disturbing to their troops that the Germans were retaliating and instead of sending their bombers on long distance flights were concentrating on the battle front. The best time for sleeping was between five and nine o'clock in the morning, and Tom was annoyed with himself for having made it necessary to get up at eight or half past when he might have had the day off. If the authorities considered him unfit, why bother? He had made a great sacrifice to pride.

It was a windy morning with heavy clouds at two or three thousand feet, but the air was very clear. The klaxon called A and C flights immediately after nine o'clock; A to carry bombs and C to escort them. The job was to go some six or seven miles into Hunland east of Arras and attack troops that were moving up in support of an attack that was developing in great strength; an attack that incidentally made it very probable that they would have to evacuate the aerodrome during the day at a few minutes notice; and everything packable in advance was being packed. All this was disturbing. The farmhouse was a pleasant home, and it was very Hunnish of the Huns to push them out of it. The place they were to retire to was a wretched barren field with only hut accommodation.

Tom had received no order countermanding Beal's tentative permission to fly, so he responded to the klaxon. It was pleasant to hear that C flight was to do the escorting. They took off and gained height and waited for A. Tom had a Camel he had not flown before and found it stiff and self-willed and needing getting used to.

Mac did not believe in crossing the lines below two thousand feet if he could avoid it, and A flight flew so high as to force their escort into the verge of the clouds, where there was at any rate no chance of being dived on. Archie got their range accurately and put up some very close bursts. Frequently he barked without appearing, having gone a little high and expended his hate in the clouds.

They flew in the angle between the Scarpe river and the Cambrai road past Athies, Feuchy, Fampoux, Monchy, Roeux, and Pelves. A flight went down in a long dive, and Beal opened out to full throttle to keep above them, hugging the ragged soffit of the clouds. They could see downwards very well, but their level view was obstructed by frequent flocculi of blown cloud. They came very suddenly on a bunch of Huns flying northwards across their front. They were going down at a slight angle, evidently meditating an attack on A flight below. Beal immediately followed them and they went away east very fast. They were Pfalz scouts and could easily get away from Camels on the level, but were not much good in a dogfight. They sometimes played the dive and zoom game, and never went into a scrap of their own accord. As they vanished into the east Tom warmed up his guns by taking a long range shot at one of them without effect. Beal did not follow them far, as C flight's job was to sit above A flight. He kept as high as possible in case the Huns should come creeping back in cloudland to try to get above them. Meanwhile the raid was going on. A flight were about two thousand below making towards a village which Tom saw by his map as one of the great Sailly family, Sailly-en-Ostrevant. There was something on a road near there . . . but Beal waggled his wings and went away in a long dive. A bunch of Huns was coming up from the east below a thousand feet. Probably it was the lot they had just driven off taking the risk of coming back low down to interfere with A flight who had gone down on to the floor to a good target. Tom's pitot showed a hundred and sixty. As they were getting near to shooting distance, the Huns dived away from them to take a crack at A flight, more to disturb them than with much hope of doing damage, for they appeared to turn away too soon to get anything particular into their sights, but the atmosphere must have been very full of bullets at that moment, with C flight also shooting at long range to scare the Huns. And then there was a further crackling as a few Pfalz dived out of nowhere on to C. The lower Huns turned away north-east and went all out. As they turned they made a good target for C. Tom got his sights on to one of them and gave him a burst that must have worried him, but heard a horrible pop-pop-pop on his own tail and saw tracers streaking past. He jerked into a turn and threw the Hun's sights off, and, looking upwards, caught a glimpse of a Pfalz pulling out of a dive to zoom away. He continued to circle, feeling uncomfortably lonely.

Another Camel appeared and followed him round. It was Skinner. Two's company. Someone else joined them. Three's better. It was Debenham. There were four or five Huns floating about overhead, and A flight was coming up underneath with noses well up. There was a strong wind blowing from the west and in circling they were getting further east. Two Camels with streamers showed up: Beal and Miller. They picked up formation and set off homewards, the two flights flying almost side by side just under the clouds. It was an uncomfortable journey. Although his pitot showed over a hundred, this was only air speed, and Tom saw the landscape creeping by at sixty or seventy miles an hour. Archie put up a black barrage for them to fly through. They pretended to dive under it, followed by some of the Pfalz taking long range cracks at them, and then zoomed cloudwards again through the smoke while a lot of Archie burst far below them, where they might have dived to. The

Huns were not enterprising, and seemed to dislike the appearance of the barrage smoke so much that they kept on their own side of it and were seen no more. Tom laughed at Archie's miscalculation that had cost about half a million marks in wasted shrapnel. It must be very uncomfortable in Hunland with all the shrapnel that rained down from great heights.

They crossed the lines and landed after having been out for just less than an hour. Tom made a bumpy landing, not getting his tail down sufficiently before touching the ground. He bounced twice and the third time turned a somersault, and once again found himself hanging upside down in the belt. What an exhibition! He crawled out, feeling a perfect fool. It was certainly windy, but he had been flying Camels long enough to be able to land properly. It was inexplicable that he had not held off until his tail dropped. It was difficult to blame the state of the atmosphere for that.

He saw the major in the distance by the office looking at him, or probably glaring at him. He hoped that someone else would turn over, but everyone else got down safely if not always elegantly. Tom walked across to the office to see what the major had to say about it. The major told him he had crashed three Camels in a week, and there wasn't an unlimited supply. Considering the circumstances of his last crash, the only reply Tom felt to be adequate was to kick his backside. As this was impossible, there was nothing to be said. The major never went up himself; what the hell did he mean by talking like that to a fellow who was trying to do a man's job?

Perhaps the major felt that he had hardly said the right thing, for he changed his tone, and hoped Cundall wasn't shaken, and thought he'd better see the wing doctor as he hadn't been well and still looked a bit groggy.

A flight said they had bombed and shot up a lot of troops with great effect. Miller claimed a Hun, and Beal confirmed that it crashed. A few drops of rain fell. Everything was packed and there were no fires. The morning wore on miserably. It soon became apparent that there would be no more flying that day. The wind increased and the rain poured. Tom put on his sidcot against the cold and lay on his bed and read. Time stood still. The rain drummed on the zinc roof, giving dismal assurance of safety. The noise of guns was not quite blown away by the wind; it was sufficient to remind that the big push was still on after a week of terrific fighting, and there was as yet no sign of its cessation. It might go on for months; what chance was there of surviving?

The doctor came to have a look at him. If he swung the lead a bit he might be invalided home. Not wind up; he would never be sent home in that disgrace. He would admit fear, but, by God, he wasn't yellow. But if the M.O. could find something wrong with him . . . sick leave and Home Establishment!

'Well, how are you?' inquired the doctor.

'Oh — er — all right. I had some — er — coeliac malaise yesterday.'

'What do you mean?'

'Bellyache, colic. It's cleared up.'

'Any diarrhoea?'

'No.'

'You've had some crashes lately. Tell me about them.'

'A week ago I turned over landing in a fog. I wasn't hurt. Three days ago I was shot down and turned over in a shell hole. I wasn't hurt — at least, beyond bruising my forehead. To-day I turned over landing on the aerodrome because of the wind up — I mean because of the wind. That was a damn silly thing to do, but I wasn't hurt. It was nothing.'

'That's three times. Have you noticed things happen in threes? You feel all right to-day? Fit for flying?'

'Yes, I felt all right up.'

The doctor put a thermometer into his mouth and felt his pulse. He looked at the thermometer and at his tongue. He listened to his chest and tapped him above the knee.

'I think you're right,' he said then. 'You seem perfectly fit. I wish I had a heart like yours.'

There was bully beef for lunch. The wet afternoon moaned and shivered on the grey aerodrome. The order to move did not come; probably authority was waiting on the weather. Tom went to sleep. Williamson went to sleep. Seddon wrote. Smith wrote.

Tea time was mail time, but no mail was delivered that day and there was no toast for tea. Driblets of news trickled through. The enemy had not been able to get to Arras, and had been repulsed in two attacks. Depression began to lift. A fire was lighted in the ante-room. The temperature rose, drink was disincarcerated, and voices joined in song.

Glorious, glorious,
One barrel of beer between the four of us.
Glory be to God there are no more of us,
For one of us could drink the lot.

People played uproarious games of slippery Sam, ludo, roulette. Towards dinner-time the move was definitely postponed. The German attacks had been shot to pieces, and they had not advanced an inch towards Arras. There was bully beef for dinner.

XVI

WHEN Tom woke up in the morning after a blank peaceful night, the rain was pattering pleasantly on the roof. How good for crops and aviators, thought Tom, and dozed, lulled deliciously by the soothing sound. He had a warm bath, put on his best slacks, and breakfasted at ten. It was a luxurious life while it lasted. There were newspapers in which to read of enormous German casualties. There were bacon and eggs and toast and marmalade and coffee, and nothing whatever to do. The padre announced a service at eleven o'clock, weather permitting; that was, weather being bad enough. It was Good Friday. Tom strolled latrinewards with Williamson.

'The padre can't be more than thirty or thirty-two,' he said. 'Why the devil doesn't he take off his dog collar and come over the lines and do a spot of ground-strafing if he's so keen on the bloody war? I've no use for these young padres.'

'He probably has a conviction that his vocation prevents him from fighting, but he wants to do what he can,' Williamson replied.

'He probably has a conviction that his skin is worth looking after, but finds it interesting to have a look at the war from close but not too close quarters. I dare say he fancies himself in khaki, and hopes to be mistaken for a hero by the more buxom virgins of his parish and so to conquer some long-lusted-after maidenheads.'

I

'Oh rot. What a lot of time you spend suspecting the honesty of perfectly well-meaning people. The padre is a decent fellow, and he is probably basing his conduct on the best standards he can work out. His standards are naturally not the same as yours, or he wouldn't be a priest, but I am as perfectly certain they are honest as I am sure you enjoy considering mankind vile.'

'Hell, that's a smashing blow for church and state. You ought to be a bishop, Bill. Still, mankind must be fairly vile, or we shouldn't be here.'

'Well Tom, we shan't be any the less here by bothering our heads about it. Let's go to this service to break up the morning. I never really enjoy bridge before lunch.'

'If you like,' said Tom. It was a long time since he had attended divine service. Since he had been in the grip of a power that assumes all men to be deeply religious in the ecclesiastical sense of the word, he had met force with guile by being a Swedenborgian; a creed very baffling to martinets.

The padre reminded them of all the Good Fridays they had spent at home. Home, what a lot that meant, and how righteous to fight in its defence! He finished with a prayer for those at home.

'Hullo,' said Seddon, when they entered the hut, 'where have you blokes been to? I thought we might have a spot of bridge.'

'We've been to church.'

'Church! *et tu Brute?*'

'Bill overcame my better nature. We are defending our homes. That's why we're in France. Smith, can you leave that letter and play bridge.'

'Righty-ho!' said the ever obliging Smith.

During the day an official document about the Royal Air Force circulated. The new regime was to commence on the first of April, which seemed to Tom an appropriate date. Bulmer, Moss, and Debenham already had the strange new uniform and when they went out in it they were sir-ed and saluted endlessly by all sorts of people. It was the hat with its decorations as of a Field Marshal that did it. There had been a rumour of an outfit allowance of £18, but it appeared that the uniform was not to be compulsory for the present, and khaki might still be worn on all occasions, so that the new uniform would be merely a replacement and the national exchequer would save a few thousand pounds. The rates of pay were not changed, but instead of being in advance pay would be in arrear, which would have the immediate effect of cutting out a month's pay. Altogether the R.A.F. seemed to be starting off in quite the wrong spirit. It was, however, made legal to wear brown shoes and slacks, but as everyone always had done so, this privilege was not a great set-off.

And then came the mail. Tom carried off a parcel and a couple of letters, one of them in unfamiliar feminine handwriting. He wondered whom it could be from; the postmark was Buxton, and he didn't know anyone there. He opened the parcel and it contained a sweet abundance of dates and chocolate. This was excellent, for chocolate had been difficult to get locally since the beginning of the push, and flying was sweet-tooth work somehow. He read the letter from Buxton.

Dear Mr. Cundall,

It was awfully kind of you to write to me, and I shall be glad of that parcel of letters. It was very thoughtful of you, I think. If you do not already know, Allen is in Hospital in Manchester. I have been to see him and he is dreadfully knocked about. It is awful, but he is not in danger I am most thankful to say. He has an arm, a leg, some ribs, and his nose broken, and his face is awful but he will be all right in a few months.

He asked me to send you and Seddon and Williamson his very best wishes for good luck and to tell you that he was flying at two thousand feet over Bapaume when something happened, he does not know what and he woke in Hospital at Manchester. Isn't it weird? he has no idea at all what happened between over Bapaume and Manchester, but it is marvellous that he is alive don't you think so? He will write to you himself when he can and will be awfully glad if you will write to him and let him know how you all are and how things are going. It might be best to write care of me in case he is moved, but I do hope you will be able to send him a line as I know he would like awfully to hear from you. He has told me a lot about you all.

131

Well of course it is splendid to know that Allen is safe now although he is so dreadfully injured, poor boy, and we both hope very much that you will all come safely through this awful war.

Again thanking you very much for your kindness,

Yours very sincerely,

PHYLLIS GIBBS.

'Well, of all the extraordinary things . . . here, Seddon, read this.' So Allen had been lucky after all, and the great love affair would die a natural death instead of putting on a violent immortality. As for a few broken bones, that was nothing: anyone would be glad to retire honourably from the war at that price.

The weather remained dud for the rest of the day and the night was peaceful, but Tom was awakened by the batman at quarter past five in the morning for the dawn show. It was quite fine enough to take off, but when they were over the lines clouds came sailing up from the west in ever-increasing quantity. Beal took them down east of Arras to drop their bombs, but there was no one about to drop them on. The fields of the recent battle were heaped with dead Germans. The slaughter must have been terrific, and Ludendorff hadn't even an acre of waste land to show for it. They went down and bombed a trench, but the Huns stopped underground in their dugouts and apparently considered it too early even to man machine guns. Only two of Tom's bombs would drop.

They climbed and wandered down the front towards Albert, which was now a little way behind the German lines. Everything was quiet on earth, and the sky seemed empty except for a solitary RE8. The day was evidently a Huns' holiday. The Kaiser's birthday, perhaps. Archie was paying his customary attentions, but he was quite a natural feature of the sky: you might as well expect the sun to take a holiday as Archie. Had the Germans done their worst and failed? Was the big push over? Or was this lull but an interval while roads were repaired and big guns and munitions brought up? Did the repulse at Arras mean that Amiens was saved and the Huns could only consolidate what they had won and dig in in the hope of being able once more to massacre anyone who attacked their strong posts? And would the war go on for ever?

132

The earth was assuming a veil of low cloud, and they went down before it was opaque everywhere and flew home at five hundred feet. Tom made a perfect landing in the commencing rain. They reported all quiet and a dud day set in. The weather seemed to have broken definitely. What with that and the sudden peace it was glory, glory, allelujah. Tom read all the morning and slept all the afternoon. Robinson was transferred to another squadron as flight commander and as he was to go that night dinner would have to be a binge in his honour and the mess must secure a few oysters or lobsters in time. The major had a congratulatory message from Wing about the squadron's sound work during the push. The brigadier was going to pay them a visit to-morrow or the next day. It rather looked as though the noble army of brass-hats considered the push to be over, and perhaps the general would have something interesting to say, and not merely call them fine fellows.

Dinner was very much as usual except for three oysters apiece, veal instead of beef, and some rather rough red wine which not everyone liked, but it suited Tom very well, and he drank pints of it and felt fit to loop round the moon, and afterwards he remembered to keep off whisky. There was Grand Marnier and Kummel, and he kept to these and port. Robinson seemed really sorry to go, although it was very nice to be a flight commander and get the first shot at Huns and have one's tail protected all the time by the rest of the flight.

'I don't want to go to this comic squadron,' he orated, 'I'd much rather stay here with you fellows and win the war in good company. The trouble with this squadron is that we're too good. This is only the beginning. You'll find they'll be sending you all away one by one to show other squadrons what to do to the poor old Hun when met flipping about miserably in an Albatros that can't catch fish and has to live on bluebottles in summer and bits of Archie in winter. That's why they put up so much Archie; to give their starving Albatri something to peck at. What a life for the poor old beans! And now I've got to go away among a lot of comic aviators that probably think the Huns are terrible big fellows bristling with machine guns and climbing turns and no tails to sit on, and when anybody shoots one down they send a telegram to the Victoria Cross department of the *Daily Mail* and get so drunk that the wing colonel has to go over and pull them out of bed next morning. But, seriously, I'd rather stay here than even be dressed by a colonel. Besides, we, that is A flight, wanted to try a new Hun-trap that I invented. It's very simple. The idea is to tow a bundle of sausages and bottles of beer on a thousand feet of cord, and when it appears suddenly in the middle of a Hun formation they all collide.'

Robinson spoke his stuff well and had them all yelling with laughter. It was a pity he was going; his fantastic mind was a part of the amenities of the squadron. Without Tommy and him humour would be scarce and rags might become noise and horseplay only.

Hudson as was usual with him under the impact of alcohol, became inassuageably aware of the tragic loveliness of life. He went to the piano cosmically vibrant and struck from it passages of Chopin whose magic of line and inexplicable sweetness of modulation expressed for him this mood of the universe. The glaucous ineffaceable music maintained itself among crude noise as if a Christian martyr, palely unaware, stood physically bound to a stake among howling heathen but integumented with facets of heaven.

As soon as his hands paused someone started the gramophone, and an ear-blasting nasal voice shouted 'The Bells are Ringing for Me and My Gal', and Tom went out into the quieter night to recover poise. He did not in the ordinary way mind the gramophone with its musical comedy blarings, but the brutish indifference to the feelings of Chopin and Hudson wounded him. But there was nothing new in it, and Hudson shouldn't try to play Chopin on a binge night.

In two minutes he returned. Chadwick entered at the same time with his mandoline and superseded the gramophone with his whole-hearted twanging. Tom always found something slightly touching in the sight of Chadwick giving himself so earnestly and completely to his mandoline. Familiar tunes ting-a-linged under his energetic fingers and the good old rackety songs once again shook the mess. Things were going well, but before anyone had got reasonably blotto the bar ran out of drinks. There wasn't even a drop of lime juice left. James, as P.M.C., was called upon to explain the unprecedented enormity.

'Sorry troops,' he said in his rich voice, *'que voulez-vous? c'est la*

134

guerre. The push has disorganized the drink supply and there is great competition for what little there is. I call upon Maitland to explain why our friends the Yanks haven't brought any booze with them.'

'I guess it's because it was notoriously the one thing Yurrup was never short of,' retorted Maitland.

Robinson's tender turned up at half past nine, and drinkless they sang 'For He's a Jolly Good Fellow', and cheered and wandered out into the dark and blusterous night to see him off; if anything could be seen. The tender was a throbbing shadow; the last they were to hear of Robinson's voice flowed out of the gloom as the shadow receded, vanishing among shadows: 'Cheerio troops. Plenty of revs'. They shouted farewells; and then the evening was over and there was nothing to do but go to bed.

XVII

IN the morning it was almost stormy. Masses of cloud were being driven along the sky by the whip of a wilful south-wester, and sporadic splutters of rain flung down. Nevertheless the order was to stand by; the enemy was attacking on the Somme, still lusting, evidently, after the city of Amiens. The klaxon summoned A flight at half past nine to drop bombs on troublesome Germans between Albert and Morlancourt and to report on the state of the war there. They returned after an hour, and Seddon was caught by a gust of wind as he was landing, and stood on his nose.

The Germans were gaining ground. C flight went off to carry on the work, but Tom did not go with them. As he was taking off with his tail well up and wheels still on the ground, his prop touched a mole hill and knocked a piece of itself off; a small piece, but sufficient to set up a violent vibration. He throttled right down, slowed down, and turned and taxied in, while the rest of the flight vanished into the east.

Tom did well to be off that job. Beal was in his most reckless mood and spent a frantic quarter of an hour at an average height of

135

fifty feet. It was a magnificent effort. They came back full of information and their machines of bullet holes; at least Beal and Miller did: Skinner had too much wind up to know anything, and Debenham did not come back at all. They had done damage to the enemy and carried out a useful reconnaissance. It was a first rate military exploit; and it was part of daily routine; a routine impossible to keep up for long; there would be no one left capable of it. Smith was warned for duty on the next job, and Dubois was sent up to do shooting and bombing practice on the aerodrome targets whenever the wind dropped. Dubois was very unhappy about it all. He had a violin which he played remarkably badly, but he would sit in his hut for hours soothing his melancholy with croonings that were tuneful to him only. A new fellow named Cross was posted to the flight, and he too had a musical instrument, a portable gramophone, by means of which he assuaged his love of British opera with songs from *Maritana* and *The Bohemian Girl*, but not including, Tom was thankful, 'I dreamt that I dwelt'; which would have made the war too horrible. Apart from his gramophone records Tom found him an excellent fellow, and borrowed *The Old Wives' Tale* from him.

The weather was hopelessly dud in the afternoon, but the sky was blown clear in the evening and myriads of stars came out whose brightness foretold more rain. Tom spent a good deal of time talking to Smith, who had a wife and was interested in nothing else. He had been married only six months, very little of which time he had been able to spend domestically, and he was aching so much to get back to his wife that life was hardly bearable, separated ineluctably from her, faced by imminent death. There was nothing to be done about it; Smith knew well enough that it was one of those situations that a man has to face with such force as he can bring to bear; but it eased him a little to make moan once into a sympathetic ear, though moaning was very other than his usual mien.

Tom told him all he knew about avoiding bullets, and moaned with him about war; admitting that the flicker of patriotism that once irradiated his mind had been damped almost to extinction by the murderous issue of rivalry in patriotisms. And the whole thing was the outcome of political wangles. International treaties were the final scores in games of diplomatic cunning played for their own hands, and as much for personal as for national prestige, by politicians who hated each other like bulls and bears. A poisonous system, and they were being done to death by it; to death, with millions of other subjects of governments that had been brought into the devil's sabbath by dominant interests they served or by bribery. To death. There was nothing to be done about it. They should try to survive if only to join in the coming protest.

But Smith wasn't interested in that sort of motive for surviving. Tom gave him the happy example of Allen, his predecessor in the same corner of the hut. He had probably earned a pension and would be able to get married as soon as he was fit for the ceremony, parents permitting, and spend the next fifty years doing nothing but gaze into her eyes, if he wanted to.

The first morning of the Royal Air Force, which was also Easter Monday, was rough and rainy, and no flying was possible, but the squadron had to stand by as it looked like clearing up and the enemy was attacking down south. They were having a lot of this half-dud weather, and it was very trying waiting about until it cleared up, or until things got so desperate somewhere that they had to go out anyhow and drop some bombs. And crossing the lines under low clouds meant that there were dozens of machine guns turned on, and you couldn't get out of range. Of course, you didn't meet any air Huns; they didn't fly in such weather.

The promised general came by car; but he only told them what they knew already: that they were fine fellows, that they were now Royal Air Force but would carry on their old traditions, and that there was a war on, but not quite such a bad war as it had been a week ago.

After lunch it was not impossible to fly. Blue lanes and lakes intermicated cloud, and it was not windy beyond all hope of landing. A and B went out; A to escort, B to bomb. They came back. The afternoon wore on to tea-time. A little longer and there would be no job for C that day. Then the klaxon spurted a call: DER-der-DER-der; and again; and yet again. The major seemed excited. Tom finished his cup of tea unhurryingly while Beal went dashing to the office. They were to hurry down to the south side of the Somme where it was reported that some low-flying Huns were helping the attack, and do a patrol at two thousand feet to prevent this sort of thing and enable British bombers to bomb unmolested. It was good to have a patrol for a change. The bombs were taken out of their racks and they sped away southwards at full throttle to the unknown country beyond Somme. It was very gloomy down there. Although the clouds were at about three thousand feet and there were patches of blue, everything looked dull or lurid. Tom flew for the first time over the straight-ruled east-and-west line of the road from Amiens to St. Quentin. It vanished, indefeasably straight, into the grey eastern limit of vision like an undefeated purpose striking through uncertainties.

They flew over the ghastly remains of Villers-Bretonneux which were still being tortured by bursting shells upspurting in columns of smoke and debris that stood solid for a second and then floated fading away in the wind. All along the line from Hamel to Hangard Wood the whiter puff-balls of shrapnel were appearing and fading multitudinously and incessantly. There was a constant coming and going of all sorts of British aeroplanes that dropped their bombs and returned for more. The desperate defence of Amiens seemed to be holding; it was a nightmare clash between half-mad armies exhausted by a fortnight's continuous fighting; and although the defending troops had been blasted almost out of existence the attackers had no force left to push through the storm. So Tom imagined the battle going on below, where no one living was visible and only machinery seemed able to go on. The unceasing rain of bombs out of the sombre sky, and all the pouncing and shooting from the air; what was the total effect of it in the battle? It seemed to Tom that it was the supremacy of the R.F.C. that was saving Amiens. If the Germans had been able to attack in the air as well as on the ground. . . .

The desolation of the dead land below them seemed to impregnate the atmosphere with gloom and horror, exhaling contagion that defiled the air and tainted the clouds with death and corruption. There was something unclean in the yellow-grey light of afternoon, as though evil were an actual spirit that here in middle air spread its throne, invisible but influential; and round it flew all the smashed and bloody ghosts made in the Somme massacres; and all their agonies and all their broken desires made inaudible deathly moan.

A flaming meteor fell out of a cloud close by them and plunged earthwards. It was an aeroplane going down in flames from some fight above the clouds. Where it fell the atmosphere was stained by a thanatognomonic black streak. Tom's engine lost its rhythm, missing on one cylinder. They went three or four miles into Hunland without encountering any Huns; certainly there were none flying low. Tom felt that things were getting on his nerves. He ought not to stop out with an engine that wasn't going properly. He was entitled to go back; anyone else would have gone already; he was stupidly sensitive. It was only plug trouble, but it gave away revs, and another plug going would be serious. He made the dud engine signal and turned away west alone.

He had about three miles to go through Hunland, which with the wind against him might take three minutes. This was nothing to worry about in the ordinary way, but the day was sinister. Tom felt as if he were being threatened. It was upsetting not to be shot at by Archie. The reason obviously was that there were no forward batteries up yet; but it was worrying because a cessation of Archie usually meant that attack by diving scouts was imminent; but in that case there were one or two guiding or indication bursts put up for the benefit of those scouts, but to-day Archie was quite silent near the lines. Nevertheless he imagined the heavy clouds full of Huns. It might be better to climb and skim along just under them instead of keeping his nose down for speed. But ridiculously enough he did not like the look of those clouds and preferred to keep away from them; also climbing would not be so easy with his engine missing. He kept his nose down, preferring speed, and then, through a small patch of blue that he happened to be watching, came some Fokker biplanes, easily recognizable by the extensions of their top planes. One, two, three, four. Now he was for it; they couldn't help seeing him, and could catch him easily. He put his nose down to a hundred and thirty. The Fokkers, who were much faster, flew over him. Huns never attacked in a hurry; they liked to have a good look round first, and a solitary scout was quite likely to be a decoy. Every second was valuable; he was nearly over the lines. His mouth was as dry as chalk. That reminded him, he hadn't bought any chewing gum yet, and the chances were that he never would now. His guts turned to jelly. The Huns turned on to his tail and dived.

As they opened fire he did a vertical turn to the left and they missed him. Then he reversed bank quickly as only a Camel could, not daring to turn so that he was going east. The rattle of machine guns got dangerously loud as he did this, so he kicked the rudder-bar and side-slipped downwards. The controls went slack; let her go! And in a second he was spinning violently. He brought the throttle back slowly. The Huns would probably think they had shot him on the turn and be satisfied: their game was dodging about among the clouds looking for strays to pounce on, and they would climb away as soon as they saw him falling apparently out of control, and not follow him down, especially as they were right over the lines and there were many British machines about. Usually it was dangerous to spin away, for a spinning machine was easy to follow down, and although it was difficult to hit then, in coming out of the spin it was apt to present an easy target before the pilot had regained complete control. And in any case he was no better off, being in the same position in relation to the attackers with the disadvantage of having lost a lot of height. Tom took a backward and upward glance (there is nothing more vertiginous than looking at your tail in a spin) and took dizzy comfort in not seeing any following Huns. In this case the trick had worked. He came out of the spin at less than a thousand feet. Which way was he going? His compass was spinning like a top, and there wasn't any sun, and he couldn't see any distance from that height.

The country ahead was quite unfamiliar but it looked cultivated, and so he must be going more or less west. Where was the battle? Looking about he found it under his tail. There was a long straight road below him which ought to be the Amiens-St. Quentin road, and as he was crossing it at a right angle he must be going due north or due south. But he couldn't be doing that, because he was flying away from the battle. He felt dreadfully confused. The earth seemed to have twisted itself askew during his spin. The engine sounded horrible. There was an intermittent miss on another cylinder, he thought. An RE8 flew overhead. It was comforting to meet the Harry Tate, but he could not tell whether it was bound outwards or homewards. More likely homewards as it was nearly half-past five, and in that case he was flying east. Hell! Should he follow the RE? He pulled out his map and studied it.

He must have been attacked a little way south-east of Villers-Bretonneux. Ah, perhaps the road he had just crossed was the Amiens-Roye road, which was a long straight streak running south-west across the map. Yes, that was it, and so he was flying south-east on an Easter trip to Paris. He whoofed with relief, and turned happily northwards on his long journey home. Another day's trouble was over, or nearly so. Unfortunately his engine was running badly enough to spoil the pleasure of it, and he had to watch the ground all the way so as to keep within gliding distance of places that looked all right for landing. Corbie, Franvillers, Baizeiux; then familiar ground all the way home. His engine was stuttering alarmingly when he reached the aerodrome, and he flew low over the mess and office to give everyone an opportunity of hearing it. He saw James come out to see who was making the noise, and there was quite a gathering to see him land.

The major wanted to know what the devil he meant by doing a circuit low down with his engine missing like that, and told him off for risking his machine unnecessarily and foolishly. He should have come straight in and landed at once. Tom was surprised at this rebuke. Theoretically, of course, it was risky to do a circuit at thirty feet with only half an engine, but after the dire horrors of the afternoon it was difficult to take such a trifle seriously. However, he admitted that the major was right this time.

Beal and the others came back half an hour later. They had been shot at by Fokkers which dived and climbed away, and they had chased a two-seater. But no damage had been done either way. Tom's narrative of his escape by spinning was well received. No one else in the squadron had ever risked it, as it was a method universally frowned on. In the circumstances, however, it was a good stroke of tactics; the more so as the very reluctance of the British to spin away from attack would make the Huns more ready to believe that he was a genuine kill; and he had gone into the spin very naturally from a turn and had not shut his engine off suddenly. The only mistake he had made was that he did not know which way he was going when he came out; he ought to have kept some prominent feature of the landscape in mind by which to steer. But it was hardly reasonable to expect a man to have everything so very well arranged in an emergency of that sort. There was nothing like the damned rattle of machine guns for numbing the brain. It was a good get-away.

No doubt the Fokkers had gone home and told how they had shot down a Camel near Villers-Brettonneux, and as there were four of them they would each be credited with a kill, and no doubt that would show in official figures as four enemy aircraft, or whatever they were called in Germany, destroyed. That was generally supposed to be what happened in all flying services except the British, in which a Hun shot down was either credited to one man, or split up into fractions according to the number of persons who shot at him.

Tom wondered what on earth had been the matter with him that afternoon. The sight of the Somme seemed to make him morbid and upset his nerves. Were his nerves going wrong? He took comfort from the reflection that he was the sort of fellow, evidently, that got away with things. His guardian angel had been very busy lately. And it was funny to think that he, quietly eating the roast beef that evening had brought forth, was probably four dead British aviators in Jerry's summary of the day in the air.

XVIII

IT was pleasant, on so fine a day as the second of April was, to be relieved of the strain of waiting for the klaxon to send them bombing. God, that low work! Fellows were getting nervy with it: Tom knew how he felt himself, yet he had been very lucky in getting out of jobs. He'd only done half as many as some of them but what he had done were, under Beal's leadership, as hot as anyone could wish. Beal was a modern hero, who, unlike Henry V, Achilles, Ashur-banipal, and other heroes of antiquity, kept so quiet about it that no one except his own particular followers really knew how terrific he was. Tom thought sometimes that it was even more heroic, being a coward, to follow a hero into his scrapes than to be the hero.

Heroes followed their temperaments; cowards sometimes overcame theirs. Probably most of them were cowards; it was difficult to tell or impossible. Not Beal; he was naturally fearless, and perhaps not Miller, but three out of four. Miller was a Canadian farmer from the Pacific coast; tough, both as a fighter and drinker. He could absorb any amount of war and spirits, and rejoiced loudly in the destruction of Huns. He wasn't exactly a Hun-hater, but he knew very well what they were for; to be killed.

But take Seddon, who had used to go daily to a bank in Lombard Street to add up other people's money: gentle, sensitive, civilized, urban, married: with sympathies oblique to the war-lines of enmity now that propaganda and tiger-tail-lashings had taken the place of patriotic fervour, and young men no longer thanked God for matching them with that hour: it was impossible for Seddon to fight for the sake of fighting, to hate because he was told to hate, to have the heart to kill or be killed in cold blood: he must force himself to do what had to be done, to act contrary to intuition and spirit, and the struggle must be tearing his nerves to pieces. He had a wife and two children, and leave was stopped. Why hadn't he gone into the A.S.C. like other married men? Pride, probably; he had felt himself fit to do what the best could do, and he was doing it.

Williamson was different. The chances of life and death seemed to matter little to him so long as he was comfortable at the present moment; and he usually was comfortable. The life suited him; there was no work to do, absolutely none, unless flying could be called work. And there were no women to fuss round him and make intolerable demands. He could read and meditate and talk and eat and drink in an unique male society; and it even pleased him to be assisting at the greatest of all battles that had come to pass in the ever-warring world. By profession he was an architect, or on the way to becoming an architect, and as there were already more English architects than there was ever likely to be work for, unless the Germans succeeded in smashing up England badly with their air-raids, he was not anxious to be a civilian again. It would be a good idea when there was an air-raid to light up all those hideous buildings that ought to be demolished, and so get them bombed. That would make the Huns really useful; but they never would have enough bombs; moreover it was doubtful if they ever hit what they aimed at. It was no world for architects unless they were French and had umpteen towns to rebuild.

Tom argued with him about this, taking the view that England would need a lot of building when, if ever, the war was over; but Williamson, who was faintly optimistic about most things, was pessimistic about his trade. His generation of architects was doomed; work would go to the wicked old practitioners of sham Gothic and stuff; how could he spend his life pretending that buildings held by steel girders were Gothic or Tudor? The only alternative was Victoria Street British. There were quite enough grey-beard loons in the profession to draw up thousands of elevations of that sort of tripe and enough engineers to see that they wouldn't fall down if built. The ghastly tradition would be handed down to youngsters whose medieval philosophy had not been disturbed by direct contact with new-style war, and sham architecture would continue to adorn this land of such dear souls, this dear, dear land.

Tom wanted to know, what about housing? Surely what was called the emancipation of women would mean that houses would have to be built of a kind that would not enslave them? But Williamson had little use for housing. There was simply nothing in it; any competent architect could give you a plan and elevation in the rough for any sort of house in half an hour. What would happen was this: a few men would be in the fashion and turn out ten or twenty plans a day each to their large drawing offices, and the rest get next to nothing. That would be the way with houses for the comparatively wealthy; the comparatively poor would be doomed to inhabit the leaky and inconvenient hutches built and decorated by speculators; and the less speculative builders had to do with architects the more profit they made. For the past century the English people had lost their instinct for style in building, and there was no reason to think that the war would revive it. They were content to live in the amorphous conceptions of beer and baccy bricklayers. They had no more idea. . . .

They were interrupted by Seddon. 'I told you so. Balloons. Wing thinks it would be nice if we celebrated our day's rest by bagging a few balloons.'

'Who's on?'

'A of course. C's coming with us to look on.'

Beal came up to warn Cundall for duty. 'We go up in half an hour to escort A flight on a balloon strafe. It's an easy job. The SEs are coming with us on high patrol.'

'Very nice for everyone except A flight,' Seddon commented.

Beal laughed. 'You'll enjoy it. Get a balloon in flames and you'll feel you've really done something; something you can see.'

'Or run into a flaming onion, and there'll be something I can really feel.'

'I know they don't look nice, but have you ever actually known anyone be hit by a flaming onion?'

'No,' Seddon admitted.

'Nor have I,' said Beal.

At this Williamson laughed, and Seddon demanded against him 'haven't B got a job?'

'I don't think so. I believe ours is the only job to-day.'

Seddon joined in the laugh against himself.

First the SEs took off, fifteen of them, and gained height; then C flight; and lastly A flight, who would fly lowest. A carried Buckingham mixed with tracer for setting balloons on fire. It was commonly supposed that the Huns shot anyone who landed on their side carrying explosive ammunition, though they often carried it themselves.

It had become very familiar to Tom, this business of flying that once had been so tentative and unnatural. The fierce intractable Camel had become tame, and as it were an extension of himself, so that flying was more a matter of volition than of conscious control of external mechanism. The ground fled past and sank away in its immemorial manner. There was nothing strange about it; always the earth has behaved thus, if not actually, then potentially; what was actual at one point of time being part of the texture of all time, as if the all-pervasive human mind was already familiar with the aroma of all experience, of which the individual items were realizations in time of its possessions in eternity, and men seemed less to learn than to remember.

The earth swung and tilted, and the horizon adjusted itself to

K   145

the laws of flight. It levelled. The dark smudge of Arras came slowly towards the stationary armada perched in the furious wind with air-screws furiously turning to save it from being swept away by the gale. The aeroplanes kept almost perfectly still, only bumping up and down a little and moving slowly a foot or two backwards or forwards among themselves. The chequered world, some of its rectangles greening with April, crept past below. It would move in whatever direction they willed; Tom sitting there in the noise and the hard wind had the c101ed massy earth his servant tumbler, waiting upon his touch of stick and rudder for its guidance; instantly responsive, ready to leap and frisk a lamb-planet amid the steady sun-bound sheep. The poet's boast was his accomplishment; to swing the earth a trinket at his wrist; the earth with all its bitter peaks and scornful seas.

Tom felt safe and happy in such company; no Huns would attack such a fleet as this unless they were one of those fifty-strong circuses, and even then there would probably be more manœuvring and bluffing than fighting; it was when five or six met five or six that real dogfights occurred; the larger units were unwieldy, and the individual felt that it was no time for him to take the initiative, for if he tried to do anything on his own he would probably get himself shot down, or at least shot up. German air strategy was intended to be scientific; they were unwilling to attack except from a winning position derived from the advantages of height, surprise, and numerical superiority, and they did not hesitate to avoid or run away from combat when these factors were not in their favour. They also avoided crossing the lines, so as to have the further advantage of fighting above their own terrain with the support of their innumerable anti-aircraft batteries, and of course they lost very few prisoners. The only Huns that did cross the lines were occasional two-seaters on special jobs and rare balloon raiders. They were also adopting the idea of large circuses flying in layers, and when you attacked one of the layers it melted away eastwards while the people above dived on you. If you tried to get above the whole lot it meant a climbing competition up to twenty thousand feet where a Camel was no good at all.

All this was very sound, and its counterpart on the ground had

146

been very successful, but it was defensive strategy, and barbed wire could not be staked to the sky. The British had the moral advantage of attacking an apparently timid foe, and were quite willing to fight on the Huns' terms. Bristols and SEs did most of their work ten or twenty miles in Hunland, and Camels as a rule looked after the first ten miles, which they tried to make safe for artillery reconnaissance machines to do their work. There was no hard and fast rule about distances, but it was working out in practice something like that, while varying with the needs of day-by-day.

The SEs went among the clouds, which started at about four thousand feet and mounteained upwards in separate masses, drifting before the west wind. Mac also led A flight into a gap among the clouds and Beal followed him. They flew through a sort of cañon whose beetling walls of granite and pale gold seemed to threaten to crash down on them. A changing strip of Hunland showed below, but Archie found them a difficult target and hardly got near enough for his bark to be heard. Mac went diving down to take a look round, and quickly climbed again into another rift, followed by Beal. In this way they explored the front down to Albert, dodging among the clouds not so much to defeat Archie, though this was something, as to avoid surprise by possible Huns that might spot them from afar off and work among the clouds and come out on top of them.

The result of the exploration was blank; there were no balloons up, probably because of the strong wind. So they went rummaging among the clouds, which was great sport; you never knew what you might meet there coming unexpectedly round a corner. The two flights played hide and seek, climbing up to eight thousand feet, which was as high as the clouds went, and diving away again and zooming and frisking like celestial porpoises. Archie joined in the game with a burst or two when he caught a glimpse of them, which added to the fun. He was a dear fellow in his playful mood, and one could get quite fond of him so long as he did not come too close: a merry entertaining fellow who enlivened many an otherwise dull hour, and so long as one remembered his bad character and did not trust him, his prattle was harmless enough.

They seemed to have cloudland to themselves. The SEs had gone away Berlinwards in the clear heights. It was past one o'clock,

Tom felt hungry and ate some chocolate he had brought with ...... No Huns were likely to be about at that time of day; they would all be at luncheon. The job was a farce, and much more restful than Wing had intended. They had nothing to do but drone for an hour along delightful valleys among moving skiey Snowdons and Scafells. It was a day of the humbler hills of spring, dull and grey at their bases, but peaked with pale gold that flowed far down their sides: the huge Alps and Apennines of summer, red-gold in the heavier sunlight, would arise later; these were their forerunners.

Looping, Tom thought, was entirely new. No birds looped, at least, so far as he had seen, and he had got into the way of watching the flight of birds with professional interest. Not even gulls, those graceful and accurate flyers, ever went right over in a loop. Why should they? It was of no use, and only the idle adventurousness of man was ever likely to discover so unnecessary an antic. But flying, ordinary practical flying, and all its sensations, were part of the unconscious inheritance of man. How many millions of years ago had archaeopteryx or pterodactyl flapped their unimaginable way through the steamy air of the young world? But this was probably quite unsound. Was there any flying group in man's animal ancestry?

A flight was out of sight. An aeroplane came round a sudden corner towards C, and at once turned steeply away, showing black crosses on its wings as it banked. It made a good target as it flew straight across Tom's bows. He got his Aldis on it and opened fire at about fifty yards range. It was a full deflection shot. He got its nose in the ring and held it there for a few seconds by using his rudder. It was an Albatros two-seater. Everyone was shooting at it. A flight, that had been chasing it round the corner, was enabled by its turn away from C to come up within range on the other side, and the unlucky Hun was in a storm of bullets. He put his nose down to dive away. The observer was either shot at once, or like the donkey in the midst of the bundles of hay, he could not choose among ten assailants and did nothing. The pilot had one chance; to disappear into a cloud; but probably he had counted on being able to run from A flight, being out of range and rather faster than a Camel, and when he had met C and come under fire he lost his nerve and put his nose down to dive away; the usual response of a Hun, or anyone with wind up, to attack. He started diving at about five thousand feet, not very steeply. They chased after him down to two thousand and then watched him go. He crashed all right. It was curious that the machine had not gone down in either a steeper dive, as usually happened when the shot pilot fell on the stick, or obviously out of control. Perhaps the pilot had somehow kept hold of the stick, but was too far gone to make a landing. Tom hoped the two young Germans they had met a minute ago so suddenly among the clouds were not killed; but there was little chance of that; they had been shot to blazes and had flown straight into the ground. They ought to have gone in flames with all the explosive stuff A flight were shooting at them. It had been bad luck the way they had blundered right into overwhelming adverse force. They had evidently been trying to do some reconnaissance work without being seen, and would have succeeded very likely but for the irrelevant condition that it had been too windy for balloons to go up.

The Camels, attended by Archie, climbed away into the clouds and continued looking for prey; a little more grimly now that they had made a kill. But they met no more Huns and turned for home soon after two o'clock. It had been a pleasant sort of job with a minute's excitement without danger, and Tom had presumably added to his score another tenth of a Hun.

XIX

In fact Tom was credited with a seventh of a Hun, as Moss's guns had jammed and neither Seddon nor Smith had fired. This brought his score to a fractional number approximating to three. This was very little, but it put him definitely on the credit side in the aerial war; he was earning his keep, and the ground-strafing he did could be thrown in as overweight to make up for all the machines he had crashed. Not that he was so very keen on being on the credit side for the sake of his country; England, my England; precious isle set in the silver sea; tongue that Shakespeare spake; and all the rest of it, was all very well: he could quite well appreciate the splendours of English literature, the beauty of some of the unindustrialized parts of

England, and the glories of fox-hunting, cricket, and the Lord Mayor's show: but everything was vitiated by the consideration that the war was a profitable gambit for a minority of speculators. Every aeroplane that was crashed, every bomb that exploded, was adding to someone's private fortune, and helping a munition-worker to acquire a ridiculous grand piano. This war, declaring itself godly, righteous, a crusade, was tainted and suspect, and the disgusting ignoble civilization that supported it deserved eclipse. It was to gratify his own egoism that he liked to be on the credit side; his own pride and the sense of brotherhood with all the other unfortunates in arms, who must not be let down. It seemed a pity that the young men of the armies could not get together and agree to go home and turn out their own war-lords and money-lords. They had no quarrel with each other; it was a lie and delusion that made them fight, and it had gone on so long as to get cold and smelly. They were fighting for a bad smell which propagandists called the odour of sanctity; and the more people that were killed, the greater and more beautiful the sacrifice, and the more holy and fishy the odour. And if the Dover Patrol was costly in life, were not shipping magnates lousy with shekels? And when the war had been over a few years who would be the better man, rich Lord Neptune the well-known shipowner, or poor Jack Tar the unknown survivor and ex-hero?

It was past three before he had lunch, and as tea was at four he went straight on after only an interval for a cigarette. He certainly was hungry. After tea he took up a new aeroplane that Cross had brought from Candas, and put it through its paces and tried the guns on the ground target. It pulled well, and when he put it over vertical and gave it a touch of elevator the horizon fairly spun round. He met Burkett out for exercise and had a furious scrap with him, round and round and round after each other's tails. It was a good Camel, and Tom adopted it for his own, hoping this one would last longer than his recent mounts.

He came down at half past six feeling hungry again, and invaded his stock of fruit and chocolate, as dinner would not be till eight. This onset of appetite was a good sign; he was always hungry when he was in good trim. He made vocal noises indicative of good spirits.

'Are you in pain?' inquired Seddon.

'Not at all. I don't think I could feel pain. I feel too dense. The world is a surface without significance or substance. I feel as I imagine stockbrokers and bank clerks and such insects feel in their Surrey homes. It was a summer's evening, old Kaspar's work was done. It's been a jolly sort of day, don't you think?'

'Not bad. I was sorry for those fellows in the Albatros. They ran right into it poor devils.'

'Oh, they're all right. After life's fitful fever, they sleep well. Dead as doornails. They were probably good Germans and didn't object to a soldier's death. *Das Krieg ist das Krieg.* They won't haunt you.'

'No, they won't haunt me. I didn't shoot at them. But I hope they haunt you, you blasted militarist. What's the matter with you this evening? Feeling proud of your seventh of a Hun?'

'Have an orange,' said Tom, throwing him one.

After dinner and a few drinks, Tom joined in a sing-song in the mess. Beal warned him for the dawn show, to leave the ground at six. Bombs, of course. These dawn shows were getting earlier and earlier. Soon it would hardly be worth while going to bed at all. To be called at five o'clock, summer time, at the beginning of April! Would the war be over by June? Beal thought that very likely it would. But the immediate prospect of resuming low work was a depressing end to a good day; but then the rain started pattering down and soon it was a good steady downpour. Had the weather really broken at last? If not, what a waste of good rain! But it would stop night-flying, and so help towards a good sleep, and it might well last to wash out the dawn show. Meanwhile the artillery was carrying on a strafe, thumping the night's dull ear with enormous rumble.

The rain stopped during the night, and Tom duly ate the early egg before an hour's trench reconnaissance. They got off the twilit earth a few minutes after six, and went straight over and bombed some third line trenches beyond Arras. Beal, who knew everything, said that most Huns lived in second or third line trenches, where there weren't quite so many machine guns as in the front line and the pits near it. You could tell by the double traverses and elaborate digging of the trenches where there would be most Huns to be awakened; which was about all that could be done to them on these dawn shows when they were nearly all asleep a long way underground. It was in fact very difficult on a quiet morning to find a target worth twenty bombs. You could only aim at trenches or the place where a village used to be and hope to damage something hidden or camouflaged; machine guns for preference. For machine guns were difficult to attack. You had to look out for them more to avoid than to encounter, for if you went diving right down on a nest, giving them a no-deflection shot, it would certainly be your last dive. The fellows on the ground could see you ever so much better than you could see them, and would have their sights on you right away. You might outshoot a solitary gunner, but not a nest of them; you had to sheer off; if you had any bombs you could try a lucky drop without diving; but the great thing was to keep turning and sideslipping when you were being shot at from close range. It was no use being heroic at these times; they would get you. The difficulty was to know when and whence you were being shot at. It was by no means easy to see so small a thing as a machine gun amid all the clutter and clobber of the battlefield, and the Huns seemed able to hide them away somehow, being cunning devils and up to all tricks of camouflage. Certain it was, they didn't see a tenth of the number firing at them, even flying low, and from above a thousand feet or so it was pretty well impossible to spot them at all, though they were still well within range. Perhaps more practice would help; Tom really hadn't spent a great deal of time studying the details of the ground, and the time he had put in was not passed in conditions helpful to nice observation; in fact, the impressions he brought back from these jobs were usually, when he came to think of it, somewhat intermittent, having blurred passages and possibly blanks where observation had been so mechanical as to leave no enduring impression on his fear-occupied mind. He must ask Beal how many machine guns he usually saw, Beal not being subject to fear.

As it happened, that morning Tom caught sight of two machine guns in an open pit by a communication trench that led towards the front line, and he went off to drop his last two bombs on them. Seeing him coming, they or their neighbours put up showers of tracers that frightened him and made him pull the plug rather too soon, and dropping his left wing he leant over and saw his bombs burst a long way from his target.

Bullets were coming from all over the earth; the rest of the flight had vanished into the mist, and he had the undivided attention of dozens of angry gunners. He climbed away, skidding and turning, to the safer height of two thousand feet, and feeling better there he did a half-roll back towards the scene of his unsuccess. He heard a noise behind him, and looking round saw four Archie bursts where he might have been if he had gone on instead of half rolling. This was funny enough to laugh at, and showed that he probably needn't bother about attack from the air at the moment. Archie only used one or two bursts as a pointer. Archie seemed annoyed and gave him salvo after salvo all to himself. It was flattering, all this attention; the enemy must consider him a dangerous man. He felt more like a poor fish himself.

Arrived about over the place where he knew the machine gun pit was, he pulled up his nose and throttled down and stalled, Archie at once bursting well away in front. He dropped nearly vertically for three or four hundred feet, spraying the earth below in a long burst of firing. Then he eased out and twisted westwards at great speed, and he crossed the lines in a few seconds, feeling that he had at least had the last say in his little battle, even if, as was very likely, he hadn't done much damage.

It was not very safe to be across the lines all alone on a misty morning with the red-faced sun making the east an impenetrable murk; it would be difficult to see any approaching Huns until they were close. He was already getting dazzled with peering eastwards, and couldn't tell whether he was seeing dazzle spots or distant enemy aircraft. But it was no use cruising about over thrice-battered Arras; he'd better go and look for the rest of the flight, which had probably gone south trench-inspecting. There seemed to be no activity save on the part of the artillery which was putting over some early high explosive hate, so he did not feel that he ought to go down and pay a solitary call on the trenches and have all the machine guns to himself. He had had quite enough of that for one morning. The thought of going below two thousand feet over Hunland made him feel wrong in the bowels. That inescapable unpredictable fire from the ground was unnerving. How the devil much more of it would he have to go through? The alternatives seemed to be death or lunacy.

But it wasn't a bad morning for a peaceable ride. There was murk up to about three thousand feet, where it ended and showed a clean horizon. It was queer, that straight, ever-receding wall that mist looked like when you got near the top of it. And where the mist ended, ruled straight as the surface of a lake, cloud began; bergs floating in ocean. There wasn't as yet much cloud; what there was glowed purple in the angry sunrise that would soon pale into watery grey-gold morning. He met a big Ak-W doing a shoot, and saw far up a bunch of specks, almost invisible except when a wing flashed in the sun. He watched them carefully. Probably they were . . . yes, there was some black Archie bursting among them; they were SEs or Dolphins: he need not be afraid of going across the lines with that protection above. They were about twelve thousand feet above him he thought. Damned cold up there. He crossed the lines at three thousand and went leisurely eastwards on half throttle. Archie put up a couple of bursts near him, and then no more. Hullo, why no more? He couldn't see anything, but turned away south. Then white Archie burst near him: warning! There was another burst above him in the east. Then he saw the Fokkers. Where were the people up top? He looked up. Archie was calling them, and they were coming. So were the Fokkers. Should he be a hero and stick it? He couldn't get away, probably, so why not stand decoy to the end? But his nerve failed, and he went away west with his neck twisted to look over his tail. The Fokkers would be on him in a couple of seconds. Faster!

He pushed his nose down and touched the rudder to sideslip. His heart was thumping. There were nine of them. He was for it. Then the leader pulled up into a climbing turn and they all went away east. They must have seen the trap. Tom pulled up and turned to watch the fun. He had done his part, and he hoped to God he would never have to repeat it. It was fine to see the SEs as they were, coming screaming down the sky; they could dive, those fellows! The Fokkers were fast and vanished into the sun before the SEs were on them, and Tom, circling over the lines, lost sight of both friend and foe. The whole thing had occupied one too exciting minute, and he was alone. He turned east again and, climbing, went to look for the fight, but could find nothing. Two dozen aeroplanes, or however many there were, seemed to have evaporated into mist. Then he saw below him towards Croiselles two machines circling in combat. He dived towards them and found that they were as he expected an SE and a Fokker. The Fokker seemed to be getting rather the better of it, having gained a little height, and so Tom fired at once to scare him. His guns gave a burst and then stopped and did not respond to immediate action with the cocking handle, and the last he saw of the fight was the Fokker going away east with the SE in pursuit. Tom made for the lines with Archie in fierce attendance. He couldn't see anything wrong with the guns; they just would not fire. Then he thought of looking at his CC gear handle, and of course it was right down. Idiot! He ought to have thought of that at once. He pulled up the handle, pointed his nose towards the Archies, pressed the lever, and the guns worked perfectly.

It was not time to go home yet, so he sailed towards Albert with the faint hope of seeing the rest of the flight. He felt that he had done a useful if rather timid and lucky morning's work; though no doubt to run from the Fokkers was as useful a thing as he could have done. No one sane would stop to fight odds of nine to one, and the Huns, always wary, would have suspected a trap at once if he had not fled. It was very lucky for him that the SEs had come down in such a swoop. It was unlikely, though not impossible, that the Huns had not seen the SEs. Perhaps they thought they had time to pick off the lonely Camel and clear out. Archie had been very useful; there were advantages in operating in sight of home. Archie, from below, had been able to see the Fokkers against the sky, before he had been able to see them against the level sun. The SEs could hardly have been so high as they had appeared. He would have said fifteen thousand, but as they seemed only just to be crossing the lines from home, they would hardly have climbed above twelve thousand at the most. Anyhow, he hoped they had been lucky, and slain the Fokkers. He didn't like Fokkers with their top plane extensions. Nobody minded that old friend the Albatros or that newer friend the

155

Pfalz, but there was something definitely repulsive about a Fokker biplane. The triplanes were bad enough, but they had bad habits and their pilots were afraid to do much with them for fear of breaking them up, and they were said to go to pieces under fire. But the biplanes seemed nearly as good as the triplanes, and to have none of their weakness. They were about as good as SEs, and it was more pleasant to encounter Albatros scouts.

Tom did not meet the flight, and after seven o'clock turned for home, and when he got over the aerodrome he saw three of them had just landed and were taxiing in.

X X

Tom had his second breakfast at eight o'clock; gloomily enough, for Skinner had been shot down. Miller had seen him go. He was hit when he was at about three hundred feet, and Miller had watched him spin into the ground. He was certainly killed. Beal had come in for a good deal of damage. His machine had a lot of holes, and a few wires were cut. Everyone was holed more or less; and the job hadn't been worth it. They had not done any certain damage, and there was really nothing to report except that the enemy seemed quiet on their front. And Tom had, or thought he had, a personal grievance. When he had reported his own doings, Beal had made no comment at all. This wasn't natural; what the devil was the matter with him? Was he feeling worried and thinking about other things? He didn't look like it, and Beal wasn't the sort of fellow to be worried. The only explanation was that he was sceptical, and thought that Tom was just telling a yarn to cover his absence from most of the job, but as he had nothing to go on, he couldn't or wouldn't say anything. Fellows often got separated from the rest on these jobs, and nobody thought anything of it so long as they got home safely; it took a win-the-war-quick merchant like Beal to start getting suspicious about a trifle of that sort. Good God, wasn't there enough to put up with in the bloody war without this sort of thing? But Beal always had been difficult, with that exaggerated sense of duty of his, which was taking the hell of a long time to get knocked out of him; although, heaven knew, he had sacrificed enough lives to it. And the irony of it all was that Tom had done a damn sight more good that morning than the rest of the flight with their precious trench reconnaissance. . . .

Tom pulled himself up. His nerves were running away with him and spoiling his breakfast. Beal came in, and Franklin and others of B flight, who were going up at nine. Tom got talking of his adventures, and made a fairly creditable story of them.

'Pretty good,' Beal remarked. 'A pity you didn't get that Fokker. What was wrong with your guns? Are they all right now?'

'Yes. As a matter of fact it was only the gear handle wanted pulling up.'

Franklin emitted one of his big guffaws and said: 'That's about the first thing to look at.'

'I know that. In the excitement I forgot all about the gear and tried to clear the guns.'

Again Beal said nothing. Damn the man. It was his place to laugh it off. His silence was a criticism. Confound it, you couldn't expect a fellow to be as cool as a snow man in the circumstances.

'Do you ever do anything damn silly like that when you're excited?' he continued.

'Oh yes,' said Franklin, 'we all do, if you ask me. I remember once fiddling with my guns for ten minutes, and then I gave it up and went home. I got the armourer to look at them, and he pointed out that I'd shot away all the ammunition.'

This brought a shout of laughter. Thank heaven there were fellows like Franklin, thought Tom.

Apparently the reign of the klaxon horn was over, and they were no longer to wait on its regal raucous voice. The major still used it, but the times of jobs were known in advance, and it was only a harmless weakness of the major's that led him to do so. He liked to hear his authority stentorophoned in a brazen voice of command.

Nevertheless, when the shout for B flight blared, Tom found that the noise was still hard on the nerves. His next job was due at half past two, but in these giddy times an emergency might develop anywhere and upset routine. Danger was apprehended east of Amiens where the Fifth Army had been smashed, and a continuous rain of bombs was to be aimed at the enemy there. After a dawn trench reconnaissance on their own front, jobs, until further orders, were to consist of bombing in the region of the Amiens road: until the danger there was considered to be over there would be no respite from low work except by way of bad weather; but unfortunately the sort of weather that would stop patrolling was not necessarily bad enough to stop low work. A sheet of low clouds, for instance, made a patrol unnecessary and impossible, but you could go ground-strafing in anything but fog, gale, or heavy rain. Low cloud only increased the risk, as you had to stop within range of machine gun fire all the time you were in Hunland; but it might be a protection against air attack as there was little likelihood of air-Huns being out and about if the clouds were below about two thousand feet.

There would be no afternoon nap, and Tom tried to get in a little sleep before lunch. This five o'clock in the morning business made the day unendurably long to jaded nerves. Time's flagging wing seemed ineffective to move the clotted minutes; and without lessening the inevitability of the next job spread out the burden of waiting for it into interminable weariness. But as soon as he lay down he knew there would be no sleep for him. He was tired, but never had he felt less able to sleep. He was restless, and had to do something. He wandered into the mess and joined in a game of poker, and not having a poker face he lost as usual. It was not his game, and it was a damned silly game anyhow. B flight returned and A flight went out. The clouds were thickening and lowering and the wind was strong. It was unpleasant weather to cross the lines in; the ceiling was down to about fifteen hundred; A flight, back to lunch, had dashed over, dropped their bombs, and dashed back again. Machine gunners were getting better and better at hitting aeroplanes; they had so much practice. Nowadays you couldn't go anywhere near the ground without getting a few holes to show for it.

Beal, marvellously, decided to take the afternoon off as his bus was still in the riggers' hands because of damage received during the early show, and the half past two job was entrusted to Miller's leading. There would only be four on the job, one of whom would be Dubois, who looked a picture of melancholy when he heard that he was on active service. Farewell, happy shores of Trois Rivières!

Tom did not attempt to give him good advice; he remembered lecturing Skinner, and Skinner was dead. The order of battle was to work in pairs. Dubois was to keep with Miller, and Smith with Cundall. Tom was afraid Miller might be feeling his responsibility and want to do an undue amount of war-winning, but it appeared that he, like most other people, had had his bellyful of low work, and was not out for suicide. Moreover, he was a disciple of his fellow countryman Mac, who was one of the most successful pilots in France, and Mac had that morning taken A flight there and back as quickly as he could. What was good enough for Mac was good enough for Miller, and unless they saw something going on that it was up to them to take a hand in, there was no point in hanging themselves in the air as targets for invisible machine guns. The rain of bombs was the thing. If they got split up while bombing they would at once rendezvous at a thousand feet, or as high as they could get, over Corbie, so as to go home together or wherever else Miller thought necessary. Miller would dip twice when he was going to let go his bombs.

They took off and touched the ceiling almost at once: it was a terrible afternoon on which to cross the lines. Miller took them over the Somme and crossed between Hamel and Villers-Bretonneux, hugging the clouds at a height of twelve hundred feet. Immediately Archie went for them furiously; the Germans must have brought up a lot of batteries as a defence against all the bombing. But they were too low for Archie to be very accurate; the real danger was from machine guns. It made Tom feel sick to be blanketed down in Hunland, unable to get out of range; the unseen, ineluctable menace was too much. All the time to know that perhaps ten machine guns were firing at them; that at any moment the fatal bullet might be fired; that to live through each minute was marvellous: to feel all this was too great a strain. It made him breathless and sick.

Miller gave the sign to drop bombs by Warfusée-Abancourt. The Germans hadn't such good trenches to protect them here as in front of Arras. Tom turned towards Hamel and let his bombs go and veered away at once across the lines to Corbie. Smith followed him, and they circled in safety over Corbie until Miller and Dubois joined them, and then went home. Miller lost height until they were nearly on the ground. It was impossible not to feel happy contour-chasing home, another day's work done, even in dismal bumpy weather. They struck a patch of rain and had to fly nearly blind through the dissolving cloud that spread a gauze of smoke and water down to the tree tops. They got through it, chased some troops off a road, chivvied a staff car, and landed feeling almost refreshed.

There was a notice on the board announcing that the squadron had created a record among scout squadrons by not sending in a single inaccurate report during the month of March; and during the same month they had broken the record for bringing down the largest number of enemy aircraft in one day. Obviously the squadron was a very fine squadron, and there would have to be some sort of celebration about it. No one was feeling very festive, however, except Chadwick of course, and those great men of B flight, Bulmer and Franklin; even James seemed to be affected by the atmosphere of strain and to have lost some of his thrusting eloquence. Williamson was another imperturbable, but Williamson was not an enthusiastic binger, being more amused by watching others getting excited than by getting excited himself.

A tender went over to Avesnes and got some Pommery and Greno, but the place seemed destitute of food, and the ordinary stuff had to do: soup, roast beef, tinned peaches. But no one was very interested in food; drink was the thing. Tom found the champagne infernally dry; the gas from the bubbles smelt almost foul. The padre drank lemonade. The wing colonel looked in for a little while and told them how noble they all were, and the major replied how very glad they were to be at all useful to the great cause. With official eloquence over and the port circulating, the mess began to get tumultuous. Things were thrown about, and everyone was shouting. Moss tried to dance a jig on the table and broke crockery. A rough house was developing. Chadwick tried to play his mandoline but no one would listen. Someone tried to snatch it from him, and there was a bit of a scrap, in which the mandoline was damaged. Burkett was swinging a chair about and he hit Miller and there was more trouble. Drinks were going round all the time, and glasses were being smashed. Tom was jumping on a chair trying to break it, but it was a stout one that wouldn't give. The mess was becoming a wreck. Everything was being thrown about, cushions, gramophone records, chairs, ash trays, fire irons. Hard knocks abounded. People were fighting mounted, or just charging about. Tom collided violently with Maitland and they clung together to recover.

'Mix me a drink that'll put me clean out,' said Tom

'Sure to hell I will.' Maitland made for the bar.

'In the American language,' Tom said with careful articulation, 'the word hell seems to be a noun, pronoun, verb, adjective, adverb, and term of affection all at once.'

'You're right. It's the joker. Ever since we joined in this rotten war of yours there's been nothing else to say.'

Tom drank his drink, whatever it was, and threw the glass at the wall as a gesture of horror. Then he felt fed up. What the hell was the point in smashing up the mess and raging around like a damned lot of lunatics? He couldn't get happy-drunk, and this was no good. He went out. It was raining fast. There was a good fire in the hut. He sat by it, feeling physically but not mentally drunk. He was tired; he could sleep for a week; but it was too much trouble to undress. He dozed in the comfortable warmth until he was awakened by someone coming in. It was Smith, rather drunk, who lighted a lamp after some fumbling, and then Williamson came in supporting Seddon who was completely soused and talking at random. He seemed to be pressing Williamson to call on him at home after the war, and they'd . . . but it wasn't very plain what they'd do.

Tom flopped into bed and slept the sleep of the exhausted and drunk. He had a bottle of drinking water handy, which was very useful at dawn. But instead of going off soundly to sleep again after the cooling drink, he lay dozing, depressed by the weight of an obscure problem, dreaming a lot of nonsense through which the feeling of uneasiness transuded. At intervals he realized that his head was worse than usual after a thick night. The problem could not be solved by getting drunk. What problem? It eluded him down long fantastic dream-ways and hid behind cloudy malaise and absurd phantasmagoria. Yet all the time it was in his belly, gripping his bowels with relentless tentacles like some monstrous parasite, draining his strength and nervous force. The flickering world, pale to its last verge, spun pendant in an abyss of fear. A lurid glare from a ghastly sun . . . over a Somme of blood. There was the hollow throne of fear, terrible with fanged emptiness, and through the eternally motionless air a black streak that went down and down and down, dragging him towards inevitable death. The earth was spinning beneath him as he fell, spinning away from him. Better to be killed than left in the blank of space. But it was gone, and beyond a phenakistoscopic veil he saw the flying moons and spheres caught in webs and dragged away. He was alone with a problem that filled the whole universe, spreading out like gas to unimaginable tenuity. He wanted to think what it was about, but the inside of his head felt as if tangled string was caught on rusty nails, and each painful molecule moved alone, eluding vision. His morning sleep was no good; he might as well get up.

Beal came and said there would be no jobs that day, as the weather was too dud. Thank God for that — but no, Beal hadn't said anything. He was dreaming. His watch said half past eight. Might as well get up. There was something he ought to do. What was it? Some problem to solve. He wasn't well enough. His head was dreadfully bad. No, it wasn't that. His father wanted him to dig the early potatoes. At the beginning of April? He knew it was early April because of the push. . . .

Tom sat up in bed, with an effort throwing off the baleful mantle of sleep. It was horrible, that state of dozing when the worlds of waking and sleep were so mixed that you couldn't tell dream from actuality. It seemed like a sort of unhealthy self-hypnosis. His head really was bad; no wonder his dreams had been unpleasant, whatever they were. He remembered speaking to Beal and looking at his watch. Surely he really had looked at his watch and seen half past eight; he could still see it in his mind's eye. No; it was five to seven. The others were asleep. It was raining and there had been no dawn show for B whose turn it was. There was no point in getting up yet, and he would not risk sleeping again. His head was too thick to read, but he had some aspirin which he took to relieve it. He felt depressed and unrefreshed. Another wretched day had started. Probably it would clear up just enough to let them go out beneath a low blanket of cloud and be shot to blazes under Beal's guidance. It had to be done to help, if they could, the poor devils in the trenches;

but the question for him personally was whether he could stick any more of it. But what was the use of bothering? If he cracked, he cracked. His head began to feel better, and he reached for *The Old Wives' Tale* and read. Useful stuff, aspirin.

XXI

THE way out was so easy. It was only necessary to pick a quiet spot in Hunland, away from where you'd been bombing, and land there, and your war was well over. The immediate future might not be very comfortable, but that was nothing. Who was to know? Your engine had cut out; you had been shot down; anything. The Germans weren't likely to be very interested; and if you had time you set your machine on fire after you had removed the spare razor and tooth brush which you always carried with you in case of accidents. The Germans' chief interest would be to get information out of you, and Tom was pretty sure he couldn't tell them anything they didn't know already, and in any case you weren't bound to answer questions, though refusing mightn't be too pleasant: that was a bit of trouble he would have to face; he couldn't expect to have it both ways.

Why not? One way and another he had borne a reasonable share of the war; and now he was finished. He would either be killed or break down if he went on any longer. There was this one way out, this one chance of life, and life with the externals of honour, for no one would know, and his own conscience, if he had such a thing, wouldn't trouble him much about escaping from a mad war which he had come to hate as the worst folly and crime ever committed by the idiotic and wolfish leaders of mercantile pseudo-civilization. He had done with it. But he hadn't a spare razor.

It continued to rain and blow all the morning; but news came through of an attack in front of Amiens, and they were all standing by: if the weather cleared they were to dash down south and bomb and shoot up the attack. The flights would go out at intervals of half an hour in the order A, B, C.

Tom settled down to bridge in the mess. He wondered how many more of the squadron were feeling as he was, and meditating landing on the wrong side. He could not tell by looking at them, and hoped that he himself did not show outwardly how dread an army had enrounded him. If only leave would re-start and give something to look forward to instead of this frightful blank: but here were the Huns still attacking. He called No Trumps without their long suit defended. It didn't matter much what you did while waiting for slaughter. He was doubled and should have been well down; but the long suit of clubs was blocked after two rounds, and a wrong lead put him in and he made his tricks in hearts and spades. It was wonderful what you could get away with sometimes. The way that dooming line of clubs had ceased upon the midday with no pain!

But they weren't to get away with a jobless day, for the rain stopped and the pall lifted somewhat and Wing wanted to know what they were doing. The major had his Camel got out of store and he ascended into the sky. He was very doubtful about sending his pilots out ground-strafing in this sort of weather; the whole squadron was getting racked and nervy. They had aeroplanes, not tanks. But it was just clear enough, and A flight set out at two o'clock. Tom wandered on to the aerodrome to see them go. He jumped into a machine-gun-pit and uncovered a gun and got the sights on them as they turned down wind. They didn't seem a very difficult shot. There ought to be armoured machines for low work. Rumour had noised of one called Salamander; but rumour was all. The new Fokkers had tubular steel fuselages. It was no longer safe to sit behind a screen of canvas and wood and trust to speed as protection against bullets; a good gunner with ring sights could allow very accurately for speed; practice was making perfect. The only protection was good luck. Probably your bus was hit every time you went near the ground; if your luck was good you didn't give an unseen gunner a sitting shot and nothing vital was touched.

Tom was still there when B flight took off. One of the rear men had his engine cut clean out when he had reached fifty feet, and he turned back to land on the aerodrome instead of going straight on. He tried to keep his nose up long enough to complete his turn down wind and of course lost flying speed and fell into a spin that only lasted half a turn before the machine crumpled on the ground, collapsing suddenly, as if the rod supporting a deck chair had slipped from its grooves. It had seemed to hit the ground slowly and gently, and might, without outraging the eye, have retained its corporeity perfect; but there was a mere strew of wreckage.

Everyone rushed to the crash, and the tender on duty came bumping over the field. The pilot was a new man named Priest. He was pulled out of the cockpit, snoring with blood. His nose was pulped and his forehead looked crushed. One of his legs was twisted. But he was not dead, and if his skull was not fractured he might live, an honourable rhinoplast, to enjoy length of days: his war was over. And if he did not wake up he was spared the pain of lingering out a few more tortured days until a machine gun got him. They put the damaged snoring body on a stretcher and the tender bumped away with it to the nearest Casualty Clearing Station. Lucky Priest.

Then A flight returned without elegant Chapman, and it was time for C flight to go. They took off into the thick and blusterous air, only able to see a few hundred yards, and unable to get above eight hundred feet. They were to go farther south than ever, into quite strange country beyond Moreuil, where the enemy was making headway. It was not easy to find the way in the mistiness. They crossed the Albert-Amiens road, the Somme, and the Amiens-St. Quentin road, and then flew straight south until they picked up the railway line that went to Moreuil and Montdidier. They passed a bunch of Camels going west, and soon came to the area of the fighting, where there were more Camels. The Germans weren't well sheltered, being massed in shallow trenches, in shell holes, or wherever they could find cover: there seemed to be no end of them nowadays. Beal went right down on them, and Tom, feeling white all through and holding himself to the job, flopped after him, letting his bombs go as fast as he could get rid of them. The machine guns were on them at once. Tom turned and sideslipped and watched his bombs go. He thought he got one good hit in a shell hole. He put his nose down towards a trench and blazed away. A bullet knocked splinters out of the dashboard and frightened the life out of him. He wriggled away westwards to a less murderous altitude, with fear spearlike through his vitals. He went across the lines and cruised about to recover his nerve. He could not go down on to the carpet again point blank into the mouths of the machine guns. It was dangerous enough anywhere under the clouds, but Beal's way of stopping at a height of a hundred feet or so was impossible.

Tom turned back to the war and braced himself to dive and fire. So far as he could see the Camels of other squadrons that were out on the same business were not going much below five hundred feet; what was five hundred feet to machine guns? It was damnably dangerous even there. He made a few skidding dives and shot off most of his ammunition without coming to harm, and cleared off into safety. God, what a life it was! He wondered how many men he'd killed or damaged. He hoped he'd distributed a few Blighties; whatever the German equivalent might be. What a funk he'd been in; shaking with fright. Where were the others? He roamed about and met a Camel marked W. That should be Dubois. He went close and waved. Dubois waved back and followed him. It was no use hanging about any longer, so Tom headed north, and they did a *formation à deux* home. Tom couldn't even be bothered to dive at anything on the way, but held straight on at two hundred feet through the grey depressing afternoon.

Miller was already back, badly shot up, having made the journey on his gravity tank. A bullet had smashed the pipe that led from the pressure-pumping propeller on the interplane strut. There was no sign of Beal or Smith. Dubois was very glad he had met Tom; he was sure he would never have found his way home alone. He wanted to know how Tom did it, flying straight back through all the mist.

'Oh just instinct,' said Tom; 'you'll get it soon.'

Beal landed a few minutes later, displeased at having been left to come back alone. He told Tom and Dubois that they ought to have kept some sort of formation or at least kept near him. It was his job to select targets to attack, and they should concentrate on the spot he chose and not go dropping bombs at random. What did they think the idea of going out in formation was? He wanted them to work as a unit and not all scatter as soon as he went down.

'I think you might have given those instructions beforehand,' said Tom. 'It's not very pleasant, coming back from a hot job like that, to be told off for such a usual thing as getting split up. Why not have a rendezvous?'

'There's no need for a rendezvous, and there shouldn't be any need

166

for these instructions, as you call them. In a dogfight it's different: but apart from a dogfight there's no occasion for not keeping together. Let's go along to the office, and I'll tell you what I want. . . .'

They walked to the office, Beal expounding, Tom fuming inwardly, Dubois impassive. Miller joined them and they made their report. Still there was no sign of Smith. Tom began to despair of ever seeing him again, and felt sick at heart. He went down to the mess. Dubois caught him up.

'I say, don't you think Beal is very unreasonable? We shall all be killed.'

Tom shrugged his shoulders. 'It's part of the job. I'm sorry Beal is such a fanatic; but he's right.'

'Well, I don't want to be killed because of Beal.'

'No. But we shall be. Unless Beal gets killed first. He won't be; flight commanders always last a long time. There's only Miller and me that have been in the flight more than a fortnight. When I think of the fellows that have come and gone it gives me the creeps. Now poor old Smith seems to have gone. It's usually the new fellows: the longer you've been at it, the better your chance. I've three times your chance, and Miller's got about one and a half times mine. But with Beal leading nobody's chance is worth a paper sou. It doesn't matter. They're turning out over two thousand aeroplanes a month, I hear, and there's plenty of schoolboys and Americans that like the idea of flying.'

Tom sat by Williamson. 'Smith hasn't got back yet. I suppose he's gone west.'

'I hope not.' Seddon spoke across the table. 'It'll be ghastly for his wife.'

'If the passion was mutual. It never does to take that for granted. She may be hooked up with an obese cloth manufacturer by now for all we know.'

'Oh, come off it, Tom. He was in a bad corner. I wish we could get really stable in the hut. Poor old Smith's corner is unlucky.'

'What about Allen? He was decidedly lucky if you ask me. Perhaps Smith is too.'

'I hope so, but. . . .'

'Listen,' interrupted Williamson. 'That's him.'

'I believe it is. Let's go and see.'

They abandoned tea and went up to the aerodrome. Someone was landing. Yes, it was Smith all right. It turned out that he had lost himself and had landed at two aerodromes to ask the way. The second one contained Nines, and they had a wash-out day, and everyone except the orderly dog seemed to have cleared off to Abbeville for a binge. Who would fly Camels?

So the quartette in the hut was intact for a little longer. Tom felt that he was extraordinarily lucky in his hut companions. He might so easily have had, in this chance association, incomprehensible colonials or boys straight from school with their usual poverty of ideas and plenitude of foul language: good fellows and all that, but better for a rag in the mess than arguments in the hut. A superstition suddenly grew up in his mind: death could only get to him if the quartette was broken, and the vulnerable corner was Smith's. So long as Smith was all right, they were all all right; and Smith's unexpected return was a happy omen. Smith was his mascot, his sure defence.

It was no use trying to scorn this secret stupid superstition; it persisted, and actually raised his spirits. Tom was too glad of anything capable of doing that to fight against it for long. It was the most queer thing imaginable that he should get relief from such an irrational and unaccountable aberration. He was fearfully and wonderfully made. And as for Beal, he would take him at his word and keep close to him all the time on the next job. It was ridiculous; but his was not to reason why; he was a soldier, and must do his Balaclava stuff. He'd show Beal.

Fortunately the next job was not quite so bad, since the attack had died away for the moment. It took place on the afternoon of the next day. It was cloudy, but flying became possible for Camels after lunch. They went down to the Somme as usual to drop their bombs. It was quiet on the ground, and Beal kept at a thousand feet while he had a look round, and did not go down until he had selected some battered trenches three miles over near Marcelcave to attack. Tom was not happy at a thousand feet, but it was better than Beal's usual reconnaissance at one hundred.

But when Beal went down in a dive to five hundred, and then right down on to the floor, the old breathless fear returned. He dropped his bombs, and where Beal went he went too, rather like a timid bather into cold water. Beal was content to do his bombing and go. He did it thoroughly, but seemed to have lost the conviction that it was necessary to do more unless there was an attack actually going on. Miller and Smith were still with them at the end, but Dubois had disappeared, and they went home without him.

It hadn't been such a bad job. If only Tom could throw off the feeling of terror that gripped his vitals when he went near the gun-bristling earth: but it was as though fear had gathered there like an invisible gas, and every time he dived into it he was inevitably overcome. There ought to be an issue of anti-fear masks or dope. The rum ration had been stopped for aviators; but who could need it more than these cold-blooded divers into the pit? Dubois turned up later. He had lost himself but had come to a town which he recognized as Arras; and so it was a day without casualties. This was good, but it was generally felt to be a scandal that they should have to work at all in such weather. All the German and most of the British flying forces were having a holiday; but they were expected to go over to the attack day after day, twice a day if it was fine enough, without ever a rest.

Tom was worried about himself again. He had almost thought he had won a battle against fear, but the haunting presence was back again: it had merely retired for a few hours about some unimaginable spectral business. The silly idea of Smith's talismanic value had faded. It was inconceivable that such nonsense had ever been able to influence him. What was he to do? He knew very well in his heart of hearts that he would never escape by landing purposely on the other side; it wasn't in him. There was nothing to do but make up his mind to die with a good grace; if one must die, better do it as decorously as possible. It was nothing more than a falling asleep. No one was afraid of going to sleep. The only difficulty was that he was fond of life. Life was good. And at home there were a lot of prosperous elderly gentlemen and persons with certified weak hearts who would go on living and living and living when all that was left of him would be a stinking mess of putrescence; these people were sheltering behind him; he was playing Isaac to their foul old Abraham;

169

where was the angel's voice? God, it was terrible; the young men were sent out to be massacred so that the weak and unworthy elements of the race might be preserved. There was no escape.

He drank gloomily a lot of whisky in the mess, and then there was a brew of egg flip. He staggered out to go to bed. He brushed past someone in the doorway. The padre's voice came through a haze:

'You know you'll ruin the lining of your stomach.'

Blast the padre! Representative of a church that backed up the war and still called itself Christian. Bloody lot of hypocrites, church people.

He turned and went back. He wanted to see the padre because he'd thought of something to say to him, but he couldn't find him. What he had thought of was 'worry about your own stomach. I shan't live long enough to do much harm to mine'.

But it remained unsaid.

XXII

ON the next day, Saturday the sixth of April, rain spread over northern Europe in the early morning, and in places continued all day. In London those with relatives in the R.A.F. hoped that this would be a real day's rest for them, and bore with patience the damping addition to the horrors of week-end shopping; but in Picardy it cleared up in the afternoon and there was plenty of flying, for the enemy was making yet another assault on the defences of Amiens, and there seemed very little reason why they should not carry them, unless it might be their own exhaustion. The British reply to the attack was to bomb from the air more intensely than ever. The clouds lifted to some three thousand feet, so that machines of all descriptions could be used. When C flight arrived at the scene of action soon after three o'clock the air was crowded with machines coming and going, and it was quite difficult to avoid backwash. An instinct made Tom aware that there were Huns about too, waiting to pounce; but none was visible at the moment.

Beal wasted no time, but went right down to a hundred feet. He had thought out a new idea, by which he and Tom would work close together in front, and Miller with the other two would follow a little after, or attack from another angle. He hoped by this to deliver a concentrated attack without their all getting in each others' way. Tom was nearly upset by a shell bursting right underneath his tail, and he lurched as though a giant had given him a push. He hung desperately on to Beal, dropping bombs where he did, not at all sure where. Then he followed him as he went nosing along communication trenches for troops going up. Tom slewed about as much as he could, but Beal seemed entirely unconcerned about bullets; he was after prey. But suddenly Tom saw something that made him go alongside Beal and waggle his wings. There was a bunch of Huns, possibly a dozen, coming down on them. Beal saw them and turned just as they opened fire. He went down in a spin, hit either from the air or from the ground. Tom completed his turn amid an appalling pop-pop-pop-pop-pop-pop of machine guns, and zig-zagged westwards. The Huns had dived and pulled out and he was still alive. His Aldis was smashed. He was aware of a group of holes in his left bottom plane. They apparently weren't going to attack again. But there was a crack-crack-crack-crack in a different key. Splinters from a centre-section strut flew in his face. A landing wire broke and the ends rattled about. Something tore a leg of his sidcot. He must be flying straight over a machine-gun nest at about fifty feet. His engine spluttered and his hand switched over to gravity automatically. There was a terrible din going on now his engine wasn't roaring. He was not particularly afraid. His body was functioning as an automaton and his mind was anaesthetized to everything but surprise or curiosity. What was happening, was going to happen? There were bullet holes everywhere. It was preposterous that he wasn't hit. He was going down. He would probably be dead in a second or two. It was impossible to live through this. Then the engine picked up, and he thought he was across the lines, but still a cracking continued. He was certainly across the lines, but the cracking still continued. There could be nothing shooting at him, but the noise went on, and fear returned. What was this unaccountable machine-gun-like row? He couldn't make it out. Was the aeroplane breaking up? Should he land somewhere at

171

once? He throttled down and glided in panic towards the shattered ground. Then he saw a strip of torn canvas that was flapping in the wind on the fuselage just behind him.

He opened out again and climbed away. He was shot to blazes, and it was a miracle that he was alive. There was a smell of petrol. Perhaps it would be better to land as soon as possible. He crept along cautiously on half throttle, and tried to collect his thoughts. What had happened? There had been a dash into Hunland, right on the floor, and here he was, dazed but alive. Beal had gone. They had been shot at from the air and ground at the same time. Beal was dead. What a rattle of guns there had been; that damned staccato chatter. He really didn't remember details.

Someone came alongside him. It was Miller, followed by Smith and Dubois. He waved and joined them, but would not fly faster than eighty miles an hour and they soon left him behind. They came back and had a look at him and amused themselves by fooling about round him. He wouldn't throw a stunt for the world. And there was a damnable smell of petrol. He might burst into flames. Beal, his admirable enemy, had gone and he remained. These twin facts swung round in his head like a planet and moon. Fate manifestly hadn't the interest of the Allies in view. Those Huns had done a good day's work. Where the devil had they appeared from so suddenly? It was weird the way things appeared from and vanished into nowhere upstairs. You had to be as watchful as a goshawk. Then what had happened? The Huns had left him alone and some of their pals on the ground had taken advantage of his preoccupation with them to finish him off; nevertheless their bullets had hit everything but him, and here he was floating insecurely home. He would like to get his bus home. It would break all records. Never had anyone been so shot up and got home. It would be amusing and dramatic if the wing collapsed when he landed, that landing wire being broken. He hoped it would. The rattling and cracking were alarming though they seemed to arise from harmless causes.

He was glad to see home at length; not so profoundly relieved as he expected to be after his unsafe journey; he seemed to have lost some of his capacity for feeling.

His escort let him land first, which he did without losing any time. He made a good landing and watched his damaged wing as he touched earth. It dropped, and scraped its tip along the ground; but this was because the whole aeroplane was tilted, not because it had collapsed. Tom switched off and swung round the pivot of his dropped wing to a standstill.

He climbed out to see what had happened. The tyre of one of the landing wheels was flat, punctured in the air. It struck him as extremely funny to get a puncture in the air. He laughed and laughed and leaned over the bottom plane and laughed till he ached, with his face over a group of six bullet holes that represented a bit of good shooting by one of those Fokkers.

Two mechanics with a spare wheel and tools were the first to arrive. Then Williamson and Hudson. Then Baker and Reeve, very new comers to the squadron, who gazed with reverential horror at the gaping wounds.

'Good God man,' exclaimed Hudson, 'what the bloody hell have you been up to? Even your sidcot is shot through. Aren't you hurt?'

'I'm all right. I've only been following Beal. He won't be back.'

There was a scorched tear in his right thigh, and a brown mark as though someone had laid a hot poker lightly on his left arm, which meant that a bullet had grazed. A piece was smashed out of a centre-section strut within a few inches of his face; he remembered feeling the splinters blow against him. Several bracing wires were broken, and the petrol tank holed near the top. There were two holes in the floor of the cockpit. The total number of bullet holes was over sixty. It must be one of the most remarkable escapes ever made. He certainly had a reliable guardian angel. For what was the angel working? Wasn't death due till next week? Miller came hurrying up:

'Was Beal shot down?'

'Yes, he went in a spin.'

'Didn't he see those Huns d'you think? Holy Jesus, you've caught it!'

It appeared that Miller had seen the Huns in plenty of time and had started climbing, but they had only dived once on Beal and Tom, and cleared off quickly because of the number of British machines in the neighbouring sky. Miller had taken a long range crack at them, but they wouldn't stop to fight. He was sorry about Beal, but he had asked for it, and had nearly done for Tom as well. They'd better go and report.

Tom felt shaky but exhilarated. This was the third Camel of his to be written off by machine-gun fire. After tea, the new wheel being fixed, he taxied the wreck in for dismantling. He cut a bullet out of a spar of the left-hand bottom plane to keep as a souvenir. The whole squadron had been examining the damage and Tom's escape was the evening's wonder. It came on to rain. Beal's decease was not particularly noticed. It was unusual to have a flight commander killed, but Beal had not been with the squadron long and had not secured a big bag of Huns. You got little credit for ground-strafing, although it was the most dangerous, nerve-racking, and perhaps most valuable work that scouts did. Assaults on the trenches were particularly trying, for they were in the most concentrated area of machine guns. It was really safer to go farther back and look for transport and troops on the march; there were machine guns everywhere in Hunland, but not so many a few miles back, and the difference more than compensated for the greater liability to attack from the air; also it was much more fun if you caught anything. Had Beal been able to devote his brief career to aerial combat, no doubt he would have shot down twenty Huns in quick time and his ghost would have been comforted with a posthumous D.S.O.; for he had all the qualifications of a Hun-getter, and his tactics were the essence of that offensive spirit which was sedulously instilled into young pilots by official talkers.

There had been a Captain Trollope, whom Tom knew, killed recently. He had, like Beal, come out to take over a flight in a Camel squadron. During his brief course he shot down six Huns in one day, which earned the M.C.; then he was missing, and men would remember him for a little while as an inspired warrior. But who would know Beal and honour his memory? He had gone out daily to confront incalculable death with risk-oblivious courage, without the stimulus of man-to-man combat; and there was no red triumph of broken or burning enemies reeling down the skies to be entombed in the perky officialese of *Comic Cuts*. He would be forgotten in a week. Bravery was nothing without publicity and popularity. Beal was not unpopular, but he had not been long enough with the squadron to form one of that more stable nucleus of older hands which the imagination envisaged when the tongue said 'the squadron': Mac, Bulmer, Moss, Franklin, Miller, Williamson.

On the fringes of this nuclear group were Tom himself, Hudson, Seddon, Maitland, and Burkett, all of whom seemed in the process of taking root. The rest were here-to-day-and-gone-to-morrow folk whose expectation of life, once they had started jobs, seemed to be about a week then-a-days; perhaps one in ten of them settled down. The more permanent people had their casualties in plenty, but if an expectation of life table for aviators in France had been compiled it would probably have been a sort of inversion of that ordinary one which assures profits to assurance companies. It was difficult to assign reasons for survival. In the first selection youth and immaturity of practical judgment were no doubt adverse factors; and then differences of eyesight and habitual alertness told; and lastly acquired tactical skill and innate cunning. But when all these things were allowed for, it was difficult amid the flying bullets to believe in anything but luck. Everyone got shot up occasionally, and nothing but luck could account for the inches this way or that which made a bullet harmless or fatal; and a succession of lucky chances that resulted in survival lasting over months took on an aspect of destiny. All nonsense, Tom thought. As a condition of war there must be some survivors. But if the survivors liked to think that the piercing eye of destiny had singled each one out as an individual worth keeping alive, why not? They might at some time try to do something to deserve it.

Tom felt more and more worried about Beal as the evening passed, and whisky could not still his conscience. It was impossible not to feel glad that Beal had been killed, and it seemed the most horrible feeling he had ever had. He hadn't realized how much Beal had seized on his imagination as the complete hero, and how much he hated him as a menace to his own life and a reproach to his half-heartedness; or feared. Into what a vile morass of shame he had wandered when his instinctive feeling about the death of one of the bravest men he had ever known was relief! A little comforting maggot of hope wriggled in his brain. It was a vile maggot, and it would not stop wriggling. Those frightful jobs sitting at fifty or a hundred feet over the trenches had probably come to an end.

Miller asked him if he was fit for the early job. They were to go up at six for the usual reconnaissance and morning message to the Huns. Cross would have to be on it.

'I hope he'll be all right,' said Tom. 'We've had enough casualties lately, and we shan't be much good till some of these new fellows have gained experience.'

That was his reply to Beal: casualties. What was the use of destroying the flight? No one had a chance to mature under a flight commander who insisted on too much heroics.

Beal, Beal, Beal: he couldn't get him out of his thoughts. He seemed to hear echoes of his voice flitting about the mess. 'Cundall!' Tom jerked round.

'What's the matter?' asked Bulmer.

'My God, you gave me a start. Your voice sounded exactly like Beal's.'

'Nerves. Too much ground-strafing. Egg flip's the finest thing for ground-strafing nerves. Hancock, bring four egg flips. What I called you for was a spot of bridge. Here's Franklin and Maitland. What about it?'

'Thanks. Till ten. I'm on the early job.'

'You ought to have a rest, but as there's only you and Miller left in your flight I suppose you can't. Probably Mac will be taking you over again to try to rebuild the flight. Cheerio!'

Tom took his egg flip. 'Personally I'd be damn glad to have Mac back again, and I know Miller would.' He went on playing bridge till eleven as it was raining so steadily and sullenly that the early job seemed impossible. Egg flips were comforting, but Beal haunted him all the time; he was always near; if Tom could have looked round quickly enough, he would have seen him. His voice was entwined in the buzz of conversation.

The batman called him at five o'clock. The morning was fair after a foul night. What a waste of good rain! He fell asleep at once, but after a second the batman was shaking him again. His eyes were glued with sleep, and he ate the hard-boiled dawn egg as if dreaming and went through the running of the engine in indifferent semi-consciousness conditioned by the operations of an automaton. The cold wind of rapid motion revived him as he took off. There was no need to think about taking off; the body attended to that and the dim mental regions of habit; the conscious mind was free to enjoy the solid lift of the planes bearing on the smooth hard morning air, the wheeling and foreshortening of things terrestrial, the trees that yielded up their splendour and height and diminished into embossed variegations in earth's colour-pattern.

They surveyed the trenches from two thousand feet or so, and everything appeared quiet on their sector. Archie accompanied them assiduously. It was impossible to see far laterally; the red fingers of dawn could not spool the intertangled filaments of mist; but above it was clear, and some black specks appeared in the eastern heights. They dropped their bombs hurriedly and began climbing.

There seemed to be six Huns, quite ten thousand feet above them. They did not want to attack, evidently, but sat up there watching. Then Archie gave them some warning bursts. Dolphins were going over above them, and they made off. Their game was to chivvy solitary Harry Tates or pick off stragglers, not to fight the main intendment of Dolphins or Camels. Miller stayed about a little longer in case they returned, and then, not being on patrol, turned for home.

XXIII

TOM was influenced by the comparative pleasantness of the dawn show to feel more than ever the relief from Beal's direction; he could not be unaware that the flight would have run a great deal more risk if Beal had still been their leader, and perhaps have achieved very little more; not enough to compensate for the risk. But that was not the real question; which was, had Beal on the whole achieved enough to justify the strain and loss to which he had subjected his command? Tom thought that, from the military point of view, he probably had; and the military was the only point of view relevant. Life was cheap and Camels plentiful, and most of the casualties had been among

M 177

new pilots, who were of little value and easily replaced. Debenham and Taylor and of course Beal himself were experienced; but he must have done a lot of damage to the enemy by his resolute attacks, and he had taken back useful information during the worst period of the push.

Yes, that was all very well, but there was a super-added reckless-ness that made all occasions needlessly dangerous . . . The theme drifted about in varying light, now a gaze-compelling globe occupying the front of heaven, now a tongue of darkness in far-down fires of emotion.

B flight went out at half past nine to bomb the threat to Amiens as usual, and returned unharmed an hour later. Tom was in the hut when Williamson came in to take off his flying kit. He had had the usual sort of job. They had dropped their bombs and then climbed towards some Huns that were playing hide-and-seek in the clouds, but nothing happened except a bombardment by Archie, who was very fierce by the Somme. One of these days he would hit something.

'It's a pity some of you blokes didn't come with C flight occasion-ally to see what Beal put us through. I don't believe any of you know what real ground-strafing is.'

'No?'

'No.'

'You're wrong. Bulmer's hot stuff when there's something to go for, I can tell you, and Franklin's quite crazy when he's leading; but I'll say this for him: he knows he's batchy and isn't surprised if other people don't imitate him too closely. There wasn't much doing to-day, and it's no use getting shot up just for the fun of the thing when all you've got to do is to drop bombs to keep Jerry nervy.'

'There's the difference. If Beal couldn't see anything doing he usually went down and put his nose in trenches to smell out trouble, and he seldom bombed from above a hundred feet. Sometimes it would seem more like a hundred inches, and he expected to be fol-lowed and imitated especially by me of all people. He used to make me wonder sometimes if it weren't better to be killed quickly and get it over. He was the most fearless man I've ever come across. I couldn't help admiring him.'

'More admirable than comfortable. You must be immortal by the way the bullets dodged you yesterday. But it's just as well Beal won't get you into any more scrapes like that.'

'Now you're touching on a point that's bothering me. I recognize that once anyhow I've met a hero; and at the same time I can't help feeling glad for my own sake that he's gone.'

'Well, what of it?'

'What of it! Well, my God, isn't it pretty foul to be rejoicing in the death of the one man . . .'

'Rejoicing in the death of my Kyber,' interrupted Williamson vigorously; 'you're not doing anything of the sort. You're glad to escape from merciless leadership, and I should damn well think so: you're not steel and granite. It's not his death you're glad about, you big boob; it would come to the same thing for you if he'd been made king of Spain and gone away to be crowned.'

'I suppose you're right about that, but . . .

'Oh, stop butting. You used to be moderately clear-headed and didn't give a damn about things; I'll say that much for you. But lately you've been hopeless, moping and worrying your head off about sweet Fanny Adams. It's since your hero Beal has been tearing the heart out of you. Give me Bulmer every time. I feel as safe as houses following him – barring accidents of course – and so do we all.'

'When you're ground-strafing?'

'Well, accidents will happen then, with the best of leaders, but I've every confidence in his judgment, and I know he's not wanting to offer me up as a sacrifice to Mars all the time. However, I don't want to crack up Bulmer and run down Beal, who, as you say, was a very stout fellow. All I want is you to cheer up a bit and get rid of this morbid stuff. If you're going to get upset about deaths, you'll be no good for anything. Bothering about the dead is selfish, morbid, and unnecessary. On any theory Beal's all right now. While he was alive I dare say life was as pleasant to him as to the next man, and the idea of death as unpleasant. But nothing is pleasant or unpleasant to him now; everything is cancelled; so why worry? Look, you've got me preaching, damn you. For Christ's sake let's cheer ourselves up. Shall we go over to Avesnes this evening and have a decently cooked meal for a change and some good claret and see what adventures the mouldy townlet offers? Not taking the wretched married men with us?'

'All right, Bill. Thanks for the sermon. If we can find adventure in Avesnes we'll be uncommonly clever, but we'll try.'

When Seddon came in after A flight's job he was looking gloomy.

'Hullo Seddon, what sort of a job?' asked Tom. 'You don't look very pleased about it.'

'Poor young Reeve went down in flames. First time over.'

'What happened? Fire from the ground?'

'No, we had a scrap. We saw a bunch of Huns drop out of a cloud on to a Harry Tate and we went after the Huns. We didn't arrive till the Harry Tate was going down in a spin, but we got three of the Huns, and another layer came down on us and got Reeve. I saw him go. I had just got an Albatros in flames; and I can tell you the two made me feel absolutely sick. Christ! what dupes we are! They tell us all this is honourable, noble and all the rest of it. Murder is murder however much we cover it up with lies and flags. I shall never forget those fellows going down in a hell of blazing petrol. I sent one of them. O my God!'

'Don't be so cut up about it, man. It's kill or be killed. You didn't start the war. You're not responsible.'

'Not responsible! Wasn't I like a lot of other fools,' shouted Seddon, 'patriotic, spoiling for a fight, at any rate for the professional army and navy. What's the good of a big navy if it doesn't do something; that's the feeling you get. When you see your big guns, you want to see them go off and show the world what a hell of a big fellow you are. That's how I was. That's how we all were.'

'That won't do,' said Williamson. 'We didn't start the war. If we'd sat still there would still have been a big European war. Would you rather we'd kept out of it and made big profits out of supplies, like America?'

'Yes, I would. France would have been knocked out quickly and there would have been peace in six months. And the people who would have made profits are making them anyhow, blast them.'

'Our turn would have come later.'

'Better to chance that than make sure of it at once.'

'Hear, hear. Well said, Seddon.'

Thus encouraged by Tom, Seddon went on, more calmly, 'What were those two fellows burnt to death for? Because now that the Allies have got America in on their side they know they can win in time, if it takes another three years and another three or four million lives. And since the politicians have already divided up the spoils and think they can get the cost of the war out of Germany, they go on. And of course the big military people will go on till doomsday at their favourite game if they're fairly sure of winning eventually; it's a fine old beano for them, and they'll mostly come out of it lords. The financiers may know better than to hope to get much out of a ruined country, but they've got so much at stake in the British Empire and France that they want victory to keep the stocks up. They put their money on us. And no doubt they hope to get ruined Germany well into their grips when she wants financing for reconstruction. That's why the murdering goes on.'

'There you are, Bill, you can't laugh that off.'

'I know that's how Seddon looks at it. I can't prove that he's wrong, but it's not the only way of looking at it, and I doubt whether a big thing like this war could be run by a gang of sharpers and bullies. It certainly started in a burst of pure patriotic fervour, and, once in, the English don't back out until they've won or lost.'

'Rot. Not so much British bulldog stuff. What about Peace with Honour?'

'And the Treaty of Utrecht, by God?' added Seddon.

'I don't know anything about them, and don't want to. You fellows are a damn sight too well informed, that's what's the trouble with you. What does it all come to? You worry your heads like a pair of old apple women, but you do your jobs like anyone else, so what's the good? Why lash yourselves with words?'

'I suppose it relieves our feelings a bit,' Tom replied. 'We can't all have no feelings like you. It wouldn't bother you if your grandmother was raped by the dustman.'

'Well, now we've got all that settled, what about letting Seddon in on our cheering-up party to-night? What d'you say to coming over to Avesnes this evening, Seddon, to cheer ourselves up a bit if we can? We all seem to need it.'

'All right, thanks; if we're still alive.'

They were all alive that evening as the rest of the day was a wash-out. A sudden thunderstorm broke over the aerodrome during lunch and lasted till past five o'clock. They set out as soon as it cleared up. Seddon and Tom were tired and not in good spirits, and Williamson was not at his best. There was no tender available and they had to walk but luckily got a lift most of the way. Smith had been asked, but he had refused.

First they went to Madame Marron's to arrange about food. Madame lived in dingy respectability with her sister and daughter in a decaying house in the main road, and was glad to improve her tiny *rente*, which probably would hardly have kept a cat in comfort in England, by catering for officers. She was, of course, charmed to see them, and would have dinner for them with three bottles of St. Julien in half an hour. Tom left her twenty francs to relieve her of all anxiety about their return, and they went away to do some shopping; first to the canteen for such commodities as tobacco, tooth-paste, Eno's. Then Williamson wanted to buy French underclothes to send to the women at home, to remind them that he was hoping for leave soon; and Seddon thought it would be a good idea to send his wife a silken surprise; and as Tom went with them he could not avoid a purchase, so he bought a refulgent jupon that would do for his sister: it wasn't really necessary to give presents to girls in war-time. Williamson, however, bought all sorts of things, and the two girls serving were delighted. No Frenchwoman was so stupid as to be embarrassed or embarrassing about clothes, and where an Eng-lishwoman was apt to be either prudish or brazen, she was natural. The French, Tom thought, were not so frightened of life as the English, and had come to better terms with it. There was more amenity in their civilization, which was based on the practical per-ception that the highest of the arts is cookery, and of virtues, economy; these had the advantage of being universally practicable, whereas higher Anglo-Saxon things, poetry and charity, left ninety-nine out of a hundred people out in the cold, and they built themselves chapels for protection against the icy spiritual temperature, and paid priests out of their own pockets to utter fervid incantations for exorcizing their spiritual and celiac indigestion; but of course they started at the wrong end. One should approach the spirit through the portals of the flesh, and remedy the higher indigestion by alleviating the lower one. It didn't work the other way round.

He realized on the way back to Madame Marron's that he would certainly never have the face to go into an English draper's shop and buy women's underclothing, so perhaps he oughtn't to fuss about the imperfections of Englishwomen.

Dinner over, Tom was led by the wine in him to ask the ladies if they read Molière. They looked puzzled, but madame suddenly exclaimed:

'Ah, Molière. C'est de la poésie,' and they all agreed that they did read it, and assented to his suggestion that the 'Voyage Autour de mon Jardin' was his best work. Hearing the word *poésie*, Tom was flooded by a mighty thought: the basis of poetry was the necessity of rhythm for co-ordinating action when people work together; and was soon led by the cogency of his argument to assert that socialism was natural to man, and individualism a disease. He had vaguely disliked socialism before, but tremendous illumination had come out of the grapes of St. Julien, trod by rhythmic, communal feet; if they were.

Seddon applauded the argument, but Williamson only betted him he wouldn't be able to repeat it in the morning. The women had sat through it with immitigably polite faces, and Tom told them that Seddon had that morning shot down a Boche in flames, and so established him as a hero. Seddon made an effort to stem their plaudits by saying that he did not like *atterrer les Boches en flammes*. This was treated as a witticism. 'Que monsieur est drôle,' they said, and laughed. Williamson and Tom joined uproariously in the laughter, and Seddon himself was infected. It was all very jolly. They talked of dancing, and a gramophone was set to make music, and Seddon, the hero, performed some steps of the waltz with mademoiselle in the small available space. Then the others took their turns with her, and Tom was considering whether he ought to ask madame to dance, when Seddon, who was making great conversational efforts, addressed mademoiselle in a loud voice as *tu*. Madame's sister was at that moment tending the lamp which had burnt dim, and she was so shocked that she turned the wick the wrong way and the lamp went out. Madame's voice hurtled in the darkness 'monsieur, c'est comme ça qu'on parle à une femme avec qui on se couche.' Williamson took advantage of the darkness to make a dive for mademoiselle, and she was frightened and gave a little scream. The worst construction was put on this by mesdames, and their voices niagraed into the dark abyss to drown the shocking impropriety with a torrent of abusive patois. They couldn't find any matches. Mademoiselle joined in the clatter to assure them that she was all right and had only screamed because of the sudden darkness.

'Look out,' said Tom, 'I'm going to strike a match before they have hysterics,' and when he struck it the men were all sitting quietly in their chairs.

'Did I do that?' Seddon asked Tom.

'Yes, you fathead. You mustn't *tutoyer* a girl unless you're intimate,' and he made apologies for Seddon. The women calmed slowly, but they could not forget that a hideous impropriety had occurred in their presence. Their precious jewel of respectability had been touched by predatory hands; it was their life; murder had been attempted with a lethal *tu*; the evening was spoilt; they went.

At the Poisson d'Or Tom recognized two Americans he had met in England. They had just come out to Miles' squadron which was near by; so of course they all had champagne together: Americans never seemed to think they were drinking unless they were having either champagne or some baleful mixture of their own imagining. They were enthusiastic drinkers, and as enthusiastic about flying and fighting. They were, translated, like the young Englishmen of 1915. Weariness and scepticism had not touched them; death in battle was glorious; they were fighting for the right and the honour of their country; they were magnificent. They did not say those things, but plainly it was so. Tom felt inclined to shed maudlin tears over these lovely and innocent victims, but fortunately he had eaten a good dinner that was ballasting the drinks.

On the way home Seddon remarked: 'by the way, that girl whispered something in my ear as we were leaving. I couldn't make out what it was, except that I caught "huit heures".'

'Good God,' exclaimed Williamson, disgusted, 'talk about pearls before swine. Evidently she was giving you a date, and that's all you know about it. She's not a bad wench, that. We must go again and do some apologizing, and if you get another date and don't want it, I'll keep it for you. If there's one thing that's wicked, it's missing an opportunity of that sort. The gods will punish you, Seddon, married man though you are.'

This led to an argument about morals for the married. Seddon talked about loyalty. Williamson said that the utmost to be expected of a married man was fidelity while actually living with his wife connubially; it was impossible in other conditions. Tom reconciled these points of view by suggesting that a man should be loyal so long as he was sure of his wife's fidelity, which was while he was looking at her.

The FEs were making their fine-night din: gunfire was flickering and drumming; Beal's ghost was laid.

XXIV

THEY had to get up at half past eight in the morning, although the weather was quite impossible for flying, as the squadron was to stand by at nine. The Huns were restless beyond Somme, as usual. There was no chance of its clearing up by nine, but one had to be up and about. This was inconvenient. Ten was the proper hour for breakfast on a dud morning. Tom, meditating with a slight headache on the iniquity of disturbing people unnecessarily in the morning, came upon a great thought, which he enunciated rather suddenly.

'When mind comes in, progress goes out.'

'What are you talking about now?' Williamson grumbled. 'For heaven's sake don't be so full of brains first thing in the morning.'

But Seddon showed interest. That was the best of Seddon, he was always interested in a new idea; and, encouraged, Tom explained that the course of evolutionary progress up to man was plain enough, but as soon as man was sufficiently developed to have intellect, all progress stopped. There were alternations of good and bad in his circumstances, but no further progress in himself. Intellect turned on the evolutionary process and stopped it. Man to-day was about the same as he had been five or ten thousand years ago, and in the west he was slipping into another bad period down the usual glissade of war.

'Nonsense,' said Williamson. 'Of course we're progressing. Whoever, for instance, has flown before?'

'What difference does flying make to a man?'

'A lot.'

'It doesn't.'

'It does.'

'It doesn't.'

'It does.'

'If flying has changed you,' said Tom, 'it must be regress, not progress; you couldn't ever have been less like a human being than you are now.'

Williamson considered this, but as no adequate reply occurred to him, he threw a boot for Tom to dodge.

The weather, fortunately, continued too bad for flying, and from twelve o'clock only A flight was standing by; and A flight was released after lunch. Spirits rose; everyone was contented; a real dud day at last. It seemed long ages since the last really free day. Noise developed about the mess in a long crescendo as the drinks went round. There were groups playing poker and slippery Sam and Australian banker, but the noisiest was a quartette of ludo players, yelling at each pipping, when a franc changed hands. No one took the gambling seriously, and the stakes were so low that they could not have interested a wealthy young man like Moss, for instance, at all as stakes. The most serious game was poker, at which the Canadians and Chadwick were exercising their faces, and raising a shout at each showing. The gramophone was kept playing the too familiar musical comedy tunes which everyone must have been utterly tired of if he had listened to them, but the gramophone's function was usually a background one; it was a backcloth shutting out the icy stare of eternity through chinks of silence, and it made things cosier. They were dependent for new records on people returning from leave, chiefly, and no one had returned from leave for three weeks; or three years, was it?

It was very necessary, Tom thought in bed that night, half drunk as usual, to have the gramophone going; all the warring world needed a gramophone to conceal blank eternity. The nations prayed officially to God, and then quickly set the gramophone playing hymns and patriotic tunes, and the world's fools felt the answer of God in their own emotions, and the world's knaves felt cleverer than ever, finding the answer of God in their own cleverness; neither could stand the cosmic silence and starry unconcern, before which . . . good God, what were they? Wasps in nests in an orchard, that, instead of enjoying the sweet essence of the plums while they might, made war; the wasps of each nest stinging and being stung painfully to death in combat with their neighbours. They did this, not because there was not enough fruit to go round, but because in every nest each wise old wasp wanted a whole tree to himself for the good of the nest; and the young wasps, being full of the nidamental spirit, and because former generations had been used to fight when the orchard was new and the fruit not enough to go round, believed the wise elders and fought.

Tom saw the embattled wasps crawling or flying in mighty array, the generals leading them from behind, the goodly priests, their stripes concealed with white shirts, making a buzzing noise behind the generals, a noise which meant that they had arranged with the wasp god to give their particular nest victory and limitless quantities of plums if the fighters were worthy and fought well. And he saw the wise old wasps busy among the plums for the good of the nest.

A huge old wasp, bloated with plum juice, indignant that Tom was wasting time looking at him among the plums when he ought to have been intent on the battle, came buzzing angrily at him. His buzz sounded like 'go and fight for freedom, young wasp, or I'll . . .' Tom was powerless against him. Although the natural sting in his tail was old and decayed, he had been wise enough to have an artificial sting put in his mouth, which was very sharp and poisonous, and Tom knew that with it he poisoned fruit which was his but he couldn't possibly use, so that no other wasp should be able to suck his juice unlawfully.

Tom was terrified. What was the wasp war to do with him? Heavens, he had wings, he was a wasp himself! The dangerous old wasp was getting more and more furious. Suddenly, sting out, he darted at Tom, his buzz rising to a raucous yell. Tom sat up in bed with a shout of terror. The klaxon was giving the air-raid warning. Three startled voices asked what was the matter.

'Sorry. I was dreaming about a damned wasp. I can still see the beast.'

The wasp faded, and only the air-raid remained. They were supposed to go into the dugout when the warning was given. The FEs, judging by the silence in their quarters, were all out at work. A faint buzz that might be a Hun high overhead was just audible above the guns. They settled down to sleep. Nothing happened.

When they woke up again it was foggy morning, and the guns were making rather more row than usual. It developed into such another day as the one before. If anything serious had happened, it might have been considered just fine enough for them to go and do a suicide show, but it was all quiet on their front, and even before Amiens, so they were left in peace to enjoy another happy and riotous day. The war seemed to be over for the moment. There were rumours of a German push up north in the region of Armentières, but it did not seem serious, and anyhow it was time the fellows up there had something to do.

In the evening it certainly sounded as though there was a strafe in progress by the row the artillery was making. The Germans, too, were sending over a lot of heavy stuff, and some of the shells were dropping quite near. If the Huns made a really big advance in the north, Arras would be left in a salient, and they would have to move. They were on the edge of the safety zone as it was. But they were all too happy together and too inebriated to care about the outside world. In the hut a rowdy gambling party gathered round the home-made table. There was Chadwick, of course, and Franklin and Miller and Maitland. There was no early job in the morning, apparently, and they played late. Chadwick, who had become a sort of assistant mess president, produced two bottles of whisky. As the night was misty there were no air-raids, and nothing to disturb them until the major came in in pyjamas and said he wanted some sleep that night if they didn't. Then they went to bed.

C flight had a job at half-past nine in the morning; low bombing, with Mac leading. A Captain Forster had come to take over A flight. It was still fairly misty. Mac crossed the lines and went a few miles over to look for a good target, but visibility was very bad and nothing at all seemed to be alive on earth. Even Archie didn't bother much about them. In the end they let their bombs go from above two thousand feet, and hoped they would do some damage. Then they went home. They were only out for fifty minutes.

In the afternoon there was a squadron show, Mac with C flight leading, with B on his right and A on his left. Everyone, that is to say, seven machines per flight, was on the job, which was as much to show new pilots the lines as anything. It was a quiet enough day for it. They did not go more than five miles over, and Tom felt perfectly safe with his tail well protected, and enjoyed the trip. As for Huns, they only saw dots in the far east, except for a distant two-seater away towards Bapaume which they chased; but it knew all about them and got away. Archie put up a lot of stuff, and two new fellows in B flight were so scared by his bark that they dashed all over the place and so attracted the notice of Archie, who gave them special individual attention in the hope they would run into someone. Bulmer gave them some sound advice when they got home, which they all did without mishap.

Tom didn't mind this sort of war. It was more like the old days before the twenty-first of March. The squadron was recovering tone, and new fellows would have time to mature, and they would all be happy together and continue to kill off Huns in the good old style. There would be occasional dud days, even though summer was coming, and, with the squadron up to strength, regular days off for everyone in turn. And leave must soon be recommencing. Indeed, anyone who urgently wanted it could put in for a week now; but a week wasn't much good, as about four days might be taken up in travelling. It was much better to wait a little longer for a fortnight, which couldn't be long delayed now. The squadron had gained a reputation in the push, and now that it was over would certainly be treated well.

The only cloud in the sky was the new push up north, which seemed, from the latest rumours, to be much more serious than had been thought. The Germans had made a sudden onslaught on the Portuguese who were holding a sector of the line south of Armentières and had chased them off the earth. It had been the usual foggy morning; did the Germans, Tom wondered, make their attacks depend on sufficient mist being available, or were they just lucky? The only time they had started an attack on a clear morning they had been smashed; he meant the attack on Arras.

But what were the Portuguese doing in the front line? Had Haig and Co. no idea there might be an attack?

Well, let the squadrons up north deal with the mess. It was time there was a change in the incidence of strain.

With the resumption of flying the squadron quietened down after its two festive days, and Tom went to bed that night almost sober and quite early in anticipation of a dawn job, which was, however, prevented by a convenient mist. In the afternoon there was another squadron show, but as only five machines from each flight were to be on it, Mac let Tom off. He went up, however, after tea for amusement, and wandered off towards the low sun. It was a delightfully calm unclouded evening and rather misty. Flying towards the sun was as if he were in the apse of an immense temple with walls of luminous gold, and the sun a present blinding-bright deity; such beauty and texture did the mind lend to mere molecules and vibrations, if such things were.

When he surveyed the dim bowl of earth from the clear and fresh heavens of ten thousand feet, its markings were unfamiliar; he had been drowsing in the remote peacefulness. He throttled right down and the features of the ground began to loom in larger scale. A small town was underneath him. He turned over on his longitudinal axis so that he was sitting at a right angle to the plane of the earth, and by turning his head to the left he was looking straight sideways on to the roofs of the town, which was as it were on a hanging map. By letting his joystick come back a little he made the world-map rotate about the hub of the town, which, slowly spinning, approached steadily. When it took up most of the visible map, he straightened things out, and went for a trip among the chimney pots. The place was not St. Pol, as he had thought it might be. It appeared given up to French civilians.

He wandered off eastwards, pleasantly tree-hopping, and came quite soon to familiar country near Avesnes. Here he found a staff car containing two comely brass-hats, and he went down to meet it, threatening it with head-on collision. It stopped and he passed a foot or so over it. Stink bombs would be useful for such occasions. Some injustice might be done, but so would some justice. He hoped he had put the fear of imminent death into their ribboned bosoms.

Thus refreshed, he landed. He was feeling almost happy without the help of alcohol. The horrible depression of a few days ago had gone. His forebodings seemed to have been wrong, and the insupportable burden of fear no longer bore him down; it had shrunk to a small packet that he might reasonably hope to carry without stooping. His self-respect was on the mend too. He had been worried about himself, thinking he was being looked upon as having wind up. By Beal chiefly. Why had he thought that? He didn't remember anything particular to be ashamed of. Of course he was no hero, but probably he was as good as most people; no, not as most people, as most pilots, and scout pilots at that. Most mere people hadn't the nerve to be pilots at all, and among those that had, scout pilots were supposed to be the pick. Besides, he knew pretty well that it required a particularly high sort of courage to do any good in the air. On the ground you had very little opportunity of avoiding troubles that came your way, but in the air you did much more in the way of making your own troubles. If scout pilots liked they could wander up and down the lines without doing anything particular; but hadn't they shot down twenty Huns in one day?

Altogether he was feeling much better. He could do with a drink before dinner, and went down to the mess. He bumped into Mac who was coming out as he went in.

'We take over a new part of the line to-morrow, Cundall. North of Arras to Nieppe Forest.'

'Oh,' said Tom; and then: 'That takes us on to the new push front, doesn't it?'

'Yes,' replied Mac, passing on.

Tom was staggered. Another push for them to stop. The brightness went out of the evening. He got a gin and vermouth from the bar, and sipped in sorrow instead of drinking in happiness. There were only one or two of the newer fellows in the room, and he did not know them well enough to want to talk to them just then. He looked absently at some stuff on the notice board. There was something from G.H.Q. addressed to the B.E.F. It began by suggesting they were all splendid fellows: an ominous beginning from which the purport of the whole might be guessed. G.H.Q. evidently had complete wind up. There is no other course open to us but to fight it out. Every position must be held to the last man. There must be no retirement. 'With our backs to the wall and believing in the justice of our cause, each one of us must fight to the end.' Tom had a momentary vision of half a dozen British generals (all that was left of the B.E.F.) with their swords drawn standing in a bed of wallflowers with their backs against their château, awaiting the charge of Ludendorff and his staff (all that was left of the Germans). The British had erected a barricade of empty whisky and champagne bottles and were encouraging each other with poignant reminiscences of the playing fields of Eton.

Tom went across to the hut. The others were there changing and cleaning themselves for the evening.

'Heard the news?'

'No, what?'

'We're changing over to-morrow to a new line. Arras to Nieppe Forest. That will give us an excellent opportunity of stopping the new push. Judging by an Order of the Day from G.H.Q. to B.E.F. that's on the board, it's a bad one.'

Smith and Seddon groaned.

'Damn it,' said Williamson, 'I thought we were going to have a little peace. Here have I been next on the list for leave for the past ten years, and now I suppose I'll never get it. If we've got to go through another month of push-stopping ground-strafing it's certain death. I might as well have spent my money on food and drink as on those clothes I bought at Avesnes. I'll never see them again.'

'It seems to me,' Seddon remarked out of his towel, 'that they want to destroy this squadron altogether.'

'They're flogging the willing horse,' said Smith. 'What does G.H.Q. say, Tom?'

'Oh, that we're fine fellows but we're up against it. We've got to believe in the justice of our cause and fight with our backs to the wall. No doubt a sound belief in how just we really are is good protection against bullets; but living at G.H.Q. is better. And where the devil do they think the troops are going to find a wall to put their backs against? High Command has given them no Hindenberg line, in spite of all the Chinese labourers. Too pig-headed to learn from the enemy until it's too late. Backs to the wall! Generals can only think in well-worn phrases, just as they are still basing their strategy and tactics on the Peninsular war.'

'That's not quite fair, Tom,' said Williamson, tying his tie. 'G.H.Q. has to speak to all sorts and conditions of men, and the quickest way of letting them know what's what is to tell them they've got their backs to the wall.'

'That's true,' Tom admitted, but the admission ran counter to his feelings, and he recovered from the check at once: 'but also it's true that it's the only way exalted warriors can express themselves. The exhortation also talks about not yielding an inch. I think that's the phrase; it should be. When, by all accounts, the Germans have already advanced about ten miles, why in heaven's name does anyone write that? If that isn't inability to think except in conventional phrases, then it's wilfully lying nonsense.'

Smith and Seddon supported this position whole-heartedly, and Williamson admitted it was rather a foolish remark, but didn't matter much.

'It matters as an indication of the sort of mentality that's in charge. Look at the results of it, if you think it doesn't matter.' (Tom had seen a sudden interpretation) 'The reason why the Germans have been so successful in this new push is because they attacked the Portuguese, who ran and left a big gap in the line. Everybody knew, even generals must have been told, that they weren't fit to stand up to an attack. Are we to believe that G.H.Q. had been given no information at all about the coming attack? I don't. They have had some idea of every other attack. And anyone with the intelligence of a platypus would know that the attack would fall on the weakest part of the line. Yet there the Portuguese were left, a gratituous weakness, and now the Germans are just walking through the open door, and God knows what's happening to the fellows on the exposed flanks. They're paying the price of idiotic generalship; and G.H.Q. sends round its kind regards, and will we please get out of the mess somehow. God, it makes me absolutely mad, and if I said this outside I'd probably be shot.'

'And deservedly,' said Williamson. 'You may be right; I don't know. But you certainly wouldn't improve the position by shouting these things about; in fact you might do more harm than whatever blunders have been made.'

'That's a sweet sentiment out of your dear Tennyson,' Tom sneered. 'Theirs is not to make reply. And so incompetence in high quarters is to be shielded for ever, and idiots in authority to shed oceans of blood . . . .'

'Tom, your tongue's running away with you.' Williamson was irritated by the sneer. 'I don't know that you're doing much good by ranting in here.'

'Oh, go to hell,' said Tom; and Williamson, who had finished dressing, shrugged his shoulders and went out of the hut.

'Damn it,' exclaimed Tom. 'I must go quarrelling with Bill.'

'I suppose he's right from his point of view,' Seddon commented, 'but I know how you feel, Tom. If you start thinking about this bloody war it drives you mad.'

'I don't know anything about all that,' said Smith, 'but I know it's getting me right down. I feel I'd do or give anything to get home. That may not sound very grand, but it's the truth.'

'Poor old chap,' said Tom. 'You've got some reason to want to get home, and so has Seddon, but I've nothing particular to bother about but my own comfort and safety. I'm the sort of bloke that gets mad on general principles. It knocks me down out of control, when I think of the fat kites at home making a profit out of it; all the well-paid war-workers who hope the jolly old war will go on for ever; the women who snivel and glory over the dead men they helped to murder; the brave officers with influence and D.S.O.s and permanent jobs in Whitehall, whom poor devils home on leave from the shambles have to salute. . . .'

Seddon broke in. 'And don't forget the financial gentry, accumulating huge wads of national debt in their own favour at five per cent which they made their frightened pals the politicians go to. That five per cent is an open admission that no patriotism is to be expected when it comes to money. Patriotism, like true religion, is very desirable for people without money. It's all a damned swindle.'

'Quite. And what are ninety per cent of the fellows out here but poor fishes without tuppence in the world and no right on the earth that they inhabit by kind permission of the money owners? None of them has the least idea what it's all about. They find themselves fighting for England in France on account of little sister Belgium, a relation none of them knew anything about until they suddenly found they had to go and be killed to save her from being raped by wicked Germans who had already done the deed of darkness. England! France! Belgium! Germany! God, what harlots the nations are! They feed their young lovers with empty promises – and how young men have loved them; they have been loved as no woman or god ever has – they send them out to murder and be murdered because they are jealous of rival whores; and all the time it is to rich and covetous old lechers they are selling themselves. I wonder their blasting sins don't wither them. . . .'

'They've found an elixir of youth; it's called Propaganda. . .' Seddon commenced, but Williamson came bursting in dancing about and shouting.

'Hullo, still at it? Well, I'm going to leave you for a bit. I'm going, oh I'm going . . . .'

'Where the devil are you going?' asked Seddon.

'Not to hell I hope.' Here he clapped Tom on the back, and sang, 'I'm going to London-don-don-don.'

'I don't know what you're talking about, but before you go, I must apologize,' said Tom.

'Oh rot. We're all strung up. My fault really. Anyway, leave's recommenced, if that's any comfort to you.'

'Leave!' they shouted.

'And that's not all.'

'Come on; out with it.'

'Bombing and ground-strafing are washed out for the present. You'll be patrolling the new line while I'm away. It's by way of a rest, in recognition of our valuable services. Now what about it?'

'By God, and here we've been . . . What about a drink before dinner? Who's coming?'

They all went to the mess and drank. Dinner was a cheery meal, and after it they settled down to drink and sing. This was like the old days. The mess waiters were rushing round and the good old songs were sung or shouted.

> Why should 'e wiv all 'is money
> Mix wiv 'er wot is so pore?
> Bringing shime on 'er relitions,
> Makin' 'er into an 'ore.

The mess began to get unsteady as Tom poured whatever was offered down his gullet. Who cared? This was a happy-drunk. He was as happy as a king. No more ground-strafing! Good old who-ever'd arranged it! Good old Wing, good ole Brigade, good ole G.H.Q., good ole Foch, good old Georgie, good ole ev'rybody, good ole Huns; hoped they'd got plenty to drink, blast 'em. Let 'em all come, Albatri, Pfalz, Fokkers. Who cared? No more low bombing.

> Drunk last night,
> Drunk the night before,
> And we're going to get drunk again to-night
> If we never get drunk no more.

Everybody was dancing about and making a row. He didn't know what he was doing, and didn't care. No more bombing. The mess was spinning. He couldn't stand up. Didn't want to stand up. He was happy.

PHASE TWO

EXCELLENT as it was that leave had recommenced, Tom found out soon that there was a spot in the sun. Only one officer was to be away at a time, and as it appeared that the major, Bulmer, Franklin, Miller, and Moss were all somehow entitled to leave before he was, it would be a long time until he crossed the Channel. Williamson should be back on the twenty-seventh of April, and the next man would go away on the same day. By the time all five had had their leave it would be July; then Tom would go, and when he came back it would be time to start thinking of Home Establishment, for six months in France on Camels was considered enough, and after seven months one was quite likely to be sent home, and after eight, certain. A few people who distinguished themselves so much that they were given command of a flight after six or seven months, did nine or even ten months, bribed by seven shillings a day extra pay, great authority, and comparative safety. Even Archie was kind to leaders, and went mainly for the rear men of a formation. However, Tom had no expectation of this distinction. If he could remain alive after the hazards of seven months' war flying without having done anything notably disgraceful, that would satisfy him. Then he would have three months in England and return to France, if the war lasted, towards Christmas, which was a suitably quiet time for renewing combatancy. He would probably have a flight in a Snipe squadron.

That was the prospect, but there was a good chance that leave would not be quite so long in coming as it seemed. The usual arrangement by which two were away at a time, one going every week, might come into force again soon if the push in the north died away, and he might even get his leave towards the end of May at the best.

It was worse for Seddon, with whom he worked out these times, for after Tom, Hudson would go, and Seddon only after Hudson, which made his leave seem an intolerable age away; and he was married and had young children whom he was needing to see.

Moved by these considerations, Tom said: 'Look here, Seddon, you're married and all that. You have my turn. It doesn't matter a damn when I go. I've nothing particular to see to.'

But of course Seddon wouldn't have anything to do with the plan. Tom reflected that he ought to have approached the matter more carefully, and not to have stated it so baldly. The only thing was to abandon the scheme for the present, and when the time was getting near he could have a letter written to him saying that something or the other had happened that would make him want leave just when Seddon would be due to be away, and then he would ask him as a favour to change places, and it would be difficult for him to refuse. Tom felt virtuous in advance. It really would be quite a big effort to put back one's leave by two or four weeks. He was entitled, like other philanthropists, to a glow of virtue in his chest for such an altruistic intention.

But he liked Seddon, for their congenial hatreds were a bond of strength, so perhaps he ought not to put down his glow to virtue, but to the pleasure of doing something for someone he liked. This was pleasure of a vastly respectable sort, but still a pleasure. To be truly virtuous, Tom thought, one had to do something for someone one disliked.

The klaxon went for the morning job at ten o'clock. This was to be a squadron show to look at the new line; all their work for the day. His thick head from last night's celebration of the new order had yielded to aspirin. Life was pleasant. Williamson had gone off to Boulogne at half past eight to catch that day's leave boat. It was nice for him to get his leave at last, but it seemed that he was going to miss an easy time. Tom hoped that when he went himself he would miss something worth missing.

It was a fine bright day with a good deal of cumulus above four thousand feet. The flights were to go out together, but as separate formations, and survey the new line comfortably. They turned north from Arras, past Vimy Ridge and Lens, in front of Bethune, over the La Bassée canal, between Armentières and Merville. From their northern limit, Nieppe Forest, they could see the smudge of Ypres in the north-east, Lille in the east, and the round eye of Dickebush lake.

There were plenty of landmarks, and the front did not need much getting used to. North of Festubert and Givenchy there was a lot of activity on the ground, but that did not concern them. Other people were to attend to earthly happenings; they had returned to their proper element.

Mac went among the clouds and penetrated a few miles into Hunland, and soon he waggled his wings as a sign that he had seen Huns. Some of the cloud-peaks thrust up to ten thousand feet; in the blue fields beyond there was an occasional flash of a tilting wing reflecting the sun. Mac climbed as fast as he could. In a few minutes they were at ten thousand, and the Huns, a mile above them, were discernable as aeroplanes, bluely translucent, and perhaps there were ten of them. They kept well above, not caring to attack so many Camels, and when they had been forced up to seventeen thousand feet they went away east. Not even a dive: evidently the Huns on this front were quite as timid as those south of Arras. Both Albatros and Pfalz had a wonderful respect for Camels, and it was necessary to go about in small formations to get them so much as to fire a shot from above, let alone dogfight.

They followed the Huns, going as far as ten miles over, but even that did not provoke attack, and they went home to lunch, having completed a day's rest-work; but Wing had found another job for one flight, and the major let C have it. Two RE8s from No. 5 were to do some special work that deserved escort.

Immediately after lunch C flight went and circled over 5's aerodrome, and the two Harry Tates took off and they all went for a long tour over Hunland below the clouds, but nothing happened except about two thousand shellbursts from Archie, especially when the Harry Tates, having finished whatever they were doing, turned for home. The sky went black with the barrage. Some of Archie's shooting was good; he seemed very accurate in these parts. Several times Tom was scared by an enormous bellowing cough with a secondary clanging note, as though it were a jinn with an iron throat coughing, that Archie sounded like when he was really close. But as usual no harm was done, and they saw the Harry Tates to the lines. Then Mac turned back, climbing among the clouds out of Archie's sight.

The cessation of Archie's bombardment evidently made the pilot of an Albatros two-seater think that danger had gone, for they surprised one quite near the lines. The pilot was shot at once, and down it went in a vertical death plunge. Archie went for them, but they climbed back among the clouds and worked their way along the nephelene valleys southwards, and near Lens they caught another two-seater. The observer saw them coming and fired, and the pilot put the machine into a steep spiral. This made it difficult for the observer to do any effective shooting, but it also made it difficult for them to hit the Albatros. They followed it down and down, firing from all angles without hitting anything vital, and getting in one another's way. Tom went within a few feet of colliding with someone, and thought he'd better be more circumspect: the Albatros wasn't worth having a collision about. And then they began to get within range of the ground. Tom slithered about, earnestly considering his own safety. The pilot of the Albatros had to come out of his spiral at last, but not above five hundred feet. Mac was waiting for this, and with superb quickness he flicked into position a dozen yards behind the Albatros's tail, and fired a burst. It dived to earth.

They climbed away from ground machine guns all out. The Albatros crashed like a shell exploding; a column of black smoke sprang up and a furnace of flames.

It was, from the point of view of military utility, quite a good afternoon's work to crash two two-seaters. It wasn't very glorious for six Camels to set about two separate two-seaters; indeed, it was, like so much of the war, mere blackguardism; but two-seaters with their spottings for artillery, their photographings, their reconnaissances, their bombings, were the real danger: German scouts were of no direct importance in military operations.

Not that they were at all unwilling to fight Hun scouts; the difficulty was to find them within ten miles of the lines, which was about as far over as Camels usually operated. SEs, Dolphins, Bristol Fighters, machines of longer range, often had to go fifteen and twenty miles over to find them. It was not easy to imagine what good the Huns thought they were doing by patrolling their own back areas; but they did, and they had a bad enough time of it there; venturing into Camelled regions was disastrous for them.

Tom was back in time for tea, feeling satisfied with the war, and sleepy after four hours flying in the delightful spring air. What a healthy life! And what a relief was the change to patrolling; in addition to the comparative safety, it was so much less like work than their late occupations. When you came to consider it, there was a lot to do on those low bombing jobs. You had to fly, managing an engine and aeroplane, in formation, keeping accurate position relative to four or five other Camels at intervals of about twenty yards; watching the leader's movements so as to turn or dive when he did, throttling down and rounding in a smaller arc when he turned inwards, or opening out to make a larger arc when he turned outwards from you; and you had to watch the floor for movements and targets and to see what was what, which involved frequent turnings-over vertically on your side to get the wings out of the way: you had to watch all the sky, especially around the sun or clouds, for Huns; you had to dodge Archie: and then you had to do your bombing and shooting.

After tea he strolled up to the aerodrome with Burkett, who was a Canadian, and would have it that beavers were quite as intelligent as men, because the dams they made showed as good a knowledge of engineering. Their only disadvantage was that they hadn't hands and couldn't talk; but their paws and understanding of each other might be almost as good.

Tom had never seen a beaver, and only knew that they used to be made into hats. He had a notion they were like badgers, which were made into shaving brushes. He argued that whereas beavers had built exactly the same dams for thousands of years, men had made a lot of progress in that time, and now they made aeroplanes. But Burkett thought that was just where beavers were superior: dams were useful to them, and beavers were intelligent enough to keep to what was useful. What was the good of aeroplanes?

'The good of aeroplanes? Well, good lord . . . hullo, look at that!'

'What?' asked Burkett.

'It's gone down behind that tree. It was a Harry Tate. It must have spun into the ground.'

As they were by the office, Tom went in and told the major he had seen a Harry Tate spin into the ground about three miles away.

'Did anyone else see it?' No one else had seen it, and the major seemed sceptical, but he sent Baker up to look for the crash. Baker

203

came back in ten minutes saying he couldn't see anything; so Tom went up himself to search, and soon came upon the wreckage of an RE8, with a crowd round it, and the dead or unconscious pilot stretched on the ground. There was no ambulance. He recognized the markings, and went over to No. 5's aerodrome and told them where one of their machines had crashed, and then home to enjoy having been right . . . at any rate, about the fact.

What a misfortune it was to fly REs! Why did they use the wretched things? Probably because they were the product of the Royal Aircraft Factory, which, for one successful machine, the SE5 and 5a, turned out lots of deadly BEs and REs, and doubtful FEs; if FEs, which were pushers, could be called aeroplanes. The Germans, largely through the skill of the Dutchman Fokker, had once obtained a great ascendancy in the air, but fortunately the inventors of the Bristols, the de Havillands, the Sopwiths, had enabled the British to fight back. But still RE8s, with their R.A.F. engines puffing out clouds of smoke from the chimneys over the centre-section, propelled at a maximum speed of ninety miles an hour, trundled lugubriously over the lines on their business of artillery observation, where they ought to have been shot down at once: or they killed their pilots by spinning into the ground; so did Camels, but instability was part of their intendedness.

The fine day was followed by a fine evening. Smith and Seddon were affected by the arrival of spring, and Smith was full of melancholy, and Seddon of irritation. The recommencing of leave seemed a mockery; Seddon could hardly hope to get away for another eight weeks, which in prospect was like eight years; and Smith was separated from his wife by a whole eternity. He had no hope of seeing her again: so few pilots lived more than two months in France. He seemed already dead and buried so far as interest in life was concerned. He moved and performed necessary actions with some appearance of cheerfulness, but his heart was dead in him; the agony was over; he was frosty with living death.

Tom liked this moving corpse, but he found it was no use trying to cheer it up. He could only hope it was being kept in cold storage, and would in the fullness of time be given back to its legal owner preserved from mortification and decay, and with only that slight loss of flavour which cold storage causes. Tom preferred Seddon's reaction to war: irritation, hatred, flames, fury. No doubt if he survived he would come out of it a very much more developed and dangerous personality than he went in. If he went back to his bank, he would probably appal the management with abominable and desolate theories of finance, and find himself in prison and penniless. That would be fine for him. He might become a great man. Tom would like to know him after the war, after the war, after the war.

There was a terrific row as a multi-engined bomber flew low overhead. Friend or foe? It went away without doing anything. There were Gothas about; the air was full of the buzz of their engines and the noise of exploding bombs and Archie's fuss. There were squadrons of night-flying Camels to deal with them, but it was difficult to see anything at night; difficult to check night bombing by raiders in dim moonlight that made the features of the earth plain enough, yet left the quick aeroplane invisible.

Towards midnight the north-east wind drove masses of cloud across the sky, obscuring the eye of night, and there was peace for a few hours until an artillery battle developed at dawn. But there was no dawn job, for the north-east wind, angered by some malfeasance against its skiey dignity, piled up with its spumy breath of rage huge cloudy tokens of malice, churning them into a ragged smother of storm-drift; and having filled the sky with tempest it came whirling and shouting against the earth, flinging spurts of rain, plucking at tender foliage with unprehensile fingers that grasped and slid away and grasped and slid again; and the giant shrieked with idiot fury against the irreducible solidity of the world.

I I

THE impatience of the north-east wind lasted for more than three days; it was in process of rapid exhaustion on the fourth, in the evening of which it became possible to do some flying. C flight went out at six o'clock in bad visibility, and over the lines there were dense masses of heavy cloud that prevented patrolling, so they returned home. It was as though the wind had been choked with its own spleen, and had died away while the heavens were still encumbered with cloudy vestiges of its malice.

The obscurity lasted over the next day, but in the morning it was possible to go out among the foggy clouds and do a blindman's-buff patrol, although it was difficult to keep in sight of each other. There was little chance of finding any Huns. They did, however, catch a glimpse of a two-seater ghostly in the mist, but it vanished immediately, and searching for it was vain. After an hour and a quarter Mac went home. Dubois was missing, but he landed half an hour later and said he had lost them in a cloud and had been looking for them ever since.

In the afternoon Wing thought they should carry bombs and do some push stopping. The squadron had only had five days' rest from low work, but those days had been a very complete rest owing to the kind unkindness of the north-easter. Things were not going well on the ground. So C flight went out in the mist at three o'clock to do a low reconnaissance and look for ground targets to bomb. Towards the lines the fog extended right down to the ground, and Hunland was opaque. They flew around for a little while, and then, to Tom's powerful relief, Mac took them home again in the thickening weather that during the night turned to rain. The rain lasted for forty-eight hours, clearing up in the evening of the second day sufficiently for a patrol of three machines per flight; a squadron show that turned out entirely comic, as the only other things in the sky were clouds. Tom was not on this job; and as sufficient new pilots had arrived during the week to bring the squadron up to full strength, he hoped for many more times off as soon as the newer people could be got on to jobs. Baker was nearly ready to go over the lines, and a newly arrived South African named Grey, who was inclined to be pompous and pious, and believed in duty and temperance, was being broken in as quickly as weather would permit.

But while dud weather relieved the strain of the war, a lot of it together made a weight of boredom. Afternoons could be slept away and mornings till ten o'clock dozed away, but this left about ten hours for gambling, talking, reading, playing ping-pong. Tom soon got tired of cards. The instruments of roulette and ludo had been smashed in the last binge. He talked a good deal and read, but came to the end of his own books and no one seemed to have anything worth borrowing. He went over to Avesnes with Seddon and found a copy of *Le Peau de Chagrin*. It wasn't, as a rule, possible to buy books in Avesnes, but there were some in a furniture shop occasionally.

The went to the Poisson d'Or for dinner, and Tom found Lucie very affectionate. She breathed on him and called him *très cher ami*.

'Voulez-vous me montrer où est le cabinet?' he asked her.

'Mais certainement.'

He went with her, and when they were out of sight he put his arms round her.

'Ah, je t'aime plus qu'un chat aime le lait. Sois à moi.'

'Ah, oui, oui, mon cheri. Suis moi. Mais il faut dépêcher, tu comprends.'

He followed her, and the matter was soon concluded, and Seddon not kept waiting for his dinner.

'You ought to have a word with Lucie,' Tom said to him. 'She makes no fuss whatever.'

'You mean . . .'

Tom nodded.

'Well, that's damned quick work.'

'Business hours,' said Tom. 'Why don't you speak to her?'

'She doesn't like me so well as she likes you. Besides, to tell you the truth, as leave actually has started, I've decided to try and stick it. So for goodness' sake don't let's talk about it.'

'All right. I'm sorry for you. This marital fidelity business must be damnably wearing.'

'It is rather,' Seddon admitted; 'but so is everything worth doing.'

'That's where you're wrong. It's the wearing things that we ought not to do. There's only one test of right conduct, and that is happiness and satisfaction. To know if you are doing the right thing, shut your mind to all considerations of law, morals, religion, convention, and concentrate on the sensations in your guts. If they are sensations of relief and happiness, you are right. Otherwise you are wrong. Like the lad in Swinburne: save his own guts he had no star. All this has only just occurred to me, but it feels right.'

'You're not afraid of unorthodoxy, Tom, anyhow. But suppose a man gets relief and happiness out of murder, what then?'

'Murder most foul, as in the best it is. If murder for the sake of murdering pleases a man, he's not human, and the sooner he's put away, the better. There may have been a few such people, but I don't think they're enough to affect the argument. If humanity were fundamentally vicious, there would be no hope for it anyhow. My argument is only an expression of belief in the fundamental decency of mankind, against the official and legal position of distrust. Mistrust and fear of strangers are hell. No one has a chance of being worthy till he is trusted . . .'

'And embezzles the funds,' Seddon interrupted.

'Well, can you wonder at that in a society that creates large quantities of goods and leaves them lying about labelled NOT FOR YOU? And the people who mustn't touch see certain of their fellow citizens of no great virtue helping themselves while they stand breathing frosty breath on shop windows. Can you wonder?'

'Then wouldn't your test make theft right?'

'It might. But there's a saying, all property is theft. I think that, given social justice, no one would derive satisfaction from stealing except pathological cases. I think all real crime must be abnormal and neurotic, and induced by anterior crimes of society. Moreover, we must remember that we personally and millions like us shall never have any respect for the legal and moral prohibitions and sanctions of states and churches that authorize and bless wholesale murder and devise every possible stimulus to turn their subjects and flocks into murderers. We've got to work out something new.'

'You'd agree that one of the essentials is redistribution of income; that is, reorganization of finance?'

'Yes. That's important.'

'I don't know about your new morality. It's a wonderful idea, the reconciliation of virtue and happiness and after all the centuries of misery and duty . . . If it were possible! But you'd never make practical politics of it in a thousand years. Yet it seems right, when you consider it. The good, the beautiful, and the true; how can we know what they are unless they are what makes us happy?'

'Children start by being happy, and their parents immediately smack and lecture the happiness out of them so as to bring them within the perverted social and religious scheme. We poison life at the source.'

'H'm. You haven't any children, Tom. I have. It's very difficult. You can't have a lot of spoilt kids about.'

'Sometimes you're quite a guide book to popular misconceptions, Seddon. Do you mean spare the rod and spoil the child, you old blackguard? Even you?'

'No, I don't quite mean that, but it's difficult.'

'A spoilt child that's been petted and fussed over, usually by an over-fond mother, isn't so spoilt, in the real meaning of the word, as the unfortunates in the charge of adults who are maddened by un-success and social prohibitions. Child torture is one of the safety-valves of our estimable civilization. All respectable people do it, and think they are being righteous. I wonder what the total effect is? Probably the creed of violence and war.'

'You're a keen critic, Tom. But it seems to me that if parents, as you say, whack their children to purge their own bad feelings, they will probably have secret feelings of happiness and satisfaction in their guts about it, and by your account they will be right.'

'I suppose so.'

'Well then.'

'Nothing.'

'Nothing?'

'Nothing. It's a dilemma. Let's talk shop.'

'No, don't be silly. Doesn't it show that we've got to get finance right first and make an equitable distribution of wealth? Then a lot of bad feelings associated with relative poverty will disappear.'

'Got to get sex on a reasonable basis as well. It's an enormous task. People aren't wise enough.'

'I don't know. The old sex nonsense has pretty well collapsed, and common sense may take its place. And surely people have had a sharp enough lesson to make financial readjustment possible?'

'Don't believe it. They won't connect the two things. And what about all these war fortunes? Do you imagine the owners will give them up after the war?'

'They may have to.'

'Not without a revolution. You know how money rules the roost.'

'Very likely we shall have a revolution.'

'Not after a victory; it will make people more excited and gullible than ever.'

'I suppose you're right there,' Seddon admitted.

'But I've another idea. To make my test still applicable, what we want is a technique for distinguishing between natural happiness or satisfaction, and the spurious sort arising from the satisfying of neurotic feelings. There must be some distinction seizable by special knowledge. This technique would enable the individual to put himself right, and abuses would die a natural death.'

'And they all lived happily ever after.'

'Yes, but in the meanwhile . . .'

'In the meanwhile there's hell to pay. It's always damn well meanwhile in this world.'

Lucie brought coffee and Benedictine.

'Dis-moi, Lucie, quoi faire aujourd'hui?'

She was, of course, puzzled.

'Nous pouvons espérer que le futur sera heureux,' Tom explained; 'mais quoi faire à présent?'

'A présent il faut écraser les Boches, n'est-ce-pas?'

'We are answered,' said Tom. 'Get on with the war.'

Soon they left the Poisson d'Or and walked home through the rough dark night, discussing ways and means of improving the unsatisfactory world and making it more like the land of heart's desire; young men excogitating schemes that, they knew, would only irritate or amuse experienced people and experts that preferred drifting into a mess to jumping in. Experience, Tom misquoted, doth make cowards of us all.

He was pleased with his new intellectual toy; the notion of a technique of intimate self-knowledge. Having some training in art, he knew the power of technique. It only had to be taught in the schools, and people would understand their real needs and feelings, and the pre-war sham of feeling and needing what one ought to feel and need would be swept away. The categorical imperative could be defined as what didn't shock old women.

The new knowledge of truth would work like a leaven within, and that was how true revolutions were effected. He noticed that he had New Testament authority for all his ideas: perhaps there were no new ideas, only new techniques, and everything depended on the ability of the people to make use of new technique. The steam engine had been invented centuries ago in Alexandria, but the age was sterile.

Yet even in a sterile age one must try; one would fail, but to have tried was something. A life of acceptance in an imperfect world was paltry; however aesthetic and stylized its reflection of modernity might be.

Seddon thought that the direction for immediate attack was against finance, or it would, with its dim, unintelligent, unintelligible workings ruin the world long before any leaven of new knowledge could do its work; but what the technique of financial reform was he had little more idea than Tom had of the technique of intimate self-knowledge. The monopoly of money and credit should be restored to the state; but what the state should do with it he did not know. All he could say was that the control of currency bearing the King's superscription by a gang of financiers, and its partial super-cession by private cheques and notes, was a sort of theft from the people, and should be stopped; it was the modern counterpart of the established theft of the land from the people. The nation ought to have the advantage of owning its own land and money. But further than this he could not see.

Here was a task for them; to develop techniques for putting the world right. They would have to think out some ideas and get a book or two published, and then form a society, say the League for Personal and Financial Reform, take an office in London with the help of the subscriptions of their supporters, and start a weekly paper. It might cost something to get going. They reckoned they could raise, including blood money, four or five hundred pounds between them. They would have to live. Tom could exist in a garret on three pounds a week by drinking beer, but Seddon would need at least five. That was eight pounds a week, four hundred and sixteen pounds a year. They would need five hundred members of the league at a guinea a year. It would be no use expecting any profits from their paper for a year or two. Tom could do drawings for it. He must get his hand in with practice, in case the war stopped suddenly. It might. There were rumours of German requests for an armistice so that peace terms could be discussed; and as they realized that their chances of victory were getting less every day now, the Germans might at any time be willing to surrender without waiting for military defeat or final starvation. Then, then would be the time. The world, or some part of it, would be ready to listen then, not at once perhaps, but when excitement had died down.

'We're optimistic to-night for a change,' Tom remarked. 'Still, it'll be worth trying.'

So they talked intermittently, while the wind shouted round them with its giant's voice incomprehensible messages of aery import that did not appertain to the solid world. Its fluid fingers clutched at them and slid away, flapping their coats; they were of the earth, solid and baffling to the boisterous spirit whose loud energy and insistent clamour about other than solid modes of being wasted itself in futilities of tempestuous non-achievement and dissolved in howls of angry despair. The established coagulations of the world remained untroubled, rooted, aedificial. Even human beings, with heads a little forward against the pressure, were, absorbed in their own dream-states and meditated desires and enveloping fears, half unaware and wholly uninterested. And the wind was disregarded like a prophet whose mantic voice is hollow with mysteries beyond the ken of the working world and all the multitudes of men involved in the immediacy of living and dying.

But Tom heard the wind's voice with a difference. There was no rage in it, and no despair in its unanimistic motion; it was a whirl of molecules left loose in the long process of the world's solidifying. It had no significance; there was in it no metaphor of the spirit or substanceless stuff of the mind grasping at baffling materiality; rather it was mind that lent to it what little definiteness it had. And so did the mind lend to all things their form and value, and by the influence of mind the world was moulded and changed. Without mind the wind was a whirl of molecules; or not that, for molecules were a human invention; it was some sort of movement in underlying reality; or not that, for movement depended on perception of space;

it was nothing; reality was in the mind. And whatever the mind could achieve as a condition of itself, that would be reality. If individual minds, self-knowing, would associate as facets of one unity, then nothing was too good to become true.

III

THE further two days' cessation of flying was felt by Tom as a lack; although war flying was an occupation of which a very little sufficed, ordinary peaceful flying was a daily delight whose absence took flavour from the empty day. A half hour's flight every morning; a dash up to ten or twelve thousand feet, some foolery among the clouds if there were any, then some contour-chasing; that was the prescription to keep a man healthy and wise. So, although there were no jobs in the morning as the clouds were thick at two thousand feet, Tom went up for amusement, and having justified the expenditure of oil and petrol by expending some ammunition on the ground target, so that his flight could be entered honestly into the books of record as 'firing practice', he set off over the countryside at a height of ten feet and a speed of a hundred miles an hour, jumping over whatever got in his way, full of the joy and excitement and unique bliss of flying a rotary scout, fleeter than wind, lighter than gazelle, more powerful than tempest. For the first time in the recorded universe this thing was possible; for the first time the power and the speed and the legerity and the liberty kissed in circumstance; for a year, perhaps, circumstance would hold, and there would survive a few hundred people who had flown with expert malice that menacing springheel of the air with licence to do what the devil they liked. And thousands would not survive; the licence was costly.

Tom found several staff cars, and, bull-sensitive to red hat-bands, he charged down upon them with all his thunder like charioted Thor, and saw them cower from his threat. Down, right down into their car: it was risky; he was trusting his judgment within inches of disaster. Who cared? He zoomed up vertically away, using his rudder to swing his tail upwards on top of the zoom so that he went into another dive. But he made no misjudgment, and, his spirit appeased, he landed.

During the afternoon the clouds clotted into local centres of darkness, leaving areas clear enough for flying. C flight went up at half-past five and sailed among the piled formidable masses for two hours that seemed very long. There were frequent mists and off-shoots among the main piles, and it was hard work to keep formation while picking a twisting way among these rocks and shoals. Tom was always either pulling up and hanging on his prop to stalling point or opening out and flying along the chord of his arc in the effort to keep in position as Mac turned sharply towards or away from him. Cutting a corner by using the chord instead of the arc was all right if the leader came out of his turn where you expected; if he came out of it much sooner you probably found yourself right in the way of the man on the other side, who that evening was Smith, Miller not being on the job, and Smith wasn't so expert in formation as Miller, and Tom had to be somewhat careful of him. Smith was quite a good pilot, but it took months of practice to be really good in formation.

They made their way miles and miles into Hunland, but there was nothing in the desert of clouds save Archie and themselves. It was not a pleasant evening. The lumped clouds were black and threatening and the air was bumpy. The westering sun peered dim and watery and seemed to have no power to touch the thick atmosphere with the glory and golden splendour proper to evening.

Archie was very attentive whenever he could see them, and his shooting was marvellously accurate. He made formation flying still more difficult. Certainly on this front he was troublesome; nothing to worry about, but he made a job more like work. It was marvellous that he should get anywhere near a group of tiny, twisting, hundred-mile-an-hour scouts hardly visible miles above him; but he did, and was accurate enough to attack individuals. He was a clever fellow, to give him due honour, and it was not owing to lack of perseverance if he never hit anything. That evening he followed them into nearly all the obscure internephelene grots and cañons that they visited in the search for elusive Huns, of whom there was not one to be found. By their rules it was still dud weather.

They did not get home till after half-past seven: the long evenings were coming when dinner would be a snack and binges and nightly intemperance difficult; the arid length of summer, time of hard work and danger. Would the war end soon?

Tom had talked with Seddon at bedtime. Strangely enough, their scheme of the night before did not altogether evaporate with the wine fumes that gave it birth; it almost seemed that they intended to do something; precisely what they did not yet know; but the thing would be talked gradually into definition.

In the morning there was a squadron show at the reasonable hour of half-past ten. C flight was to be the top formation at fifteen thousand feet, A flight in the middle at ten thousand, and B flight underneath among the clouds which were that morning fairly frequent between about four and seven thousand feet; and from among these they were to attempt to go down on balloons by surprise.

C flight took off first and climbed straight as they could for the zenith, crossing the lines at twelve thousand feet. It got colder and colder; on the ground it had been fairly warm, but the climb to fifteen thousand, which took about twenty minutes, meant a drop in temperature of sixty Fahrenheit degrees; but the purity and sparkle of the air were wonderful; Tom sang.

A flight were usually clearly visible below them against bright cloud, but B, down in the murk, tiny with distance, kept vanishing and reappearing. There was no sign of an enemy: Archie gave C a certain amount of attention, but seemed able to range A better. C had nothing to do but keep above A and wait for whatever might happen. Tom caught an obscured glimpse of a trail of smoke far below that might have been a balloon going down. They all moved away northwards, and for a long time nothing else happened. B flight were evidently active underneath, but Tom could not see whether they accomplished anything. Suddenly Mac waggled his wings and dived. A flight were going down also. B had run into some Huns in among the clouds and were splitarsing about in a dogfight.

They dropped with wires shrieking at a hundred and sixty miles an hour, down and down towards the clouds, past the upper cloud-layers. Tom's eardrums crackled with the changing pressure and he had to keep on swallowing. A flight got to the place of action first, and

215

the Huns had all vanished at their attack by the time C arrived, and all C could do was to climb up again to their position on top, while the others went searching among the clouds for Huns that did not reappear.

When they got home Tom heard that two balloons had been shot down by the united efforts of B flight, and Seddon had got an Albatros scout. He was acquiring a reputation as a Hun-getter. Tom congratulated him.

'I couldn't help it,' Seddon answered. 'I didn't want to kill the poor devil. I just shot at him and down he went.'

'You must be a damn good shot. I occasionally shoot at Huns myself because what else can you do, but they don't go down like yours do. If you go on like this, you'll have a flight in three months.'

'Thanks. I'm not ambitious.'

There was nothing else to do that day. Tom found that the air of the heights was very soporific, and he slept soundly till tea. A rumour was spreading that von Richthofen had been shot down in the British lines on the Somme. At first the rumour said that machine-gun fire from the ground had done it; but later this was contradicted, and it was said that an RE8, of all things, was responsible. It did not mean a great deal to the squadron, as Richthofen had not lately come as far north as their front. Tom had never had the dangerous honour, so far as he knew, of meeting him or his circus.

The next morning the rumour was again amended, and it was said that a Camel had got him. This was more reasonable. The name of the pilot was said to be Brown, flight commander in a naval squadron. And when Tom went out with C flight in the afternoon, it seemed as though the Germans must have dedicated the day to mourning for their lost hero, although when they first crossed the lines Mac waggled his wings and started climbing towards a bunch of specks in the north-east, which, when they turned into aeroplanes, were Camels, and when they came near, were A flight that had gone out earlier.

They went down six times to look at two-seaters doing shoots and the two-seaters were always RE8s. But the most extraordinary thing was the total silence of Archie. At first Tom was always expecting his woof-woof, and wished to goodness he'd get on with it, Archie being more trying in expectation than in actuality, for the danger from the heard burst was over. But after an uneventful hour it became possible to believe that the irrepressible hobgoblin was for once ceasing to trouble; and the second hour was almost boring. It was fine weather, and they flew up and down their front steadily and uselessly. Was it that Archie was short of ammunition, and the Huns were frightened to come out without his protection?

After tea there came with the mail news of another death, the death of Captain Thomson. He had gone, after his leave, to Castle Bromwich to do some instructing, and the first time he went up his machine came to pieces in the air. Poor old Tommy! This news was far more depressing to the people who knew him than Richthofen's death was encouraging.

But life in the squadron had returned to normal. There had been no casualities for ten days, the flights were up to strength, and the newer fellows were settling down and everyone was getting to know everyone and the distinction between old and new hands was becoming less marked. They were all, if not happy, at least comfortable and confident, or appeared to be; and the Huns were certainly encouraging them to be so. For after failure to recapture command of the air in March, if the attempt had really been made, they seemed to have retired from the struggle; whether to gain strength for a new attack or whether in despair, the future would show. Their wind-up was enormous; they were exceedingly difficult to find and never attacked without odds of four to one in their favour and the advantage of height, and they ran like rabbits when attacked. The SEs sometimes found them patrolling their own back areas in formations of thirty or forty; it was difficult to know what for, unless to practise flying. The only people with any fight left in them seemed to be Richthofen's crowd, and now Richthofen had gone.

If the March push had been a bad time for the squadron, the period immediately following was being extraordinarily easy. They were not even troubled with dawn shows, and on the next morning C flight took off at ten o'clock. It was windy and bumpy, and a few clouds were moving across the sky from the east. Before they reached the lines Dubois turned back with a dud engine. They went straight over in the direction of Douai, climbing to fourteen thousand, where the wind was so strong that the earth seemed to stand almost still; but it was a pleasant change to have the strong wind from the east, so that they could get back quickly. Archie took very little notice of them, and it seemed another of those quiet jobs. Mac went steadily eastwards. When they were about ten miles over, he waggled his wings and turned north. It took Tom some minutes to see what he was after. Archie put up a few bursts, and Tom saw a couple of his smudges away below and in front of them. He was warning a small formation that was heading westwards apparently unconscious of them. Mac soon went down in a dive. For the Huns, they were in the eye of the sun. As he dived Tom counted five. They were queer looking machines; by Jove, triplanes; very splitarse buses by reputation. He felt nervous. It would be a dogfight nearly ten miles over. However, there were only five of them against five Camels, and nothing else in sight. The triplanes circled about; they couldn't avoid the attack and were apparently going to make a fight of it.

Tom got one more or less in his Aldis and went in with a long burst, turning on to its tail. The thing reared up in front of him in a sort of upward roll. Tom pulled up and then dived again as it went on to an even keel. His firing didn't seem accurate, judging by the tracers. But it flopped into a spin; evidently he had put the wind up the pilot. He dived after it. It was safe to follow it down as all the other tripes would be too busy to get on his tail. It was certainly spinning like hell; must have the engine on. He had to dive steeply to keep near it. He had shot it at somewhere about nine thousand feet; he chased after it to three thousand where it spun into a cloud and he lost sight of it. Had it crashed, or had the pilot come out of his spin in the cloud, and crept palpitating home? Tom thought the spin was rather fierce and long for an intentional one; and anyway it was a moral victory. He put his nose up and climbed away towards the lines, but, searching the sky, saw three aeroplanes circling together. Two of them were Camels, and he went to have a look at the battle. It seemed a long climb before he reached them, his nose up to eighty miles an hour, and aeroplane vibrating. The triplane was putting up a good defence, turning in very small radius and firing every time its nose was pointing anywhere near a Camel.

But the pilot was afraid to come out of his turn, and the fight was gradually drifting with the wind towards the lines. He would have to do something soon, but was still turning, turning when Tom came up within range and took a shot at it.

Startled by the fire of a third opponent, the pilot of the triplane put it into a twisting dive, and then pulled up in a tremendous zoom that the Camels could not follow, and he might have got away, but a fourth Camel dived from nowhere and shot it on top of the zoom, and it spun away. They followed it down, Mac, who was the latest comer, taking difficult snapshots from vertical dives at it. Down and down it spun, falling clear of clouds. Then it crumpled with a sudden flop, its wings tearing away and fluttering in the air while the body of it fell sheer. There would be no need to bury that young man; he would dig his own grave.

Then Archie tried to avenge the slaughter and blackened the sky with his malice. His shooting was excellent, and he nearly blew them out of the sky. It was surprising that no one was hit. They twisted towards the lines without much attempt at formation, and he put up a complete barrage in front of them. Mac played his usual trick of pretending to dive under it, and then zooming through the smoke where it had been, and as usual Archie wasted a lot of stuff on the deserted air below them where they might have been; and that sort of thing always made Tom laugh.

They crossed the lines and collected into proper formation. All five were there. Then they went on with the patrol, but nothing else happened except that they chased a distant two-seater that got away, and were again heavily bombarded by Archie. He might be a joke, but he was also rather a nuisance sometimes in those parts.

When they had landed, Mac was all smiles. It had been a fine show; they had cleaned up the whole durn bunch of tripes. They weren't any more good than the rest of them. He had seen Cundall going down after his spinner; that was a crash all right, he'd swear to it. He'd got two himself, and Miller one, and there was the last one they all shot down. That'd learn 'em. That was the stuff to give 'em. Bloody fine, said Mac.

'I WOULDN'T swear to it that I got that Hun to-day,' Tom said to Seddon and Smith that evening. As it was a dark night, the Germans were putting over a lot of heavy stuff, and the hut was shaking with the explosions. 'But on the other hand I should hardly think he'd have dared spin a tripe like he did, for fear of pulling his wings off. He'd have been far safer letting me shoot at him.'

'Well, if Mac says he was gone, isn't that good enough?' said Smith.

'What the flight commander says is right,' added Seddon. 'But couldn't you have gone through the cloud after it?'

'No damn fear. I don't like going through a thousand feet of clotted cloud; it's dark and depressing and you don't know what you are doing. And suppose I got moisture in the jet ten miles over? You're liable to, flying in wet cloud. Besides I might have come out too near the ground for comfort, and I'm not going near the ground on the other side except when I have to. I've done enough of it. No, I'm not keen enough and I'm too timid to go after Huns to that extent. He's welcome to his get-away if he made it. It was only because he was a tripehound that I went after him at all. There's some thing particularly revolting about a tripehound, don't you think?'

'I've never seen one,' said Smith, who hadn't been on that afternoon's job.

'What d'you mean, revolting? They're very splitarse.'

'They are. The fellow I'm supposed to have bagged did an upward roll when I shot at him. I don't know that it was much good to him, but it scared me to see all three stories stand up and whirl like that. It wasn't as if he did it on the zoom. It was marvellous. I was afraid he'd just stand on his tail like a kangaroo next and shoot up at me somehow, and I pulled up out of it. What a blessing height is! He just flattened out after his stunt and I had a fairly easy shot at him, which I thought I'd made a bawls-up of, and when he spun, I thought it was just wind up. However.'

'How did you manage to catch them?'

'We were up in the sun, and they didn't see us in time to get away. Mac's lucky that way. I didn't see how the others got theirs; I was too busy with mine. There weren't any flamers, thank goodness. I hate flamers; it always depresses me for the day to see one, even if it's a Hun. I suppose I'll get hardened in time.

'The last Hun we got was a nasty sight. It was spinning down at the hell of a lick, looking like an aeroplane, and in a flash it turned into a fluttering floating jumble of canvas and sticks like a broken kite, and the fuselage went . . . my God, it just went. It had put up a good fight, too. I think our shooting must be pretty good on the whole. Can you imagine five Camels getting wiped out? I wonder what happens in a German squadron when a whole flight goes west like that? Suppose B flight just vanished; what the hell should we feel like? No wonder the Huns aren't very enterprising just now. They must be feeling completely dithered with the losses they've had.'

'Yes,' Seddon remarked, 'and yet it's not so very long since they were having it nearly all their own way in the air. I suppose it's the type of aeroplane that does it. When the old Albatros first came out with its two machine guns it used to shoot down everything without much trouble, and Richthofen and such people had a damn good time of it, I should think, knocking down BE2Cs and such rubbish. Think of it; chasing a slow defenceless old washout like a BE in an Albatros scout . . . my God, what a war!'

'Well, all that's over,' said Tom. 'But if it's the type of aeroplane that counts, it's very pleasant to know that we've got these newish Fokker triplanes beat with our old Camels; and if these marvellous Snipes that we've been hearing about for so long replace Camels, we ought to have a high old time. I don't suppose the Fokker biplane will make much difference even if it arrives in quantities, though I must say I don't like the look of it any better than a tripehound. But I wonder if it's altogether the type of aeroplane, or whether the Huns are feeling whacked, and have lost their nerve.'

'Judging by their pushes on the ground, I should think not,' said Smith.

'I don't know. They are probably the last effort of desperation,' Seddon argued. 'They may suddenly collapse as they have not made a real break-through, and, except for chasing them home, the war may be over in a few weeks.'

'And you'll go home and see your wife and children. By the way, how are they? You don't say much about them.'

'Fine, thanks. I had a new photograph of the kids yesterday if you'd care to see it.'

Seddon offered them a picture of a girl of three and a baby of indeterminate sex. The girl was full of that ineffable charm peculiar to very small girls. Tom was not so fond of sheer babies, but those enchanting and wicked other-worldlings of three, four, five . . . Seddon must certainly have his turn of leave.

'Lucky man,' he said. 'There's nothing like children. Trailing clouds of glory do we come. I must have children, but I should hate to have to get married to do it. I must manage somehow else. Smith, why the devil don't you desert and go home and have children? It's much more important than fooling about out here.'

'I wish to God I could. But is this the time for having children?'

'All times are right for having children.'

'Rot. You don't know what you're talking about. Wait till you're married. And if all men were like you, the earth would be full up in a few years. You can't do it.'

'All men be damned,' Tom retorted. 'I'm not talking about all men. I'm talking about us. We're the fit blokes who do the fighting, and we ought to have the privilege of populating the land. Read Plato. We ought to be able to pick and choose what maidens we will impregnate. . . .'

'I don't want to,' Smith interrupted.

'All the more for me. This damned combination of moral respectability with murder is too damned silly. It's broken down partly, but a bastard is still a bastard, even if it's the child of a fit warrior. If our race is to live by war, then the fighters must have their rights, and the can't-fight weaklings must submit to vasectomy. It would preserve the race and do them good.'

'What is it?' Seddon asked.

The door opened, and Mac put his head in. 'Squadron show at six-thirty in the morning. Good night.'

But low clouds and mist prevented the show, and they persisted all day until a thunderstorm cleared the air in the evening. The SE squadron produced a football of the spherical kind and challenged them to a game. Tom played outside-right, and after a lot of energetic scrambling they won somehow by one goal to none. This was a great improvement in the way of passing a dud afternoon, even better than sleeping, and Tom felt fine after some real exercise, and after tea walked over to Avesnes with Hudson and Burkett and Cross, and having talked a lot of shop and had a long argument in which Burkett would have it that man-made music was no good, and that the only noises worth hearing were those made by water and birds and wind and such things, walked back through the rain. Lucie had been so terrified by the thunder that she had needed a good deal of comforting, especially by Hudson, who had clean-cut features and something of an air. When he was older he might develop the decision of character that his appearance and manner at present somewhat prematurely indicated. He had served as a Tommy in the infantry: the experience had smashed his development as a sensitive aesthetic young man with a passion for playing on church organs that drove him into even ugly red-brick suburban churches, and it had left him, like many others, rudderless, foul-mouthed, scornful; dead to all humanizing influences except drink. Tom felt rather cut out with Lucie, though her largesse was great. He did not mind this.

Burkett always had what seemed to him a queer point of view, but he found him more comprehensible than most Canadians. He was proud of his cap, which sat on his head very rakishly, and he went so far as to denounce Cross's as a pip-squeak's hat. But Cross hadn't so much experience of cap-wearing as the others, being a youngster who had gone straight into the R.F.C. Very few wore the R.F.C. cap and tunic, for the fashion was to wear wings and regimental badges; and those that hadn't served with commissioned rank in another branch of the forces conformed as nearly as they could by wearing the universal tunic with R.F.C. badges. There was a queer mixture of uniforms; or rather there was no uniform; and the new R.A.F. outfit was intended to impose order on this chaos; but as no outfit allowance had been made, and the uniform was generally disliked, progress was not rapid. The typical R.F.C. bloke still wore his wings on his dirty regimental tunic edged with leather at the cuffs and scented and stained with castor oil, a pair of oily but elegant breeches or slacks, a soft topped cap pulled on with infinite negligent rakishness, and an expression of hard-bitten, sardonic wisdom. But many new pilots coming out were lads with last-week commissions and nothing to wear but the new uniform; and the old order was, though slowly, passing.

Rank too was a mix-up, when a major might, for love of flying, give up majoring with his regiment and take on second lieutenant's duty with a squadron, where he was, presumably, entitled to be saluted by his compeers and even his flight commander. There was, however, no known instance of its having been tried on.

In the morning C flight went out on an early bombing show in the mist. Tom wasn't on it, having a day off. Dubois, as usual, didn't come back with the flight. Smith had a flying wire cut, probably by Archie, and crept home frightened to death his wing would collapse. It was a stagnant, depressing day. Tom felt wooden, dis-inclined to do anything at all, possibly as a reaction from his unusual activity in playing football and walking to Avesnes and back on the day before. Smith felt the depression badly, and leaned against the hut doorpost for hours, plump, Yorkshire, unhappy. There were thunderstorms in the distance.

Tom took a letter up to the office after breakfast, and franked it with the rubber stamp *Passed by Censor No.* 554. Grey, the newest member of C flight, was censoring the men's letters, being orderly dog for the day. Tom picked up one to read, to help Grey. It was the usual sort of nonsense that the men wrote home. If the enemy had seized the entire batch, they would only have found out that the writers were all in the pink, remarkably fond of their wives and mothers and sisters and brothers.

As Tom folded it, he noticed that it was numbered.

'Here's a methodical bloke,' he said to Grey. 'He numbers his letters home. This is number forty-four.'

'Forty-four,' Grey exclaimed. 'I am glad to hear that.'

'I'm glad you're glad.' Tom wondered if Grey was mad.

'You see, forty-four is my lucky number,' Grey explained. 'I hadn't come across it for some time. The last time I saw it was in England when I was on my way to early flying one morning. It was

224

on a milk cart. I was on Avros then, and when I was taking off just after seeing the forty-four, my engine cut out, and I hit a tree and crashed the Avro badly. But the marvellous thing was, I only sprained my wrist.'

'Very remarkable,' Tom agreed. 'But I should try not to go up to-day if I were you.'

The telephone bell rang, and Tom answered it. Dubois was on the line.

'What is it, Dubois?' he said, imitating the major's voice.

Dubois said he had got lost because of the mist, and had landed near Frévant.

'Frévant! What the hell did you go to Frévant for?'

'I was lost. It's very misty up.'

'Well, you know where you are now, so you'd better fly back. D'you expect me to come and guide you?'

'I'm sorry, major, but my undercarriage is damaged.'

'Undercarriage damaged! Disgraceful! Can't you land yet? I've had enough of this; I'll have you court martialled.'

Dubois' voice showered arpeggios of explanation. The major came into the office and glared at Tom.

'Hold on a minute,' said Tom. 'This is Cundall speaking. Here's the major.'

He made way. 'Dubois on the line, major. He's had a forced landing.'

The major grunted and took the receiver. Tom walked out past Grey, who looked altogether astonished.

'Who d'you think you're calling a bloody fool?' he heard the major shout down the telephone.

Tom returned to the hut and leant against the door-post opposite to Smith. The klaxon sounded for A flight three times. Usually the major only sounded it twice.

'Bad temper,' Tom remarked; but it was too much trouble to explain.

Seddon came in to put on his flying kit, and called them weary willies.

'Don't get lost,' said Smith. 'It's thick up.'

Tom had had a parcel of food from his sister the day before, and it included a bag of nuts. He saved himself from complete inanition by cracking them between the door and its frame, an occupation that lasted till lunch and diminished his appetite.

Of A flight, only Moss got back. The atmosphere had thickened so much while they were out that they all lost themselves and each other. Tom thought of his own pleasant sojourn at the Corps School. He must write to the padre there as he had promised. It was time he had another adventure like that. During the afternoon, telephone calls came in from all over the place from lost aviators; also a complaint from Archie via Brigade and Wing that someone in a Camel had dropped bombs near one of his batteries that morning. C flight was suspected, Dubois in particular, but the complaint was met with denial.

It cleared up in the evening, and some of the forced landing people flew back. Seddon had landed on an aerodrome, and had been entertained by a Harry Tate squadron. They thought a lot of Camels for the way they kept the Huns off, and Seddon had the experience of flying blotto. He said it was miraculous. There was nothing a Camel wouldn't do then. When he landed he found a strand of telegraph wire trailing from his undercarriage; had no idea how it got there.

Tom went with Bulmer and Franklin and Moss to dinner at the SE squadron. It was a binge for Corton-Rees ne of their flight-commanders who was returning to England. He had been with the squadron for eight months, and had a bag of twenty-eight Huns in that time. He looked about seventeen, and had a shy, virginal manner: he would tell yarn after yarn of foul humour with an absolute seriousness and as though he had no idea of their import. Meeting him for the first time, he seemed a timid simpleton; for the tenth time, a lunatic; for the twentieth time, one of the finest fellows on earth.

The binge for this hero was terrific; Tom remembered very little about it next morning. They had sung 'Auld Lang Syne', and a lot of the fellows were all but weeping. The rest was headache.

BREAKFAST was impossible for Tom. Fortunately the first job was not till half-past ten, so there was some time for recovery. And then glad news came that the job was washed out because of low clouds and mist. The remaining forced landing people were collected, excepting Dubois. Transport went to Frévant and found his crash, of which 'damaged undercarriage' was a very adumbrated description, but Dubois himself had vanished. Late in the afternoon he telephoned to say that someone had collected the aeroplane but had left him behind.

Tom went up for fresh air after lunch. There was a thick layer of clouds at a thousand feet, and as it was rather oppressive underneath, he thought it would be a good idea to get through them into the clear above. He flew into them and went on climbing and climbing at ninety miles an hour. The cloud was dense; he could hardly see his wing-tips. Watching his altimeter he climbed five hundred, six hundred, seven hundred, eight hundred feet. He was sideslipping, and the cloud wasn't getting appreciably lighter, as it should if he were reaching the top of it. The speed shown by the pitot dropped to eighty. There was vibration. He pushed the stick forwards, but it didn't seem to make any difference. Then – God, what a jerk! His head banged against the centre-section of the top plane. What the hell was happening? He managed to push himself down and get hold of the joystick spade-grip with his left hand. He pulled himself through the loose safety-belt back into the seat and got his feet on the rudder-bar. He was out of the clouds and the earth was all round him – spinning like hell. God, the engine was on, he was done for. He pulled back the fine adjustment and put the stick right forward against the dashboard with full left rudder. The engine stopped. He was diving vertically: no room to get out; death. The stick jerked back; he was pressed hard, hard into the seat. Christ almighty, he'd pull the wings off. The earth was shooting past. The whole bloody aeroplane would collapse with the strain of it . . . no, it was standing it, the strain was easing. The earth had gone. He was out of the dive gliding not a hundred feet up. He tried to open the fine adjustment, but his hand couldn't do it. He had to look at the engine controls and put his shaking hand against the adjustment lever and push.

He was trembling and sick. It had seemed certain death. Another half second taken in getting back into his seat would have killed him. That was the worst seven seconds of his life so far. It was worse than being shot at; it was worse than that appalling escape when Beal had been killed; it left him limp and shaking as nothing before ever had. He could only fly straight and wait to recover; as he soon would, for the relief of escape was great as the menace had been terrible: it swept over him like a wave of new life, blessing him with a moment of paradisal bliss, so that he half-closed his eyes with the divine solace. Death had come so near him, had seemed so certain. All his nervous force had gone into that thrust against the centre-section with his right hand that had enabled his left hand to grasp the spade-grip and pull him against thrusting centrifugality into the seat. It had been almost miraculous, the quick vital action of the will to live. It had taken charge of him and concentrated all the energy stored in him into a tremendous effort. He felt as though it had not been he that had informed the effort, though it was manifest by his exhaustion that his was the force used; it was as though something external had taken charge; as though some spirit had intervened from the timeless realm where it dwelt and at leisure had bent his muscles to the necessary flexions; but the action, translated into time, had been incredibly, superhumanly swift and consuming. Had he lived when such things were credible, he would have seen some bright form of god or genii or angel or demon or saint come down through the centre-section window and help him back into the seat; if he had not seen it at the time, he would have been convinced a little afterwards by his sensations of bliss that there had been a supernatural visiting. But, angel or instinct, he had damned nearly pulled the wings off coming out of the dive.

He flew straight, pending recovery. He would never know exactly what had happened in that cloud. The instability of a Camel made it impossible to keep on an even keel flying blind for more than a minute or two; for him, at least; a very sensitive pilot might do somewhat better. Probably it was stalling into a spin that had thrown him out of his seat, but from what position he could not tell. He was taken by surprise and not braced to withstand the great jerking flop. He would keep out of clouds of that density. He ought to have known better than to have tried to get through. There might be two thousand feet of it.

He soon recovered sufficiently to take interest in the world. He was flying westwards at six hundred feet. There was a town in front of him; the same one that he had come to a few evenings previously. He had found out that it was Frévant. In a field to the north-west he discerned the wreck of an aeroplane that was being dismantled sufficiently to be packed on to a waiting lorry. It was a Camel; Dubois' Camel. There was an interested crowd of onlookers, khaki and civilian.

Tom, feeling exhilarated now, went down on that crowd and scattered it; and again and again. People ran for shelter, crouched against the lorry, got underneath it, lay flat on the ground, ran about gesticulating. The Air Mechanics stopped work to watch him. They knew him, and he could see they were roaring with laughter. He hoped they would have the sense not to tell anyone who he was, in case some of the Frenchmen were indignant and might try to stir up international trouble.

He waved farewell to the crowd and went to look for other prey, and dived on several lorries and cars and made people lie down. But the aeroplane wasn't flying quite as it should. It was a trifle slack on the controls and was pulling too much to the right. He went home and investigated. There was nothing very noticeably wrong, except that the centre-section was wobbly. He got the riggers busy on it.

Dubois was back to dinner, even more melancholy than usual. He had been fetched from Frévant by a motor-cycle combination and the major had been nagging him.

'Where did you hide?' Tom asked.

'I got to know a very nice family in Frévant, and they invited me to stay in their house. The men guarding the crash knew where I was. You see, I naturally went into Frévant, and as I stopped there my friends sent a boy with a message to the guard to let him know where I was.'

'Any daughters?'

'Yes, three. Very respectable. I told them about my home in Trois Rivières.'

'I suppose you'll be going over to Frévant for the night quite often?'

Dubois shook his head and breathed heavily. 'It was nice to be with a French family, but it makes me feel too much how I want to be home.' He seemed to have forgotten all about his telephone talk with Tom.

Dinner was noticeably better than usual. As the major was going on leave next day, James would have additional work, and the job of P.M.C. had been given to Chadwick temporarily, and Chadwick was playing the part of a new broom. The most noticeable improvements were English biscuits (the French could not make eatable biscuits), Camembert cheese, and nuts and oranges for dessert. He even seemed to have stimulated the cook to make a slightly better job of the roast.

During the evening Dubois caused a stir by walking into the mess wearing spectacles, unheard-of accoutrement for a pilot. He was in a dream, whether of Frévant or the thousand isles of St. Lawrence, and awoke to embarrassment under the disturbing stare of forty eyes.

'I wear them sometimes for reading,' he explained to the world. He had a cell of a compartmented hut to himself, and spent most of his leisure there, playing his violin when his neighbours were not at home, and he had emerged in abstraction from this seclusion without taking off his glasses. Doubtless a partial explanation of Dubois was that his eyes were weak. It was marvellous that he had with this disability been allowed to fly; but it was typical of him to achieve what he wanted when anyone else in similar circumstances would be barred. There was an amiable, absent-minded, melancholy undeniability about him. He sleep-walked past all sorts of barriers, and no one had the heart to wake him up to their reality.

In the morning the weather was misty and depressing again, Tom felt as though his head were full of fog and darkness. There was nothing to do, nothing worth doing. The idea of bridge or any other game was repulsive; reading was a bore; talking – what on earth was there to talk about? His pipe tasted foul; he had no nuts left to crack. The morning lingered like an unwanted guest. The everlasting roll of gunfire seemed to set the atmosphere vibrating slowly and heavily in sordid waves that beat upon the very brain.

He walked up to the hangars to see if the rigging of his aeroplane had been trued up. He found it still trestled up into flying position. The sergeant explained that they were going over everything very carefully while they had the chance. The fuselage was just a little twisted.

'I was over at Frévant yesterday, sir,' said the sergeant. 'You didn't arf put the breeze up some o' them Frenchies.'

'Oh.'

'One old girl fair 'ad 'ysterics. Of course we didn't know 'oo you was, sir. We nearly died o' laughing the way you chased 'em.'

Tom grunted. He must be careful about diving on mixed crowds. It was all right strafing men, but women . . . that was getting on towards caddishness. He was sorry he had given that woman what the rigger called 'ysterics. Hysterics . . . the word was derived directly from the Greek *hystera*. Curious that the possession of hystera should have such queer effects. A womb . . . practically all mammals were viviparous: why were women alone among females weaker and stupider than their males? There seemed no biological reason. Was there a female, from elephant to marmose, that was less formidable than the male? It was all bunkum, this weaker sex stuff. They simply weren't entitled to be weaklings and spoil-sports. They were human beings, as men were, and the differences between the sexes weren't sufficient to. . . .

An answer to his rhetorical question suddenly popped up in his mind. Yes, cows were very much less formidable than bulls.

'. . . ready in two hours,' the sergeant was saying.

Tom wandered down to the mess and looked through *Bystanders* and *Spheres* and *Tatlers* and *La Vies;* the gramophone played the 'Cobbler's Song' and 'Three Hundred and Sixty-Five Days' for the ten thousandth time. He came across a short story about a flying hero who, after shooting down a lot of Huns, had one of his own wings shot off. But his luck held, and he was able to reach his aerodrome.

Why the devil was such stuff published? What a rotten trade authorship was; spreading misconceptions and lies. He challenged Seddon to a game of ping-pong, but the supply of balls had given out. He sat and looked at the fire.

The major came in to say cheerio before going on leave, and they all turned out to see him off. He was going in his car to Boulogne, and Williamson would make the return journey if he could be found. It had been arranged that the car would pick him up at the E.F.C. Officers' Hostel.

Then Tom had the idea of borrowing a horse from the stables. As there was no flying, there was no reason why the beast should bolt as on the occasion of his last equestrian effort. There was one available, a self-willed animal; and as Tom had neither whip nor spurs he spent most of the ride sitting still while it browsed, and returned home when the horse would. But it was better than sitting in the mess, and the shaking up when it trotted did him good. But he wished he could sit a trotting horse properly.

The atmosphere cleared during the afternoon, and B flight went out on a tentative patrol. They were to have a look round and come back if conditions were impossible. Then Wing found a job for C flight, to be done in a hurry. It was reported that the Germans had a headquarters of some sort at a farm called Paradis, north-east of Béthune, and they were to go and bomb it. The place was marked and named on their maps as it was not in a village. They were to surprise it. The clouds were no higher than a thousand feet and were too uniform and thick to go through. They would have to go six miles into Hunland and back at a murderous altitude. It was a damnable job. They would be shot to blazes.

'One dive and away,' Mac instructed. 'Keep in formation and bomb all together. When I go down keep with me and loose all your bombs as fast as you can and pull out and make for the lines like hell. Fire if you can while you're diving, but don't shoot down the fellow in front. There won't be any Huns about upstairs a day like this, so all you need watch is the ground. Rendezvous over St. Venant.'

Bombs were put in the racks, which held them in such a way that the vanes could not rotate. When they were released, the vanes, whirled by the wind of falling, screwed the plunger into position in contact with the detonator. They stood round watching: Mac, short, sturdy, authoritative, completely confident, his small grey eyes seeing everything: his admirer and deputy leader Miller, tall and lean and tough, with brown, soft eyes in a red, weathered face; Tom Cundall, English, with his clear red and white complexion and unemphasized features; Smith, fair, plump, plain, honest: and Cross, boyish, slightly diffident, disfigured by a scar across his right cheek where a piece of flying glass had laid it open when he crashed into a greenhouse.

These individuals, each with his own world around him, ran their engines and taxied out and got into position and took off into the heavy air. They went away north on their preliminary journey of about thirty miles before they crossed the lines. When they reached Béthune Mac circled over it: it was being shelled heavily, and it was curious to see the buildings leaping and crumbling, the huge fountains of debris, the fires and clouds of dust and smoke. Tom saw the tower of a great building that might have been a church suddenly hurl itself down and crash into chaos. Why had the Huns taken this sudden deadly dislike to Béthune?

A little further north and they would have to cross the lines, and the bullets would start flying. And then fortune decisively and incredibly favoured them, for at the very place where they must turn east they found a narrow rift in the clouds through which the blue sky peered gloriously. God, how splendid! The rift was the sort of thing that was usually called a hot air hole; they occurred very rarely in cloud-blankets on warm days, and were held to be caused by ascending currents of hot air.

Into this cleft they climbed, and crossed the lines out of range of machine-gun fire, and they were able to continue in this security almost to their objective. When they had to go below the clouds they were only a mile away, and they put their noses down and got to it in a few seconds. It was a group of farm buildings partly ruinous, but with enough left standing to make an interesting target.

The raid was a surprise. Tom could see soldiers about; they vanished at the diving approach of the raiders, but probably hadn't time to take proper cover.

The target was easy. They dived steeply at it, firing and letting go their bombs. If they all dropped, there was a rain of twenty bombs in two or three seconds, besides the fire of machine guns, which no doubt went through the old roofs. As soon as he had got rid of his bombs, Tom pulled out of his dive, opened out, and turned away. He circled round in time to see the effect of the bombs, his downward wing not blocking his view. He saw the farm, peaceful and in parts solid enough; the aeroplanes, lightened of their load, were scattering away from it, their bombs as yet in air; and almost at the instant of its swinging into sight, the buildings crumbled in the almost simultaneous bursting of the swarm of bombs. It was fantastic, the sudden upspringing of spurt after spurt after spurt of grey smoke and the hesitant collapse of old walls. The silence of it all added to the strangeness; ears were so used to the steady roar of the engine that it became a normal condition, almost translatable into silence; and all these things happened without breaking the loud quietude – a farmhouse collapsed, or Béthune was smashed into its constituent bricks and stones. Their silence made them unreal. Violence lived with noise, and Tom found it difficult to be convinced of the formidable realness of these merely visual catastrophes.

He climbed away west, and very soon came to the hot air hole and safety. One clump of Archie appeared in front of him; that was all. It had been a most successful job.

They picked up formation over St. Venant and went leisurely homewards. Tom dived out of formation to have a look at Vimy Ridge when they reached that famous place. He went right down and contour-chased up the long eastward rise. It was the usual desolation of churned earth with a lot of rank ragged grass which, especially near the old trenches, was variegated with stains of bright red-brown. The million shell-holes were filled or half-filled with water. Miles of barbed wire lay tangled, and rifles, tin hats, dud shells. One of his friends had been killed there.

V I

FRANKLIN was shot down. B flight had been doing their ridiculous patrol at a thousand feet, and they only crossed the lines once, when Franklin had seemingly been hit from the ground. He had glided towards the British lines but crashed in no-man's-land just outside the British wire. He probably hadn't been killed unless the Huns had shot him before he could get into cover.

His going would be a considerable loss to B flight. He was a fine deputy leader. Everyone liked his good humour, his bulk, his imperturbability. Without him, Tom thought, the squadron would be like a menagerie without its elephant. Fortunately they had pinpoints of the crash, and an urgent request was got through to the battalion holding the line there to rescue him.

Williamson was back to dinner. He looked tired out. Tom and Smith and Seddon listened eagerly to his account of what it was like to be in England. There wasn't enough to eat, but there was still plenty to drink, though most whisky was poisonous and all beer pretty bad. London was crowded; you could hardly get into a musical show or a popular bar or a night club. Everyone was still doing well, from newspapers owners and prostitutes to hot gospellers and cabinet ministers. An officer on leave, especially one with flying pay, was charged double for everything.

'God, I've had a bust. I haven't slept these last three nights. I'm tired out and I'm more than broke. I'm glad to be back in this peaceful spot, away from all the whores, touts, and profiteers. I'm glad to see you fellows again: really, we're happy here. I never want to go inside the Savoy or Murray's again.'

'Of course, if all you do on leave is go round the London shows . . .' Seddon began.

'And now we're going to have one of our arguments,' Williamson interrupted. 'That's fine.'

'After dinner,' said Tom. 'There's the gong.'

But after dinner Williamson lay down on his bed and fell asleep. He didn't wake up till seven o'clock in the morning, when he undressed and went to bed. As it was a quite impossible morning for flying he slept on undisturbed till lunch.

Franklin telephoned early from Arras, and the squadron car went over for him. He had washed and brushed, but his clothes were torn, his face bruised and cut. He had abandoned his sidcot. He was a little queer: not quite the Franklin they knew. His engine had cut out, he didn't know why, and he hadn't been able to get back, but crashed into a big shell hole just outside the British wire. It was muddy and had three feet of water at the bottom, but it gave him immediate cover. The bus was upside down with its tail in the water, and he crawled out and lay on the mud, and kept slipping down till his feet were in the water. The Huns didn't take any notice of him at first. He thought he'd better let his own people know he was alive, so he put up his arm and waved his handkerchief, which was at once shot at. He heard someone shout 'keep there'.

Then the Huns started bombing him. They didn't make very good shooting, but it was damned uncomfortable lying there in the mud with grey sky for the only view, waiting for the next crash. He saw something dropping slowly out of the sky at him, and he couldn't run from it. It was unbearable. He scrambled up the side of the shell hole. There was a whistle of bullets as a machine gun fired at him, and at the same time a splash behind him, and a machine gun rattling from the British line. He had slipped back. The thing that had fallen into the water didn't explode. He was all right for a little longer. After a few minutes there was a crash near by: the Huns were still amusing themselves by keeping him pinned in the hole and bombing him there. Dirty lot of swine. Some time later a whizz-bang came sailing right into his hole where he was clinging to the earth, wishing to God he could burrow like a rabbit. It splashed and burst smashing the tail of the aeroplane, covering him with filth but not doing him any great damage. He felt he couldn't stand any more of it; better to run for it; probably he would have if he'd known a way through the wire; and been killed for certain.

Then shells went overhead, eighteen-pounders bursting in the direction of the German trenches. He yelled 'Give the bastards hell.' The Germans replied after a little with five-nines. He lay there with his face in the mud, pressing his body into the earth to obliterate himself. It was mind-shattering, lying there in the open amid the din and concussion of high explosive, but perhaps it was as well they didn't use shrapnel.

Things quietened down after a while; he didn't know whether ten minutes or an hour. He wasn't troubled by bombing for a long time, but by thirst. He lay longing for darkness, when perhaps a patrol would come to his rescue. Thank God he was a good deal nearer the British than the German front line. Or he would try to get back by himself, but he would probably get stuck in the wire and be caught by a flare. He dared not put his head up to take an inventory. It wouldn't be dark before half past eight. His wrist watch was going, but seemingly at a tenth of its usual speed. God, for a drink!

And then, towards sunset, they started bombing again. He had kicked and scraped for himself a shallow lair in the soft earth, and he clung there. An explosion was so close as to half-bury him with mud and daze him with concussion. He didn't know what happened after that, but he must have had enough sense to push the dirt sufficiently from his head to let him breathe.

It was dark. Something struck his shoulder. He grunted. 'Hst! Can you walk?' someone whispered.

He wriggled out of the mud and scrambled from the hole. There was a sudden light. He flung down instinctively and lay still till it faded.

'Come on.' He followed the dim silhouette of shoulders and tin hat. There were others behind him.

'Mind the wire. Follow me carefully.'

Then they were through. Another flare. They lay still. A machine gun suddenly rattled. Then they were up and over the parapet. He fell over and lay on the boarded bottom of the trench. They sat him up. He got to his feet.

'I'm all right. Bit dizzy. For Christ's sake give me a drink.'

They took him down a dugout and gave him whisky and water. He soon felt better. Things looked a bit funny, but he felt all right. They found him some grub. Then he wanted to get back home. In the morning he was coming back to bomb those Huns. God, what bloody swine. He was grateful to the infantry for rescuing him; they must look out for him getting his own back in the morning.

He went back, and got transport to Arras. He stopped there at the Rest House for the night, and here he was. All he wanted now was an aeroplane to go back and bomb and shoot up those swine. He knew exactly where they were. His crash would be a landmark.

'You can't go in this fog,' said Bulmer. 'You couldn't see a hundred yards. Leave it till after lunch and I'll come with you if the weather's possible, and we'll give 'em hell.'

The spirit of vendetta was infectious, and nearly everyone clamoured to go on the expedition. It looked like being a squadron show. Tom kept quiet. He could understand how Franklin felt, and it was perhaps all right for him to ease his bosom of perilous stuff by doing a strafe at his own risk, but the thing was growing into a private war. And they wouldn't do much good. The Huns would go down their dugouts, and they'd only waste a lot of bombs. That didn't matter in comparison with the risk of someone being shot down by neighbouring machine guns. Franklin couldn't have people killed for his private revenge; not that he himself wanted it. Bulmer, who was senior flight commander and the chief fount of authority in the major's absence, ought to stop it.

Then Mac took part. 'Are you authorizing this as a squadron show, Bulmer?'

'No, certainly not.'

'Then I'm not having anyone of C flight go. Understand C flight,' he turned about, 'you're forbidden to go on this stunt. I'm not taking the risk. You do as you like, Bulmer and Forster, but I'm not going to have my men and machines risked without orders.'

'Bloody good, Mac,' Tom said to him quietly. 'I'm glad some-one's got some sense.' He admired Mac's decision amid the wavering excitement. He was solid.

'Ay. It's all damn silly. Franklin doesn't know what he's doing.'

Mac's intervention had a decisive effect. Franklin said his idea was to go alone, and he hadn't suggested anything else. Bulmer said he was going purely as Franklin's friend, and that two were quite enough. Forster said he wouldn't authorize anyone of A flight to go. And so it was left that Bulmer and Franklin alone would do the strafe.

It cleared up a little after lunch, and orders came through from Wing to stand by. Bulmer left Williamson in charge of B flight, and he and Franklin set off amid the cheers of the whole squadron. The SE people, who weren't standing by, proposed a return game of football. A north wind had sprung up, and although it cleared the mist away, it made flying impossible, except for desperately needed Camels, by driving dense masses of low cloud across the sky. A team was, however, got together, and Tom secured permission to play, thereby avoiding the risk of a low-flying job. But the stand-by was soon washed out, so that the football was mere exercise.

Bulmer and Franklin came back after forty minutes, satisfied and shot up. They had dropped their bombs first, gone away, and then dashed back and done some shooting when the Huns thought the raid was over and had come out of their holes to look round. Franklin was sure they had hit two or three. The thing was elaborately planned. They had dived simultaneously from opposite sides to counteract the traverses.

James had given Wing an account of Franklin's adventure in no-man's-land, and after tea the doctor came to have a look at him, and packed him off to hospital. He looked queer now that the excitement was over, and was a little bit vague. Williamson became deputy leader of B flight, and Tom's leave came one place nearer.

Williamson was feeling ever so much better after his long sleep, and more inclined to regret the passing of his leave. It wasn't like him to binge so thoroughly, but he was glad he'd drunk to the dregs of pleasure once in his life.

There was an entertainment of some sort in No. 64's quarters, where there was a large hut for the purpose, and everyone went there after dinner with the exception of Tom, who was bored by concert parties, and of Dubois. The supply of coal was too low for fires in huts, which the cold north wind made untenable.

Tom was glad of the deserted mess where he could sit in peace and read. Dubois came in with his violin, hoping to find the place empty. He did not mind Tom, whom he felt to be sympathetic, and he sat down on the other side of the fire and made his noises. Tom was not pleased with the scarcely musical sounds that floated through the room, but he hadn't the heart to interrupt him. He liked Dubois, and, realizing that, he wondered why. They were opposites in most respects. He delved into the attributes of Dubois as he saw him, and came to a stratum of gentleness. That was it; he was radically gentle, and that was lovely in the midst of harshness. After a time he found himself trying to recognize the tunes Dubois was nearly playing.

'By jove, I recognize this one,' he said suddenly, 'it's "Come and Cuddle Me".'

'You don't mind my noise, do you?' He looked almost beseechingly at Tom: black, lustrous, melancholy, myopic eyes.

'No. Go on Monsieur Dubois de Trois Rivières.'

But Dubois did not go on. He sighed at the mention of his home.

239

The music they had there! His wife, his friends, they all made music, and this war had broken up their happy evenings and their simple pleasures.

Tom rather wondered what on earth happened on their musical evenings if all the musicians were of the same sort as Dubois; but he kept his expression as sympathetic as he could.

'You must be happy at home.' There was a great deal of noise going on, heavy guns roaring, big shells crumping. Both sides were shelling back areas.

'We are. Very happy. We have musical parties, and sometimes we go out in our boats to one of the islands in the St. Lawrence. It is so lovely there in the evening. The songs float over the quiet water. We picnic on an island. We go back in the dark when it is all black and silver. . . .'

Tom noticed in the quietness of the mess how the windows shook. Outside, flash after flash was red-gold on the surly clouds. Everything was rattling, rattling; the drum, drum, drum in the air could be felt as much as heard. The north wind cried as if in horror of the desolate uproar.

'And when the moon is bright we go on and on, sometimes all night. It is so beautiful and still. You know how water sounds, rippling against a boat. It is like a quiet song we could go on listening to hour after hour. . . .'

Dubois was inexhaustible on the subject of home. Tom asked him to stroll up on to the aerodrome to watch the flashes for a little while. Outside, the noise was tremendous. The crashes buffeted them. Big shells were falling regularly a little way east. They had set fire to the village of Haute Avesnes, perhaps there was a dump in that direction the Germans knew about. All along the eastward horizon there was a flicker of field guns, outshone from moment to moment by the mighty wings of fire of the nearer giants, that clapped with sharp thunder, and the quicker brighter spurts of bursting shells. The nearer guns were like the terrible brass of some plutonic orchestra flaunting above the steady ostinato of distant tympani.

It was the clear atmosphere and low driven clouds that made the gun-flashes so noticeable. The ragged sky flared ghastly for an instant on the sight and was obliterated in obscurity. And again; like smoke from a mouth of Dis illumined by nether fires; then occluded with darkness, and for a brief interval there was only the flicker, flicker, flicker far away and the burning houses in Haute Avesnes.

For years the guns had been firing. Long ages ago he had first known them, when he was a private among the Londoners at the almost forgotten slaughter known as Loos; then at the unforgettable holocaust of the Somme, during which he was for a few days in command of a platoon, and for a few hours in command of a company, until a bullet hit him in the foot; the wound had given trouble, but now was only a red mark on his instep that ached sometimes. All the time the voice of the guns had been swelling in a mighty crescendo. He was back among them, though not, thank God, forced to hide in the earth from their terror, and now they were a multitude so clamorous-powerful, that men were pismires to them. The earth was theirs; they ploughed it, they manured it with the flesh and watered it with the blood of their slaves; and all that came of their husbandry was a stink.

VII

The major being away, Wing seemed to think that the squadron needed supervision. The colonel himself telephoned at 8 o'clock next morning and demanded of Wall, one of B flight's newest men, who was doing orderly dog and so answered the telephone, what the squadron was doing. Wall answered, with truth that is fatal to diplomacy, that the squadron wasn't doing anything. Wall was a captain in his regiment and had seen a good deal of service, and had no use at all for hot-airing colonels who sat at telephones a long way from the war and chivvied combatants. Perhaps his voice sounded a trifle laconic; the colonel demanded to know who he was, and told him to fetch the adjutant at once. Wall strolled down to James's hut and roused him, and James went hurrying to the office in pyjamas and British warm imploring deity to spare his teeth. The colonel asked him why the squadron was doing nothing when a patrol was due to go up at eight o'clock. James explained that the weather was too bad; there was a thick layer of clouds not above a thousand feet, and they had decided a patrol was impossible.

The colonel considered the weather was fit for flying. The patrol must go up at nine and take bombs.

It was C flight's job. Mac was furious when he heard of it. He cursed Wing with every curse known to an erudite Canadian. He had been called at seven, looked at the sky, told the batman not to call anyone else, and gone to sleep again. There was no chance of meeting any Huns, so he left Miller and Cundall to their repose, and had Smith, Dubois, Cross and Baker roused, and at nine o'clock they took off.

Tom got up leisurely soon after the noise of their engines had died away. What on earth was the good, he wondered, of sending people out on a morning like that? It was as bad as their worst days of ground-strafing on the Somme. The clouds must be below a thousand feet; there was a fresh north wind; drops of rain fell occasionally. Well, thank the Lord, Mac was decent enough to let him off it.

He shaved peacefully, discussing with Williamson and Seddon the progressive foulness of nearly everyone as they rose in rank and removed further from contact with the enemy. How they all loved to win the war for their own honour at other peoples' risk. The bravery of back-area generals was terrific, and of base colonels very little less. Look at their decorations and their pay.

C flight came back while they were at breakfast; evidently Mac had found it quite hopeless to stop out. Cross was the first to come in to second breakfast.

'Hullo Cross,' Tom said lightly, 'enjoy your trip?'

'Bloody awful. Had to cross the lines at five hundred. We just dropped our bangers and came back. Smith's gone.'

'What!'

'Yes, poor old Smith. I was flying behind him and he suddenly did a sort of roll and then spun. He crashed near the German front line. He's killed right enough.'

Others confirmed this account. Smith had been hit by machine-gun fire from the ground, and spun with his engine on. He'd be smashed to pulp. The job had been no use at all. Mac wouldn't have crossed the lines if he hadn't had bombs to get rid of.

It was chilly, and Tom felt shivery. He had caught a cold, he thought. Some others were sneezing and feeling off colour. He spent an hour feeling wretched, and then decided to do a little flying. It wasn't at all the sort of day for joy-riding, but fresh air might blow his cold away, and action might help rid him of the depression that had settled on him, and stop him from thinking of the waste of Smith's life. Would he never get used to death? 'Afflictions induce callosities' – perhaps there was something lacking in the chemistry of his hide.

He went up and amused himself by dropping four dummy bombs on the target and made the indifferent score of 15, 18, 10, 16. The numbers denoted distance in feet from the bullseye. The wind must have something to do with it. He took off again to do some firing. It was bumpy and unpleasant up. He pulled up his gear handle and loaded his guns by pushing the loading handles, levers that in turn actuated the cocking handles. Then he climbed as high as he could get, which was to about eight hundred feet, where he ran into mist, in order to have a long dive on to the target. He dived and fired and pulled up to climb again. The engine spluttered and cut right out. He was at three hundred feet and had no room to turn into the wind, being over the northern edge of the aerodrome, where the firing target was. He would have had to turn south for room and then north again, and he hadn't height for the manœuvre. He could turn into the wind at once and come down on ploughland, but after his previous experience of it he preferred to take the chance of landing cross wind on the aerodrome. It was blowing fairly hard, and as he neared the ground he saw how much he was drifting. He sideslipped into the wind sufficiently to counteract the drift, and settled down quite nicely, as he touched ground lifting the wing he had lowered for sideslipping. Then the engine buzzed feebly, and the aeroplane, almost settled down, gave two stalling kangaroo hops, and stood slowly and gently on its nose.

Tom turned off the petrol, switched off, and climbed out. What a fool he was! He had been considering himself quite a pilot lately, an old hand; and here he was, standing a bus upon its nose like any novice. Would he never learn to fly? Fortunately the machine didn't seem to be damaged very much. Possibly a truing up and a new prop would put it right. Mechanics came out and hauled it down, and, its tail on a trolly, they wheeled it to its hangar. The air-screw and engine cowling seemed to be all that was injured.

Mac, not in a good temper, demanded to know if he choked the engine.

'I don't think so. I'll try to find out.'

It was a wet, cold afternoon, Tom, anxious to justify himself, went over the engine with the sergeant fitter. It didn't seem to have been choked; and Tom was pretty sure he hadn't choked it. The ignition was all right, the petrol was flowing freely, the carburetter was clean and the jet was not blocked. But the sergeant said there was a trace of moisture in the jet.

'I reckon that's what did it, sir. Moisture in the jet.'

'Very likely. I ran into mist, and it was as full of moisture as a sponge. Look what's coming down from it now.'

'Yes, sir. You can depend on it, that's what caused it.'

This was, at any rate, a good enough official reason for the crash, quite sufficient to whitewash him. He had gone up to practise bombing and shooting, as a zealous pilot should, in spite of the rough weather; and the moisture in the low clouds and the strong wind had done the rest. Officially he was blameless. The aeroplane was in a worse state than it looked, as several spars in the right-hand main plane were broken or cracked, and it would have to be dismantled and sent away. This did not matter greatly as the squadron was up to strength in *materiel*, but it was as well to have a good and sufficient reason for a crash for the benefit of those purple majors at the base.

Nevertheless Tom went down to the mess for tea feeling dissatis-fied with himself: he ought to have made a better attempt at landing. If he had switched off as he landed, and so prevented that final splutter of the engine, he might have succeeded. He ought to have thought of the risk; he had had enough experience of the cussedness of things. It was a typical trick of circumstance, that blind nescient jester. He had once again made a fool of himself in the sight of men; nothing was more irritating and depressing to him. He, an experi-enced pilot, an old hand.

He became aware, from the talk that was going on, that dinner would be a binge. He had been so wrapped in his own affairs that he had missed hearing during the morning that Bulmer was posted to Home Establishment and Moss to another squadron as flight commander. Bulmer would not be leaving for a day or two, but Moss had to go to his new squadron that day, so a joint binge was to be held at once.

There would soon be nobody left in the squadron. Losing Bulmer, Moss, and probably Franklin was a mighty depletion. There was a chance that Franklin would get over his concussion or whatever it was, quickly, and return, but it was more likely that he would be sent home, as he had been out for six months. Tom found some satisfaction in the fact that his leave was put forward another two places. He felt he could do with it as soon as it came. He certainly had a cold. So had Burkett and Jones and a new fellow called Lewin, and they all looked as though they would be better in bed; but it seemed too silly to go to bed with a cold when there was a war on.

Williamson wanted to play bridge till dinner, and gathered in Seddon and Hudson and Tom. They played till seven in the mess as there was still no coal for private consumption, and then broke up to change for dinner. In the hut the fact that Smith had gone was more painfully felt. Tom, preoccupied with his own misadventure and damaged pride, had scarcely felt aware that Smith had been killed. Now his vacant corner with all his personal things awaiting his use and occupancy that would never come, reminded him poignantly of it. Smith's watch was still ticking away. He had two watches, a wrist watch that he wore, and a pocket watch that hung by his bed.

Tom and Seddon talked about their projected League. Seddon had made some progress and outlined an analysis he had thought out of some evils of money.

'You're a great man, Seddon,' said Tom: 'This is original thought. You are in advance of your time.'

Williamson had been listening with interest. 'If one may inquire,' he said, 'is this surprising scheme of yours something you've been at while I was away? I don't seem to have heard of this particular stunt before.'

'Yes. We thought of it one night at the Poisson d'Or, and we still think there's something in it,' Seddon replied.

'I can understand your thinking of it at the Poisson d'Or, but aren't you sober yet? I can see I ought not to go away and leave you two together with no one to look after you. You lead each other on.'

'Oh shut up, Bill,' said Tom. 'I know it sounds mad to a Philistine, but so does every new idea and a lot of old ones.'

'The trouble is that you lose all sense of reality,' Williamson continued inflexibly. 'You puff yourselves up with gas and float among the clouds. One of these times you'll get a bad puncture apiece and crash.'

'That's a rotten metaphor. How can you get a puncture among the clouds?'

'Oh well, your skins will burst in the reduced atmospheric pressure.'

'That's unscientific. Don't you see that . . .'

'Oh, all right. Have it your own way. What a quibbler you are, Tom. Go and get on with your whatever it is, and when you're broke and finished, I'll give you both a job on my farm as ploughmen. That'll teach you what's what.'

'Farm?'

'Yes. I've decided to farm after the war. In Wiltshire probably.'

'Do you know anything about farming?' Seddon asked.

'No, but I'll soon learn. It's a decent healthy life, and you're really doing something.'

'And when you've gone broke through not understanding your trade, we'll give you a job as office boy.'

Chadwick had provided a good meal, and had hired a French-woman to cook it, so that the veal was tender and tasty. There was Veuve Cliquot, and even the port was drinkable. Chadwick had his uses.

James presided, and when the King had been remembered he opened the speechmaking. He stood up wearing his usual expression of slight worry. However much Jimmy drank, it made no difference to that; even when he laughed, as he occasionally did, loudly and sophisticatedly, that fundamental expression showed through the rident surface. He only lost it when something was worrying him.

'Gentlemen,' he said, 'we are gathered together and getting tight for the dismal purpose — dismal for us, that is — of saying good-bye to two of our stoutest pilots (cheers). It isn't dismal for them. One is returning to the bosom of his native land and of all those fair ladies whose letters to him here have so swollen our mail. He goes covered with glory (cheers) and when he arrives at his destination I am sure there will be a large and — er — quarrelling crowd to meet him (cheers and laughter).

The other one has been given his well-earned promotion (cheers) — his well-earned promotion to the appointment of flight commander, a distinction which, we can certainly say, is only gained by men. I don't pretend to know what rank the appointment carries; in the Flying Corps flight commanders were *ex officio* captains; but now that we are *poissons d'Avril* — pardon my foul language — now that we are R.A.F. I expect flight commanders in scout squadrons will be called scoutmasters (prolonged laughter). They will carry poles, have bare knees, and stop the troops from swearing . . .'

The champagne and the eloquence of Jimmy, standing solemn and worried at the top of the table, had set them all rocking with laughter. Tom appreciated this sort of thing; there was some style about it; it wasn't like the ordinary horseplay and mess-smashing binge, though no doubt there would be some of that soon. That was all very well, but here was something better. But Jimmy wouldn't get much backing now that so many of the old nucleus had gone. Robinson was a loss, and Tommy. God, poor old Tommy: one of the best fellows on earth, and now . . . best not think about it. And Smith. He wasn't a Thomson, but he was one of those fundamentally decent fellows that gave one hope that the world wasn't so bad as it seemed . . . oh damn. And now Bully was going. He wasn't an orator, but he had presence; he was the sort of bloke that made a binge good by his mere catalystic presence.

'. . . and if our friends across the lines knew that part of our tears to-night,' Jimmy was saying, 'were for the departure of Bulmer to England, it would not be a dismal night for them. They would say "Ach Himmel, Richthofen dead was, but Bulmer gone home is," and they would start flying again.

'Bully's successor is posted to the squadron, and will presumably be with us in person very soon. I am going to make a suggestion which, for the benefit of B flight, I hope Bully will be patriotic enough to adopt. My suggestion, made earnestly and not unhopefully, is that he will give the new flight commander his historic watch . . .'

This inevitable allusion of course created an uproar that overwhelmed the speaker for two minutes; and then he turned his wit on Moss.

'. . . no one could more deserve the honour that is his. He certainly is one of the most enterprising scout pilots in France (cheers). Many of us here will remember his unrivalled exploit of shooting down simultaneously two Huns that were sitting on his tail (uproar).

'I have personally always had a particular regard for Moss. I remember his arrival long ago in the days before Cambrai, before the Huns knew they were beaten. This young pilot reported at the office, and asked me a lot of questions; I began to think he thought I was the man from Cook's. Among other things he said, "Is it right the mess here's rotten?" I replied "I am PMC. It's not for me to say". I admit I sought to abash him. I was not successful. He replied "Oh well, I'll soon find out" . . . ' (shouts and laughter).

'I'm sure you will all agree that I am not alone in my failure to abash Moss. The Huns certainly have failed, and I must say that on the contrary he has done a great deal, a very great deal, towards abashing them, and I know you all wish him great success in carrying on this good work. . . .'

In due time Bulmer got up to reply. He was slightly bald, blue-eyed, and ineffably benevolent. He didn't say much; he made the conventional remarks about his happy time with the squadron, and the wonderful support he had had. He congratulated Moss and he wished them all a safe return home. Then he sat down and was cheered as though he had delivered a splendid piece of eloquence; and in a way he had; he had somehow delivered himself.

Tom noticed that Bulmer wasn't so blotto as he usually was by speech-time. Perhaps he felt the sadness of farewell, and it sobered him a little. A man might feel regret at leaving hell if he left friends

248

there — no, there was no champagne in hell. Champagne bubbles flew upwards.

But Moss was rapturously tight. It was his hour of triumph, and he loved it. He stood leaning with both hands half clenched on the table, dark, aquiline, handsome, flushed, his words coming in gusts. He was a fine animal. Tom had always been slightly amused at him. One of his earliest memories of the squadron was Moss coming back from leave and holding forth on his bad luck. For the last few days of his leave his favourite mistress had not been in condition, and he had tried to desert her for a more useful if less desirable concubine, but she had made such a scene and shindy that he had had to swear to remain faithful; and, within limits, he had. The whole affair had upset him. Why the devil were women so unreasonable and clamorous?

He said the same sort of things that Bulmer had said, but more emphatically. Tom, unusually sensitive to-night, detected that it wasn't quite the same thing to the audience to be called fine fellows by Moss as by Bulmer.

He retorted on James by saying that he was sure he had always treated him with the respect due to a ground officer by a mere flying bloke. This stroke was applauded heartily, and he qualified it unnecessarily by saying that good old Jimmy had done his time in the trenches.

Finally, all he hoped was that the squadron he was going to was nearly as good as the one he was leaving.

He was cheered vigorously; no doubt he was a stout pilot and a nice enough fellow; but Tom thought that, whereas the applause for Bulmer had shown unclouded admiration and liking, there was a very faint trace of tolerance in that for Moss. But it was very faint; far too faint for Moss to notice; and Tom might have been mistaken.

They crowded into the ante-room and made a row. Forster came to the fore, being something of an acrobat. He walked about on his hands, crowing like a cock. He leapt wonderfully high, crossing his feet twice in the air. He squatted on his heels and kicked out first one leg then the other, like a Russian. Everyone tried to imitate him, and the scene became quite lunatic. Then he made queer rhythmic movements with his knees and feet that looked easy but were quite impossible when you tried them. James, who usually did some fooling of this sort at a binge, was quite outclassed. But the best turn was when Hudson played a Chopin waltz and Forster performed mock Pavlova stuff. The delight was so undeniable that Forster got Hudson to improvise something like Le Cygne, and floated and strutted and died so exquisitely extravagantly that the more drunk actually fell down with laughing.

Then Moss had to be off. He was assisted to his tender, vowing eternal friendship for everyone, and he vanished from their ken into the rainy night.

VIII

THE morning was fair. The wind had veered to the north-west and diminished to a slight breeze driving flocks of white clouds slowly across the sky. Tom felt a little better after last night's drinking, but his cold had not gone. It was his turn of duty as orderly dog for twenty-four hours from eight o'clock. This meant that he would have to censor the men's letters, which normally wasted the hour after breakfast, walk round the men's quarters twice ('any complaints?'), and sleep in the squadron office. Officially he would take the early parade at six o'clock next morning; actually he would, he hoped, be asleep then. Also he was liable to have to attend to anything that needed official attention if the right person to deal with it was not available, and he must not leave the aerodrome. The job was a necessary bore that was given as far as possible to new pilots before their fighting days, but as no one might be given the job more than once a week except by way of discipline, other pilots had to take an occasional turn. It did not carry any exemption from flying duty; a substitute had to be found while the orderly dog was up.

The flights were to go up in the order A, B, C at 9.30, 10.30 and 11.30 and there would be a squadron show after tea.

C flight, six strong, got off to time and met A flight coming in. Mac was in a pugnacious mood. He zig-zagged on and on into Hunland till they were twelve miles over. The clouds were becoming heavier as the day passed, and their golden stooks enabled Mac to hide frequently from Archie. There were no German scouts about, it seemed, and Mac was looking for two-seaters.

Tom was far from happy so far over the lines with the wind against their return. He did not trust the blank blue emptiness of the sky. Aeroplanes so quickly materialized out of nowhere. He shut one eye and put his thumb up against the sun. He twisted his neck to study the region behind his tail. He stared at the zenith, and watched the clouds suspiciously. It was a lovely noon; the sun overpoweringly brilliant in the southern height; the clear sky decorated here and there with wisps of alto-cirrus miles above; the splendid still masses of the clouds. But none of this was lovely for him; he was too far over Hunland. Yet the realization did break through his mind's surface-tension of anxiety, that to him, sharing the way of the wind, the clouds were the anchored platform of the universe, and the bowl of earth a floating fleeting thing, passing and changing.

They went on and on, searching the waste of sky; above, among, beneath the bright islands and peninsulas of cloud. He had never before thought of them as steady: always he had retained his earthy notion of their movement, movement. That was because his own condition of remaining aloft was one of unceasing motion; some time he would go up in a free balloon on a breezy day and see the immobile mountains of the dead-still air and watch the changing of the inconstant windy world.

This new way of vision had for him something of the quality of revelation; it performed a subtle slight transmutation of heaven and earth. Some meaning in the loveliness of the dazzling scene beat against the portals of his anxiety-barred mind. The indifferent splendour flamed around his path of destruction. It mattered nothing whether he killed or was killed. There was no ethic in nescient heaven: the amoral glory of young summer neither blessed nor cursed human conduct; it knew nothing of heroism or depravity. And beyond all this there was a deeper and more physical indefiniteness. It could not be said, this moves, that stays; so much lay in the beholding mind, so little in outward things. Could it ultimately be said, this kills, that is killed?

They were diving from the clouds. They had surprised two aeroplanes flying west over Carvin, apparently in company. They were two-seaters of the type known as LVG. Mac went straight down on one of them. Tom, on his left, was in position to attack the other, and he veered to get it in his Aldis. He opened fire and the observer replied. He found himself in the unenviable position of fighting a two-seater single-handed, as all the others had followed Mac. The observer was doing some good shooting, and Tom had to sideslip away. He dived, still sideslipping, for position under the LVG's tail. The pilot saw him, and turned steeply to keep him in the observer's field of fire. He could out-fly the two-seater, but it was extremely difficult to do so with the observer's tracer coming so near. He had to sideslip and twist so much that he could not make effective reply, but he fired whenever his nose was pointing near the enemy, to put the wind up the pilot. After one of these bursts the LVG reversed bank as quickly as it could and in doing so put Tom in the observer's blind spot, and he was able to fire a more dangerous burst, and this was more than the pilot could stand. He put his nose down to dive away. At the same moment two other Camels came up and fired, and all four aeroplanes went careering earthwards. But the LVG was hit vitally. Smoke poured from it, and it hit the earth a blazing pyre.

The victorious Camels climbed away in the direction of La Bassée. The other LVG must also have been shot down. Tom felt he had done good work in holding one of them until reinforcements came to him in his lonely battle. He was still shivery with the excitement of it. He had dived on a two-seater alone and survived; he had not intended to; Dubois and Baker should have followed him, as they were in position to do so; leaving Miller and Cross with Mac. God, it was exciting, this aerial combat; the flash of tracers, the cracking of guns; the dread of being hit, of hideous fiery death. Every movement of stick and rudder had to be right or lucky; it was flying in horrible earnestness. And the sight of that wretched LVG plunging and burning filled him with horror and ghastly triumph. It stirred some primal lust of murder at the same time as his mind abhorred it. Poor devils, said pity: you have killed them, you are the strong cunning man, said unreason, the hero bathed in the blood of enemies. O God, what was he, man or beast?

It was past one o'clock. Someone else would have to do his tour of the men's quarters. Archie burst right in front of him, and he flew through the smoke. They turned for home, and landed at half past one. Mac had something to say about the fight. It didn't take five Camels to tackle one two-seater. Why the hell hadn't the other fellows on the left gone after the second one? If Cundall hadn't held him, the bastard might have got away.

Tom felt that this was praise, and praise from Mac was worth having.

The next job was timed for 4.30, and after lunch Tom went to the hut to have an hour's nap. But he was restless. The chill, or whatever he had caught, made him feel queer and slightly shivery. The queerness seemed rather of excitement than of illness. The world was unusually vivid to him. The morning's job presented itself in clear visual detail to his memory. He wanted to forget, to think of peaceful things, but his imagination was not under control. He was glad to go to tea at four o'clock.

The 4.30 patrol was a squadron show of three machines per flight. Bulmer's successor, a naval man named Large, had arrived. Bulmer would be going in the morning. Although officially off the strength of the squadron he wanted to have a last look at Hunland. It was a fighting patrol that went out. Forster, Seddon, and Maitland of A flight; Bulmer, Williamson, and Hudson of B flight; Mac, Miller, and Cundall of C flight; all experienced men. They went in layers, A underneath, B in the middle, C on top.

They went straight over, miles over. If there were any Huns about they were going to find them. Archie bombarded furiously, but a group of three was very mobile, and they dodged him easily. Tom and Miller understood each other very well, and when Mac turned sharply, if Tom was on the inside he dived under him and came up on the other side, while Miller flew across the chord of the arc to where Tom had been; and vice versa; it was quite good fun. Tom was shivering with excitement.

There were Huns about, lots of them. But they were too far over even for this aggressive patrol. The Huns must have seen them, for Archie was sending up a lot of stuff. The two forces flew up and down opposite each other, trying to lure each other farther east or farther west.

After a long time some of the Huns drew nearer. Tom felt in his belly that there was going to be a fight. His tail was exposed to all the sky as no one was flying behind him; he watched minutely for Huns. A half dozen Pfalz scouts came over above them. They circled and climbed, and the Pfalz circled above them. A and B climbed up to them. The Huns would not attack so many Camels except by surprise. They cleared off east, and the business of marching and countermarching began again. Tom watched and watched his tail. The sun was westerly, so there was no danger of surprise from out of its dazzle.

The other flights had gone down again, and more Pfalz, nine of them this time, came over just on top of them, and again they splitarsed about waiting for attack. Suddenly and surprisingly Mac disappeared. He had gone down vertically. Tom and Miller fell after him. There was another lot of Huns on top of B flight, and Mac took the opportunity of dropping out of the sun at them. At the same time the Huns attacked B, and the Pfalz on top came down on all of them, while A flight climbed to the scrap. Mac got an Albatros in a spin at once. Tom fired at another, but did not get it, and had to dodge a Pfalz that was diving at him; he was not so keen to get a Hun as to neglect to watch his own tail. Some of the Pfalz dived and zoomed, but others came down and were involved in a dogfight. For a minute there was a mix-up, a proper dogfight with everyone firing at everyone and as much danger from collision as anything else. Then the fight quickly spread out. A flight had climbed to it and made the odds better. There were about fifteen Huns, Albatros and Pfalz. Tom caught a glimpse of another one going down. He shot at several and sideslipped away from several dangerous rat-tat-tats. Then he got to circling in earnest with a Pfalz, and no interruptions. Round and round and round they went. He could turn better than the Pfalz, and felt he was winning the duel. After its tail, round and round. It straightened and he fired but it immelmanned away. He went after it, but it dived away all out. He got it in his Aldis and fired, but it went away too fast for him, and he gave up a chase that would take him miles and miles east.

He pulled up and looked round. No one was in sight. There were

two black vertical streaks in the sky; two had gone down in flames·
He climbed westwards. Then Archie opened fire, blackening the
sky in front of him. Archie was fond of going for single machines.
He didn't give a damn about Archie; in fact it helped him, for he
saw other clouds of its bursts in the distance, and flew towards one
of them, and soon saw two Camels which he went and joined. They
were Forster and Maitland.

With the help of Archie six of them came together, one missing
from each flight. They wandered up and down the lines for Archie
to shoot at, and after half an hour went home.

When they had landed, they gathered in an eager group to discuss
the fight. Miller was there; he had gone straight home with his
engine missing. Someone had gone down in flames. It must be
Seddon. Bulmer was certain he had seen Williamson later, but what
had become of him nobody knew. Yes, it must be Seddon.

It emerged from the discussion that at least five Huns had been
shot down; one in flames. The flamer was Miller's; he was elated
about it. Mac had got one, and was annoyed because his guns had
jammed when he was likely to have got another. Bulmer had secured
his thirtieth victim. Poor Seddon had got one, and it was possible
that Williamson had also; or a Hun might have got him. He was
fighting when last seen. Forster had seen whoever it was go in flames;
he was too far away to know it was Seddon. If it was Seddon he had
just got a Hun, and another one had attacked him when he was
probably looking after his own victim, and it had got him. It was a
great pity about Seddon, who had just become deputy leader of A
flight and was doing well. And about Williamson if he also had gone
west. They had lost one, or perhaps two, of their most promising
men for five or six Huns. It wasn't quite good enough.

Tom reported at the office, and then went to his hut, which now
he had to himself. Williamson would probably turn up later. He
couldn't get used to the idea that Seddon was gone. They had so
much to discuss. Surely to God he would come in soon and curse
the war and they would talk about their wonderful scheme.

There was a knock at the door. It was the orderly sergeant looking
for him. He put on his Sam Browne and cap and shook himself into
shape and went to the men's messroom. There wasn't much occasion

to worry about Bill yet; very likely he had had a forced landing somewhere.

'Orderly officer. Shun!' The noise ceased. Tom walked round. Seddon was just charred and bloody garbage; get used to the idea. There were no complaints. Every one of his friends got killed. Surely Bill would come back. He couldn't face the idea that they had both gone.

He changed for dinner. His cold was getting worse. He felt rotten. Smith, Seddon, Williamson . . . He hurried to get out of the intolerable hut. He drank some whisky and sat down to dinner, but couldn't eat. People saw he was upset and left him alone. The sun set in a watery haze: no word came from Williamson.

After dinner he sat in the ante-room looking at a book. Then he got up and went to the office, where, as orderly officer, possibly it was his duty to be. He might hear Bill's voice on the telephone. The orderly corporal was there. He sat waiting for the telephone bell. He waited and waited. It was half past nine; if Bill was all right he ought to have got through by now. The bell rang . . . hullo . . . the Wing adjutant wanted Captain James. The corporal went to fetch him.

James talked business with Wing. 'You know we got five Huns this evening? . . . One man down in flames, one missing . . . not a bad show, but we've lost two of our best men. . . .'

Tom got sick of waiting for the telephone and walked aimlessly towards the mess. He saw a light in the hut; who was there? Of course, the batman. He went in. The batman was making a bundle of his bedding to take up to the office. Tom sat down on Williamson's bed.

'Dreadful thing about Lieutenant Seddon, sir.'

'Yes.'

'And 'im married and got a fam'ly. Dreadful thing. I 'ope no 'arm's come to Lieutenant Williamson. There's nothing 'eard of 'im yet, is there sir?'

'Nothing at all.'

'Don't look promising, do it, sir? And what with Lieutenant Smith being killed yesterday this 'ut fair gives me the creeps. If I was you sir, I'd be glad I was sleepin' in the orfice to-night.'

The batman went with Tom's bed and bedding and came back after a few minutes.

'Bed's all ready, sir. Anything else to-night?'

'Nothing thanks. Good night.'

'Good night, sir.'

Tom got up to go. Where to? He sat down on his chair. The hut was haunted. There were faint echoes of dead voices. Smith's watch was still going. Who had wound it up? Surely the others would soon be coming in for the night. No, he must accept the fact that they had gone . . . for ever. He must face that knowledge. He wouldn't have any more friends. He must be self-sufficient. Friends went, all of them, and he couldn't bear losing any more.

The light of his lamp showed dimly the three empty beds, the three ownerless washbowls and chairs, the shaving tackle and other personal stuff. The social table stood in the middle, covered with the green tablecloth that had been their joint property. The dull light peopled the hut with shadows, grotesque caricatures that bore scarcely any resemblance to the objects that cast them. They were a society of ghosts immobilized by his human presence, waiting to crowd into deep penumbra for some damnable purpose. As long as he watched they were harmless. But he couldn't watch them all. Some behind his back flitted . . . what the devil was he thinking? But there seemed to be a congregation of shadows in Seddon's corner. God! He sprang to his feet. He had seen Seddon sitting on his bed. He was going mad. But no, he had known all the time it was pure illusion. He was sane enough. Overwrought. But it had seemed real. Had Seddon really gone down in flames? Was there no possibility of a mistake? It might have been another Hun. Forster might have made a mistake. Impossible. Seddon was dead. Yet there was just a chance in a million . . . 'Oh, Seddon, for God's sake come back,' he said aloud. The door opened. His flesh crept. Someone came in. The door slammed. It was Williamson.

'Bill! my God, Bill, is it really you?' He felt weak and sat down.

'Of course it's me. Don't I look like it?' He'd been drinking.

'Thank God. Thank God to see you.'

Williamson walked across the hut, bumping the table as he came. 'Damned nice of you. Think I'd gone west?'

Tom nodded.

'Not me. Though it might have turned out worse.' He flopped down on his bed. 'I'll tell you. You know all about the dogfight, of course. Well, I found myself scrapping with a Pfalz and an Albatros. I didn't care a damn about the old Pfalz of course, and I went for the other fellow. I got right bang on his tail. I could see him looking round at me. I could see I shot him, for he went flop suddenly and down he spun. Then the Pfalz got in an angle shot at me that wasn't so bad. I don't know what he hit, but oil started flying about. It got on my goggles and I couldn't see what the hell I was doing. I was so flustered that I got into a spin. I got out all right and the old Pfalz hadn't followed me down, bloody fool. I'd have been cold meat. I could make out where the sun was, and flew west. I couldn't take my goggles off of course. I kept wiping first one side and then the other with my handkerchief. Even Archie for some reason didn't bother me. Damn funny that. Just the one time when he might have been a bit of a nuisance.

'After a bit the engine began to sound wrong. It was getting hot. That did put the wind up me. I was shouting away at it "Go on, go on, go on, you ———" and it heard me and bloody-well did go on. I began to think I should get home if I could see my way, but suddenly it stopped with a click. Seized right up. I pushed up my goggles, and you can imagine my relief when I saw I was well over our side. In fact I was up by Houdain, only a dozen miles away. I came down on rough ground and stood on my nose. I was right alongside a farm, and a couple of fellows came dashing up to me before I could climb out. And what the hell d'you think? One of them was Barraclough. Of course you don't know Barraclough. I hadn't seen him since I left school, but he was just the same. He was always called Spotty, so I sang out "Hullo Spotty! Fancy running into you!" He was a bit startled at this, and wanted to know who the devil I was. I got up on the centre-section and jumped. "Don't you recognize me?" I said.

' "Of course not," he said. "I wouldn't be able to recognize you if you were my favourite aunt in that flying hat and your face all over oil."

'So I took my helmet off and wiped my face a bit, and he soon knew me. Just then I noticed he had crowns on his shoulders and a row of ribbons a foot long, so I thought I'd better call him Barraclough, anyway in public. The bloke with him was just a bloody lieut., and he was looking a bit amused about something. God, fancy old Spotty a blasted major, D.S.O., M.C. and bar, Croix de Guerre with cabbage leaf, and God knows what all. I always liked him, but he was a bit of a silly ass at school.

'However, there it was. And old Spotty was all right. He greeted me like a long lost brother and dragged me off to his mess in the farmhouse, filled me with juice, cleaned my face and we had a damned good jaw about old times. He's a stout fellow. Wouldn't hear a word when I tried to congratulate him. Said every show he was in, practically everyone else was knocked out, and there was no one else to take the rations. The Pomme de Terre was the only thing he'd earned — protecting a station-master's wife, he said.

'Then I had dinner with them. They were resting after a hectic time in the line. They'd been in support at Fleurbaix on the British right flank next to the Portugoose when the big break-through came. Jerry put over the most marvellous bombardment. There wasn't a headquarters or a dump within range that he didn't know all about. Then they saw grey uniforms come running out of the mist and turned the Lewis guns on them. And when they saw it was the Portugoose running they didn't stop firing. Then Jerry came through. They started retreating at Fleurbaix and finished up at Hazebrouck five days later — at least, a few of them did. And, by the way, they're quite sure no one had the least idea of a push coming there. Jerry caught us properly.

'After we had yarned away some time, they produced a car and ran me here, and here I am. I didn't telephone as the understanding all along was that they would send me back, and I didn't expect to be so late, but you know what it is once you start yarning. I hope to God they'll guard the aeroplane. I forgot to mention it to them. It isn't worth much, but someone's bound to help himself to the watch if there's no guard, and you know what a hell of a fuss that means. You can crash a dozen aeroplanes and very likely no one says a word, but lose a watch and G.S.O.s shed tunic buttons about it.'

'Well,' said Tom, 'that's all right. I suppose you haven't reported or anything yet?'

'No, I came straight in here. I'll show myself in the mess.'

'Then you don't know Seddon went down in flames.'

'No. By God, did he? Oh hell, I'm sorry to hear that. Old Seddon. No wonder you were looking blue when I came in. Here, I've got some ammunition.' He undid his sidcot and fished two bottles of whisky from his pockets. 'Got a corkscrew?'

''Fraid I haven't.'

'Never mind.' He held the lower part of the neck of a bottle in a gloved hand, and smashed the top off with the heel of a boot used as a hammer.

'Where's your tooth mug?'

Tom held it out and Williamson filled it with whisky. 'That'll do you good. Mind there's no broken glass in it.' He poured out some for himself.

'Well, here's to you. May you always come back.' Tom swallowed a mouthful of neat whisky.

'And you.'

They drank and talked and talked and drank. Williamson was already a third tight, and he made Tom drink the larger share of whisky. They talked about Seddon.

'What a hell's that idea you two prishlesh idiots had 'bout shome damn league bizhness?'

'Oh God knows. Shome bloody rot I shpozh. But we'd ha' done it. By God we'd ha' done it if the bloody fool had had the shensh t'look after his tail. Sheddon you damned idiot, wherever you are, why t'hell didn't you look after your tail?'

'Shut up you fool. Don't shout. You're batchy. Hold out your mug 'f you can.'

''Member how he upshet thozhe ole women in Avesnes by shaying *tu* to the girl?'

They laughed about it, laughed drunkenly and long. Someone, hearing the noise, opened the door and looked in.

'Holy Christ, here's Williamson back, tight as ———' called a Canadian voice. People began to come in. Williamson was telling his yarn. Shouts of laughter. Tom sat drinking himself dead to the

world. There was a crowd. What was it all about? He . . . he . . .
didn't know. Didn't want to know . . . Someone killed . . . Bill.
No, there was Bill. Someone dead . . . didn't know. What was the
crowd about? A voice penetrated his coma. 'Don't forget you're
orderly dog, Cundall.'

Yes, orderly dog . . . office . . . get there. He got to his feet.
The hut was all wrong . . . it hit him. He tried to get up. Hands
helped him. He was clinging to Bill. Bill was clinging to him.
They were outside. A lot of people were laughing. Damn funny.
He laughed. He was on the ground. He swore. He couldn't walk.
His feet got tangled. Bill was as bad. They were rolling in a ditch.
Hell. The world was spinning. Couldn't get out. Sleep there.
Then he was in bed, alone. The pillow was sinking, sinking down
endlessly. He opened his eyes. A face was looking at him. He had
seen it before . . . ugly . . . who the hell . . . don't know you. . . .

I X

TOM opened his eyes in the morning light. Where was he? What had
happened? There was a large-scale map pinned to the wall. It had
reddish marks on it. He drowsed. Blood. Blood on the map. Blood.
What had happened? He'd murdered someone. He'd seen a face
he didn't like and murdered someone.

He came to some time later. There was someone there. He sat
up.

'Good morning, sir,' said the orderly corporal. Tom looked at
him. That was the face.

'My God, you're alive. I thought I'd murdered you.'

The corporal looked startled, and then smiled. 'I think you must
have been dreaming, sir.'

'What are those red stains on the map?'

The corporal looked and then pointed. 'Those ones?'

'Yes.'

'They're just some dirt. I'd call them brown, sir.'

'So they are. Look, corporal, I was tight last night.'

'Yes, sir.'

'Anything happened during the night?'

'Nothing at all, sir.'

'Good. What's the time?'

'Twenty to eight, sir, and it's raining.'

'I wish you'd find my batman for me and tell him to bring me a gallon of drinking water and my Eno's.'

The office was supposed to be clear of the orderly officer's gear by seven o'clock, so having drunk much water Tom put on some clothes and went to the hut, leaving the place clear for the batman to get straight. His head was aching and still swimming, but he hadn't mixed drinks and didn't feel really ill. He found Williamson in a bad way, his mouth a kiln and his head one throb. He got him to take a dose of aspirin and left him to doze. His foot kicked an empty broken-necked whisky bottle.

Tom took a long time over toilet, but arrived in the mess for breakfast, or rather for a drink of tea, before anyone else was about. He didn't want anything to eat, but drank four cups of tea. Whisky was nourishing stuff. No need to eat breakfast after drinking the distilled essence of an acre of barley. He could still drink himself insensible pretty quickly, thank God. There was always that way out. The real horror of living would come when he reached the stage of being able to pour whisky down his gullet without its having any effect except to ulcerate his stomach and calcify his liver.

It was May-day and raining steadily. His nose was blocked up on one side. He would never again believe in the whisky cure for a cold. There was no known cure once the damned thing had got hold of you. Humanity was a thousand times better at finding ways of killing than of curing. His neck was still sore with all yesterday's twisting to watch his tail. He ought to have vaselined it last night. There was nothing whatever to do; there was nothing he wanted to do. The last fumes of intoxication began to fade from his mind, and time and the grey world engulfed him like a cloud. What on earth did people do that was worth doing? He picked up *La Vie*. They fought, they consumed food and drink, they slept; but these occupations left blanks, as this one, when life was blankly intolerable. A houri leered at him from *La Vie*. There was one thing missing from this war — rape. The soldier's lot was harder than it used to be: more fighting and no rape.

Rape . . . love between men and women was unknown to nature; sex was a fight in which women were the chattels of the strong men; and how happy they must have been; how they must have enjoyed sudden fierce changes of ownership. When police had stopped fighting and raping in the interests of that disease, commercial civilization, and priests had inculcated a commercial code of morals, young men and women, their natural instincts thwarted, prim and lying, began to imagine they loved each other; a respectable, cowardly, slimy, hypocritical passion suitable for a society of the same qualities. And when their instincts were still further thwarted during the lugubrious progress of this sham passion, they took to religion, drink, vice, suicide.

His head was getting more and more clotted. And this was the sort of fighting civilization led to: unrewarded butchery. And the sort of rape, the twenty-franc prostitutes of the licensed house or the twenty-centime drabs of the ditch. This miserable substitution was the achievement of Christian civilization and morality. In this Devil's Smithfield fellows like Seddon were burnt to death for their faith in themselves.

Tom jumped up and banged *La Vie* on the table . . . and then sat down again. It was no use raging. He must keep hold of himself. He was like a midge caught in a spider's web. It was no use flapping and squirming; he was stuck there: and when the gorged spider had room in her swollen maw, would have his juice. Or might disdain him and shake him, damaged, from the web.

In the afternoon, with Williamson, he packed Smith's remains. They put out his cigarettes and toilet stuff for the batman to dispose of, and burnt a lot of correspondence. There was nothing harmful in it as far as they looked, but you never knew. His watch was a good one, and it wouldn't do to pack it: someone at the base would find it. So they hung it up as the hut timepiece. Tom would take it with him on leave and post it to Smith's wife. The rest of his stuff would have to take its chance.

There was some rejoicing during the afternoon at Franklin's return from hospital. A day in bed had put him right, and he was too noisy to remain at a Casualty Clearing Station when he was feeling well. He was transferred to A flight as deputy leader, and so William-son kept his streamer. Williamson was pleased with his new flight commander, Large. He was R.N.A.S. but he was good. He had some new funny stories, and seemed to have flown every sort of aeroplane that had ever left the ground. He had certain information that Camels would be washed out in favour of Snipes within two months.

Franklin's return made a week's difference to Tom's leave, as he was next on the list and would be off in three days' time. Then, a week later, on the major's return, Miller would go. As it was im-possible for both Miller and himself to be away at the same time, since that would leave C flight without anyone of sufficient experience to act as deputy leader, he would have to wait till Miller's return, which would be on the twenty-sixth or seventh of the month. Almost four weeks to wait; it was an age. Leave was always like that, elusive, and the nearer it approached the more slowly time passed. And he had resolved to put it back still further by changing with Seddon. He was released from that.

But Seddon had not gone yet. He was still somewhere about the place. At any moment his voice might ring out, 'I say, Tom . . .' or he would walk into the mess, or Tom would find him in the hut and say, 'My God, Seddon, I've been dreaming you were dead' and the day would brighten and his heart beat in its old rhythm. And Seddon would laugh and say, 'Not yet', and they would talk. How splendid it would be to talk to Seddon again. Splendid now that it was impossible, and he was utterly gone, swallowed in the ocean of no-being. Was there anything in those queer fancies or inspira-tions that sometimes visited him that death was an illusion? Those queer notions that came to him sometimes when he was flying . . . produced, no doubt, by the fantastic airyness of the skies and the excitement of battle.

He must get used to the fact that Seddon had gone for ever, and nothing of him remained. But it was hardly possible yet; Seddon was still almost present to him. Oh for a last talk with him, if only to say good-bye for ever and ever . . . no, it was better as it was, that he should go, if he must, suddenly, unknowingly. He had been something; he was nothing; it did not matter to him. It mattered to a few of those that were still something; but their time was quickly passing, and soon the utter blank of forgetting would destroy the very fact that he had ever lived. Indeed, who was he? Identity lived in names and in other people's perception of it. These gone, the dead was no more one person than another; he was merged in indeterminate community.

The next morning Tom and Williamson cleared up Seddon's effects. When they opened his kit-bag they found on top of everything an envelope addressed to Cundall and/or Williamson. It contained a letter and a sealed envelope marked *For my wife if I am killed*. The letter was dated March 22nd, 1918.

'Dear Tom and Bill,
'If you read this it will be when I am wounded, missing or dead. If you know for certain I am dead, please send the enclosed letter to my wife, and I should like you to let her know any particulars you can of my death. If I am a flamer, don't say that, say shot down and killed.
'If there is any doubt about my death, please burn the letter to my wife.
'Burn all correspondence, especially a bundle of letters and papers tied up with a bootlace. Please be certain of this. Put it as it is on a hot fire, if you can. If I am wounded will you please keep the bundle if you can till I write to you. If you can't, then burn it.
'I would like you to keep something in memory of me. There is nothing very valuable among my stuff. Have my silver cigarette case and my fountain pen or anything else you like.
'If I am alive when you read this, au revoir. If I am dead, good-bye, and may you both be more fortunate. If there has been any bright spot for me in this war, it has been living with you two blokes.
                                                                    'P. B. SEDDON.'

They found the bundle of papers tied up with a bootlace, and put it in the stove with a lot more correspondence. They found the cigarette case, but not the fountain pen.
'You have the cigarette case. He was more your friend than mine,' said Williamson.

Tom shook his head.

'Of course he was. You'd even arranged some sort of partnership.'

'Well, what will you have?'

Williamson considered. Then he said: 'I'll have that new razor of his. It's not a very orthodox memorial, but it'll certainly keep him in daily memory, and be much more useful than that case which you'll never use.'

They closed the kit-bag. Tom went and sat on his bed with his head between his hands. Williamson rolled up and strapped the valise. 'Well, that's done. I've had the job often enough, and I thought I was quite hardened, but I must say I haven't liked it this time.'

Tom did not reply for a minute. Then he burst out: 'It isn't only losing Seddon as a friend, but it's such a bloody waste. He was a man in a million. He had little opportunity, caged in a bank. The war brought him out, gave him courage to think, and now . . . And look at the way Smith's life was thrown away.'

'Yes, I know. Authority always lets you down sooner or later. But the personal grief at losing a friend is bad enough. Don't, for your own sake, mix up other things with it. You'll only make yourself mad and do no good.'

'But I can't help seeing these other things that are so obvious . . .'

'But don't upset yourself about them; it's no good. You have to take things as they are. People who can't stand it say that heaven will put everything right. You don't do that, so you must face things as they come, and not shout about them.'

'Things will never get any better if no one shouts.'

'That's different. Raging and getting upset don't do any good. If you want to make things better, you must store up your energy and direct it into action at the right time, not dissipate it by shouting as each emotion comes along.'

Tom weighed this before he spoke. 'You're right, Bill. You're squarely and solidly right. I must seem pretty feeble sometimes. I wish I had your good sense.'

'Oh —. There's something about you that inspires me to preach sermons. God knows why. I wish you'd stop it, whatever it is.'

'No. They're the only ones I've ever heard that are worth listening to.'

'Anyway, I can tell you're feeling bad, because you've agreed with me without arguing for an hour.'

They went for a walk, and came to Izel, where they had coffee and cognac at the little estaminet. People were flying around for practice or amusement, but there were no jobs. The sky was covered by a light grey blanket of cloud, weather which effectively prevented patrols without being unpleasant.'

'D'you remember the last time we came here with Allen?'

'Yes, centuries ago,' Tom replied. 'In February or March wasn't it? It's a different world.'

Madame and mademoiselle remembered them, and were surprised they were still alive. Everyone had been killed in the push. Was the monsieur who was had been with them before also living?

'Mais oui. Il est blessé, mais it fait bon progrès. Il est en Angleterre et bien heureux, ou il l'était il-y-a deux semaines quand il nous écrivait.'

Mademoiselle was interested and wanted to hear all about him.

'D'you remember those two gunners who told us how they were going to shoot up the advance?' Tom said on the way back.

'Oh yes. I bet they had to leave their guns and run for it. They reckoned without the fog. Anyhow, that's over, and we're still alive. That's something to be thankful for. It must have been the biggest. . . .'

'Hell,' Tom interrupted, 'for God's sake talk about something else. I'm fed up beyond anything that ever was with this bloody war. I never want to say another word about it. Let's talk about books, women, religion, any damn thing.'

'Oh, all right. Did I ever tell you the one about. . . .'

X

Tom felt quite ill with his cold. Several others were similarly troubled. Jones, the horse-like Canadian, had become feverish and had gone into hospital. There were no jobs that day. After tea a new pilot named Bruce arrived and moved into Seddon's corner, which he preferred to Smith's on account of the comparative longevity of its previous occupier. He was quite a youngster and wore the new uniform. Tom thought he was a poor enough substitute for Seddon. He was a nice looking lad but that was all.

'Have you been in any dogfights lately?' he asked Tom and Williamson, anxious to know all about this new world and to air his knowledge of the overseas slang term, dogfight.

'Sh! We never speak of the war in this hut, do we Tom?'

'No. Damn the war. You'll have enough of it.'

'Oh,' said Bruce, and kept quiet. But Tom, not wanting the boy to feel snubbed, asked him about himself, where he had trained, how long he had done on Camels, and so on.

The weather continued too dud for jobs until the afternoon of the next day, when the cloud-blanket was broken up by a westerly breeze and drifted in misty masses. Tom had been up in the morning in the hope of clearing his head a little. Thorpe, one of the more recent additions to A flight, had gone to hospital, and Tom felt that he might have to do likewise. It was something more than an ordinary cold; it was 'flu.

A patrol of three from each flight went up at five o'clock. Mac took Tom and Cross. It was difficult to keep together owing to the foggy clouds, of which there were irregular layers up to nine thousand feet. Mac made little attempt to keep with the other flights, and they went creeping among the fogs looking for two-seaters.

But the first thing they found was an Albatros scout, conveniently five hundred feet below them. It was most extraordinary how lucky Mac was at surprising Huns. It was impossible that he should have had any idea of the presence of the Albatros before they came into a clear space right over it. It seemed to be alone, and it was very unusual then-a-days for a German scout to be alone within a few miles of the lines. Perhaps he was attempting a balloon raid, trusting to the cover of the clouds. Or perhaps he was lost.

Mac dived on him at once. The Albatros saw him coming and turned, and there was a duel. Tom remained above in case more Huns appeared; it was probable that the rest of the formation, if there was one, was not far away. But none came.

The duel was quickly over. Mac got on the Hun's tail at once, and fired a burst that sent him down in a vertical dive. He disappeared in a cloud after some two thousand feet, but he was going too fast ever to pull out.

Later they found a two-seater. This time Tom went down with Mac. The pilot turned away, but only succeeded in making it difficult for his observer to take aim. The Camels followed easily and riddled him. The aeroplane flopped over, one of its wings broke away from the fuselage, and it went down in a jerking fall. They followed to see it crash.

Nothing else happened. Archie shot at them when he could see them, but was not accurate enough to be interesting. In spite of all the murk in the air, the western light was pale yellow and lurid. The chaos of clouds was livid or gloomy as it was lit or shadowed; the earth underneath was yellow and scabrous, gashed with trenches, dark regular-twisting lines in lighter marges, maculae of disease, sometimes strongly marked, sometimes fading into the general ravage: earth and sky harmonious in desolation so hideous as to be flaunting.

They landed and reported their successful show. Cross was a little unhappy because he hadn't actually done damage to the Huns.

'Why worry?' Tom said to him. 'You're still alive, and that's the main thing, especially your first month over.'

An Australian named Watt moved into the fourth corner of the hut. He was tall and massive, with a great blue-shaven jowl. He and Bruce got on famously, having at some period of their careers been at Northolt together. Tom found them slanging each other heartily; Bruce had a wonderful flow of navvy's English. Watt was posted to B flight, Bruce to C flight.

Tom ate an ill-cooked and tasteless dinner, and talked to Grey, or rather Grey talked to him. He found that Grey, like nearly everyone, improved with more knowing, and wasn't unbearably pious-pompous, although his solemnity was so marked as to set him apart. He seemed to have a liking for Tom, and was in the habit of making serious slightly deferential remarks to him, which Tom, not prepossessed with his bearing, had not particularly noticed. He was tall and thin and grave, abstemious from drinking, correct in speech, and his face had the genteel drooping misery of a camel's. Tom would have placed him among the provincial dissenting clergy. Grey had noticed that Tom sometimes read what he called Good Books, and was anxious to discuss English Literature with an Educated Englishman; so few Englishmen, he found, were really interested in their heritage of Great Literature.

'I'm reading *Pendennis* at the moment,' Grey remarked.

Pendennis? Tom seemed to have heard the word before. Grey assisted his memory by naming Thackeray as a great portrayer of the English Upper Classes; as great as Dickens was of the Lower Classes. Would the present century produce any such Great Figures?

This was certainly a change from the ordinary conversation.

'A novel I very much enjoyed — I call it a novel although it is in verse — is *Aurora Leigh* . . .'

'Hell,' Tom interrupted. 'There's a letter I absolutely must get written, if you'll excuse me. I'd forgotten.' He sheltered behind pen and paper. It was flattering to be taken for an Educated Englishman by a wild man from the Orange River, but the duties were too heavy.

Soon he went to bed, and fell asleep while the hut was rattling with the concussion of gunfire. He dreamed a lot of unpleasant nonsense, in which Seddon was vividly but unwholesomely present. He had not been killed: he had escaped in some vague dream-way. He was changed. His face was scarred and puckered, and there was a gaping wound over his left eye. He was dressed in an old brown suit. Tom wished he hadn't come back; the dead shouldn't return. But he wasn't dead. They had packed all his things and sent the letter to his wife; why had he come back? There was nowhere for him to be. . . .

Tom woke up with the dream images still in his mind. He kept himself awake so that they might fade before he slept again, fearing to dream.

In the morning he had breakfast in bed and stayed there to lunch, it being his day off. There was no flying as it was raining. Williamson was there most of the time, absorbed in *Nostromo*. They exchanged occasional comments.

'Come to think of it, we're having a pretty easy time of it now. No dawn shows or ground-strafing to speak of, plenty of dud weather. . . .'

'And 'flu,' Tom added.

'Yes, that's a nuisance unless you're bad enough for hospital, but we're in luxury compared with a month ago.'

'Not in this hut,' Tom objected briefly.

'Now you're mixing one thing with another. In the way I mean, we are in luxury, comparatively.'

'Count your blessings one by one. I suppose I'm too fed up to value it. I'd like to get out of this hut. I wish we could have a hut for us two.'

'There aren't any. It's pretty comfortable here. Those two blokes seem harmless.'

'Oh I don't mind them. They're just patent digesters. The hut gives me the blues.'

'You'll get over that. It's the 'flu.'

There was a knock at the door. 'Come in,' they both shouted.

Grey's head came in and looked about, and then his diffident body.

'Good morning. Good morning, Cundall. I was given to understand you were in bed, so I though I would inquire. I hope you are not unwell.'

'No. Just lazy. Very kind of you. Sit down. Gasper?'

'I don't smoke thank you,' said Grey, folding himself carefully into Tom's chair. 'Not that I think it wrong! By no means. But I don't wish to form a habit to which I shall always be subject if, by not commencing, I can do quite well without it.'

'Oh quite, if you feel like that,' Tom replied.

Williamson, who had been lounging on his bed, sat up to look at Grey. Grey pulled a small book bound in blue leather from his pocket.

'I wondered if you would care to borrow this,' he said to Tom. 'I expect you know it, and I should be glad to have your opinion. I must admit that at present I can admire rather than enjoy it. I find the language and thought both very puzzling.'

'I'll be glad to borrow it,' Tom answered. 'We'll have a talk about it some time.'

Soon afterwards Grey arose to leave, apologizing for possible intrusion.

'My God, man, this isn't Buckingham Palace,' exclaimed Williamson. 'You don't have to talk sammy here.'

'Er — quite. Of course not, old fellow. But I don't feel very well acquainted with you yet. That is a privilege I hope for.' Grey smiled horribly and went.

'Whatever's the matter with him?' Williamson asked.

'He sounds as though he's sat too long alone in the wilds reading English Literature, especially Scott,' Tom guessed.

'He's probably a town-bred clerk. What's he lent you?'

Tom handed him the book.

'Were you being polite or are you going to read it?' asked Williamson when he had looked at the title.

'Read it, of course.'

'What foul taste you have.'

'Just because your mind is too soft to bite on anything harder than novels and romantic poetry. . . .'

'That's more like your style. You're feeling better.'

Tom got up to lunch. His head was a little clearer. Franklin had gone on leave. Another week and Miller would go; then a fortnight, and he would go. The rain left off, and he was able to go up for fresh air during the afternoon. The daily flight seemed almost a necessity. It blew away for a time the dull depression that clogged him on the ground. He tried to keep the thought of what was still pleasant steadily in mind. There was flying (non-duty flying, of course); there was being friendly with Williamson; that was about all. Everything else seemed shrouded in a fog of depression. If he could somehow last through the next three weeks, he would have a fortnight's leave. The only thing to do was to look forward resolutely to that; past the thirty odd jobs he might very likely have to do in the interim. Thirty jobs was probably a good deal more than the average lifetime. Perhaps it wouldn't be as many as thirty, but the weather must soon clear up for summer, and the long days would mean two jobs usually. Why didn't the damned war end? The German thrust had been brought to a standstill all along the line. Surely to God there wasn't anything else on that scale to come?

A squadron patrol of nine machines went up after tea. Grey

went with Mac and Miller to have his first look at the lines. Williamson led the B flight trio, with Large following, as he wanted to have a look round before taking over the leadership. When they came back after an hour-and-a-half's quite useless cloud-dodging, Large showed them what he could do. He looped off the ground and rolled with his wing-tip a few feet above the squadron office; he seemed to hate going above a hundred feet; every movement was smooth with expertness; and after showing them all what novices they were, he put his bus down almost in the hangar mouth with a pukka sideslip Gosport landing that reduced his forward speed to ten miles an hour, or so it looked. Tom wished he could fly like that. He knew he never would; *nascitur non fit*. Large must have been born like it. If Tom tried to loop a Camel off the ground, it would just be suicide. Yet there was no reason why one shouldn't gain height on a loop. He hadn't the nerve. He might practise on a cloud, though.

Tom felt that he wasn't brilliant or ever likely to be brilliant, either as pilot or fighter. He was a careful hack. By mere survival and accumulation of experience he was becoming a slightly useful hack; he could give a mite of the experienced support that the real fighters needed. He could follow Mac, and possibly Mac might feel that he'd someone behind him who need not be nursed and could fly well enough not to get in the way. He said something like this to Williamson.

'You may not be a brilliant fighter,' Williamson replied, 'but you're a damned lucky one. You get away with anything. You ought to have been killed about a dozen times over since I've known you. If your heart was in this war, you'd follow up your luck and do a lot.'

'My heart's certainly not in the war; but whose is? Take Tommy for example. He was brilliant, but you can hardly say his heart was in the war. No, I'm afraid my mediocrity lies in personal qualities and in my fear for my own skin. Not that I give a damn anyway.'

'One never runs oneself down except in the hope of being contradicted: translated out of the French. I won't disappoint you altogether. Tommy hadn't your detachment. He was a simpler character. Before making up your mind about yourself, wait till you find something to do that you'll throw yourself into bald-headed. It may be you're no good, but you don't know yet.'

'What the devil is there ever likely to be that I shall want to do?'

'Aren't you going to reform the world?'

'Damn the world. There's perhaps one thing I'd like to do. Have children. A dozen illegitimate children. And tell them the truth.'

'Will you keep them and their mothers all together in one house? Or will you be a millionaire, and run several different love nests?'

'Let them keep me.'

'Immoral earnings?'

'No. Charwomen.'

'Well, don't forget to find out what the truth is before you tell the children.'

'Oh shut up.'

The beef was like leather. It was probably horseflesh, anyway. There was some green stuff, but no potatoes. Bread was scarce, and dog-biscuits were offered. There were lashings of whisky. A sing-song developed. Large had quite a voice, and so had a new Welshman named Griffith, but he didn't know the songs. Things were thrown about, and the mess got a bit wrecked. Grey stood about looking puzzled, as though it was all literature to him. Tom felt he wanted to do something for him. He jumped off the table into collision with him, and waltzed him round. It was like embracing a telegraph pole. They sang about the parson and the other heroes of ribald romance. Tom went to bed nearly tight again, and woke in the morning with a thick head.

'All this drinking is getting me groggy,' he said to Williamson. 'Look at my hand. I'll have to cut it out.'

'That's nothing. Once I got so bad I saw spotted snakes crawling about my bus over Bapaume. One floated in the air in front of me, and I tried to shoot it down.'

'Liar.'

Rain was drumming on the roof, and the day was quite dud. The rain-soaked hours lingered and stared. There was no aim or meaning in life. Cards . . . that damned gramophone. Williamson had brought some records of Gilbert and Sullivan songs back with him. Once Tom had liked these ineffably English airs. Outside, Cross was making an opposition noise in his hut. 'In Happy Moments Day by Day'. Tom went up to the office to write up his log-book from the official records. He looked at some stuff labelled 'ıst Brigade, R.A.F. Summary of work. 4 p.m 3rd to 4 p.m. 4th May'. He was in it.

'. . . Later the same pilot (Captain MacAndrews) attacked another EA this time a two-seater, NW. of Harnes. He and Lt. Cundall fired many bursts into it. The right-hand planes were seen to fall off, and the EA crashed at Estevelles.'

The brigade claimed to have destroyed twelve Huns during that rather dud twenty-four hours. God, it must be rotten to be a Hun pilot. They were now being sent to the front, it was believed, with hardly any training, and their morale was gone to pot.

During the afternoon the wind increased to a gale, and blew the skies ragged and bare. There was some excitement when Griffith and Lewin, returning from Candas with new machines, had to land in the fierce wind. Lewin got down all right, but Griffith stood on his nose.

X I

BUT the morning was again overcast, and low clouds remained until the late afternoon. Tom went up before lunch for his usual fresh-air trip. His cold had almost gone. The clouds prevented his going above eight or nine hundred feet, so he contour-chased. He saw red hatbands in an open car, and made his habitual strafe. He stopped the car by meeting it head-on and pulling up off the radiator. The occupants looked scared.

After lunch he joined some fellows who were shooting on the range. They set a Very light with its base as the target, and if it was hit, it went off. It made a good mark at a hundred yards with a service rifle. They also used their automatic pistols, but the things kicked so much as to make one's hand shake, and they couldn't shoot anything like straight after the first two shots.

Then, after tea, the usual patrol of three machines from each flight went up. The sun had put on robes of glory; all the air was full of his splendour, and the vast clouds were his galleons of state. Amid this mighty fleet the aeroplanes soared and darted and dived like falcons among Andean slopes and precipices, as fell and significant in their minuteness as the magnificent clouds were unmeaning in their huge pomp. For an hour they hawked and hunted up and down the empty cloud-walled corridors. They climbed high into the cold vacancy above the top-gallants of the shining argosies. Strips and scalenes of the far-down earth, its bitter pallor filtered out by the gauze of air, showed dim and blue between the faintly misted edges of the clouds, which, cut sharp against the sky, yet showed a trace of unmarmoreal nature at their bases.

From sixteen thousand feet over La Bassée they saw two, three bursts of white Archie away in the north-west. Mac went down to them in a long dive. Tom, following, saw his pitot show a hundred and sixty, seventy, nearly eighty. His rev. counter went nearly to fifteen hundred. Mac would melt their engines. It didn't matter, they could glide across the lines. And they would get there first. The other flights, below them, could not make the pace. They crossed the lines. There was a Hun two-seater on their side, flying west. Tom had never seen such a thing before. The terrible excitement of it: the screaming wires and roaring engine: he pulled the gear handle fully to the top: the aeroplane blackish against the clouds, whose occupants had not seen them against the sky. At last down on to it, ahead of all the others. They were seen. The pilot turned sharply, the observer fired at Mac, streaks of phosphorous smoke showing his incendiary bullets. Mac went down and pulled up under his tail. Tom fired from above after Mac had started firing from below. Burst, burst, rattling burst. The observer shot at him. The aeroplane was huge in front of him, he must turn. He did, with pressure pressing him into the seat. The observer had crumpled. He lost sight of the Hun. There it was, spinning away, smoking. They'd got it, got it, Mac and he. In flames. Oh God, poor devils. They were shot. Hundreds of bullets. They did not know. Spinning and burning it disappeared. Other Camels had come up. A flight, B flight, some from another squadron. But Mac and he had got it. It wasn't the usual Albatros or LVG. The air seemed full of Camels that had seen Archie from afar.

They finished the patrol without more incident, and went home a quarter of an hour early. Mac was anxious to get home and claim the Hun, as another squadron had come up and might have taken a long shot at it. The occasion was unique, a Hun two-seater three or four miles west of the lines at twelve thousand feet. As a rule they only came so far over at about twenty thousand feet where nothing except Dolphins could chase them. It was one of the new DFWs — a nice looking, very splitarse bus. This was the first to be shot down in British lines. It had gone down just south-west of St. Venant. Forster had landed somewhere up there. He had glided away giving the dud engine signal by dipping and pulling up repeatedly.

'Come on, Cundall,' Mac said, when they had reported, 'we'll go and see if we can find the remains.'

There was still more than an hour's daylight. They went north and searched the ground in the region where the Hun went down, but all they found was Forster's Camel, which had made a good landing in a field near a village. Mac went down and landed by it. Tom flew round and round waiting for him, dived on some Tommies, ran his wheels along a road, and did some vertical turns with his wing-tip nearly in the grass. There was a lot of troops about, and a crowd collected to watch him. They scattered when he dived at them. They fled in all directions. He had great fun chasing them about, and then did some half rolls and slow rolls and side loops to amuse them. Still Mac did not take off, and at twenty to eight Tom waved good-bye to his crowd and made off home feeling pleased with himself.

He got home late for dinner, which, anyhow, was hardly worth eating. It was very different on earth. There was a dismal two hours before bed. He was sick to death of cards, he didn't feel like reading, and didn't want to get drunk. Hudson was allowed to play the piano for a little while. There was still excitement, exhilaration, oblivion to be found in the air, but on the ground there was depression, reaction from the over-excitement of fighting, and weariness. But the burden of fear that had nearly broken him a month ago had not returned, though the frightful strain of that time must have left some mark. The conditions of the pre-push period had returned, but not the atmosphere. The squadron was not so good; it only had ten experienced pilots instead of twenty, and they weren't such a wonderful crowd to live with. Nothing amusing seemed to happen; the war in the air used to have a funny side. The food seemed worse; the songs seemed stale unless he was tight.

He went to bed. God, how he hated to see young Bruce in Seddon's place . . . He would be better for some leave. Three weeks, almost. He'd fade away before then, or go mad. Then he couldn't get to sleep for raiders. There was a continual row of bombs and Archie and FEs The artillery was quiet, but it was a fine night for bombing.

It clouded over in the small hours, and there was peace, and when Tom woke up again rain was pattering on the roof. He got up late and lounged away the blank morning. Grey kept coming up to him as if he had something to say, and then he would make a futile remark about nothing. There was something wrong with Grey. If Tom answered him he did not attend. He was distracted. What was the trouble with the weird bloke? Had he got wind up after one look at the lines? It hardly seemed likely; Grey wasn't human enough to experience fear. At last he nerved himself to speak.

'May I speak to you confidentially, Cundall? I need advice.'

'If you think I can be of any use.'

'I'm afraid I'm — I'm being punished for wrong-doing.'

Mad, Tom thought.

'I knew it was wrong. It was against my convictions, but I was led away, and I knew I should probably never have another opportunity. It seemed hard to die without knowing what is often called life's supreme experience, though I realize now how disappointing it is when sinful.'

'What the devil are you talking about?' said Tom irritably. 'Do come to the point if there is one.' He wished the fool would find someone else to talk his nonsense to. It had no interest for him.

Grey blushed quite vividly. 'When I was in France — I mean London — before coming out to France, I — er — I . . .'

'Well, what did you do? Shoot an A.P.M.?'

'No, no, I committed — er — sexual wrong.'

'Oh. What exactly does that mean?'

'Surely you can understand?'

'If you're upset merely because you went with a woman, my advice is, don't be. I hope you enjoyed it.'

278

'But the consequences, Cundall, the consequences!' Grey's voice was agonized.

'Do you mean you've got a dose?' Tom looked at him with more curiosity. After all, he was a suffering fellow human.

'I'm afraid so.'

'Good God! You! Grey, I believe you're human after all.'

'If it's human to sin and be punished, I am.'

Tom was afraid Grey might burst into tears; he certainly was suffering. This sense of sin, Tom thought, that the religious make so much of, was no use for keeping a man out of trouble, it only made him miserable when he was in it; and that was what the religious liked to see.

'Look here, Grey,' he said impressively, 'I'll give you my advice since you ask for it, and that is first of all to dismiss the idea of sin and punishment. I assure you you're more sinned against than sinning. Treat it as a purely medical affair, and don't get wind up. Millions of people have been in your position before, and the trouble is easily curable if taken early. See the M.O. as soon as possible, and you'll be quite all right in a month or two.'

'Thank you, Cundall, thank you. You do indeed help me. I'll try to take your advice. How do I see the doctor?'

'He comes round every week at least. You'd better tell James you want to see him as soon as possible.'

'Yes, but — won't Captain James want to know what's the matter?'

'I dare say he'll ask you. So will Mac and other people. Say you feel queer. But you won't be able to keep it to yourself for ever, although you don't drink.'

'Thank you. I'll see James at once. I'm very grateful to you, Cundall. You have done me a lot of good.'

Later Grey told him the M.O. was to visit the squadron some time next day. Tom told Williamson about it.

'Don't say anything to anyone else yet, Bill, but Grey confided to me this morning — what do you think?'

'That he's lost his virginity.'

'Not a bad guess. He's got a dose.'

'Good Lord!' Williamson roared with laughter. Recovering, he said: 'and I suppose it was the one and only time he strayed?'

'So I gather.'

'He would. But I ask you can you imagine. . . .'

The sunset promised fair weather, and Tom went early to bed in expectation of an early job; C flight was to go up at six o'clock in the morning. But the job was washed out. The day was warm and pleasant, but there was a screen of misty clouds at about fifteen hundred feet. During the morning the warmth increased, and it was possible to sit comfortably outside the huts among the trees. There was at last an aestival quality in the air; behind the curtain of mist the sky was being garnished for the long festival of summer; which for them would be a festival of death, and the heavy glory of the sun would gild their enskied murderings.

Mac and Forster returned at midday, having obtained help from a northern aerodrome. They had found the remains of the DFW, which had come down in a wood. There wasn't much of it left after falling ten thousand feet in flames. One of the occupants had been an officer of the Prussian Guard. Mac had his Iron Cross.

After lunch all the Canadians set out for Izel, to the horse show and sports of one of the Canadian Divisions.

'Let's go and worry the Canadians instead of going to sleep,' Williamson suggested to Tom.

The took off and circled above the village. The Canadians were gathered in a field on the opposite side of the village to the aerodrome, against the village wood, and their athletes were running races. They dived and joined in a race, and jumped the wood and went back to do it again and perform a few stunts. The Canadians stopped their athletics and watched them. Tom dived on a group of brass-hats, charged the wood, and zoomed more or less straight up the side of it. At the top of his zoom his engine spluttered and stopped. He flattened out and got his nose down. He was just over the trees with no engine and very little speed. He stalled over the tops of a bunch of tall trees, put his nose down for speed and zoomed some more trees. This took practically all his flying speed, but he was at the edge of the wood. There was a sort of high brushwood hedge between him and open ground. He put his nose right down to regain flying speed, and pulled up a little, crashing through the top of the hedge, stalled completely and pancaked fifteen feet on to a track, hitting it with an enormous plonk that bounced him in a somersault, and he fell upside down.

He undid the safety belt and crawled from the wreckage as two mounted Canadian R.A.M.C. men dashed up, expecting to find a corpse. Tom shook himself. He was unhurt, but the aeroplane was shaken to pieces. He felt a perfect fool. A motor ambulance rolled up, followed by a huge crowd of Canadian troops. He certainly had provided a spectacle. All he wanted was to get away out of sight. Mac and Miller and Burkett were among the crowd. No one seemed annoyed with him; they were glad to find him alive. Someone told him he had made General Currie duck. Mac fought his way to him.

'I guess you've made a proper mess of your bus this time,' he said.

'And a blasted fool of myself,' Tom muttered. 'I want to get away out of this.'

'Well, cut along, and tell them to send and collect the bits. You'd better lay claim at once to that new bus that came from Candas yesterday.' Mac was practical.

Tom pressed through the throng and made off round Izel towards the aerodrome, coming to the far side of it. As he was walking across, Williamson dived on him and made him lie down. He reported his crash, cause unknown, at the office, and put in for the new Camel D6585, and it was allocated to him. It was brand new, and would be the best bus in the squadron, at any rate for looks. He had done well out of his crash. He had a wash and then went to the mess for tea. On the way he met Grey.

'Hullo, Grey. Seen the doctor yet?'

'Yes, thanks. I saw him this morning. Everything's all right.'

'What! Haven't you . . .?'

'No, he says it's only an impetiginous pimple.'

'An impetiginous pimple!' Tom burst into laughter. He held his sides, he staggered about, he clung to Grey. Something funny had happened at last. 'Oh Grey, you are the limit. You'll be the death of me. Come and have tea, and don't look so deadly solemn! You ought to offer up a prayer of thanksgiving for a damned lucky escape.'

'I have already done so,' replied Grey, solemnly.

The Canadians came back from their sports, and the weather cleared sufficiently for a squadron patrol of nine to go out. Neither Tom nor Williamson were on this, and they sat outside the hut enjoying the warm evening.

'D'you mean to say you haven't even got a bruise from that crash?'

'Nothing at all but a tiny graze on my right arm that I can only feel if I rub it.'

'You know, Tom, you must be awful big med'cine man.'

'Eh?'

'There must be something special about you, if one could only see it. You're being kept for something. Not even allowed to bruise your precious self. And you even manage to get hold of the best machine in the squadron through your crash . . . .'

'Look, there's a squirrel,' Tom exclaimed. 'In that tree there.'

They watched the squirrel. Hundreds of cockchafers were buzzing among the trees. The grass was yellowed with a million dandelions. The trees were vivid with delicious green. The grey stone and red-brown tiles of the farmhouse helped the pleasant scene. Only the huts were ugly. They were part of the war.

'By the way,' said Williamson, 'how's your pal Grey? He's still about I notice.'

'I'd better tell you, but keep it to yourself, or he'll be ragged to death. He's seen the M.O. and it's only a pimple.'

Williamson roared with laughter. 'My God, what a comedian! Have I got to keep that to myself?'

The patrol came back early as conditions were bad, and soon afterwards Miller came up to them.

'Hullo, Miller. Enjoy your comic patrol?'

'Durn silly. It's a fog up. But see here, Tom, I've got something I wanna fix with you. I had a letter from my brother by this evening's mail, and he's expecting leave at the end of this month. That's when you're due to go.'

'Anything I can do?'

'Waal, as we haven't set eyes on each other this last two years, near enough, how'd it be if you and I changed places? Then I'd see my brother, and you'd have your ticket a fortnight earlier, and get away in style in the major's car. How about it?'

'My God, what d'you think? I'm all for this. We'd better tell Mac about it.' Then he added, 'I suppose you really have heard from your brother?' It was a silly question to ask, but it had occurred to him suddenly that this was very like the scheme he had planned for Seddon's benefit, and the question popped out. The whole thing seemed slightly eerie.

'What the hell! You don't imagine I'm putting my leave back two weeks for the fun of it!'

'No. It seemed too good to be true, that's all.'

'Waal, it's true sure enough, so I guess you don't want to bother about that. I've fixed it already with Mac and Jimmy, so as you're agreeable, it's all OK.'

'Oh yes, I'm agreeable all right. And give your brother my best love.'

'Didn't I tell you just now you were lucky?' said Williamson emphatically. 'If anything can go right for you it does. In spite of your nose, I believe you're a Jew.'

'Certainly everything's come right to-day, even if I have smashed one more Camel. God, only four days till leave! It seems about six months nearer. I'm going up to the shop to see if they've found out what was wrong with that engine, and to talk to them about the rigging of my new bus. Coming?'

The cause of the engine failure seemed to be a broken pressure pipe. It had snapped at a fault.

'See how they endanger our lives, sending us up with faulty pipes,' said Tom.

'H'm. I bet you starved the engine,' Williamson replied. 'That pipe broke when you crashed.'

'You're only jealous because I've got D6585.'

'Oh, you'll soon smash it up.'

XII

THE morning sky was covered with a slight translucent patterned mist that looked as though Orion had slain some starry dragon in the night and spread its squamous skin for the morning sun to dry. Soon

283

it faded and vanished, leaving clear sky. B flight went up at half-past ten, and C at half-past eleven. Tom had to borrow Dubois' machine, whose day off it was, as his own was not yet ready. The air was clear and cloudless, and Archie had plenty of ammunition after all the recent bad weather. He followed them all the time, and there was no cover from him. There were Huns about: they could be seen as black dots far away in the east, and sometimes a wing flashed in the sun high up and nearer. It was difficult to see them against the bright sky, and near the sun there was an area it was quite impossible to be certain was empty.

They had not been out long before Tom made out some of the Huns, seeming transparent and tenuous, almost invisible, coming up behind them. Mac had seen them, and he waggled his wings. They vanished in the sun. Mac circled and circled, waiting for them to come down. Miller, Cross, Baker, and Grey made up the rest of the flight, and they were all circling waiting for the Huns, who, seeing the Camels were not to be surprised, would not come down. Then Mac left off circling and put his nose up to climb at them. They climbed and climbed. The Huns were able to keep above, but after reaching 18,000 feet, they went away east, and Mac chased after another group which he saw miles away beyond Merville. Archie gave them warning, and they fled. Yet another bunch, or possibly the first one returned, came up from the south, and sat in the sun over them, but were driven off by some more Camels that arrived high up. These turned out to be B flight, and they all kept together till B went home.

So the manœuvring went on without any actual fighting. Tom watched his tail and the region of the sun with unceasing vigilance. He was determined on one thing; he would not be surprised. He had constantly to be turning his neck, and it was sore. He would look round to his left and then turn his head through as nearly complete a circle as he could, surveying everything, especially Mac, on the way. Mac was twisting a good deal, and Archie was bursting uncomfortably close. If they were going to have four hours of this sort of thing day after day through the summer, the strain would be terrible. What, he wondered, were the other fellows feeling about it all? Mac and Miller, of course, were out to get Huns; they had a reasonable regard for their own skins, but they had a real desire to be great Hun-getters; further than that he could not penetrate into their minds. But Cross, flying there behind and outside him; had Cross any desire beyond surviving without disgracing himself? Tom could not believe that this quiet young man who listened day after day to the same Balfe and Wallace tunes on his gramophone was anything of a militarist at heart: he certainly did not profess to be.

Baker he hardly knew. He was superficially lazy, sardonic, war-weary, but there was at times a keenness about him that might arise from a carefully hidden thirst for glory. He had a D.C.M.

As for Grey, it was impossible to guess what went on in the darkness of his mind. No doubt he had imbibed correct sentiments about loyalty and patriotic duty and the Old Country, if they called it that in Africa, and no doubt he did not doubt the correctness of correct sentiments, but accepted them as a child accepts the moral tags of grown-ups. For him it was an ordered if not understood world, where truth sat on the lips of Great Men, and Commanding Officers were right. God dwelt in some sphere of light above the darkness of the world, heeding the strife and giving aid to the right side. He had to let the Germans win a few battles or there would be no virtue in fighting for the right; it would be too easy.

And Grey probably lived in a world of high lights and black shadows, full of spheres and cubes and regular polyhedra and precise classifications and categories; a serious, unfluctuant, child's world.

Tom's thoughts ran on while his senses were engaged in flying and watching. It was as though he split in two parts, one active, one meditative. Flying, war flying, was having that effect on him. When he was at length shot down and killed, his active part would cease and his meditative part would go endlessly wandering above the earth, homeless, deathless, lost; durable beyond all life, meditating above the dark eventual rock.

Mac was manœuvring to get between the sun and a dozen distant Huns a little below them in the east. He climbed south-east, and, the Huns going south-west, came into position to dive on them. But there were more Huns above; it was a dangerous position. Never-theless, Mac took them down on the lower group, fired without doing damage, and turned away. The higher group, which was Fokker triplanes, followed down, and it looked as if there would be a dog-fight, but only one of the triplanes actually attacked. It fired at Baker, who dived under the formation with the Hun after him, and Miller turned quickly and shot at the Hun, which went on down and down. It was not difficult to see its long fall through the clear air, and at last it crashed by the La Bassée canal.

The other Huns were content to sit above them and take an occasional long shot. It wasn't a comfortable position, ten miles over with so many Huns about. At any moment those above might receive reinforcements, and, finding courage in numbers, abandon their strictly defensive tactics. Mac took the chance of diving away westwards. The Huns followed at a good distance, as if they were frightened of a trap; and as it happened a half-dozen Bristol Fighters appeared rather suddenly in a cloud of Archie, and the Huns liked Bristols even less than they liked Camels. The Bristol Fighters held on their eastern way, and the Huns vanished except for a group sitting up in the sun.

The Camels continued patrolling. Their job was to keep the lines safe for lonely two-seaters doing shoots and photographing trenches, not to go dogfighting miles away in Hunland. From time to time Huns approached, and there was circling and skirmishing, but they were not actually attacked, and did not get into position to attack. They went home at half-past one.

Baker's tail-plane was full of holes. Miller was pleased with himself: 'Got that durn tripe with one burst.' Grey had only seen that one Hun. They were all hungry, and left reporting till after lunch, when they went to the office and put the vague events of the morning into official shape. Tom was always interested in the great difference between the queer exotic reality and the terse official narrative which recorded that reality for the practical world. It was typically human, the reduction of cloudy magnitudes to formal succinctness; the rejection of all experience that was not for the practical mind essential. A Fokker triplane had been shot down and seen to crash: it did not matter that it had been a tiny blue-grey translucent thing above them, shaped like its plan; then had come suddenly large and colourless out of the sun-dazzle, its tiers of wings showing in frontal elevation, alarming with gun-flashes and the streak of tracers from it, shining silver and green as it came close, and dulling into whitish grey as it went down in a steep jerking dive; that the projection of its course against the background of earth was deceptive, and it was impossible to guess where it would crash, appearing to move in an irregular arc, first going miles away east, then in a continuously steepening path to curve more and more back towards and underneath them, fading with distance from its proper shape into a moving mark, falling long after it looked about to crash, its movement looking then more like a slow horizontal one than an almost vertical dive; stopping suddenly and unexpectedly, a broken spread of wings on the ground, just discernible.

Then Tom went to the hangars to have a look at his new machine that the riggers were busy on. It would be ready for a trial flight next morning. And then it was tea-time, and after tea there was only time for a quiet pipe before getting ready for the half-past five patrol. Life seemed a rush.

Soon after they had taken off Mac gave the dud engine signal and turned back, and Miller took the lead. Soon after they had reached the lines Miller also went back, and Tom took the lead. Then Baker went back, and Tom patrolled the lines with Cross and Grey. He did not feel it necessary to go far into Hunland, though he was rather tempted by a balloon that was left up alone within reach, but thought it might very likely be a dummy put there for some unpleasant purpose. There did not seem to be any Huns out; they were perhaps resting after their morning's activity. It became very boring dodging Archie for nearly two hours with nothing to do but inspect a couple of Harry Tates and watch shells bursting on the ground, and he was glad when it was late enough to go home. They were at twelve thousand feet over Merville, and he dived away towards Béthune, and turned due south from there for home, flying low. When they came to the long straight road running north-west from Arras to nowhere in particular he dived on some troops, and his engine would not pick up after the dive. There was a narrow strip of grass bordering the road, and he had to get down on that. There was not much room, but fortunately he made a perfect landing. At once troops came flocking round, mostly Canadians, and he was soon the centre of interest of a crowd. He waved to Cross who came low to see if he was all right. Canadians seemed to have a bad effect on his engines, somehow.

There was no lack of help, and he gave two volunteers some instruction in swinging the prop, but they could not get the engine to start. There was a motor-cyclist among the crowd, and Tom got him to go to the aerodrome at Caucourt two miles away for help. He was at the end of a village called Estrée-Cauchie stretched along the road. He passed the time conversing with a Canadian sergeant, a huge fellow. Tom felt almost overawed by such physical splendour; they certainly bred some fine men in God's own country. He was glad that he himself had the prestige of being an aviator, and had just made a landing that must appear wonderful to a layman; he felt able to meet the sergeant on equal terms; as one fine fellow to another.

The sun set. Help was a very long time coming, as usual. He walked to the village and had a cup of coffee and a glass of vin rouge that cost half a franc. That sort of stuff was still cheap. It was getting dusk. The Canadian sergeant wasn't a backwoodsman, but something on the railroad at Montreal. He returned to the aeroplane, and when it was too dark for flying a tender arrived and two mechanics got out and saluted Tom.

'You've come too late. Why have you been so long?'

'I only had orders to come a quarter of an hour ago, sir.'

'Well, it can't be helped, but I'm afraid it means you'll have to guard the aeroplane for the night. I'll go back on the tender and explain to your people.'

Tom had dinner at Caucourt, and discussed the war with his hosts, who were Bristol Fighter merchants. They did quite a lot of fighting twenty miles over, and shot down great numbers of Huns near their own aerodromes for few casualties. Last week one of them had been smashed by a direct hit from Archie; it had been a nasty sight, but fortunately an exceedingly rare one. Altogether Bristol Fighters were useful and safe machines to fly, but there wasn't the fun to be got out of them that there was out of Camels. They were sufficiently splitarse and did all the stunts, but there was nothing like a Camel for lightness of touch and accuracy to inches. The Bristol people agreed that a Camel might be all right for fun if you didn't mind the engine conking every few days, but not for war flying.

At any rate, a Camel hadn't a radiator to be shot up, Tom said.

Then a tender from home called for him, and he went back on it and spoke to Dubois about his unsatisfactory engine.

'I know it's rotten,' said Dubois. 'I wish you'd crashed the bus and got rid of it.'

'Thanks. You do your own dirty work. I've crashed enough Camels. I'm trying to give it a rest before I break my neck.'

He set out at nine o'clock in the morning with Dubois and two mechanics for Estrée-Cauchie, but the engine would not start until they had tinkered with it for two hours, and then it sounded wrong.

'You fly it; it's yours,' Tom said to Dubois, 'then you can crash it how you like.'

'I think you ought to fly it. You brought it here.'

'No. It doesn't like me. It knows you.'

As it was plainly Dubois' duty to fly his own machine, he yielded to persuasion and got sadly in. He had to take off along the side of the road, cross-wind, and with only just enough run-way before the grass ended in the village. He ran the engine a long time before he waved. There was quite a crowd looking on. He opened wide out quickly and got away all right. Then the engine started popping.

'My God, he'll be into that house!' Tom exclaimed. The crowd held its breath. Then the engine picked up and Dubois staggered over the village and climbed away. The crowd let out its breath.

'Struth, I thought 'e was for it. . . .'

'I wouldn't fly one of those goldarn buzzers for all creation. . . .'

'Eh, that were my billet 'e tried to knock over. . . .'

Tom got back to lunch, and afterwards took up his new machine for a test flight. Dubois had got back safely. He had lost his prop landing and the engine would not start again, so they had pushed the aeroplane into the hangar and were working on it. Mac wanted Tom to have his own machine ready for the evening patrol if possible. There was quite an epidemic of engine trouble. Tom found his machine pretty good. It was a trifle stiff; no doubt it wanted some pulling about to loosen its joints, and he did several rolls and a spin with this intention. Anyhow, it looked nice. He would try to avoid crashing it.

The squadron went up fifteen strong after tea. Clouds were

coming up from the north-west, and the atmosphere was thick. It was clear above eight thousand feet, but they soon had a condensating floor of cloud below them, and had to go underneath it. As it was no use patrolling the murky air below two thousand feet, they soon returned home.

'I find that war flying hardly terrifies me so much as I expected,' Grey said to Tom.

'That's good. But don't let that stop you from watching your tail all the time, or you'll be frightened to death one of these days,' Tom replied.

Grey seemed comparatively pleased with life. People were getting to know him, and although he was laughed at as an oddity and ragged a little, he was so very harmless that it was impossible to dislike him. Moreover, everyone had a comfortable feeling of superiority in his presence, and this was quite likely to give him a spurious popularity.

That evening in the mess Tom noticed that Burkett and Hudson and one or two others were trying to make Grey drunk. Grey looked rather like a daddy-longlegs terrified but flattered by the attentions of wasps. It had to come, of course, for no flying man could live in France and remain sober. Nevertheless Tom went over to Burkett when he was forcing Grey to have another.

'I say Burkett, I met a fellow-townsman of yours last night. He told me there were more breweries and more drunkenness in Montreal than all the rest of Canada put together.'

This lie had the effect of diverting Burkett's attention and starting him arguing. Tom drew Hudson into it with a wink, and Burkett spoke for some time. Grey had plenty of opportunity to escape, but he did not take it. Instead he made a grave contribution to the discussion:

'Without knowing the right and wrong of the question, I must say it seems a remarkable statement for a man to make about his home town.'

'It would be if he'd made it,' Tom said, and abandoned Grey to his fate, which was not drunkenness that night, for Mac came in and shouted for poker players, and the gang broke up.

XIII

TOM awoke next morning with the thought uppermost in his mind that this was his last day before leave. He would be glad when it was safely over. There was little chance that the weather would prevent either of the jobs, for the sun was shining gloriously in a sky of pure blue. A light cool breeze was blowing from the north-west, a veritable zephyr. It was a morning to make the heart glad – sweet day, so cool, so calm, so bright. The rhythm, matching the morning's perfection, ran in his mind. He would soon be hearing a different rhythm, that of his engine, on the indefectability of which his chance of safety would depend. He would spend anxious hours listening for the least irregularity, and the lovely clarity of the day would be a burden and a weariness.

C flight took off at half-past eleven, and climbed away over Arras, a dark triangle attended by a satellite star that was the ancient citadel. They reached the lines at ten thousand feet, seeming the only occupants of the sky. The battle area, two miles below, dirty brown and foul yellow, gashed with tortuous lines of trenches, pencil-marked with the queer blue of wire entanglements, littered with ruins of towns and villages, might have been a picture done by a mad painter, a map of desolation, rather than anything real, except that there were puffs of yellow-grey smoke and red flashes, and fires smouldered here and there. There was no movement.

Towards the horizon France resumed its normal summer appearance of a bronze and green patchwork, melting into misty grey distance. Far away in the north there was a just perceptible brightness indicating that the English Channel was there. To-morrow he might cross it. His engine was roaring regularly and rhythmically. Archie was not interested in them. There was nothing to do but sit in the empty sky and wait for whatever might turn up. They wandered up and down between the Scarpe and the Lys. Lens, Béthune, La Bassée, Merville, Armentières. The great bulge in the line north of Neuve Chapelle along the Lys. The line swinging east again in front of the huge patch of Nieppe Forest by Mount Kemmel and Wyschaete to the scar that had been Ypres.

Then out of the east a large formation appeared. Mac headed towards it, although perhaps a thousand feet lower. He would get right underneath them miles over Hunland. Tom felt his guts melt. What the devil was Mac playing at? This was asking for trouble. He wouldn't get his leave after all. He had waited nearly five months for it, and — God, they were SEs! He expanded with a mighty breath of relief. His vitals re-coagulated. The SEs, seventeen of them, passed overhead. He shook his fist at them for giving him such a scare. They must have been the devil of a long way over. Why hadn't Archie been going for them? The Huns must be having one of their days off.

Then WOOF WOOF loudly behind him, too close to be pleasant. Looking round at once he saw Cross go down in a dive. God, was he hit? Tom turned outwards vertically and watched him. He pulled out and climbed back into position. Good. They turned and twisted, but Archie did not trouble them any more.

The reason for Archie's sudden action seemed to be to give warning to a two-seater working along the canal. They chased it, but got nowhere near, and soon went home to a late lunch. Cross was looking rather white. Archie had burst right under his tail and up-ended him, nearly throwing him out. There was a big tear in his tail-plane. Mac washed him out for the rest of the day.

Tom spent the afternoon fiddling with his machine. B flight went out and got an LVG, which Williamson shared with Large. After tea he sat outside the hut talking with Williamson about leave. He would stay with his sister, a war widow, and they would cheer each other up. Nearly everyone he used to know was dead.

At six o'clock he went up on his last job. They were five strong as Cross was not with them. As soon as they reached the lines they were warned of Huns by a burst of white Archie, and they saw two formations away east of Lens, the top one about on their own level. Mac climbed towards them, and the Huns, Albatros scouts, climbed away northwards. They followed them, reaching the chilly height of eighteen thousand feet, which was too high for a Camel to fly properly. The Huns put their noses down and went off eastwards. Mac worked down to fifteen thousand, and the Huns came back very cautiously, and then turned away again, and they lost sight of them for perhaps half an hour. Then they showed up again quite near. There were eight of them higher than the Camels and five lower. Mac, as they were right in the sun for the lower group, took a chance and dived on them. Tom was more interested in keeping an eye on the top layer than shooting at the lower, but he took an ineffective shot at one. Mac got one in an irregular spin and zoomed away as the upper formation dived towards them. They climbed and the Huns did not actually attack, but crossed over above them to get in the sun. Mac flew straight west watching them, knowing they would not go too near the lines. Suddenly he turned sharply towards Tom as the Huns dived. Tom went under him, pulled up, and half-rolled after him. The Huns fired. Tom sideslipped away from a too loud rat-tat-tat-tat. He caught a glimpse of someone stalling. Whoever it was fell into a spin, hit. The Huns zoomed away, and, apparently satisfied with their success, broke off the attack and sat over them. Mac's blood was up, and he left off splitarsing about and climbed at them, zooming occasionally to take an upward shot at them. Suddenly they made off east as hard as they could go, and soon afterwards a dozen SEs came up from the west all out after them. The Camels followed, but could not make the pace, and the hunt vanished into the east.

The remaining four Camels picked up formation, and Tom had leisure to look round. The spearhead of Mac, Miller, and himself was intact. The other Camel was following in the middle behind and above. Tom could not at first see whether it was Baker's or Grey's, as its letter was concealed from him by the bottom plane. He opened his throttle and pulled his nose up until he could see the fuselage. The letter was X. Baker. So Grey had gone. That which had been Grey was a still warm mess of carrion somewhere on the unreal map below. Dead before he had been properly alive. Probably he had known nothing of the attack from above, had been occupied with following Mac, had been plunged from his half-light into total darkness too suddenly for knowledge. But poor Grey! was anyone on earth more innocent, more inoffensive, less deserving of being murdered in this obscure quarrel between rival gangs of merchants, imperialists, usurers, and megalomaniacs?

As they went home the sun was reddening in the west, and the day was preparing for its death in misty pomp and magnificence as though it were a supreme day among days, with title to kingly honours. They were flying into a sea of liquid light that always receded before them, too dazzling to look into. Tom watched the ground changing underneath, the familiar villages appearing and receding; well-known roads, woods, farms; distinctively shaped patches of cultivation. The aerodrome appeared, and he floated down and landed from west to east, there being no wind, so as to be able to see. The stick came softly back, the tail settled down, and he touched ground, wheels and tailskid together, without a jolt, and taxied in. The job was over.

'Well, Grey's gone west,' they said, and then discussed the scrap. Mac was fairly satisfied, as he had picked off a Hun in rather difficult circumstances. He was sorry that the top layer hadn't come down to dogfight. A pity about Grey, but he couldn't play for safety all the time; had to take a risk sometimes.

They reported, and Tom went to the hut to get ready for dinner. Williamson was sitting outside reading.

'Hullo, Tom. Had a pleasant final job? Any damage?'

'Mac picked a typical flight commander's Hun out of a crowd. Grey's killed.'

'Grey! What, did a Hun get him?'

'Yes. I don't suppose Grey saw him. Mac went down on five Albatri under eight more, and the top lot came down on us. There might have been a scrap, but some SEs came along and the Huns ran for it. The SEs chased them home. We couldn't keep up of course. That sort of thing's all right for the leader, but it's not comfortable for the rear fellows.'

'Quite. But there it is. You're not blaming Mac, surely to goodness?'

'No. But I'm sorry about Grey. I'd got used to him. It's beastly to think of that poor innocent being killed. Last night in the mess I stopped him, possibly, from getting tight for the first time in his life. God, fancy reaching the advanced age of — what was he? twenty-three? twenty-four? — without having been drunk. And I interfered with his last opportunity. It's a lesson to me to mind my own business.'

'Then for God's sake take it, but don't start worrying that weird head of yours about your part, whatever it was, in Grey's lifelong sobriety. His next of kin would probably send you an illuminated letter of thanks if they knew. Now look here, I've never smoked opium, and I'm quite prepared to pass out without it. What opium is to me, getting drunk was to Grey. So what's the harm, you big flop?'

'Still, I wish I hadn't. Perhaps, underneath, he really wanted to. You never know.'

Tom found that it was difficult to eat any dinner. Afterwards he sat with a book, until Williamson insisted on his playing bridge. There was another ghost about the place. A tall awkward ghost, a nervous pompous ghost with a deep voice — 'pardon me, Cundall . . .' Why the devil did he always hear the voices of the dead? No one else seemed to be troubled by the ghost . . . 'That long streak Grey's gone west.'

'So I hear. What'll you have? Queer sort of bloke. Hancock! Two Scotches. I bet you can't put your ears between your knees — like this . . . .'

Had he ever enjoyed playing bridge? He was partnering Wall, who was the sort of player who knew where every card in the pack was after the first round, and expected his partner to know also. Tom stood it for some time with the help of a few drinks. Then he broke away and devoted himself exclusively to drinking for a little while and went to bed.

The hut was empty, but the batman had left a lamp alight. He stood by the bed where Seddon's used to be. The grief and bitterness that had seemed to be ebbing came surging back. He went to his own bed and threw himself down in the immemorial posture of grief until he had regained some ascendancy over the blind force of regret.

The door opened, and he sat up quickly. It was Williamson. They looked at each other. Something had to be said.

'Well, it's the last night in the old home, Tom, for a fortnight.'

'Yes.' Good God, Williamson might be gone when he came back . . . But no, Bill could look after himself.

Tom looked at him as he sat on his bed taking off his boots. He seemed not to feel the strain of war. His was a well-balanced body, his hands firm and not too large, his movement precise but not meticulous. His eyes saw keenly, yet were always kind. A man entirely without meanness, yet without the usual temperamental instabilities of magnanimity. By God, what a friend to have.

'It looks as though it'll be calm enough. You won't be sea-sick.'

'Not me.'

No, Bill wasn't the sort of fellow to go west. Grey hadn't a chance, poor devil. It was grotesque to drag that figure of fun, that poor comedian into the tragic scope of war and cut short his comedy with murder.

'I shan't forget my last leave in a hurry. I went nutty. I properly had the last day on earth feeling. . . .'

Grey was a child who could just read story books, knowing almost nothing of life beyond fairy stories and the conventional lies official adults told him. They had given him a story called War, with a lot of words such as honour, duty, God, heroism, in it, and he had read it, fatally. It was child murder.

'. . . in St. Martin's Lane,' Williamson was saying; 'the old bird went on jawing us about the wickedness of being blotto in the midst of Armageddon, till I sang out "Go on, old dear. Armageddon fond of you", and somehow we made a song of it and danced round the old bird singing "Armageddon so fond of you" till he shook his head and . . .'

Hell and damnation. He would get out of this murderous and hypocritical civilization, with its swinishness and murder at one end, its lying sentimentality at the other. If he survived. . . .

'. . . you'd have laughed, Tom. I wish you'd been there. One day we'll have a bust up together. . . .'

He'd live among simple primitive people somewhere, who ate fruit and lay in the sun and bred children and weren't worth commercial exploitation; who had no churches or armies or money.

Crash. Watt and Bruce burst in singing and making a row.

'What yer, Cundall,' Bruce called out. 'Lucky old man, going on leave in the morning. Feeling good?'

'Not particularly.'

'God almighty, you ought to be feeling like . . .'

'Who the devil are you to be telling me what I ought to be feeling?' Tom snapped.

'Hullo, you're feeling a bit fresh to-night aren't you, Cundall?' Watt joined in.

'For God's sake, you fellows,' said Williamson, 'can't you leave a man alone when he's feeling cut up?'

'Oh. Sorry.'

'My God, I'm damned sorry, Cundall, really,' Bruce protested. 'Naturally I expected you'd be feeling fine. I'm sorry.'

'No. It's for me to be sorry,' Tom replied.

'Well, let's forget it,' said Watt, and they turned in, Bruce and Watt arguing about whether you could gain height on a roll, flying level, or not, and the others kept silent.

Whenever Tom woke up depression returned like a load in the pit of his stomach; he felt sick with it. In the morning breakfast filled him with nausea. He ought to be able to throw off his malaise; he was losing resilience; his nerves were jagged. Perhaps leave would put him right. He must forget. No, not forget. He must remember without rancour. God, how could he? He loathed utterly this damned war and the sordid system that created it. He must endure till he was killed or could go away, clean away from the disease of civilization. He would never forget, but time would blunt the harsh edge of remembrance; he would grow old and callous; it would be a dream.

The excitement of preparing for the journey invigorated him. He packed his kit-bag, put Smith's watch in his pocket, received a number of letters for posting in England, had a final quick drink with Williamson and Miller and Burkett and Hudson and Maitland. Then he got into the squadron Crossley and set out, waving good-bye to the fellows who had turned out to see him off. The car went through Izel, near the scene of his recent disaster, towards the St. Pol road. A Camel with a deputy leader's streamer came roaring over the tree tops. It was Williamson. He couldn't get down to strafe because of the trees. They waved, and Williamson vanished.

Tom arrived in Boulogne soon after one o'clock. His bag was put on the quay, and the car went to the EFC to look for the major. Tom had an hour and a half before the leave boat sailed, so he had lunch quietly at Mony's. Then he went on board and put on his life-belt. He avoided talking to people, not being in the usual going-on-leave mood. The crossing was calm and uneventful. Three destroyers were in comforting attendance. It was a fine hazy day, and the English coast was not visible until they were within four or five miles of it.

Folkestone. He had spent summer holidays there as a youngster. He remembered the Leas, where people walked about while a Blue Hungarian band played, conducted by one Herr Wurms ("her worms" most people made of it), reputed to be a ladies' man. The steep cliffs, the lower road, the shingle, the switchback, the penny-in-the-slot machines from one of which he remembered an alarming pennyworth of electric shock, the pier, Cardo's Cadets . . . he was coming home.

The ship moved to its place alongside the quay, and a train was waiting. After enormous delay it started and rattled inland among the chalk hills. The evening was delicious. Hedgerows again, white with hawthorn, between golden-green meadows and brown-green cornfields on the wooded greensand. Beyond Ashford, the Weald. This was his native land. Wandering lanes, hedged and ditched. This was England. He had forgotten how lovely England was. All this incredible, jocund, casual beauty . . . it was difficult to keep back tears. He resented the emotion, fought it, called it murderous, deceitful. If it had been a dull and rainy evening — but it was useless. The emotion constricted his throat; it seemed deep and real; all his other feelings appeared shallow and meretricious in the shock of discovering how unquenchable, how real was his love of England.

PHASE THREE

'Hullo, Bill.'

'Why, hullo, Tom. So you've managed to get back. You're a day late.'

'Yes. I went to Izel. A particularly ghastly journey. I think the pace of these damned French trains has dropped from five to four-and-a-half miles an hour since the push. After twenty-four hours in trains I reached the old aerodrome yesterday. I barged straight into our hut and found perfect strangers in possession. I nearly fainted. I thought you'd all gone west.'

'Not all. Bruce has.'

'He didn't last long. Anyway, they gave me dinner and put me up for the night. I couldn't get through to the squadron by telephone, and after I'd pestered them all the morning they gave me transport and here I am.'

'And here you are. This isn't a very beautiful spot, but there's plenty of accommodation. We've got this hut to ourselves.'

'That's fine. A Nissen hut for two, eh? Plenty of room, anyway. Well, how've you been getting on?'

'Oh, as usual. You did well to miss the move. We had to get up at half-past four, and had two jobs besides the enormous labour of moving. We hadn't a mess, and had to go round begging food. And there was bombing all night. It was a lovely day.'

'Three days ago, wasn't it?'

'Yes. We're just getting settled. Your usual luck.'

The batman brought in Tom's kitbag and unpacked it as much as was necessary or possible. Tom had a wash.

'Well, are you coming to tea?' he said, and Williamson got up from his bed where he had been having an afternoon nap and they went out into the rain. The aerodrome was in bare flat country. The officers' accommodation consisted of a row of Nissen huts on each side of a sunken road that went to Estrée-Blanche, a village about a mile away. Outside their hut, the last but one towards Estrée in the row across the road from the mess, there was a steep bank down to the road about ten feet below. Immediately opposite was the squadron office.

'The padre has bagged the hut next door for a church, you'll be pleased to know,' Williamson informed. They walked past several huts along the top of the bank, which rapidly became shallower as the road climbed towards ground level. Opposite the mess entrance it had decreased to two or three feet and there were steps cut in it. The two large huts that were the mess-room and ante-room were placed parallel to the road with a narrow cindered path between them, and the doors faced each other across it. They went into the mess-room where people were having tea.

'Hullo, Cundall. Hullo, Cundall,' said everyone.

'Hullo, chaps.'

'Cundall, there's a job at half-past five in the morning. Miller's gone on leave, so get a streamer fixed on your tail.'

'Righto, Mac.'

As well as Bruce, Black of B flight had been killed. It was not, however, certain that Bruce was dead. He had just vanished during a scrap with some Albatri. Burkett was wounded, but had got down safely before he lost consciousness.

He was in hospital. He had an explosive bullet in his thigh, and would probably lose the whole leg.

On the credit side, the squadron had bagged, Tom gathered, something between a dozen and twenty Huns, scouts and two-seaters. Mac had three and some shares, and was definitely the squadron's biggest Hun-getter, and possibly the most successful of all Camel pilots. Williamson had got a Pfalz and some shares in two-seaters. Watt had got an Albatros in flames his second time over; this was probably a record.

After tea Tom went to the hangars to look over his bus and have the deputy leader's streamer fixed. Then he went for a walk with Williamson. It had stopped raining. A flight would probably be able to do their six o'clock patrol.

It was corn country. They walked along a footpath through barley fields towards a distant windmill whose arms were rotating in the fresh south-west breeze. They came to the mill and stood watching the ancient device for trapping wind power.

'It's curious that these old things should be working still in France,' Tom said. 'A commentary on the Revolution.'

The door was open, and the miller looked out at them.

'Voulez-vous que nous entrons, monsieur?'

The miller professed delight at their visit. They climbed into the dim interior and looked at the primitive machinery at work. There was a tremendous noise of creaking and groaning: a great turning of wheels by mighty force. It was far more impressive inside than outside.

They talked to the owner and exchanged information about milling and flying. His name was Maugredie, and he had three sons in the French army. One was still alive.

'The French have got something to fight for,' said Tom when they had left the mill. 'They do own their country. The land doesn't belong to a set of dukes and millionaires whose only interest is rent. Louis Quatorze was beaten; Henry the Eighth won. The English haven't the intelligence to discriminate between thieving and government.'

'H'm. I don't know much about the history of it, but the French don't seem so wonderfully happy about it.'

'The French don't want happiness so much as security and respectability, and they would have achieved it if they had left the Germans alone. Internally they have. But we English have almost destroyed our peasantry and made a race of urban slum-dwellers who have neither happiness nor security nor respectability. But they make cannon-fodder.'

'You've touched on a point there. It sometimes bothers me to think of them dragging fellows out of slums to fight for their country. You'd think they'd want to fight against it: though I believe some of 'em volunteered. Not that I know anything about it. Like most people, I've never seen a slum.'

'Funny you should say that. I tried to have a look at some while I was on leave. I should think the volunteers wanted to get away from the slums.'

'Good Lord. That's the most original way of spending leave I've ever heard of. What on earth for?'

'It takes a bit of explaining. When I went away on leave I got across to Folkestone on a lovely evening, and going through Kent with the country looking gorgeous got me groggy. I expect you know what I mean. I had the hell of an England my England sort of feeling . . .'

'I know. The sight of England does get you that way after months in this dismal country.'

'Well, it made me think . . .'

'Everything does. It's a disease with you.'

'Was I a jingo at heart still? I thought I'd better take a corrective, so I went to Hoxton and Stepney and had a look round. I'm no good at slumming. I felt out of place. I couldn't go poking into tenements or down back alleys where people had got washing hanging out and all that sort of thing. So I got nothing but a general impression of dirt and gloom. But it was enough to counterbalance a fine evening in Kent.'

'And now you're quite sure you're not a jingo, I suppose?'

'I don't know. We never know what we are until something tests us. I'll put it like this. I suppose you've heard the story of the fellow who fell in love with a woman for her beautiful voice. They got married, and the first time he saw her undressed he said, "Mary, for God's sake sing." Well, as long as I can think of the English countryside, English Gothic, and some English people I've known, as England, I can be reasonably patriotic; but when I think of poor devils in squalor at Bethnal Green, the bloody fools of Mayfair, English profiteers and propagandists, then – for God's sake sing.'

'That's a reasonable feeling. I suppose you didn't spend all your leave slumming. What shows did you see?'

'Oh, *Maid of the Mountains, Chu Chin Chow* again, the George Robey show, Delysia in *As You Were.*'

'If you could care for me, as I could care for you-oo,' Williamson sang. 'What else did you do?'

'Kept fairly sober for a change.'

'Good man. How's the women?'

'Very womanly. They've properly come into their own. If the war goes on much longer there won't be a virgin left in London outside Balham.'

'So that makes up your leave; slums, shows, and Sallys.'

'And children.'

'What, have you begun your illegitimate family?'

'Not yet. I made friends with all the kids I could in the short time. Seddon once hinted that although I theorized a good deal about them I knew nothing of children. So I amused myself by trying to learn.'

'What's the verdict?'

'They've all the vices of adults which are within their compass except pride, and none of their virtues. That's why they're so charming, until they get tiring. I suppose it's their charm, credulity, weakness, lack of pride, that's led to all the sentimental tosh that's been talked and written about them. Even friend Jesus was wrong. No Kingdom of Heaven could be made up of children: it would be a kingdom of jealousy, squabbles, and attempted murder. Sophistication is essential in heaven.'

'Well I'm damned. I went on leave, and all I came back with was a thick head. You go, and back you come with a complete set of new ideas, including sophisticated angels. But what's the moral of all that?'

'Anything you like. Never leave till to-morrow what you can drink to-day.'

'I thought you might say our troubles are because the nations are like a lot of squabbling kids.'

'Oh God, no. A child's world might be full of squabbles, but their murder wouldn't be organized. I like the wickedness of children. When holy adults aren't bullying them into goodness they've no hypocrisy or shame about it. Perhaps I shouldn't say wickedness at all, but naturalness. They're so much the same thing. Anyway, when they're quite young they don't bother about right or wrong, and that's very nice after the slime of hypocritical church-godliness we adults are dirtying-over our quarrels with. When they get a bit older you can see the morbid influence of parents; they learn to state a case for putting themselves in the right like any damned propagandist.'

'For the past fortnight I've heard and talked practically nothing but shop, eternal shop,' said Williamson; 'this is a relief. But you're praising naivety and sophistication almost in the same breath.'

'Well, isn't sophistication the art of being simple? I think I've thought of a moral.'

'Let's have it then.'

'Be clever, sweet maid — no; be intelligent sweet maid, and let who will be good.'

'That's an excellent moral. Does it go on: do wicked deeds, don't just day-dream about them?'

'And be scared. If you want it to.'

'The trouble is, in my experience, so few sweet maids have any noticeable intelligence to be intelligent with.'

'I dare say you're right,' said Tom. 'But can you be good without intelligence? You can be obedient, of course, and I suppose that's the same thing in the eyes of the people we're expected to obey. We know what a good German is: one who obediently hates everything English and French. But a good man is one in whom the bond of universal human sympathy does not fail.'

'For Christ's sake don't talk like that in war-time,' Williamson exclaimed with a quick flash of feeling. And then he went on in his former tone: 'I thought you'd given up wanting to put the world right. I believe you're as bad as ever.'

When they got back they went into the ante-room, at the far end of which a bar had been rigged up. It was a bare shack after the comfortable farmhouse. The ping-pong table was in use with a new supply of bats and balls. The furniture was very much the worse for wear, and there weren't enough chairs. Mess-smashing had to be paid for, either in cash or discomfort, and discomfort was considered preferable. Mess bills were quite heavy enough, without a whip-round for furniture, which was infernally expensive. In fact mess bills were the subject of a lot of grumbling. Very little beyond rations for eating seemed to be provided for the fifty or sixty francs a week which the P.M.C. collected; and it might go up to seventy or more if there was a big binge. If anyone said anything to James, he called it the price of intemperance.

Altogether it wasn't inexpensive to fight for one's country. There were no free drinks provided for aviators: brewers and vintners and distillers could not brew and vint and distil for pure patriotism. Indeed, as they alone made it humanly possible for the war to be carried on, they well deserved for this service to humanity the fortunes they were making.

After dinner Tom enjoyed being rowdy in the mess. It was fun, till you got sick of it, this life of inebriation, irresponsibility, foolishness, and noise. It was a relief to the nerve-racked; a diversion for the sane. *Dulce est desipere in loco*; the war was certainly a *locus*.

Then he went to bed and read one of the books he had brought back with him. Night-flying started: there was a row of the raiders of both sides. Bombs dropped. The hut shook with them. There was a distant rattle of machine guns: apparently raiders were doing some shooting as well as bomb-dropping. Archie barked.

Williamson came in. 'There's a good moon for them,' he said. 'We seem to get it every night here.'

'I say Bill, do listen to this.' Tom read out: "Even they also whose felicity men stare at and admire, besides their splendour and the sharpness of their light, will with their appendant sorrows wring a tear from the most resolved eye: for not only the winter quarter is full of storms and cold and darkness, but beauteous spring hath blasts and sharp frosts; the fruitful teeming summer is melted with heat, and burnt . . ." He left off for a moment for the crashing of a nearer fall of bombs. ". . . with the kisses of the sun her friend, and choked with dust: the rich autumn is full of sickness; and we are weary of that which we enjoy, because sorrow is its biggest portion: and when we remember that upon the fairest face is placed one of the worst sinks of the body, the nose, we may use it not only as a mortification to the pride of beauty, but as an allay to the fairest outside of condition which any of the sons and daughters of Adam do possess." Isn't it fantastic — oh damn those bombs — that marvellous best period prose leading to a serious meditation on the nose?'

'What the devil are you reading?'

'It's Jeremy Taylor's *Holy Dying*. Appropriate, don't you think? I picked it up for tuppence. Not much demand.'

'The stuff you read,' said Williamson. There was a noise of aeroplanes quite close. He opened the door and looked out.

'Hi! mind that light,' someone shouted, and he shut the door after him. After a few seconds his voice came through the chink of the door. 'Tom, put out your light and come out. I want to show you something.'

Tom blew out his candle, got out of bed, and went outside.

The night was cool. There was a north wind that driveth away rain.

'Look in the road,' Williamson whispered. Against the bank opposite could be seen three dim crouching figures. The major, James, and someone else.

'God, these groundlings,' said Tom. They stood on the bank looking into the sky for the raider, but it was invisible, though the row it made showed that it was near. There was a slight hiss of falling bombs, and two loud detonations two or three hundred yards behind them, and the raider faded away. The major remained in the road. Tom and Williamson went to bed. The row went on at intervals all night. At half-past four Tom was called for the early job.

I I

IT was strange to Tom to be up at daybreak once again, and to eat the hard-boiled dawn egg. They were all very sleepy after the noisy night. It was a clear cold morning that promised a fine day. It had started to get light at four o'clock, and would continue light until about half-past nine in the evening: and C flight's second job would be from 7.30 to 9.30 p.m.

They took off into the sharp air. Besides Mac and Tom there were Dubois, Cross, Baker, and a new fellow called Robson who was on his first job; he was flying in Miller's usual place on Mac's right. They climbed steadily east towards the unspectacular sunrise. The new aerodrome was behind Aire-sur-Lys and the westernmost bulge in the line south of Nieppe Forest.

There seemed to be nothing in the sky. It was too early for Huns, who seldom finished breakfast before six o'clock. They spent an idle-busy hour sailing up and down four or five miles over, dodging Archie, while the sun climbed out of the horizon mist.

Then Mac waggled his wings and turned southwards. Tom could not see what he was after. Mac had the most marvellous eyesight. Then he made out a group of moving dots hardly visible against the grey world. They were perhaps three miles away and below to the south-east.

When he had gained enough height, Mac put his nose down to a hundred and thirty to catch them. They were ten Albatros scouts, and, seeing the attack coming, they turned east to avoid it, but the Camels had enough height to make a final dive at a hundred and sixty, by which they were able just to get a shot at them. Mac was successful in picking off one of the rear ones before they got away. Tom did not hit anything, but he saw Mac's victim go spinning, spinning down out of sight. He had started at above fifteen thousand feet, and it was not possible to see him crash in the far-away world, but he spun at least ten thousand feet, and would hardly spin so far intentionally when he was not being followed down.

The Albatri vanished into the east and stopped there. The Camels resumed patrolling their beat and saw nothing more of them or any other Huns. Archie barked, the sun climbed and brightened, the earth looked more real, guns and shells puffed. A fleet of Nines and Bristols came back from a distant errand. Some Dolphins appeared high up. There were no Huns.

They landed at half-past seven. Tom performed an infinitely leisurely toilet as quietly as he could. Williamson, having no job till midday, was sleeping late. Then he ate a large second breakfast, starting at nine o'clock and spread out by conversation till ten; conversation about the decrepitude of the enemy; about the Albatros and the Pfalz and the Fokker tripehound and the Fokker biplane; the last an elusive sort of machine that only appeared now and then, but seemed pretty good. Perhaps they were experimenting with it. They needed to experiment with something; if they didn't make an effort soon they would be pushed out of the air altogether. They seemed to be concentrating on night-flying, to judge by the nightly racket. They dropped a great number of bombs; it was remarkable they didn't do more damage. They kept people awake and made it difficult to get up at dawn.

A flight went up at ten o'clock. Tom watched them take off, and then wondered what he would do all day. It was distressing to realize that, at ten o'clock in the morning, he had already been up for five hours, and it was more than twelve hours till bedtime.

The long day passed with talking, reading, eating, ping-pong, cards, and, between lunch and tea, sleeping. A flight got a two-seater on their morning job. Dinner was at seven, and a squadron show at 7.30; an uncomfortable arrangement. There wasn't a Hun in the sky; only SEs, Nines, Harry Tates, and clouds of Archie. It was fine, but visibility was bad owing to mist, and Mac turned for home at nine o'clock.

The next day was the same sort of thing, except that C flight did not have the dawn job, and Tom got some morning sleep after a disturbed night. He went up at eleven o'clock, but they did not see any Huns except two separate two-seaters which they chased but did not get near. He was glad they did not have to fight, as it was Cross's day off and another new man named Hole was with them as well as Robson, and the formation was rather comic. Hole was ugly, red-faced, festive; good company but a bad pilot. Tom hoped to God these two would soon settle down to flying; apart from them, C flight wasn't so bad. Mac of course was a first-rate leader. Dubois, if he didn't do much damage to the enemy, could fly: Cross was reliable; Baker might become really good. Tom missed his opposite number Miller in formation; other people's leave was a nuisance. And when Miller returned Mac would be off, and then both would be overdue for Home Establishment; but Miller would probably get a flight, and Mac very likely a squadron of Snipes and become a great man, another Bishop.

In the evening C flight again went out alone. A few clouds had formed during the day, and the atmosphere above five or six thousand feet had a peculiar mistiness and glow. Tom wondered if there had been a big eruption somewhere and volcanic ash was arriving. There were no Huns about. As the sun sank the light changed to a sinister and depressing purple. Clouds were evil; endowed with bad life. Archie had a more awful significance. Yet there were no storms threatening. Nature seemed to be uttering some apocalyptic warning above meteorology. Even Mac was affected by the horribleness of the gloomy light, and he went home at quarter to nine. As they approached ground the menace faded; on earth there was an ordinary glow of sunset.

They had all been disturbed by the evil glare, and gathered to talk about it. While they had been out a fellow named Walker, who had only arrived the day before, had spun into the ground and killed himself; but that was nothing to have such a sunset about.

C flight's first job next day was at 11.30. It was still fine, with a light easterly breeze and a few white clouds between five and six thousand feet. Tom was beginning to feel a little tired, with four hours a day over the lines and nights of bombing. Although the Huns were giving them an easy time of it, to be over the lines was always a strain. Even Archie's continual barking during all the clear weather became irritating.

Again there seemed to be no Huns out. They serpented up and down the front between five and ten miles over. It was impossible to feel comfortable; continuous and exact watchfulness was necessary. Tom was glad to feel that Mac saw everything. They went on, twisting, turning, up and down, interminably. Dubois was opposite Tom, and Cross, Robson, and Baker were behind. He was getting hungry. It was quite pleasant at fifteen thousand feet this weather, very different from the bitter cold when he had first visited the heights. Robson came barging up, and dipped and turned away for home. Archie was very accurate between ten and fifteen thousand. The height seemed to suit him. He was pretty good down to a thousand and up as high as they could go, but that was his best patch. Without Archie it was difficult to believe in the reality of the war, or anything else earthly, at this height.

Mac waggled his wings and put his nose down towards Armentières. There was a bunch of Huns well below them but miles and miles over. Mac evidently intended to attack. Down and on at the hell of a lick. It took over two minutes at a hundred and forty to reach them. They were beyond Armentières, a good fifteen miles over, at about eight thousand feet.

The Pfalz flew towards them. Perhaps they did not see them coming. There were eleven of them in one large formation. It was nearly a head-on meeting. At the last moment some of the Pfalz started splitarsing round. Mac got one at once. Tom, close behind him, found one in his Aldis and fired, allowing plenty of deflection. As he closed on it in a steepening dive it turned on its side and fell over flop into a dive, and Tom pulled up in a zoom, watching it go streaking down. But his engine spluttered. He glanced at the pressure gauge and saw that the pressure had blown on the dive. Hell, fifteen miles over. He flattened out and switched with a touch of a finger over to gravity, and was for a terrible three seconds without engine. Then it picked up and he climbed westwards.

He saw the three other Camels a hundred feet above him. There was a loud pop-pop-pop of machine guns behind him. He kicked the rudder as by reflex and skidded out of the line of fire. There was no one on his tail, but looking down he saw half a dozen Huns following about fifty feet below, and as he looked one pulled up and took a shot at him. It didn't do any damage, but he felt very uncomfortable. He wasn't at all sure that a Pfalz couldn't climb better than a Camel. But they did not follow far. The leader took another snapshot, and then they all turned away. The followers all seemed to be quite tame. Several had just been slaughtered, and the rest were probably too scared to do anything but long for home. They did not know how scared Tom was also. It must have been a shock to be attacked by Camels so far over. Archie had given them no warning.

Tom tried to pump up pressure, but it was no good, so he made for home, and the others followed him in. Mac was anxious to claim two Huns for himself; Tom, Cross, and Baker were credited with one each. If all the claims were good, it was a massacre. But it was difficult to be certain so far over. They looked genuine kills, and that was as much as could be said.

The Germans seemed to put all their worst pilots on Pfalz, whose job, presumably, was to chase lone two-seaters when they could and keep away from Camels and SEs. Nevertheless Tom was very glad his engine hadn't taken another two seconds to pick up.

When they had reported the combat it was two o'clock, and Tom was starving. He ate a huge lunch and then felt sleepy and slept till tea-time. In the evening he was lucky enough to break his tailskid while taxiing out to take off, and so avoided the job, which, however, was uneventful. But a job was worth avoiding, and the nervous tension of flying a long way over Hunland; things happened so suddenly, and there was always the chance of meeting a Hun circus anything up to fifty strong. Only to be over there was a strain to war-tired nerves, and was cumulative in its effect.

Yet Tom was finding that there was an attraction about the area of the lines. Here was the stage of tremendous events, here was frantic excitement in comparison with which nothing else had much flavour. Two hours at a time over there following a leader like Mac was too much; nevertheless, all other places were unreal and uninteresting.

When they went over the lines at noon next day it was pleasantly fresh in the heights, and not too cold. There were enough light clouds to be decorative and to hinder Archie without making formation flying difficult. Archie, having perhaps wasted too much ammunition lately, did not trouble them much, and the Hun flyers seemed to be having a morning off. Mac did not go far over, but cruised gently at half throttle, occasionally floating down to three thousand to look at the ground.

And again in the evening it was quiet and pleasant. There were some Hun scouts miles away in the east, just visible from time to time as tiny dots at the limit of vision. But they showed no inclination to come any nearer. The heavens glowed in light of sunset that turned the western surfaces of clouds to compact flame; and bright whisps of alto-cirrus, seen through a clear mist of light, seemed at stupendous altitude beyond dizzy imagining.

But on the ground heavy guns were busy, and towns on both sides of the lines were being yet more smashed up; ruins were being yet more ruined, and bricks pulverized. From towns where there was anything left to burn long inverted pennons of smoke were streaming.

They went home at dusk, and as they were passing the line of kite balloons one of them, perhaps half a mile away, caught fire, and Archie put up a lot of stuff near it. Mac turned, and they saw a Pfalz making off eastwards. They chased, but it was too fast and got away. It was a jolly good effort on the part of the Pfalz, Tom thought. If they had seen him a minute earlier it would have been his final effort.

An order had come through that bombs were to be carried on all patrols and dropped in Hunland not less than three miles over. They need not go down and aim at anything. The idea seemed to be to create a demoralizing racket; each squadron would drop about a hundred and twenty bombs every fine day. They were also instructed to use up ammunition by firing at the ground. They did a good deal of this already, by way of warming up guns and just for fun. Tom had taken a fancy to the square at Merville for shooting at. The first of the new bomb-dropping jobs would be under his command, as it was Mac's day off on the morrow, the first of June, and C flight had the early job at 6.30.

It was a quiet enough job. There were a few Huns out, but they kept away in the far east, and Tom was not at all desirous of their doing anything else. He got rid of bombs at once. Archie was leaving them alone, and Tom wandered along three or four miles over very cheerfully. It was fine to be leader and not have to keep formation and to know that his tail was well protected, and it was very much easier to keep a good look out. He hadn't Mac's cloud-piercing eyesight, but was confident that he could see well enough in the air to avoid surprise; and that was the great thing. He wasn't Hun-hungry. So long as Huns kept away beyond a ten-mile limit they were no business of his, and he hoped they would stop there.

Occasionally he did a half-roll, to give his followers something to do, and fired at Hunland on the dive. This aggressiveness irritated Archie, who put up quite a lot of hate about it. Tom would dive and zoom and half-roll again, leaving Archie miles away, and shoot again just to annoy him. The rest of the flight tumbled after him as best they could. It was great fun. There didn't seem to be any reason for keeping sedate formation in the empty sky. God had sent a cheerful hour, and Tom would not with superfluous burden load the day.

At quarter past-eight he turned homewards to breakfast. He was hungry, and he put off reporting and attending to flight commander's stuff until he had fed.

'Eh bien, monsieur,' he said to Dubois, 'did you enjoy it?'

'I never enjoy jobs,' Dubois replied, 'but it wasn't so bad. You splitarsed about rather a lot.'

Tom threw his gear on to his bed, brushed his hair and went to breakfast. There had been a lot of bombing during the night, and they were talking in the mess about a hospital near St. Omer that had been badly smashed. The newspapers were making a lot of fuss about the wickedness of Huns in bombing hospitals, as though it were done intentionally. But the fellows of the I.A.F. on night-flying said it was quite impossible to see Red Cross flags.

Then he went to the office to report, and afterwards shaved and settled down to nearly nine hours' rest till the evening job at seven o'clock. He sat outside the hut and tried to read, but it was difficult with the continual row of flying and shooting, and it was natural to look up when a change of engine tone indicated that someone was doing something. He grew tired, and wished that the times between jobs could be passed in oblivion. B flight took off at 11 o'clock. Cross and Baker came and talked to him. There were unpleasant stories from the south. The Huns were pushing and had got within thirty miles of Paris. There was no end to it. The war would go on for ever. There might be another push on their own front at any time, possibly by them to relieve the pressure in the south, and they would have the job of push-helping instead of push-stopping. There had been a small push a fortnight ago when Tom was on leave, to straighten a bit of the line between Béthune and Nieppe Forest. But that time the squadron had not been involved.

They strolled along the road towards Estrée-Blanche, and after a few hundred yards came to a concrete emplacement with a man on guard. They investigated. It was the entrance to the local bomb-store, and contained half-a-million or so pounds of high explosive.

'Good God,' exclaimed Tom; 'I'm going to sleep with wool in my ears in case Jerry gets a direct hit on this place.'

'That man,' said Cross, as they walked back, 'was East Lancs, but he seemed to have more of a Yorkshire accent. He had a signet ring on the little finger of his left hand. The bottom button of his tunic was undone. He had a mark on his cheek where he had nicked himself shaving I should think two days ago. His left shoulder was slightly higher than his right . . . ' He went on for some minutes.

Tom was astonished. 'It's all right,' said Baker; 'he's taking a course of mind training. It keeps him amused.'

'As long as it keeps him amused. But I don't quite see the point.'

'Well, what's the good of eyes if you don't use them?' Cross argued; 'or ears? Stand still a minute and count all the different sounds you can hear.'

'Thanks. I use my eyes quite enough looking for Huns, and my ears listening to my engine.'

'You don't know how much you miss,' Cross insisted.

'Not nearly as much as I'd like to.'

B flight came back to lunch. They had run into a mixed Hun circus at least thirty strong about twelve miles over. Williamson h ad got himself involved and had shot down an Albatros in pure self-defence before he got away. The Huns had shot at them from a distance and let them go. Williamson had one bullet hole in his top plane and that was all the damage. Huns were queer fellows.

III

Tom slept till tea-time and was awakened by Williamson, who brought him letters. There was one from a girl he had been friendly with on leave. She told him her mother had died; and when she went to register the death, the registrar had refused to sign the certificate because she hadn't brought the dead woman's sugar card to surrender.

He ate a lot of bread and honey for tea; dinner would be a snack after nine o'clock. He spent the two hours before the evening job sitting outside the hut with Williamson. Boring as these long unoccupied intervals were, he preferred doing nothing to doing something, such as playing cards or writing letters. He never wanted to play bridge again, and couldn't be bothered to write letters: most of the fellows tormented themselves daily with this duty. He was fighting for his country, and that was quite bad enough without writing about it. Field cards were the greatest of the war's ameliorations. It was interesting to see what messages, unintended by the inventor, could be sent by skilful crossings out.

C flight went out at seven o'clock, and they dropped their bombs and chased a couple of two-seaters and fired off a good deal of ammunition at the ground and that was all. The R.A.F. seemed to have won the war in the air. Tom wished the people on the ground would be quick about winning their war also.

By the time he had finished his flight commander's clerical work it was half-past nine and he was so hungry that even bully beef went down easily. He heard that Wing had warned them provisionally for a period of low work, starting in the morning at the chilly hour of half-past four. Tom was glad it was his day off, but the outlook was gloomy. Presumably a push was contemplated, and they were to help it.

He was very tired, and went to bed soon after he had finished eating. Williamson came in before he was asleep.

'Well, how have you liked your first day in charge?'

'It's all right upstairs,' Tom replied, 'but I don't like all the bumf to sign when I come down hungry.'

'Think of the honour and glory. Hullo, here we go.' There were air-raid noises in the distance.

'Good night,' said Tom. 'I'm going to sleep before they get here.' And he did, but was awakened several times in the night.

When he finally woke up at eight o'clock in the morning, Williamson, back from the early job, was shaving.

'Good morning, Bill. Been ground-strafing?'

'Washed out, my dear, washed out, thank God and all his angels. We just dropped routine bombs from ten thousand and wandered around chasing a few Huns home.'

'What, isn't there going to be a push?'

'No sign of it. Perhaps the pressure down south has eased a bit.'

'I hope so. God, I'll enjoy my day off better than I expected.'

Cross had used Tom's machine for the early job as his own was out of action, and had had a forced landing five miles away near Rely. He had come back to breakfast, leaving the mechanics that had gone to his assistance wrestling with the engine.

'What did you do to it, you greenhouse smasher?' Tom demanded.

'Nothing. It gradually petered out.'

'I don't believe it. It's a good engine.'

'Very likely it is for you,' said Cross seriously, 'but haven't you noticed how an engine gets used to one man, and goes perfectly for him; yet when someone else tries to run it, likely as not plays hell.'

Tom went over to Rely after lunch. Owing to the shortage of sugar they had to sweeten the after-lunch coffee with golden syrup. The mechanics had got the engine going, and Tom bumped off the very rough ground into the air without breaking anything. He went

317

and had a look at Aire and the Nieppe Forest from a hundred feet. There were all sorts of things hidden in that forest when you looked into it closely, from big guns and tanks to dumps of, perhaps, jam and Maconochie. But it was all very well camouflaged, and from a little higher it was just a wood with a few gun-flashes. The line ran close in front of it, sweeping south-west towards Robecq, and it was very uncomfortable flying low over its eastern edge, because of all the explosions going on. So he climbed away up to five thousand feet and went across the lines and took a long dive at Merville, firing a few hundred rounds at the square. When he pulled out Archie started firing at him and was very accurate. Tom circled, and Archie actually followed him round. He tried to loop round a burst, but flopped out sideways and nearly spun. He hated to spin unintentionally. Camels were brutes to loop. Archie was wasting a lot of shells on him. He dodged about, and Archie did not get near enough to be unpleasant, but he was very persistent. It was fun having a bombardment all to himself. He would dive, zoom with rudder, circle, half-roll, loose off a burst at Hunland, and Archie would be all over the sky trying to anticipate. There was no ill feeling about it, and Tom went home when he had had enough, with Archie barking round him like an excited dog until he was out of sight.

He was back in time for tea, and afterwards walked over to Estrée-Blanche with Williamson to explore. It was a pretty village, with a rivulet and a calvary. They went to a cottage for food and conversation, and the woman gave them plenty of eggs and fried potatoes and coffee for two francs each. Williamson had done his second job in the afternoon, and they had caught a two-seater and crashed it behind Lestrem. The woman had two little girls that looked at them in silence, and a cat that had given birth to three kittens three days ago. The elder girl, nine or ten, was interested in Williamson's hair, which waved pleasantly, and after profound study she remarked, 'Monsieur se coiffe à la mode'. They thought it would be nice to keep a kitten in their hut, and madame was quite willing to give them one, but it would not be old enough for a fortnight to be taken from its mother.

They were back in time to see C flight take off for the last job, and managed to eat some dinner. As there was a squadron show at six o'clock in the morning Tom kept sober and went to bed in good time, but could not get to sleep for noises. He was becoming used to night noises and it took a particularly loud crash to wake him up once he had got to sleep. The trouble was to get there.

In the morning he spent two hours at work with the squadron and went miles and miles over, but there were no Huns. The same thing in the afternoon from half-past three to half-past five. These squadron shows weren't much good, for if the flights kept together no Huns, in whatever quantities, would go near them. They dropped seventy or so bombs and fired a few thousand rounds at Huns in general, and cost the enemy a lot in shrapnel. But the whole thing had an air of futility. Once the war might have had a purpose, heaven knew what, but some sort of purpose; now it was just damned silly.

It had been a hot day, and it was pleasant to sit outside the hut smoking peacefully in the cool evening. Four hours a day of war flying were tiring even if there were no Huns to fight, and made the neck sore. And the first job in the morning was at half past five, and it would be a grand night for bombing. Hudson came back from leave. Chadwick had been to St. Omer and came back in the same tender bringing a musical instrument called a one-man-band. Maitland had gone on leave.

It was impossible to sleep before about one o'clock, when the moon, set and the Huns went home. At half-past four they were called. Tom's engine would not give its revs, and when Mac opened out he was left behind. It did not matter, for they did not see any sign of Huns, who almost seemed to have retired from the war in the air by day, but it added to the nervous tension. And it was the same in the afternoon, when C flight went out alone from one to three o'clock. Mac cut both these jobs short by ten minutes as there was no purpose in stopping out. When Tom had finished for the day he was too tired to take off his sidcot. He flopped on his bed and fell asleep at once.

Tom's engine was doctored and it seemed to be running all right in the morning when he took off for the six o'clock squadron job, but after they had been over and dropped their bombs, the revs dropped so much that he turned back to go home. But before he reached the aerodrome it picked up and was running quite well, so

319

he turned east again. Rotary engines were mysterious and wonderful things. He saw some Camels away beyond Merville and went to join them. It was B flight. They were busy shooting down a two-seater. Tom saw it go down and crash near Estaires; and as he could not see his own flight he tacked on to B. Williamson was not there, it being his day off. There were some clouds this morning, and later they caught another two-seater among them. It dived away north-wards but not in time to escape. The pilot was hit and the machine zoomed up, flopped over, and spun away. They followed it down and saw it crash at Neuve Eglise.

Tom could not make out what was the matter with his engine. It had periods when it would not give full revs, and then it would pick up and run well for a time. But it did not seem likely to cut out altogether, so in the afternoon when C flight went out alone at four o'clock, he determined to hang on if he possibly could.

There were continents of cloud between five and ten thousand feet. Some Hun scouts could be seen occasionally a long way away but they would not come within range. The clouds hindered Archie from bothering them much, and they went up and down their beat for a long time in peace. Then a two-seater, an LVG, came nosing along towards Lens to do a shoot. They saw it from fifteen thousand feet creeping among the clouds, and went down in a steep dive, dropping on it so suddenly that the observer did not see them until too late. He fired and hit Robson who plunged earthwards, and then the LVG, shot to blazes, toppled over and spun away into a cloud. Mac dived down past the cloud like a gull down the face of a cliff, till he came out below its base, and Tom, following, saw the LVG spinning down with flames wrapping the fuselage. Robson was avenged.

They climbed and went south to Arras and then north again without seeing any more Huns. But Mac had tasted blood, and as there were no aeroplanes, he went for a couple of balloons up behind Steenwerck where the clouds were helpful. Tom hated this balloon game; the Huns put up so much filth. They came from the clouds two thousand feet above the southern balloon and went down on it in a very twisty dive. Archie woofed all round them at once. But they got through his barrage. Tom pointed his nose at the balloon and fired: couldn't miss. The observer jumped. A flag of flame from the balloon. The observer's parachute opened a little and then collapsed and he went straight down. Mac made for the second balloon which was being hauled down quickly. Archie put up a black barrage in front of them. They zig-zagged through. Stuff was coming up from pom-poms in smoky streaks. But the second balloon went, and Tom saw the observer jump and his yellow parachute open, so that he floated down to safety. Flaming onions, phosphorous patches of smoke that it was fiery death to touch, floated up past their wing tips in strings, and things like Very lights. The stuff seemed only to miss them by inches. There was another Archie barrage in front of them as they turned west. They dived under it, but Archie was all round them again immediately, making a row like a mad Cerberus. They got through safely and went home.

Tom found that his mouth was dry and foul. The way the Huns protected their balloons was wonderful. It was miraculous that they had all got away. The sky had been full of death. He hoped Mac was satisfied.

When they landed they had been out nearly two hours and a half. Everyone but Tom had had to switch over to gravity. Perhaps his engine didn't get enough mixture. As he was taxiing in it stopped, and ten minutes was wasted trying to get it to start again, but it refused.

Very little damage had been done by all the hate. Mac's bus was untouched. Tom had a hole through his rudder. Cross had a tear in his top right-hand plane and a fragment of Archie embedded in a strut. Baker had a slit in a plane and some wires had been cut. Yet Archie must have used a thousand rounds and seemed to have their range to a foot; and God knew how much stuff had been put up by pom-poms, besides all those ghastly bubbles of fire that floated round them. They all swore to having missed some of them by an inch, and it was said to be certain destruction to touch one. Yet they were all safe, if scared — except poor Robson who had the unworthy fate of being shot down by a damned two-seater. It was spectacular to light those huge balloon bonfires in the sky, but none of them was at all keen on repeating the feat, unless it was Mac, who by some inscrutable twist of nature was master of his fate and safe in the midst of a furnace while he followed his star. He was going on leave in a few days and wanted to do some damage before he went. Tom marvelled at him: he was an example of that mythus Tom had never believed in, the man of destiny. The stories of a Marlborough or a Napoleon immune and invulnerable became credible; of Nelson or Achilles, safe till their destiny was fulfilled, and perishing at once when fate had used and abandoned them. He didn't believe in this sort of thing; it was anthropomorphic interpretation of chance; but he marvelled, and had a wash and changed for dinner.

A and B flights went out together at 7.30. Tom had many drinks after dinner as the morrow was his day off and he needn't bother about being fit for an early show. He yarned in the mess with Cross and Baker and Hole. Chadwick earnestly produced music from his one-man-band, assisted by Griffith at the piano. Griffith also sang. He was quite a good baritone, and gave them clean fun such as 'Clementine' and 'There is a Tavern'.

The patrol came home at quarter-past nine. They had met a lot of triplanes and Albatros scouts and had shot down four. Large, Franklin, Williamson, and Jones were credited. Thorpe, a newish member of A flight, was missing: he had just vanished.

'Two casualties to-day,' Tom remarked to Williamson when they were in bed listening to the night flyers and the row of bombs and guns. 'Things aren't so good.'

'Both new fellows. You're bound to get that.'

'Poor blighters. Thank God we came out in winter, and had time to get acclimatized.'

Williamson yawned. 'Hell, I'm tired. When the devil is it going to rain? It seems to have been fine for months.'

IV

TOM lazed away his day off. As B flight only had one job, an uneventful job before breakfast, he had Williamson's companionship. They talked of what to do after the war.

'Are you serious about your farm?' Tom asked.

'Yes. At least, I'm keen on the idea. Why don't you come in with me? It's a good life. We're both unattached.'

'I'd love to. But I don't know the first thing about it.'

'You'd learn in six months,' Williamson declared.

'What, all about crops and cattle and markets and God knows what?'

'Yes. Nothing in it for a man of your intelligence.'

They argued about it for some time, and at length Tom said:

'Look here, Bill. Let's say it's fixed we do something together, but don't let's absolutely fix on farming. There's plenty of time; there may be other ideas. I've more than half a mind to clear out to some other part of the earth for a time, and it would be fine to go together.'

'Well, if anything definite occurs to you. . . .'

Mac warned him for flight leader next day. The first job was at the reasonable hour of eight, so he would have a chance of several hours' sleep after the racket had ceased. The second job was at 2.30; both single flight patrols.

There was a formation of Huns about when Tom invaded Hunland in the morning. He climbed to fifteen thousand, but they were still two thousand feet above and well east. He counted seven of them; Pfalz scouts. They showed no inclination to come down, and Tom considered fifteen thousand feet high enough for a Camel; they lost liveliness rapidly above that. They would go up to twenty thousand, but weren't any good up there.

He cruised up and down, watching the Pfalz, who kept at a respectful distance. It was good enough; he was preventing their going down on any lonely Harry Tates, and if he tried to get at them he wouldn't be able to.

Presently he saw a spot moving about in the distance towards Lens that might be an aeroplane doing a shoot. He opened out and put his nose down to a hundred and thirty to get between it and home if it was a Hun. He kept an eye on the Pfalz, but they were miles away.

Suddenly Archie put up a couple of bursts. They must be to warn the two-seater. Tom went down more steeply; a hundred and forty, fifty. They would intercept it. It put its nose down to go home, but the Camels were coming down at a hundred and sixty. Tom got it in his Aldis and opened fire at rather long range. The official idea was to hold fire until you couldn't miss, but Tom wasn't a hero and liked to put the wind up the enemy as soon as he could. After all, a couple of machine guns at a hundred yards, aimed with correct deflection, must put the fear of death into the crew of a not-too-lively LVG.

Baker, on his left, was well up with him, and Tom heard his guns rattling, but the others had lost some distance. The LVG turned sharply away, throwing the observer's aim out, and he fired at random. Cross headed it off, and the three of them put burst after burst into it. A yellow flame came from the tank amidmost. The observer stood up, leaning from it with his hands over his face. The pilot put the machine into a vertical dive, and the observer jumped or was jerked out. He went down in the dreadful wake of the aeroplane with legs and arms asprawl in the unresisting air. Tom felt sick. O God, why did they do these things? He lifted his misted goggles, remembering the Pfalz, and searched the sky. They were dots, miles away and above. 'You bloody skunks,' he yelled at them. Christ almighty, what were they doing up there, leaving that wretched LVG to look after itself? He hated them and climbed and climbed at them. His engine wouldn't give its revs. It was no use; he couldn't get at them.

He calmed. He was being a fool. But, O God, this bloody war, this lawful holy murder.

He went away west and cruised about over the lines, keeping an RE8 in view. Protection was all very well; he had had enough of the other sort of thing.

In the afternoon it was misty. There were no Huns about and Archie could not get their range. They wandered about at twelve thousand feet where it was cool and refreshing after the oppressive heat on the ground. At last it felt as though a storm were gathering that might break the weather. They were back by half-past four, and they had tea and Tom signed the forms and finished the day's work.

Tom fought his depression. It was no use being upset. War was like that; the human brute had an instinct for murdering strangers: itself a stranger in a universe that would in time, long cosmic time, kill it. Meanwhile it was sometimes possible to be happy with the help of dope. He did not want to get tight, however, as there was a job at six o'clock in the morning, and the possibility of a break in the weather seemed remoter in the cool evening. So he got half tight.

A flight met the evening circus over Fleurbaix and got shot at rather a lot; but the Huns were no marksmen, for they could only find one bullet hole among them, in Lewin's rudder. Forster got a Pfalz in a spin.

Sunrise was reddish but it was quite fine enough for the early job, and B and C flights took off at six o'clock. Hun scouts began to appear after they had been out for half an hour. Tom, watching the sky overhead, saw a sudden flash in vacancy. He pushed up his goggles and peered. Yes, there was something there, so high as to be invisible unless the eye was suspecting that precise spot. He had seen them before Mac, he thought, and was pleased with himself for this feat. It might be Dolphins, but he had an instinct that it was Huns; triplanes, at that height.

He opened out and drew level with Mac, moved the joystick two inches left and two inches right to make one wing-waggle, and stretched up an arm to point out the Huns. He saw Mac look up, and at once waggle his wings.

Mac climbed all out. With his feeble engine Tom could not keep with the rest, and they climbed further and further above him. He went on climbing, and reached eighteen thousand feet, where he was three hundred feet below the others. The triplanes were still high above, perhaps at twenty thousand. They seemed to be waiting for them, knowing that the higher the Camels went, the greater would be their own advantage; they were twice as good as Camels at twenty thousand.

Tom's engine began spitting and missing. He fiddled with the fine adjustment, and succeeded in reaching nineteen thousand. His Camel was very floppy on the controls there, the engine was spitting and popping badly, and he had a queer sort of feeling that he must hang on to the joystick tightly or he would fall out of the sky.

A little above nineteen thousand his machine stopped climbing and seemed to move slowly along horizontally with its tail down, almost stalling. The others were five or six hundred feet above. He moved the fine adjustment a little too much and choked the engine. Immediately he stalled and spun. He let her go, pulling the fine adjustment right off to clear the engine. He came out of the spin at fourteen thousand feet over Carvin, and opened the throttle and fine adjustment. The engine picked up and ran in its usual half-hearted way. He was fed up with the damned thing. They kept on tinkering with it, and then on the ground it would give its revs, but in the air it had no guts. It wasn't due for overhaul until it had done another fifty hours. It was worth while crashing the bus and writing it off; but he had sworn to stop crashing.

Archie, pleased to have a lone Camel to worry, came woofing all round him. He cleared out of Hunland across the lines and circled about looking up for C flight, but the sky seemed empty. He flew up northwards past Béthune, where two stray Camels from another squadron tacked on to him, probably because of his streamer.

Having a following, he turned eastwards and soon saw a two-seater behind Merville. He chased it off, not very seriously, as he didn't know his assistants and was sick of shooting at two-seaters.

Then he climbed to sixteen thousand, looking for C flight. He sighted a formation of Pfalz below him in the east. They were quite a dozen miles over. Mac would have gone for them at once, dived and shot one down, and away. Tom hesitated. He lifted his goggles to examine the brilliant sky. It wasn't easy to see against the morning sun, but he thought there were some specks high up. Then he saw about ten aeroplanes in two close layers at his own height coming from the south, but to the east of him. Then a flash high up. Probably those tripes again. He studied the dots in the south. They became large enough to recognize: Camels; and they were after the Huns.

Tom had another look upwards, and as the triplanes were still keeping in the heights he put his nose down to attack the lower formation. They had turned east and were going home as fast as they could. He took a long shot at them without expecting to hit anything, for he had missed his opportunity through over-caution. As he was doing that a Camel came vertically down out of nowhere on to one of the rear Huns and sent him flopping down in a full-engine dive, turning as if in a slow spin.

It was Mac. He seemed able to make his bus jump. Then all the others were there, B and C flights. The triplanes had come down, six of them, and they did some diving at the splitarsing Camels, but couldn't hit anyone, and soon went off upstairs and weren't seen again.

Tom followed C flight with his little formation, but one of his followers drew up to him and waved good-bye and they went away west.

It was soon time to go home, and B flight disappeared. Mac seemed reluctant to go; perhaps he wanted to bag another Hun and make sure of going on leave with a score of fifty. What a man! He kept them out twenty minutes longer than the regulation two hours and they chased a two-seater, but it was warned in plenty of time to escape.

They landed at twenty past eight, and B flight, waiting to make a joint report, cheered Mac ironically as he climbed out.

'How many Huns did you get after we left, Mac?' Large inquired.

'None.' B flight made noises of derision, and they all went and reported; then had second breakfast. Those tripes and Pfalz had probably been trying to work a decoy. They hadn't the guts for it. All they were good for was to chivvy artillery buses or unescorted Nines bombing thirty miles over. Tom retold the story of how they had got an LVG in flames the day before with seven Pfalz sitting over them frightened to interfere. What a crew! Still, they were showing themselves more now.

C flight's second job was to be at three o'clock, but during the morning clouds came up from the west and spread over the sky a monotonous grey screen. By eleven o'clock it was raining steadily, and had obviously set in for the day. There was a general rising of spirits. Rain at last, thank God; half a day's rest and perhaps a peaceful night.

Mac came round shouting for Tom and Dubois and Cross and Baker and Hole. He was going to St. Omer; had a tender; C flight first choice of places; the afternoon show was bound to be a wash-out; a good feed together before he went on leave.

So C flight, except Dubois, spruced themselves up and went to St. Omer; Forster and Franklin with them. They lunched at the Treille d'Or. The cooking was excellent, and Tom had a bottle of Chambertin he would remember for ever. Then coffee and cognac and a Romeo and Juliet and everyone talking away; young eupeptic bellies sleek with content.

Some of them wanted to shop. They went out into the narrow street in which the Treille d'Or was concealed. It was raining fast.

Soon Mac cursed the rain. 'I got no goddarn shopping to do. Who's for a bottle of fizz? Franklin? Cundall? Come on Tom. Come on Baker.'

327

Tom and Baker and Hole went with Mac into the drinking place that had attracted his notice, and the others would rendezvous there when they had bought their stuff. It was a private house except for a sign CAFÉ over a bottle of champagne in a ground floor window, and the open front door. Madame *bon-joured* them graciously and showed them into a comfortable sitting-room.

'Champagne, messieurs?' She began to enumerate her stock.

'Apportez bon, très bon,' Mac commanded briefly. He was removing his trench coat and madame saw his wings.

'Ah, des aviateurs! I love ze brave flies!' She embraced them each in turn.

'Madame est très gentille,' said Tom politely.

'You 'ave my Pommery. It ees ver' good. Mil neuf cent douze.' She smiled knowingly and left them.

'A pity she's not forty years younger,' said Hole, his short sandy hair bristling with sudden lust.

'Randy old bitch,' Mac commented.

Madame returned with eight bottles on a tray, and stayed talking to them in Anglo-French until she perceived accurately that they had had enough of her. The Pommery was good, too dry for Tom's English palate, but it was exhilarating, and that was everything. They were soon all very pleased with each other. Tom tried to retain a spark of reason in the centre of his rotating brain. He could do it so long as he refrained from talking. He closed his eyes to feel better the swaying and falling of the world. It wasn't possible to keep from talking for long at a time. He noticed that Hole, his pale blue eyes wonderfully bright with conviviality, tended to talk about General this and Lord that; about binges at the Savoy, the Piccadilly, Prince's; he was *fruges consumere natus*. Baker talked about Eastbourne, where he lived, and the school he had been to; he shed off layer after layer of his quickly acquired scepticism and sardonic war-weariness and groped back towards his former glory of being captain of the cricket eleven. Fours came from his bat, late cuts, off drives, a pull over square-leg's head.

Mac had never seen cricket played: had heard it was the slowest game in creation. The western slopes of the Rockies towered behind him; hemlock, spruce, huge Douglas fir; the crash of falling giants;

328

lumber floating down to the mills of the Pacific coast; the yell of bandsaws; prime clear and merchantable red pine and white pine; spruce, that was used for aeroplanes.

Aeroplanes: the present did not peel off; he was a fighter all through; he had found the life that chimed with his temperament exactly; while others were sick with longing for dead days, spirits opaque with dread, he was content and limpid, catching the fierce rays of war like a clear lens and focusing them to a point of fire.

The spark of detached observation spluttered out. 'I say Mac; what about that blasted engine o' mine. It never goes properly. It's putting years on me.'

'General Boodle was completely blotto,' said Hole to Baker. 'He was showing us bayonet drill with a knife tied on the leg of a chair.'

'Can't get shot of it unless you crash the bus.'

'I've crashed my allowance. I'll be breaking my neck.'

'He did an at-the-stomach point at a waitress and lunged a bit farther than he meant.'

'Ay. You've sure said it, Tom. I tell you what. Fly mine while I'm on leave, but don't crash it or I'll drink your blood.'

'Thanks Mac. Damn good of you.'

'Good job she wore corsets.'

'I'll fix it. Yours'll do for new fellows to practise with. That'll get the bastard crashed.'

'A month ago I thought I'd got the swell bus of the squadron.'

'A good thing it was only at the stomach,' said Baker.

'It's no durn good going by looks. They're like women; you got to work 'em to find out.'

Forster came in and Tom shared another bottle with him. The stuff had got hold of him. He would drink himself out. Franklin arrived soon after and the room at once was crowded. They talked and cross-talked, and lapsed into song.

> Take the pistons out of my kidneys
>   The gudgeon pins out of my brain
> From the small of my back take the crankshaft
>   And assemble the engine again.

That song was damn funny when you were tight. And he was tight;

tight as ———. Didn't matter. Tender all the way back. Hadn't been really tight for a long time. Felt good.

And assemble the engine again.

Here was Cross at last.

I went up in an aeroplane and crashed into a farm.

What was Cross shouting about? Stopped raining? Sun? Christ, and there was a job. Mac was bustling about. Fifteen miles to home. Forty minutes before the job, someone was saying. Had he got to go up blotto as he was? Where was the tender? Mac seemed to know. Outside. Sun shining. Bloody marvellous. Could only just walk. Stagger, rather.

Tender. Eyes shut, lean against next fellows. Jolt, jolt, jolt. Thing was moving. Damnation, what had thrown him out of his seat? My god, what a blotto patrol it would be. Jolt, jolt, jolt. . . .

Back already. Didn't feel much better. Ten minutes, ten minutes, ten minutes. Put head in water. A bit better. Get sidcot on. Best clothes, damn it.

Climbed in all right, anyway. Felt better in cockpit. Comfortable. Couldn't fall out. It'd be damn funny doing a blotto patrol. Wouldn't be any Huns about so soon after rain. Contact. Giving her revs all right on the ground. Could see the rev-counter. Not so blotto. They were all pretty tight except Cross. Let go. Could he taxi? Yes, easy. Open fine adjustment. Throttle. Off we go. Hold her nose down then zoom. Up, up. Pulling nicely. Roll. Left stick and rudder. Throttle back. Here's the horizon coming straight. Stick and rudder central. Throttle open. God, trees. Just over. Near thing. What the hell, rolling at that height in formation. Bombs on too. Christ, he'd forgotten. No wonder he'd lost height. Tom, you're blotto. Sit tight, you loon. You know you're blotto, so don't play the fool.

It was easy flying. The bus flew itself. He was asleep with his eyes open. Didn't know what was happening. Bus was flying without him. Damn these clouds. Spots in the sky. Huns or just spots? Didn't know, didn't care. He laughed like hell; it was damn funny flying with the sky all knobbly and floppy and swimmy not knowing or caring a cuss about anything. The old bus was going

330

a treat for a change — nothing like alcohol for making an engine go, but you had to fill up the driver, not the tank. Get rid of bombs. One, two, three, four. Good-bye bombs, blow up wicked old Jerry. Glory glory alleluia; glory glory alleluia; glory glory alleluia; as we go. . . .

Christ, no mistaking that blasted pop-pop-pop-pop of machine guns. Which way up was he. The bus was splitarsing about like a loose kite. There was a flaming tripe shooting at some one. Nasty looking things. Shoot the bastard. Hell, guns wouldn't work. Loading handles. Rat-a-tat-tat-tat-tat-tat. That was O.K. Now where was the tripe? Where the hell was everyone? Not an aeroplane anywhere. Damn funny how things vanished. Where the devil was he? Better beat it westwards. Oh God, tripes between him and home! What a life! Better creep off south if he knew which way. Were those really tripes or was he seeing things? Christ yes, they were tripes and they were after him. Get the hell out of this. Nose down. Thirteen hundred revs. Where was he going? God, they'd catch him. Down, down. Four tripes, getting damn close. Cloud. Into it. Plop. Like jumping out of a window into a fog.

Couldn't float around in a cloud till the war was over though. Too bloody thirsty, for one thing. Blast those tripes, setting on a man who wasn't in condition to look after himself. And he must make water. Awkward in a cloud; might spin. But the bus was still flying itself, bless it. And certainly nice and private. Flick. He'd come out of the cloud without meaning to. Half-roll back. Best thing would be to float down and come out low and contour-chase home. Throttle back, gliding at ninety.

God, it was funny the way those tripes must be dashing about like wet hens trying to watch all the cloud. Cats with a million mouse-holes to watch.

There was the ground. Out of the cloud. Below three thousand. Now, away out of it. Sun would be southerly. Three-thirty summer time. Could guess about where the sun was behind the clouds. Where the devil was he? Couldn't recognize a thing. There was some transport. Must be the hell of a way over. Get along, Camel. Twelve fifty revs, hundred and ten miles an hour, a thousand feet. When the devil was he coming to the lines? Holy God, an aerodrome, buses with crosses. Must be twenty-five miles over. Take a shot at it while he was there. Two-seaters. One just going to take off. Down on it. Rat-tat-tat-tat-tat. It swung round, turned over on its back. That was a shock for them. What a joke, shot down taking off. Good old Pommery.

He'd been flying with the sun on his right, bloody fool. All wrong. Couldn't think, but try the opposite. A car. Strafe it. God, the real thing. Trees lined the road, damn it. But down on it. Better than strafing brass-hats. Rat-tat-tat-tat-tat-tat-tat. Three in it. One at the back got up to jump, but collapsed. It swerved into a tree. He lost it. Sudden burst of grey smoke ahead. Gun. That would be firing west, anyhow. He was heading right. He'd just shot three men in a car. Rat-tat-tat-tat-tat at that gun. Couldn't see any guns, but it looked a bit unnatural where that burst had come from. Camouflage. Let 'em have it and then swerve away in case another gun fired. Must be fifteen-inch all that way back. Pretty good to think of swerving.

He'd shot three men in a car; very likely killed them. Queer thing to do. Quite right, but queer. Damned annoying for them, probably German brass-hats lording it. They were going to visit a general and drink brandy and arrange the deaths of a few hundred or a few thousand more men, and up bobs a Camel from nowhere and kills them. Damn funny that.

He contour-chased along, looking for targets, but the exhilaration faded suddenly, quickly. Fear half-blinded him; miles away over Hunland alone. He came on a handful of grey soldiers marching. Came on them quite suddenly. God, he couldn't. It would be crude murder. He pulled his nose up and flew over them. He saw their faces looking up at him, some mouths open with astonishment. One of them stopped and the man behind bumped into him. Some were unslinging rifles. They did not break ranks. He passed on.

The ground was broken and pitted and ruinous. He climbed, searching the sky, but could see no aeroplanes. Yes, a two-seater coming from the lines. He didn't mind that, and kept his nose up to get out of range of ground machine guns. There was La Bassée. He followed the canal and then crossed the lines at Givenchy.

God, he'd been lucky. He got away with a lot. He'd come perhaps thirty miles all alone across Hunland, and no one seemed so much as to have fired at him. Pure drunkard's luck. And, hell, he seemed to remember rolling with bombs on at a hundred feet or so. He'd never go up tight again. He'd got away with it this time. He'd take the lesson. But who would have expected a solid downpour out of an all-grey sky to leave off so suddenly? And what a thirst he had. Well, he was nearly home.

Then he realized he'd only been out an hour, or rather less. Hell. He couldn't go back over the lines with that thirst. He circled over Hinges wondering what to do. There was certainly nothing to drink three thousand feet up in the air. Was a man entitled to land for a drink during a patrol? Probably not. He'd never heard of such a thing. If only his engine would miss, but it was going well.

He saw something floating down towards him; a Camel. It circled with him. Dubois. Oh damn; that meant he must lead Dubois to battle. He couldn't see properly. The edges of things were blurred; there were spots. But Dubois wasn't a fire-eater; wouldn't mind at all if they didn't go more than five yards over. So they wandered up and down the lines for half an hour without seeing anything but clouds, Archie, and an Ak-W; and then Tom, fed up, turned for home. On the way they picked up Hole.

After landing, Tom and Hole went to the mess and drank tea, and then back to the hangars to wait for Mac. Hole confided that after the scrap with the tripehounds he had lost everyone and had come back across the lines and stopped there, feeling too blotto and bleary for anything else. What ought he to say about it?

'Just keep quiet,' Tom replied. 'I've got a sensational yarn that'll occupy attention.'

Mac and Baker came back twenty minutes later.

'So here you all are,' said Mac. 'I thought the whole durn bunch of you'd gone west. See that tripe I got?'

They shook heads.

'You sure are cock-eyed. Take my tip and go on the wagon for a while.' He grinned. 'You oughta seen it. I shot him up and a bottom wing came off. He flopped over that side and then all the other wings just peeled off and floated around together. He must have felt peculiar sitting up there without any wings. Where's Cross?'

No one knew.

'The only sober man on the job hasn't come back,' Baker remarked.

'I was sober,' Dubois said gently.

'Anyone done anything?' Mac asked, starting to walk to the office. Tom told his story amid a lot of comment.

'You were drunk sure enough,' Mac said. 'Where was this aerodrome?'

'I don't know. I came to near La Bassée. I suppose it's somewhere east of there, but I really don't know.'

'It's a sight too good a reed to waste. You ought to go out tight every day. But how the hell to make a report if you don't know where it all happened has me beat.'

They went to the office and Mac claimed his Hun, and then Tom repeated his tale.

'It's my fault he was a bit oiled, major,' said Mac, shouting through the row of A and B flights taking off. 'Can't rely on this goddarn climate two minutes together.'

The major turned to James. 'Got the list of Hun aerodromes?'

James found it. The most likely aerodrome seemed to be Cardin.

'They're DFWs there unless they've moved in the last week. Was your two-seater a DFW?'

'Very likely it was,' said Tom.

They concocted a report. 'Lieut. Cundall engaged five Fokker triplanes inconclusively and entered a cloud. He emerged over an enemy aerodrome at Cardin and attacked a two-seater which was taking off. The Enemy Aircraft crashed. He returned at a low altitude, attacking suitable ground targets on the way.'

God, what a distillation, Tom thought; his bullock in a bottle of beef extract. He flung himself down on his bed and slept till dinner.

v

NEWS came that Robson was not dead; he was unconscious in a CCS. Somehow he had got out of the dive which Tom saw him go down in and had got across the lines and crashed. There was a bullet in his left shoulder.

Nothing had been heard of Cross by eleven o'clock, when Tom and Williamson went to bed.

'I'm afraid those tripes must have got Cross,' Tom said.

'Very, when you disappeared into a cloud.'

'What the hell — oh, don't be funny. I'm sick to death of this bloody war.'

'So you've told me before. So am I. But I wish I could feel I was as lucky as you are. You invade a Hun aerodrome single-handed and quite blotto, and you get away without even a bullet hole.'

'No. They've found a couple of holes to patch.'

'Well, they were harmless ones. If you want glory, you've only to sail over Hunland and shoot down everything you come across. It's my belief that the bullet's not made that can touch you.'

It was a comparatively peaceful night. There were a few FEs up, but it was too cloudy for the Huns to fly. The guns weren't busy. They slept well and woke up to the sweet music of rain on the roof and a grey sighing morning.

Tom lay on his bed in reverie or meditation or somnolence most of the long blank day. There was never a sign that the weather might clear, and no threat of work to be done. The long tension of waiting, waiting for the next job, was relaxed. No sound of gunfire disturbed the peace; the outside world was all gentle rain and wind. Tired brain and nerves sank into lethargy with the soft influence. In the quietness young men, sick of fighting, ill with unacknowledged ravages of excitement and fear, dreamed of past times that seemed perfect in happiness; or imagined the joy of going home, wounded, on leave, on Home Establishment, or after the war. Peace: if peace returned to the world it was difficult to imagine that anyone would ever find anything to grumble about; no one could help being happy in peace time. And, this one ended, there would be no more war.

It seemed to Tom, thinking of the strenuous period since he had been back from leave, that there was some difference between these flying days and those before. It was as if some tattered flag flying over the fortress of his mind had been finally shot-hackled or storm-blown to fragments. There had been a glory in the bare or cloudy skies; there had been joy in the lifting wings of flight: those things were gone; he had grown suddenly older, and beauty was dumb. And yet this was summer time, with its train of kingly days, when the blue tent of heaven was rich with gold and purple spilt by the royal

335

sun. His brain was wooden: fatigue burdened his eyes and hummed faintly in his ears.

And now Cross had gone. Tom had a book of his, a cheap edition of *The Old Wives' Tale*, with his name, H. Lawrence Cross, in it. He would keep it. He had Grey's blue leather *Religio Medici*. Seddon's cigarette case. Perhaps it was Seddon's death that had frozen his mind into this numbness. It still excruciated him to think of Seddon being burnt to death; the last thought of his tortured screaming brain would be — *in the interests of usury*. O God, O God — but what was the use of crying out O God to the deaf void? A martyr's death at the stake was sweet peace to his; pitiable proud sacrifice for a cause he abhorred.

He must not think of it: he would go mad. Or he must think: he died for England; who dies if England live? He must think: he died willingly that others might live; fighting for all he held dear. He must think that God had care of him, that he was a hero, that his death would help to bring lasting peace to the world . . . O curse those damned lies plastered over the brutish face of war. He must endure the truth he saw; the naked beastliness of this harpy; hating the system of lies and grab that brought it forth. There was yet one iron god that could make life noble: truth.

He heard that another piece of ribbon had been awarded to Mac. He would soon rival a base colonel for ribboned magnificence. It was a D.F.C. this time. Tom almost envied Mac his simple murderousness; his ordered world wherein Germans were vermin and it was decorous and ought to be sweet for men between fifteen and fifty to die for their country or for the sake of a scrap. There would be a binge.

'I've a feeling I shall get tight beyond everything to-night,' Tom said to Williamson, 'so I hope you'll be sober enough to bring me across the road when I fade out.'

'Feel like that? Well, I hope it keeps dud for you in the morning.'

The binge was lunatic, and developed into a delirium of mess-smashing. It wasn't safe with fellows like Mac, Franklin, and Watt, the hefty and warlike Australian, charging drunkenly about like bulls intent on destruction, and several of the less mad retreated to their huts. Tom yowled and frenzied as long as he could and woke up at five o'clock in the morning with a raging thirst and only his shoes removed. It was still raining. He went to bed and stopped there till ten o'clock.

He felt better for his drunk once the immediate after-effects had worn off, and was not greatly worried by the clearing of the sky that made the four o'clock job possible.

When the time for this job came Mac was missing; he had gone out before lunch and had not returned; so Tom took charge and found a pilot to make up the formation. This was a new man named Fuller who was religious and parted his black hair in the middle and always seemed to be thinking of something else. It was a good opportunity to show a new man the lines, as it wasn't likely there would be any Huns about; as in fact there were not when they arrived over Hunland; and Archie could not range them accurately. They wandered among the foggy clouds for an hour and then Tom decided to waste no more oil and petrol, and went home. Although nothing had happened, a lot of flight commander's stuff had accumulated during the day, and Tom was kept busy till dinner. Mac reeled home at about eleven o'clock. He had been to St. Omer and met some Canadians he knew and they had celebrated his fame.

The next day Mac went on leave and Miller returned. It was again dud in the morning, but the squadron went out at 7.30 in the evening. Tom led C flight. There were some Huns about, but they kept away from fifteen Camels. A few two-seaters were chased off, and B flight caught one and shot it down. The sinking sun shone red-purple and promised a fine morrow, but Tom did not mind this as it was his day off.

Williamson also had the day off, and in the morning they went to St. Venant. The mess had been so badly smashed in the last binge that there were hardly any serviceable chairs, and something had to be done. Someone had the bright notion of sending a lorry to St. Venant to see what could be found there. The Germans dropped a few shells in the town most days and it was being slowly wrecked and burnt. The inhabitants had fled, leaving most of their property, and it was better to make use of it than to leave it to be smashed. So the major agreed to let a lorry go there unofficially, and Williamson and Tom, being at leisure, took charge of the expedition.

Y
337

They obtained quite a good cargo, and kept a comfortable chair each for themselves, and a carpet. Tom also had a stool or *priedieu* for squatting on, and Williamson a good-looking Empire clock which they found would not go. The mess was greatly improved; a few more such raids would enable them to live in comfort.

In the afternoon they had a tender and went to St. Omer for tea. Patisseries were, unfortunately, of the past; they could not even buy chocolate, such was the shortage of sugar. The world had concentrated on producing alcohol, TNT, and petrol. Tom bought a feather pillow, eau de cologne, writing paper, salts, fruit, tobacco, and some books.

In the Rue de Dunkerque they recognized a snub-nosed face.

'Hullo, Marsden!'

'Hullo, Williamson. Hullo, Cundall, I heard you were killed.' Marsden sounded annoyed with Tom for being still alive when he ought to be dead. His wound, the ideal blighty which he had picked out of the March retreat, had healed quickly and he had just got back to France. He was waiting at No. 1 ASD to be posted to a squadron. He wasn't returning to the squadron if he could help it. He had had enough of Le Rhones, and was trying to get on the new Bentley Camels.

Then they drew money from the Field Cashier, had a bottle of champagne, and went home to dinner. Food had been rather better lately, owing to the nearness of St. Omer.

The jobs for the next day were squadron patrols at 7.0 in the morning and 7.45 at night, which should be comfortable enough. It was too cloudy for bombing during the night, and Tom slept well on his more comfortable pillow, but it was sufficiently fine for them to be wakened at six in the morning. Nevertheless there was doubt if it was clear enough to take off, and the major made one of his rare ascents. He told them to go to the line and see how it was there. So fifteen aeroplanes flew as far as the front line at fifteen hundred feet and then flew back again.

By the time this comedy was over it was eight o'clock, and a good morning for stopping in bed quite spoilt. Tom made a leisurely toilet and went in to second breakfast. Vick, one of A flight's new Americans, asked him to pass the pepper, and he shook it over his bacon, saying that it made it taste more like water melon. There was another American in A flight called Cable, who had a passion for flying upside down; but the major had forbidden him to practise below two thousand feet, so he had to go away from the aerodrome to contour-chase. Having now three Yanks, Tom called it U.S.A. flight. He thought them first-rate fellows to have in a mess; cheery, sociable, extraordinarily modest. Not very long ago he had imagined Yanks were uncouth barbarians who rattled dollars and boasted through their noses. Perhaps the war was doing one good thing; letting young men find out that their own nation hadn't a monopoly of good qualities; that there were good fellows all over the earth. Even a sense of humour wasn't exclusively English.

Miller had brought some new records for the gramophone, including 'Softly Awakes My Heart', of which he was very fond; surprisingly, Tom thought; Miller seemed so very tough and impenetrable. He had also obtained a set of dice, and spent a good deal of the morning rolling the bones with other transatlantics who understood the mystery.

After lunch Tom slept, and after tea sat in his pillaged chair on the bank outside the hut, reading, talking with Williamson, watching occasional passing troops and transport; all the time waiting for the late job, which was certain to take place, for the clouds had lifted and were steadily decreasing; and there was a promise, or threat, in the air of another fine period.

'Seven months ago to-day I came out,' Williamson remarked.

'You'd better see about going home, unless you want a flight. You're the oldest combatant member of the squadron except Mac.'

'Franklin came the same day, and Miller a week later. Then I suppose you're next.'

'I've still a fortnight to go before my six months are up. If you fellows would clear off I could start agitating.'

'I'm quite willing to go as soon as they like to send me, but I'm damned if I'll put in for it.'

'Hell. I would. You've done a month more than you're officially supposed to.'

'Oh, the records merchants will notice me soon.'

The squadron took off at ten to eight, and skirted the southern edge of Nieppe Forest, climbing as three loosely associated groups to ten thousand feet; and onwards above Merville and Estaires to fifteen thousand. Tom had dived and warmed his guns on Merville and dropped his bombs thereabouts. Once again they were out to kill; to kill by means of machinery; they were lever-moving controllers of mechanisms. Was this fighting? There was no anger, no red lust, no struggle, no straining muscles and sobbing breath; only the slight movements of levers and the rattle of machine guns. The poor strength of soft human bodies and the thin trickle of force derived from slowly digested grass was replaced by hard steel and the instantaneous combustion of explosives. He imagined the unimaginably swift reciprocating of the flying pistons in front of him and the solid whirl of cylinders which, compared, made the pinions of a hawk in full flight motionless and the wings of a hover-fly sluggish.

Looking north-westwards towards the rayless sun set in the glowing sky like a red-hot cannon ball, he saw the cloudy verge of France and the thin reddish streak that was the heaven-reflecting Channel and a shadow that was England: England, his task mistress, his Beatrice: 'kill Claudio'. How easy was it for the proper-false to set their image in men's waxen hearts.

But the evening's job would be short. Another hour. Archie was active; red-black in the blue-gold air. It was cold. The wind had veered northwards. There were Huns far away in the east. Why didn't they come and fight, get it over? They had to die some time. Better die fighting than admit yourself outclassed. Was life so precious? Yes, life was so precious; nobody, by actions, believed in heaven.

Then there was a great deal of wing-waggling as a bunch of Huns came towards La Bassée. There were six of them: Pfalz scouts. They had seen, probably, a couple of DH4s doing an evening reconnaissance at five thousand feet amid clouds of Archie. But not the fifteen Camels above in the sun. There was a scramble to get at them. Archie warned, but too late. B flight was nearest and got first shot. Tom circled above and watched the slaughter. Two stalled and spun at the first onslaught; then another smoked and dived for the earth and blazed. Tom saw its long fall, wondering what sort of a fellow was being burnt to death this time. Another went down in a full-engine dive, vanishing away at so preposterous a speed that the eye seemed tricked.

He did not see what happened to the other two, but they had

gone, and the scattered Camels picked up their formations. Archie left them alone, as though he felt that the slaughter was too calamitous for his weak comment.

The swollen couchant sun touched the horizon in the north-west, and the Camels turned homewards, flying easily on third-throttle with their tails up, losing height gradually, as it were strolling; their pilots relaxed after the strain of the long day; victorious. Drifting downwards serenely they came into the warm lower air, with air-screws at five hundred revolutions a minute visible to the pilots as a haze. The earth, not here scarred, was friendly with yellow patches of corn and deep green of woods turning black in the evening light.

It was so comfortable drifting gently down towards the aerodrome, cushioned on half a mile of still air. Tom felt almost drowsy. He heard a whirr and looked up and quickly pushed the joystick forwards, giving himself an uncomfortable jerk as the nose fell. Someone's wheels just touched his centre-section. God, that was a near thing. It did not excite him. He chased after the offender and saw the letter N on the fuselage. One of B flight had been gliding at a steep angle without looking where he was going.

Tom landed and taxied in and hurried over to B flight hangars and saw Jones getting out of N.

'You should try that on a Hun.'

'Eh? What? Try what?' Jones's horse-face could not express surprise, but a nostril twitched.

'Digging your wheels in his top-plane.'

'I guess I don't get you.'

'Did you get a Hun?'

'Sure. I got a Hun orl right, but what's this other?'

Tom felt that it was too much trouble to explain.

'Oh, nothing.' Seeing Williamson, he called out: 'Did you get a Hun, Bill?'

'Yes. We've all got Huns to-night.'

They walked to the office. Forster, Franklin, Miller, Large and Hudson all claimed Huns as well. Everybody agreed that there were six Pfalz and that they were all shot down, but the total claimed came to seven. This was awkward. No claimant would admit that he could have been mistaken.

'One of them must have been shot down twice. Damned hard on him', Tom said.

They tried to persuade themselves that there must have been seven, but they knew there hadn't. In the end the major put six Huns and a blank into a hat, and Jones drew the blank.

'You're just missing things to-day,' Tom said to him.

VI

THEY had a night of bombs, near and distant, and were called at half-past four in the morning. At five Tom crept out of bed and sponged his face to wake himself up; and stimulated Williamson to do the same. They ate hard-boiled eggs and took off in the squadron show at half-past five.

It was misty. They could not see the ground at all looking east, and it was useless to patrol the empty sky. But they stopped out for an hour. Then Forster took A flight home, and Large and Miller followed him.

They were home before eight o'clock, and there were just twelve hours till the next job. There was nothing to do but endure the slow creeping of the sun to west and sleep away as much as possible of the blank time. Nerves could not quite relax; it was difficult to concentrate on a book for long at a time; there was little to talk about but shop and the war: silence was better.

Tom felt sorry for the Huns. Their life must be horrible, with the wind-up that must result from the catastrophes that happened to them. God, fancy flying a Pfalz! They probably sat about with twitching faces and woke up at night sweating with dreams of malignant SEs and Camels and Bristols. It was humane to shoot them down quickly.

But even the amusement of picturing the misfortunes of the enemy palled. There was no refuge from the long glare of summer. Day-time sleep was only tiring, leaving a depressing sediment in the brain: and even in sleep the mind seemed to know about the waiting and waiting and waiting.

The long day turned unwillingly to evening, cloudless and quiet. The squadron crossed the lines, dropped its bombs, warmed up its

342

guns, and searched for Huns, twisting among black ghosts. There were Huns away in the east, but they would not fight. A high patrol of Dolphins was out, and Huns were not likely to risk going under them. The very look of a Dolphin with its sinister back-stagger was enough to terrify a timid Hun.

For an hour and a half they offered battle without being able to draw the enemy, and then, the Harry Tates and big Ak-Ws having finished their shoots in comfort, went home to bed.

But there was unpleasant news awaiting them. Next midday they were to attack a Hun aerodrome somewhere beyond Douai. They were to surprise it by flying low and appearing suddenly over the tree-tops, and bomb it and shoot it up. A lot of new Fokker biplanes was supposed to be there, and they were to be exterminated. A strong escort of SEs and Dolphins would protect them from interruption; but what a hell of a game, bombing twenty-five miles over.

Tom had a few drinks, but went to bed feeling wrong in the stomach.

'It's your fault,' Williamson said to him. 'Your drunken effort has put ideas into somebody's head.'

'God, I'll have to give up drink. Only I can't.'

Tom was kept awake so much by night-flyers that he slept till past nine in the morning, and did not finish breakfast till half-past ten. They were to take off at 12.45 and meet their escort over Béthune. A flight would lead, with B following and C last; so that C would presumably come in for most of the machine gunning. If Mac had been there, no doubt C would have lead. Forster had the responsibility of taking them all straight there, and he spent the morning gazing at 1-in-40,000 maps. Tom fiddled with his bus, looking for frayed control wires, seeing that the guns were clean and oiled. The engine had been going quite well since he had flown it drunk, giving plenty of revs, and he had not needed to use Mac's. It was always a nuisance getting to know a new machine.

At last they took off, hoping to catch the Huns at lunch and blow up their mess. Tom felt shaky. Damn this low bombing. He wished to God he could get out of it . . . There was a terrific crash. The windscreen smashed, the engine stopped with a jerk, the guns were bent. He put his nose down to glide, wondering what the devil had

343

happened. The prop stood still, the engine-cowling had vanished, there was a great gash in the left-hand top-plane, and fabric was fluttering. What a mess! But he was gliding all right, and was profoundly happy to have avoided that job.

He was too far from home to glide there, but another aerodrome was right underneath, where No. 22 lived. He had about eight hundred feet to lose. The glide seemed quite normal in spite of the ragged top-plane. It was good fun, landing in such a mess. Had a cylinder burst? He made S turns to lose height. People were watching him from the aerodrome; must have heard the crash or seen the fragments fly. Time to glide in. He found he had lost too much height to land on the aerodrome itself, but floated on to some rough ground right by the mess. Not so far to go for a drink. A crowd of people waiting for him. Now for a good landing. The stick came gently back; tail down, down, down; wheels and skid slowly on the ground together; perfect.

The Bristol Fighter people gathered round.

'Holy saints!'

'What a smash.'

'Damn good landing.'

'What's happened?'

'I don't know what's happened,' Tom replied, climbing out. 'Something came loose and the engine stopped.'

The engine wasn't so badly damaged as he had expected. The high tension leads were all stripped off, and a tappet rod and rocker arm were missing. The tappet rod had cut off the cowling like a wire going through cheese, bent the gun muzzles, and departed through the top-plane. It was a good thing that whatever had smashed the safety-glass windscreen had not jumped it and hit him on the head.

Though there was nothing in it, Tom gained a slight temporary fame for having made a perfect landing in such a state, and, when he had telephoned home and told the major what had happened, there was quite a rush to supply him with drinks, and he had lunch.

One of the Bristol merchants was Christie, whom he had known at Croydon, and they had a talk about old times; about Trollope who used to be the stunt merchant there. He had shot down twenty Huns in a fortnight, breaking all records; Christie said he had done it on

344

Bristols, but Tom felt sure he had come out on Camels. And they talked about Biheller, who had flown away from Wye and was supposed to have landed in Holland: the board of inquiry that sat on his affairs found that he was a German spy. Biheller had been a great fellow. Tom couldn't see why a German spy should land in Holland.

Then the major arrived in the squadron car to collect Tom and look at the wreckage. He was congratulatory about his escape. Tom thought he wasn't a bad sort of bloke when he wasn't playing at being C.O. and a big fellow, for both of which parts he lacked natural ability. On the way back the major said that the raid had been a success. Aeroplanes and huts had been blown up and hangars set on fire. Everyone was back except Wall. Someone had seen him go down on the other side and make a landing, so probably he was alive.

'Thank God they haven't the guts to retaliate in kind,' Tom said.

'Don't you be so sure. I'm trying to get labour to make a dugout, but it's all busy digging trenches to hold up Jerry's next push.'

Tom wished a tappet rod would often fly so conveniently. It was queer how the event pleased him, cast a light of cheerfulness over the rest of the day. He began to wonder why he felt so happy about the misadventure. Was it because he had missed a low job? Was he still terrified of going near the ground that he reacted so definitely to an escape from it?

'Bill,' he said that night, 'I'm beginning to get worried about myself again.'

'Oh? I thought you seemed pretty cheery this evening.'

'That's just it.'

'What's that to worry about, you lunatic?'

'Well, it must have been because I missed that aerodrome raid.'

'A damned good reason.'

'But it shows what wind-up I've got about ground-strafing.'

'Who hasn't? You needn't plume yourself you're anything out of the ordinary that way.'

'Ordinary or not, I'm certain I'll crack, go yellow, if we have another dose of it.'

'Rot. You won't. We may gibber and sweat our flesh off, but we shall stick it, and live to get tighter than anyone's ever been

345

on peace night. Then we'll retire to a comfortable madhouse and live happily ever after at ratepayers' expense.'

'Sounds very nice. Hullo, here they come.' There was a row of a multi-engined Hun bomber, and a series of crashes not far away. They settled down to try to get to sleep before the shindy got too bad. All these light summer nights seemed good for bombing, moon or no moon.

During the night Tom was awakened by a terrific crash. Stuff plonked and rattled on the roof. Other receding crashes followed: that was over. But a stark revelation of the horror of the thing flared like a baleful *lusus* in his mind: that human beings should organize to destroy each other. It was failure. Man had failed; God had failed. No use bringing God into it, though; might as well blame a differential equation for mechanical breakdown. He longed and longed to be out of it all, somewhere infinitely remote where nothing stirred.

'What's the matter?' Bill's voice asked in the darkness.

'Matter? Nothing.'

'You groaned.'

'Did I? Sorry.'

They went to sleep again. In the morning they heard that a hospital at St. Pol had been badly smashed. Some of the fellows were beginning to think it intentional.

A flight took off at nine o'clock. Griffith did not get his engine running properly at first and was left behind. He fiddled with the fine adjustment. The engine roared and he hurried to get off the ground, doing a climbing turn with bare flying speed. The weight of bombs made him stall. His nose dropped. The aeroplane hit the ground and crumpled. The ambulance dashed out. He was pulled from the wreckage, broken and bloody, his face smashed by the guns.

C flight left the ground at ten o'clock. Tom, flying Mac's machine, dived and fired at Merville. As a result of the dive the pressure gauge leaked, and he had to be using the hand pressure pump continually. He dropped his bombs and went home.

When the gauge had been put right he took off again, but before he had found the flight pressure trouble recurred and he flew home on gravity, and that was another job done. The others shot down a two-seater. He was not sorry to miss the affair.

346

They went out again at 6.30 for the evening job. Miller flew steadily east over Merville and Estaires. Archie made no objection. They patrolled eight or nine miles over, and a flock of just perceptible Huns patrolled another eight or nine miles east. Tom hoped they would stop there, for they were many.

Miller climbed to seventeen thousand, keeping the Huns in sight. They became more perceptible. Tom shivered; it was cold up there. The Huns were certainly approaching. He tried his guns. They fired single shots, but after he had used the loading handles three times they warmed up.

Then he saw a cheering sight: two flights of SEs coming up underneath them. But the Huns did not scurry off. This must be a circus. Tom was able to do some counting before the clash. Seventeen Huns, Albatros and Pfalz, he thought. Ten SEs, five Camels. They were all about on a level perhaps twelve miles over in front of Harbourdin, when the head-on meeting came.

The SEs got a little in front and engaged first. An Albatros spun away. The Camels went into the confusion. Tom fired at an Albatros. Something fired at him. He splitarsed and nearly hit an SE that he zoomed over and then dived at an Albatros but lost sight of it underneath him. Tracers flashed about. A Pfalz appeared in front and he snapped at it with a full deflection burst and then turned on to its tail, but saw another Pfalz getting on to his own tail. He seemed to be alone with the two Pfalz. A Camel appeared and went after one of them. He caught a glimpse of a streamer and knew it was Miller. He circled with the other. The dogfight had spread and they were fighting a duel. He was quite sure the Pfalz could not get him in a level scrap and his heart was calm. It was faster, but he could turn inside it and take snapshots to worry the pilot, who could not reply.

Tom looked on at his body automatically flying and firing short bursts. The Pfalz pilot ought to dive away and chance it. He could not hope to beat a properly handled Camel at vertical turns, and he must realize by now that this Camel was being handled competently.

They fought down and down, losing height all the time. Tom wished he could end it. He fired a long burst and the Pfalz tried to turn away from it, and gave Tom an easy shot while he was reversing

347

bank. Tom fired, but got into the Pfalz's slipstream which threw him all over the place. Nevertheless the Pfalz slowly dropped its nose and turned over on its right side. It was the end. The angle of its dive increased until it was going vertically down with the terrible impetus of a full-engine dive.

Tom looked to his own tail and saw that there was no threat. He looked down for the Pfalz again, but could not find it.

His right arm ached. Archie blackguarded him: but Archie was nothing after machine guns. He turned towards three SEs which he saw making for home. One had its tail up, holding straight on in spite of Archie. Its engine was probably shot up and it was limping towards the lines. They could do nothing to help although they were within a few yards. If his engine conked he would have to go down in Hunland and they could only look on.

They were at nearly eight thousand feet over Laventie, flying south-west towards Béthune. The nearest part of the line was about six miles away. Tom remained two or three hundred feet above to keep out of the way of all the Archie that was being put up at the lame SE, but some of it came his way.

The unfortunate SE had to dodge, or it would have been hit: Archie was too good for straight flying. He was losing height; down to four thousand over Lacouture, with three miles to go. But he would do it. Safe in two minutes. Then Tom saw his prop stop. The engine had seized. Three thousand feet and a mile to glide. He would do it all right if Archie or machine guns did not get him. A burst of Archie bumped him badly, but he could carry on. He had to lose valuable height dodging, or Archie would certainly get him. What ghastly wind-up he must have.

Tom noticed that his own muscles were tensed and he was grunting and jerking about to help the SE with sympathy. He had even forgotten his own tail. He looked round; there was no danger. The SE went on down and down, gliding at eighty miles an hour. Tom would not go below two thousand; there was no point in making himself a target for machine guns. Archie was getting erratic with the lessening range. At about a thousand feet it left him alone and put up a barrage in front of Tom. He was about to throw a derisive roll; he didn't give a damn for the old blackguard: but he remembered his rule of never throwing a stunt after a scrap, so he played Mac's trick of pretending to dive under the barrage and then zooming through the smoke. He smiled at Archie bursting hundreds of feet below. He crossed the lines and dived after the SE which, thank God, was safe. He saw it land on the flat marshy ground in front of Béthune, near Essars. Its undercarriage was wiped off, but the pilot was all right, for he climbed out at once and waved.

Tom waved good-bye to the other SEs and climbed away over Hinges. Later he picked up the rest of the flight. They were all there.

Miller, when they reached home at half-past eight, was jubilant. He had bagged an Albatros and a Pfalz. Baker had got an Albatros in a spin. The SEs had done still more damage, it was thought, and very few of the eighteen Huns had got away. It was another tremendous victory. Miller himself was doing very well; he was sure of a D.F.C. and a flight. He had a score of fourteen or fifteen Huns; possibly more, but James had been too lazy to work out the exact totals recently.

Miller marched at the head of his men to the office, full of glory and elation.

'I guess we've smashed up that goddarn circus, major.' While they were telling the story, the C.O. of the SE squadron rang up and confirmations and congratulations were exchanged. The SEs claimed six Huns, and their man who had landed near Béthune had probably got another. That made ten or eleven altogether, and for no casualties. This certainly was victory.

Tom was affected by the general exhilaration, and but for the fact that he was to lead the flight on the early job at half-past six in the morning, would undoubtedly have got happy-drunk. What a hell fire scrap! What a slaughter! What warriors they were! Miller and Baker and he were stout fellows. Dubois had been with them, and Dubois was all right though he didn't get Huns. Fuller had been the fifth, and all that was expected of him for the present was not to get shot down.

But it was absurd to have to go to bed sober after such a victory.

THE reaction was sudden and violent. He kept Williamson awake for a long time talking. Who were these wretched Pfalz people they shot down? They must be fellows very like themselves, dragged, like them, into a quarrel not theirs. To hell with it. He'd never shoot at a Hun again. He'd drop his bombs into the canal if he could.

'But Huns will shoot at you,' Williamson replied, 'and drop their bombs on you.'

'I'll have to put up with that, and dodge as best I can. Retaliation is no use. It only leads to a series of counter-attacks; vendetta.'

'It's no use, Tom. You're in it, and you won't do any good by turning conchy. Suppose you have an opportunity of shooting down a Hun and you let him go. Very likely he will shoot down one of our fellows next day. Your position's impossible.'

Tom shuffled and argued, but could not escape the fact that to spare the enemy was to fight against his own friends. In the background loomed the unspoken word treachery. Tom saw well enough that the logic of his position would compel him to refuse to obey orders; he could not go out on patrol and sham; that would be treachery. But the other course might lead to his being shot unless he was sent home as a case of wind-up.

Wind-up, nerves: was that all it was, his hatred of murder? Did this sentiment of brotherhood with all men, especially Germans, arise from nothing but funk? He thought of his own dictum: the higher the sentiment, the lower the real motive. It wasn't easy to apply his own cynicism to his own conduct: but he must make the effort.

'Of course,' Williamson said, 'I know you'll do your jobs however much you grouse in private. I'm arguing largely for my own benefit; to get the thing straight once more in my own mind, and confirm myself. You needn't think you've the monopoly of doubt.'

Tom replied: 'It's just struck me that my real motive for not wanting to fight is just wind-up. My nerves are ragged, so I rant about the wickedness of murder when all I'm actually worried about is being murdered.'

'God, what a fellow you are for extremes. But look, Tom; why bother your head? You know damn well there's no way out. You've known it for years now, so why go over it again? I want to see you come through, and I don't want you to get rattled now. Keep cool and watch your tail and you've a fine chance. I want like hell to live myself, and if you like we'll clear off out of it when we're free. . . .'

But Tom went to sleep thinking: I'll tell the major I'm finished. I'll refuse to go up. There'll be no lack of guts about that. Let 'em shoot me if they want to. Good finish to three years' service. . . .

'Half-past five, sir. Leave the ground at half-past six.'

He grunted.

'Six o'clock, sir.'

He tumbled out of bed and put on clothes quickly; his old smelly oil-soaked R.F.C. tunic; no collar and tie with that. He brushed his hair and teeth and went out into the still fresh early-morning air and across to the mess.

Dubois, Baker, Hole, and Moore were there. He was taking Moore on his first-time-over. 'Watch your tail and keep formation.'

They were grumbling about the bombing during the night.

'I didn't hear any,' Tom said.

'You must have a clearer conscience than I thought if you sleep like that.' Hole's wide-open watchet eyes glittered at him. Hole always looked jovial, even at six o'clock in the morning.

'It went down in flames long ago,' drawled Baker.

They went to the aerodrome and took off. Moore was all right in formation, and Hole was settling down to it. The sun-gilded morning was peaceful and smiling. There were no Huns. Tom wandered up and down the lines, flying easily at half-throttle, not going far over. He saw one solitary two-seater and chased it home; this was the only time Archie fired at them. There were perhaps a few scouts away over their own aerodromes, but it wasn't possible to be certain looking against the sun; anyhow, they were of no interest to him as long as they kept there.

It seemed, indeed, a Huns' holiday. No one saw anything that day except a few timid two-seaters and some remote specks in the eastern sky. Tom got down from the last job at half-past nine, tired and hungry. It had been quiet enough, except for Archie, and there seemed little malice in his quaint apparitions on so pleasant an evening. The sky was a deep peaceful blue seen from the heights, cloudless except for a few misty golden whiffs of alto-cirrus at un-approachable height: the earth a print done in dirty brown and dirtier yellow, becoming grey to the north and south, and greyish-green to the east; the west was a grey mist, until the dying sun ensanguined it. The floor, too, was peaceful; only active were a few guns ranging on new targets.

Miller had gone to bed and had left a message asking Tom to go and see him. He was feeling bad, he said, and Tom had better be prepared to look after the early job at 4.30 in the morning.

Miller was not the only one feeling queer. Several fellows were shivery, and people were hoping for an epidemic of 'flu. Tom drank some whisky and went to bed cursing the war. Wake up at half-past three. Summer was intolerable. He went to sleep at once and after a moment woke up to a noise of bombs and Archie, and in another moment the batman was shaking him.

The business of wandering about the empty sky began again. Time would not pass. He cursed the sun: 'Get up the bloody sky, blast you.' But his voice was not Joshua's. The sun sat on its curtained eastern throne kissing with the white goddess of dawn, and morning waited. The long drag of goitred minutes maddened him and the fleering eternity of an hour. He dived and shot at the stupid world spread like a burnt pancake under his nose. Dived and fired, dived and fired. And then they caught a two-seater. His guns stopped. The observer fired at him. He couldn't stand that, and pushed his nose down sharply and went away out of it, vertically, engine off. He dived the pitot right off the dial. They'd think he was shot down; and, God, would he ever get out of this dive without pulling his wings off? He eased the stick back a millionth of a milli-metre, and the devils in the streamlined wires sirened moaningly with the strain of it. His guts tried to go straight on down and pushed his backside into the seat, hard. The silly earth, all wounds, pustules, scabs, cantered past like the docile hack she was. Why didn't she scratch off all these dirty humans making stinks and itchings in her epidermis? A bitch could scratch at her fleas, but not milch-cow earth.

On the dive, pressure had gone. He switched over to gravity and went home. That was one way of ending an intolerable job: dive till the pressure gauge gave out. But what was the good of being at home at six o'clock in the morning with an infinite sun-brazen day in front of him, and nothing whatever to do till half-past seven in the evening? He wished he'd kept himself on the leash and finished his job.

God, he was going mad. His nerves were vibrating minutely, excruciatingly. He wanted to run in a circle, run and run till his heart burst. He bit his under-lip, pressed his finger-nails into his palms, held his breath at pressure in the larynx; and the torment passed.

Baker returned next with a stuttering engine.

'I thought the two-seater had got you,' he said to Tom. A high tension lead had been cut by a bullet, and there was a tinny sound as though something else were wrong. They had shot down the DFW but Baker had stopped a few bullets with his engine. A valve-stem had been hit, probably with ruinous effect on its guide and seating.

The rest of the flight came back following Dubois. It was absurd for Dubois to be Tom's deputy leader; Baker was obviously the man. But had he authority to interfere with the sacred rights of seniority? He was fond of Dubois and would hate to hurt his feelings. Probably Dubois wouldn't care. He would speak to the major about it if Miller continued sick.

Miller did continue sick, and three of A flight, Forster, Lewin, and Cable, were down with the same illness. The M.O. called it PUO. There was a good deal of it about; a bacterial infection emanating from the soilure of war. Alternatively it was nameable 'flu; and by any other name it would provide a week's holiday. It wasn't dangerous, the M.O. said, if you went to bed and stopped there, and everyone was waiting hopefully for preliminary shivers. Dubois was transferred temporarily to depleted A flight.

So Tom found himself with the job of acting flight commander for a week or till the shivers came on. It would keep him busy. Looking after a flight was a hundred times more than looking after an aeroplane. Returns, records, reports; N.C.O.s chasing after him about this and that; being father to his pilots and seeing that new fellows did plenty of target practice, for shooting was nine-tenths of the battle.

He wasn't fit for the job. He was sick of the whole vile business of war. A leader should be enthusiastic, bloody-minded, courageous, cunning, a dead shot, a real pilot, a tree leopard, a buffalo, an eagle, a steel-gutted killer — but he'd soon fade out with 'flu or go crazy or land in Holland or Hunland or Hell.

And now, more than ever, he must not get tight except on the right occasions. While his brain was seething like a hot bitumen lake, his heart and belly clamouring for anodynes, he must be nonchalant, seeming to accept the war as sport; nothing for anyone to get wind-up about, anyway; be a fine fellow whom new young pilots would have confidence in, so that they would be confirmed in courage, and write home how wonderful the R.A.F. in France was; cheery, not a sign of wind-up, Huns whacked, and everything so much better than they had expected. Well, others had done as much for him. Then they would go out in good heart to slaughter or be slaughtered, or to break their blasted necks by spinning into the ground. God damn the bloody war.

He must hold himself, find strength somewhere. He could only find it in himself; strength of pride; he would not crack. But was this strength or weakness? Ought he to refuse duty? If only he could get drunk, dead drunk, and wipe out thought.

Till half-past seven . . . and not only that day, but day after day of racking inanity. The desire ever to do anything had left him. Human activity led only to disaster. Whatever men did, others were injured by it. Greed and envy and lust were the only motives of action; the friction of egos competing in the penumbra of hypocrisy bred heat that blazed into war. And after conflagration it would start all over again. The little hatreds of individuals, denied the old-fashioned purgations of assault and libel, confused themselves into the terrible group passion called patriotism, and the nations were spearheads of malignity.

At half-past seven he must go out to get on with the mechanized slaughter which was the vicarious purgation of the accumulated irritations of their elders; irritations arising from unsatisfied greed, suppressed lust, sexual impotence, dyspepsia, and hatreds all colours of the Union Jack.

But that was only half of it. The successful people had got hold of the war, generals, politicians, usurers, industrialists, and a crowd of lesser parasites raking in the shekels; it was a fine old war for them, blast their souls. God knew what secret arrangements had been made between the national leaders, but it seemed that the war wasn't going to end until one side or the other was beaten to a state in which it could not resist the worst that plunderers could devise.

At half-past seven he was going out on patrol: no, not he: he had been murdered long ago. This fretting cursing wreck was not he. He was a young man filled with joyous life, one of God's Englishmen, captains of the earth, loving the glory that was England, responding to England's call with gladness . . . now God be thanked who matched us with this hour. He was that young fool; not this tired, scared, nervy, old cynic.

He felt calmer after his sleep and the refreshment of tea. He was like an old woman, with his nap and his tea drinking. Time picked up the step again and marched on towards the next job. And if they shot down any Huns, so much the better. Every Hun killed brought the end nearer, and that was the only thing to do; get the war finished. The Huns deserved all they got; they were the aggressors; they were on French ground; you couldn't get away from that; and as long as they remained there they must be shot at. They were the immediate cause of disaster, and they could be attacked; other responsible people were unassailable, unless the Huns dropped bombs on them, as he hoped to God they did sometimes. So, down with Huns.

But, good God, how he vacillated.

The sky was clear of Huns, but Archie nagged them all the time, keeping them turning and twisting. It was a good thing Camels were so light on the controls; Archie-dodging in heavier machines must tire the right arm till it ached as though it would drop off. But a Camel, all lightness and mobility, frisked and frimmicked in the air as evasively as a house-fly.

It was fun watching Archie's mishits for half an hour; then it was boring; then exasperating. Stupidity had reached its limit. To sit there and be shot at for nearly two hours by gangs of infuriated and weary gunners with red-hot guns, who achieved nothing but showers of fragments falling on the heads of their own troops; nothing could be more futile than this. A bad-tempered small boy trying to hit flies with a pea-shooter and only littering the dining-room floor was a fair simile.

He turned for home slightly early, but it was ten o'clock before he had finished with all the flight commander's stuff. There was welcome news that C flight had no job next day till the evening, so he went to the mess and spent an hour drinking whisky and making a row. Then he went to bed and kept Williamson awake by cursing at the stupidity of war and then at his own stupidity. For he had gone into it at first with as much zest as anyone: now God be thanked, and all the rest of it. He realized now that a thing started with an accompaniment of fine feelings couldn't be stopped just because the fine feelings had evaporated, however rank it turned. The whole blasted universe had had a fine creative push once, and now it was going on and on and on down some unintelligible slope.

Williamson had a job at 6.30 in the morning, but he was gentle with Tom nowadays, and instead of telling him to shut up and go to sleep, listened patiently and gave his usual advice: get on with the job, watch your tail, and don't bother your head.

'You're a damn good fellow to put up with all my yowlings, Bill,' Tom said fervently.

'Not a bit of it. What you say is all true enough, but it's not practical, and it does me good to talk practical stuff in opposition. It sorts of binds me to the practical point of view, if you get what I mean.'

'Sounds as though you've found a new phrase for a lie: practical truth. Forgive me. I'll be better in the morning. Good-night, Bill.'

Bombers did not make enough row in the night to disturb them. Williamson got up at six, and Tom was awakened soon afterwards by aeroplane noises, and could not get to sleep again, but lay dozing until Williamson came back at half-past eight.

'Anything doing?'

'No. We chased a couple of two-seaters and got dived on by half a dozen Albatri. Nothing happened.'

Tom had breakfast late and felt sleepy after it. He dozed away most of the morning and afternoon. After tea the news spread that the aerodrome at Izel had been bombed in the night and several fellows killed. Franklin was shivering enough to shake the mess, and the major told him to go to bed. Hole was feeling queer. The plague was spreading.

Tom took up Baker, Fuller, and Moore at seven o'clock. They

saw a good many Huns about, but none of them would come west, and Tom did not go more than five or six miles over with his small and inexperienced force. The Huns were not doing any harm.

THE coming of the plague, PUO, quite altered life. Everyone was waiting for his turn to go down with it and did not take work very seriously in the meanwhile. On the next day the Wing M.O. visited the squadron and weeded out all the incipient cases and packed them off to hospital. A flight was reduced to a fighting strength of one: Maitland; and B and C to four each. The major and James and Chadwick survived; PUO was benevolent, discriminating in favour of those that needed a rest.

There was a squadron patrol in the evening for the nine active survivors, Large, Williamson, Tom, Maitland, Dubois, Baker, Watt, Moore, Wharton. They went out in threes *en echelon*, Large in command and Williamson and Tom leading the other threes. The Huns were too scared to go near nine Camels all together, but Large caught a formation of Pfalz ten miles over, and dived out of the sun. The Pfalz saw them coming and put their noses down eastwards, but Large got a burst into a rear one and it flopped into a dive. No one else got near enough to fire.

Tom was sick of seeing Pfalz shot down, or hearing about it. He wished to God he could get 'flu and go away to hospital for a week and have nurses looking after him. He wanted the gentleness of women. He was so tired of violence. Violence would beget more violence, until the end of all things. Everyone would perish in war after war unless some miracle of gentleness supervened. That was so clear to him that he ached with the intensity of sad knowledge.

But the spread of infection seemed to have been stopped by the drastic clearance. Tom felt worn out, mentally rather than physically. He was listless and dull, incapable of decision or initiative; procrastination was his master. Days passed and he forgot in the evening what had happened in the morning. Events died out as soon as they were over, so passive was his memory, so cold his blood. He slept and dozed and dozed and slept.

Then Large and Baker succumbed to PUO, and the squadron was given a task called wireless. This was a new idea. It was apparently possible to determine from what direction wireless waves were received, and special listening stations were set up at suitable intervals to listen for Hun two-seaters doing shoots. Bearings were taken and telephoned to Wing, which plotted the cross bearings on its map and telephoned the resultant reading to the squadron detailed for the work. This squadron always had two machines ready to take off immediately and proceed to the place where Wing had deduced the presence of a two-seater.

This work was boring in the extreme, for the pilots on duty had to be waiting at the hangars by their aeroplanes. Engines were kept ticking over or warm, and as soon as Wing telephoned, they set out. The actual jobs were not very troublesome. The two-seater was seldom discoverable. But they were on duty from daybreak till darkness; as one pair took off the next went to the hangars and ran engines and waited. If no call came through they were relieved after two hours by the third pair.

For three days there were not more than six calls during the day; once only four. Tom had Moore as his partner, a youngster of eighteen with a slight lisp or lallation in his speech. They went out together twice a day and only once saw their two-seater, and then it was hurrying away in the distance. On other occasions they could only suppose that a mistake had been made or that the two-seater had been chased away by someone else during the ten or fifteen minutes that elapsed between the hearing of its messages to its battery and their arrival at the given map square. There was always the possibility that Wing, fearing that they might be tired of waiting or that they were having too easy a time, might have invented an Enemy Aircraft.

But a batman came round at half-past three each morning and woke them up. 'Stand by at half-past four.' No job ever came through before eight o'clock, by which time clouds had appeared in sufficient quantity to give cover to prowling two-seaters and Wing was awake. On the jobs they did not go far enough over to meet those reluctant enemies the Albatros and the Pfalz. As for triplanes, no one had seen any lately anywhere, and rumour had it that they

358

were definitely washed out; their place was to be taken by the latest D7 Fokker Biplane.

On the fourth day the weather was dud and work was washed out and they all cleared off to St. Omer — except Wharton, who was orderly dog — and cheered themselves up. It was still very cloudy next morning, the twenty-third of June, but there was a call at 9.25 for Tom and Moore. The two-seater was said to be in the neighbourhood of La Bassée. They searched about among the clouds but could find nothing there except Archie bursts. Tom worked in widening circles and at length met an LVG rather suddenly over Lorgies. They were all on a level. The observer opened fire at Moore. Tom ruddered it into his Aldis but only got in a short burst before it vanished into a cloud. Moore also had vanished. Tom circled round for some time, but could see neither of them. He did not want to meet the Hun again, as he hated to attack a two-seater alone. But he wished he could find Moore; fearing that the observer had hit him.

He returned home after an hour without Moore. He waited another ten minutes and then reported that they had found and driven off the two-seater, and that Moore was missing. Then he slept for an hour, but woke up still tired.

Dubois and Wharton caught the plague during the day, leaving only four to carry on the work of the squadron. Moore did not return.

Tom went out with Williamson after dinner to find a two-seater north of Merville, but it was undiscoverable. They wandered together among sunset-purple valleys of cloudland until it was reasonably time to go home. Once Tom had liked to wander among clouds. He could not remember why.

They landed a little before 9.30. Although there was plenty of whisky and few to drink it, it was impossible to get drunk when one would be called soon after midnight and was a quarter of a squadron. Tom drank about a third of a bottleful. It only increased his apathy and tiredness. Why the devil did the plague continue to pass him by? Never was a man more in need of a week's rest. He flopped into bed and slept profoundly through all the noise of night-flyers, and then: 'Half-past three, sir'.

359

'Good God, man, I've only just come to bed.' He slept again. 'Four o'clock, sir.'

He sat up. 'My God, Bill, what a bloody awful life.'

'And I bet there won't be a smell of a blasted job till ten,' Williamson grumbled. 'O for the 'flu.'

Somehow the blank morning passed. The first call came through at nine o'clock, and Williamson and Tom went out among the clouds. But the only two-seaters they could find were a couple of Harry Tates. There were Hun scouts visible far away in the east: they stopped there.

Maitland and Watt had a job at midday, with no result, and that was all. The clouds increased and consolidated, and Wing had mercy at five o'clock and let them wash out. Tom had spent the day dozing on his bed or sitting in the cockpit waggling the controls about. He had never known such utter boredom and weariness, such mental numbness. It was worse than his fits of rage and fear; for then he knew at least that he was alive and wanted to be alive: but now he knew nothing. It was unlikely that he would ever again find anything worth doing. Both action and inaction were intolerable. Grey time pressed on his brain and nerves like an ache.

About seven o'clock it started to rain. The barometer had fallen a good deal. He'd chance it and drink. The morning would probably be dud. After dinner he soaked whisky steadily. The mess was more full than it had been lately; several fellows had recovered sufficiently to be about, though they weren't passed fit for flying. Quite a drunk developed; but Williamson and Maitland kept themselves sober. Watt, like Tom, speculated on the weather.

'For Christ's sake, Bill,' Tom said when the whisky had loosened him up, 'what does it matter if we can't see where we're going in the morning? Drink up and blast the bloody war. God, man, we can just tootle out and tootle back and say "no Hun".'

'Oh all right, Tom. What's the hurry? Drink slow, drink long.'

'A drink in the belly's worth two in the bottle,' Tom countered.

There was a Scot, whom everyone called Jock, newly arrived; a delightful Harry Lauderish sort of bloke, whose expression of infinite jovial cunning was in itself a feast of humour. He had introduced a new song of his own composition, and everybody was singing:

Down in the sewer
Shovelling up manu-er
Everybody's spade goes flippity-flippity-flop.
Oh it gives us great delight
To be shovelling up the ——
I'm the leader of the gang, Gor-BLI-me.

Tom, happy with whisky and song, danced a reel with him. Jock could do it properly, and he supplied 'ochs' at the correct places. In the midst of this feat footing, Watt, who was tremendously strong, made a dive for them, and, tackling them low, lifted them one in each arm and performed a dance of his own that might have been called a kangaroo hop. Jock clung to Watt's head and Tom clung to Jock. Watt tripped and they all went down with a crash. Tom picked himself up, seized a chair, and charged at Watt, who dodged, and he hit the side of the hut. He turned and saw that Watt had also armed himself with a chair. They both charged and met with a shock that made Tom sit down bump on the floor. Watt stood swinging his chair triumphantly. Tom lay flat, as that seemed about the safest thing to do. Watt was dangerous. People started throwing things at him. He parried some of them with his chair and some fell on Tom, who crawled out of the way.

'Have a heart, Watt,' Maitland shouted above the din. 'Hancock can't bring the drinks round.'

Watt calmed down and the whisky went round. They got singing again, 'For my name is Samuel Hall'. Tom went on drinking all he could get, and was soon charging whooping about the mess, shoving, throwing hard things about, and being such a nuisance that drinks were offered him in quick succession to put him out. 'Come on Tom, drink up.' He would drink it and then someone else would put a drink under his nose. Watt had quietened down and was seeing how long he could stand on one leg with his eyes shut. Tom pushed him over twice, and then Watt pushed him over and sat on him for a minute till he got up to have a drink. Then they had a competition in standing on one leg but were both too far gone to do it at all. Tom was beginning to stagger heavily, and a little later he was aware of starry sky and Williamson's supporting arm. He was talking affectionately to Williamson and cursing the stars. The weather had let him down. Someone shook him. The batman was saying it was half-past three.

He swore and slept again. The batman re-awakened him; but it was preposterously unreasonable to expect him to wake up. Then Williamson was bothering him. Why the hell couldn't people leave him alone?

'Come and drink some tea.' Something splashed cold on his face. He sat up, annoyed.

'You've only got to get your tunic and boots on.' Williamson was putting his tunic on him. Knowledge of the outer world glimmered dimly in his mind. God, he couldn't fly in that state. Williamson helped him with shoes and piloted him across the road. Maitland and Watt were in the mess.

'I guess half this squadron's incapable.' Watt was fast asleep with his head on the table. Tom drank a lot of tea, but hated the sight of an egg. Williamson and Maitland went to the hangars to take first watch; God knew what would happen if jobs came through. Tom shambled back to the hut and went to sleep.

'It's gone eight,' said Watt, shaking him. 'Those fellows have been down at the sheds since half-past four.'

'Good God.' He felt all right, and they hurried off, Tom still half asleep, to relieve Williamson and Maitland. They found them sitting on boxes playing some sort of gamble with cards, using Williamson's tail-plane as a table, and heaped gratitude on them.

'Say, you don't think we do this for nothing? You won't see us till after lunch.'

'That'll be all right.'

But they returned after two hours, no jobs having come through, and there was an argument. It was agreed in the end that Tom and Watt should be off for an hour, to wash and shave.

The day was fine but there was a dearth of work. Tom felt much better at first after his drunk, but lassitude returned in the afternoon. Williamson and Maitland went out at two o'clock, but did not find the enemy. No other jobs at all came through, though they were kept on duty till 7.30.

At eight o'clock a tender took them over to Therouanne where a concert party was giving a show called *Maid of the Mountains*. It was something like the London play, but funnier. There were topical jokes about such things as munition workers, PUO, sergeant-majors, and when one of the actors came on looking very battered, the funny man said, 'You do look as if you've had a whack'.

Here was an evening passed pleasantly without getting tight. And Williamson and Tom were left in peace till 7.30 in the morning as Forster and Cable had returned to duty, taking first watch. Miller, although the first to go down, was still groggy, and had a slight cough left over. Tom felt a little bit tired at the knees, and began to hope he was ill. As the morning passed, he was quite certain his knees were shaky, and he thought he was becoming sore bronchially.

'Bill, darlint, I can feel it coming. PUO,' he said, as they were leaning against a fuselage, regarding the cloudy breezy sky.

'You'd better wash out and go to bed.'

'I don't feel bad enough yet. I shouldn't notice anything if I didn't know what to expect. But I'm a bit funny in the knees and chest. I caught it at the show last night. Damned good show that.'

'Well, if we have to go up we won't rush into danger.'

There had already been two useless jobs for the others that morning, and soon afterwards, at 12.20, they were ordered out to Calonne district. It was very dud up and they spent an hour among the thick clouds between four thousand and eight thousand feet without seeing any kind of aeroplane except a patrol of SEs high up.

The edges of clouds seemed a little brighter than usual. When they had landed, Tom noticed that all edges had a faint brightness. He was slightly giddy. There could be no doubt that he had caught the plague. In the morning he would see the M.O. and have his long-awaited rest; in hospital he hoped, where it would be clean, and there would be no mess bills. He felt happy and excited.

Wing was very active, and Tom had another job at 3.30. Forster and Cable had actually caught and killed a Hun, though probably not the one they were looking for.

'Are you sure you're well enough?' Williamson asked him before they went up.

'Yes. I'll enjoy saying good-bye to the lines for a while.'

So they spent another hour, or rather less, among the clouds. Tom wasn't interested in hypothetical two-seaters, but kept in sight of Williamson and dived and zoomed and stalled and rolled and skimmed along craggy golden cloud-surfaces like an intoxicated pigeon. They came back low and scattered some troops on the march near Bergues and held up a column of transport and strafed a car. Tom laughed so much that he nearly hit a tree, and heard his undercarriage swish among the leaves.

He felt so well after this pleasant expedition that he wondered if he had been mistaken about the 'flu. He could still feel a very slight chest soreness, but it hardly seemed enough to be significant. This was depressing.

He ate gentleman's relish and honey gloomily. He got up; and had to hold on to the back of his chair for a moment of giddiness. Splendid. No mistake about that. He felt better at once. Then he felt rotten. The excitement of it passed off. He was shaky, sore, and giddy. He began to hope that he wasn't going to have it too badly. Some of the fellows had been quite ill, and as he had been rather run down lately, perhaps he would have a bad dose. He might even be invalided home as he had just about done his six months, and that was a blessed thought. But no; he mustn't give way to happy dreams; a week's rest was as much as he could reasonably hope for.

He sat about talking, doing nothing, till dinner. Williamson insisted on telling the major that he wasn't fit to fly, and the major made a kind inquiry and washed him out till he had seen the doctor in the morning.

After dinner he felt so weak and giddy and sore and shivery that he went to bed, ill but happy.

I X

He dreamt that he had a son, a fair boy of four years old. He went searching among cloudy nothingness for the boy's mother, who was always somewhere else. He was alone, carrying a straw that was much thicker and heavier than it looked. He woke up thinking he had wet the bed. He heard the guns and knew where he was, and then dreamed and dreamed on between sleeping and waking. He was aware of Williamson getting up by lamplight. Thank God he'd done with that.

He slept or dozed till the batman asked him about breakfast. He had tea and a slice of bread and butter, and then tried to read, but soon relapsed into dozing. The M.O. came to see him some time during the morning and put a thermometer into his mouth.

'Have I got PUO?' he asked when his mouth was free.

'Yes, you've got it. Your temperature's just over a hundred and three, so you must stop where you are and keep quite quiet. You'll have to get out to go to the latrine, but move as little as you can. Drink as much water as you like, but don't try to eat to-day. Just go to sleep.'

'Fine, doctor. I'll do that. But I wish you'd tell me what PUO means.'

'What do you want to know that for?' But the M.O. overcame his professional love of mystery, and added: 'It stands for Pyrexia of Unknown Origin.'

'Good name for the whole blasted war,' said Tom by way of a joke.

'You mustn't worry about things like that.' The doctor seemed to restrain a push of irritation in consideration of his patient's temperature. 'You can forget all about the war for the present. Just keep quiet.'

When the doctor had gone Tom sank into semi-consciousness wherein dream and reality were emulsified into a giddy cloudiness. He woke up in the evening and talked to Williamson. There was going to be a low-bombing show in the morning in support of a minor line-straightening push at Robecq. It was worth while being ill. Mac had returned from leave and would lead the squadron, now eight strong.

He dreamed all night that he was searching for someone who was ill, always searching. It was Seddon. It was Beal. It was half a dozen different people as his mind strove in the heavy smore of sleep. He would wake up from one dream into another at some different level of the visionary world, and, seeming to realize that he had been searching in the wrong place, go on looking anew, troubled all the while by a feeling of horror, passing among great crowds of alien faces, appalled by vivid inimical landscapes, himself lost beyond the verge of known things, for ever seeking vainly.

But in the morning he seemed better and could read. He still felt weak and had swimming sensations in the head, but the doctor told him his temperature was down. He lived on a dose of salts and a glass of lemon squash that day, and still did not feel hungry. But the idea of eating became more and more pleasing, and he contemplated breaking his fast on the next day. There was no need to hurry.

Williamson told him that the low-bombing job had been hindered by mistiness; there had been no casualties, but they might not have done much damage. The push was officially reported successful, all objectives being reached.

Tom heard of events with distant unconcern. He felt impassible; rather like a log of wood would feel. He was concerned with nothing but his own sensations of weakness and dizziness; he speculated only about eating and how long he could remain ill.

After another night of heavy sleep distained with smoulder of dreams, he felt more normal in the morning. The doctor did not visit him. He made the experiment of eating some lunch, and after tea got up and titubated to the mess where he drank a little whisky and ate roast beef and felt much better, but crept back to the hut after a quiet rubber of bridge. The sun was setting in heroic splendour. There was a cold wind from the north-east which pierced his racked defence. It was said that snow had fallen in Germany, but that was probably only a rumour. Chadwick visited him in the hut. He had obtained ten days' Paris leave, and was going in the morning. He was disturbed because he had only twelve hundred francs to spend.

Tom did a sum. 'That's about five pounds a day. Isn't that enough for Paris? Heaven preserve me from Paris leave. Can I lend you two or three hundred if you're short?'

'Thanks Tom, but I won't borrow. It's such a hell of a job paying back. I don't get flying pay, you know.'

'Swop jobs?'

'No damn fear. I've done with fighting. By the way, isn't it about time you had a rest from it? You seem to have been out the hell of a long time.'

'Just about six months.'

'Quite long enough. How many survive six months on Le Rhone Camels? If I were you I wouldn't go up again in France. Tell the doc you're *fini* and want to go home. He'll do it.'

'I'm no *bon* at swinging the lead. Besides, there's Mac and Miller and Franklin and Williamson; they've all been out longer than I have.'

'I hear they're going to send Mac home and put him in charge of a Snipe squadron; at least, that's the rumour. Miller's groggy. I expect they'll send him home right away, though he deserves a flight if anyone does. As for your pal and Franklin, I suppose they're waiting for flights, and they'll get them when our push comes. So there's no need for you to wait, unless you want to hang on for a flight. But you'll be a fool if you do. Clear out before low bombing starts again.'

'I'll see how I go on. Your advice is sound, laddie. I hope you'll find what you want in Paris.'

Tom's temperature was normal in the morning, and the doctor made no objection to his getting up so long as he kept perfectly quiet; no bingeing. He expected to feel much better, for his appetite had returned and he had slept well. But he was weak and listless; very weary in mind and body. He could only read a very little, as his mind would not keep to one train of thought for more than a few seconds at a time. The past was a blank, as though the function of memory had left him, the present a burden, and the future a menace. Physical weakness did not worry him so much as his mental impotence. He sat about wondering why people objected to dying, which could not be more unendurable than living.

Aeroplanes roared overhead, but he was not interested. Williamson and other people told him about jobs that were done. His mind wandered while they were speaking. As it was Sunday there was a service in the church hut in the evening, and he drifted there. He stood up when the harmonium played and hymns were sung, and felt dizzy. The padre's round Os irritated him.

He went to bed soon after dinner. Williamson came bursting in full of excitement.

'News,' he cried. 'Mac's going home in a week's time, and as Franklin's still sick I'm taking over C flight when I've had seven days' special leave.'

'Congratulations.' Tom spoke as brightly as he could. Indeed, he felt faintly glad that Bill would be his flight commander. Williamson shouted for the batman.

'I'm off as soon as I've packed. Tender to Omer, where I can get a night train to Boulogne and get across in the morning. Damn that batman.'

While packing he told Tom that he had made a bargain to put in two more months' service in France, till the end of August, as flight commander, and he would definitely go home then. Nobody knew for certain what was to happen to Mac. The rumour was that he would be promoted major and given command of a Snipe squadron of picked men, a sort of circus. Mac himself did not know.

'I'm not leaving you for long. I hope you'll be fit by the time I'm back. I'll know you'll be safe while I'm away, anyhow. Good-bye, Tom.'

'Good-bye, Bill. Have a good time.'

The hut would be very lonely for the next week. Bill was the chief fixture in his universe. And now he had taken on this two months' flight commanding. If he had gone home Tom would no doubt have tried to follow him, but this made a difference. What to do?

His mind veered from the problem, and he fell asleep, but was half-awakened soon by a noise of bombs. It seemed as if they were the padre's round Os crashing about him. They bounced up in clusters. They were white grapes growing wild in the middle of a footpath leading to Cox's bank, and he picked them for someone who was ill.

In the morning he decided he was strong enough to get up to breakfast, feeling, not hungry, but as though he could eat. His brain was less frozen; conversation was not a labour. He walked to the hangars and looked round his aeroplane: he might even be able to fly in a day or two. The squadron had twelve active pilots now and was working as two flights. He watched a patrol take off with Mac leading. Mac was bent on raising his score to sixty before he went home and Tom was not sorry not to be among his 'flu-jaded followers. There was a rumour that the squadron would have a fortnight's rest soon, in view of its bad condition. But half the war was rumour.

The 'flu seemed to be prevalent all over the war-sick world. The Huns were said to have it badly; and Mac might not be able to find ten to shoot down. Tom had a letter from England saying that it was difficult to buy anything as nearly all shop people were ill or dead.

Mac caught a two-seater and was awarded the whole of it. There were strawberries and cream for tea. It was arranged to employ a Frenchwoman to cook for the mess. Tom had a few drinks in the evening, keeping well on the hither side of a drunk, and went to bed convinced he was almost well. He did not like the loneliness of the hut. There were air-raids as usual; the thought of being blown up all alone was unpleasant.

But when in the morning he asked the doctor if he might go up for a joy ride, he was forbidden.

'You won't be fit to fly for some days yet. Keep quiet and eat well; that's all you've got to do.'

Tom did his best to keep quiet. He expected he'd be very good at this, but actually he found that he was restless; he was absurdly uncomfortable because he was not doing his share of the flying when he felt able to fly.

There were others in a like state. Miller had been doing nothing for so long that he had forgotten how to fly, he said, and was sick to death of it. He was as ill with boredom as anything else; he wanted glory and a flight.

Hudson was another idler. Tom walked over to Estrée-Blanche with him in the afternoon, conversing about the eternal young men's subjects, books and music. They had a feed of eggs and chips. The kitten was old enough to be taken away, but he didn't want the bother of transporting it then; he was a little fatigued with the walk.

He was quite tired when they got back, and drank some whisky; but he felt all right after dinner and joined in the singing and the row. But the hut was depressing, dirty, full of earwigs. There were worse things than earwigs and he did not like killing them, but he would have to do something about it, for they were increasing in numbers and invading his bed. The usual thing was to burn them nightly with a candle as they roosted on the roof. Tom did not enjoy this sport. He wondered how it was that such stupid, conspicuous, clumsy beasts succeeded in surviving; possibly it was because they lived at peace with each other and bent all their vitality to reproduction; wise beasts after all.

It was too windy and cloudy for night-flying, and he hoped for a peaceful night. A mosquito was buzzing in the darkness and he was as defenceless against it as against bombs. He flapped once or twice at its increasing hum, and in the morning found a small bump on his temple. It was pleasant to wake up with no weight of pending jobs in his belly.

The day was very cold for July. The doctor told him he was still far from well and must keep quiet. The rumour that the squadron would have a rest was superseded by one that they would only have one soft job a day for the present. A demand came from Brigade via Wing to be informed how long each pilot had been at the front, how many flying hours he had done, and what his performance had been, so there was much adding up of figures in log books.

And immediately fresh rumours started. There had been a strafe because pilots were not being posted to Home Establishment at the right time. They were going on night-flying. Pilots were wanted to form a circus. They were going to England for Home Defence. They were to have Snipes. They were to have Salamanders. They were to have Bentley Camels . . . Tom's opinion was that some base-wallahs were earning D.S.O.S.

He went to St. Omer in the afternoon with Mac and Miller. Mac had seen Snipes in England and was burning with desire to fly them. Give him a Snipe and another six months of war and he'd score a century. They'd do a hundred and fifty on the level at ten thousand, would climb like lifts — fifteen thousand in ten minutes — were better than Dolphins at twenty thousand, were as splitarse as Camels: hell, the Huns would be driven right out of the sky if only they'd get the goddarn things out to France.

They had tea, did some shopping, and then dinner at the Treille d'Or, drinking champagne, healer of all ills. Even Miller cheered up and showed them a photograph of his girl. The M.O. had promised that morning either to pass him fit for flying or to get him posted to Home Establishment within a week. He wanted to know why Tom hadn't a photograph of his girl.

'My album's too heavy to carry about,' Tom replied.

'Waal, who do you write home to?'

'There's my aunt Jessica . . .' Tom began.

'Stop that kiddin', Tom,' Mac interrupted. 'You'll get him mad. He's serious minded about women.'

'By Jesus, I don't think I'd ever bother to shoot down another Hun if it wasn't for her.'

'Why, does she like you to get Huns?' Tom asked.

'Sure. What d'you think?'

Tom kept reasonably sober and arrived home at dusk feeling well and laden with writing paper, strawberries, shaving soap, peaches, apricots, *Le Rouge et Le Noir*, mouth wash, muscatels, nuts. Cherries would soon be in. The guns were banging away, but it was too windy for the Huns to raid, and only the FEs would be flying; a cold northeast wind.

Tom had been sick for a full week, and still felt very lazy, but he was not sure whether it was hectic or the effect of 'flu. The doctor did not visit him in the morning. He spent the day reading and talking. The squadron did two patrols, on one of which Mac went right over to Harbourdin after some Pfalz, and three were shot down. Lewin was missing. Tom thought he ought to be taking part in the war and not occupying space in a squadron and doing nothing. Flying would probably buck him up; there was nothing like the air above ten thousand. He would again demand of the doctor in the morning permission to go up for a joy-ride. It would help him to throw off laziness. He had no great desire, in fact no desire at all, to shoot or be shot down, but to hang about indefinitely in the midst of activity, doing nothing, was intolerable.

The doctor went over him carefully with his stethoscope; grunted; but said nothing.

'Do you think I can do a spot of flying now?' Tom asked.

'I don't think you're by any means up to flying standard. In fact, I'm sending you away for a week's rest to Le Touquet with one or two others.'

'That's fine. When shall I go?'

'To-day. You can pack right away.' The M.O. nodded good-bye and hurried off.

Soon afterwards Tom received a summons to the office, together with Miller, Jones, and Hole. James gave them instructions to proceed to No. 1 Red Cross Hospital. A tender would be ready at two o'clock.

'And of course you know that mess bills must be settled before you leave. Twenty francs each.'

'Why, durn it, I only paid a mess bill yesterday,' Miller expostulated.

'That's why there's only twenty francs now,' James replied unmoved.

After lunch Tom said good-bye to Mac, who would have left the squadron before he was back from Le Touquet.

'Good-bye, great man,' he said. 'I'm sorry I shan't follow your victorious streamer any more.'

Mac grinned. 'You might, some day. Anyway, Tom, take care of yourself, like you always do.'

Miller was upset at losing his admired leader: but there was an understanding between them that Mac would get him into his squadron, if he had one: he expected a Snipe squadron, but official secrecy withheld definite information.

Then they embarked. Hole's pale eyes were starry with pleasure at the unexpected holiday, especially as they were going to the Duchess of Westminster's Hospital. Even Jones's horse-face looked a little brighter than usual, and he was inspired to comment: 'Say, ain't this a notion?'

'Plenty of oats there,' said Tom.

Hole misunderstood him. 'Oh no, nothing like that.'

X

IN hospital Tom found it impossible to sleep after six o'clock in the morning; the full clatter of day-time started then. He seemed to have been awake most of the night, for night nurses, seemingly wearing army boots, tramped about on merciless errands of mercy and medicine. The ward was lighted by a vast skylight that bent the light of dawn into his eyes like a lens.

The hospital building used to be the Casino; it was still splendid with white paint. But there were no ghosts of former nights and days; the too vital spirit of wartime was a potent exorcist. Here the weary came to rest, returning briefly to the world of baths, dressing-gowns, slippers, and civilized food. And there were no air-raids, for the Huns never bombed No. 1 Red Cross Hospital, though they must know about it. The guns were inaudible unless the wind was in the east.

Outside were pine-woods and the sea; the low-toned, clean façade of Paris-Plage, with its mile of deserted promenade; and the sands on which the far-receding tide left multitudes of tiny crabs. There was nowhere to sit down. Tom explored the place with Hole during the morning after their arrival, and had a few strawberries and cream at a little café. The proprietor explained that it was illegal to sell cream, and charged seven francs.

They were examined by a doctor in the afternoon. Tom hoped that he was ill enough to be sent home; he felt tired after his wakeful night. But there was nothing wrong with him except that he was a little run down. The colonel commanding the hospital would pronounce finally upon him later. A week's rest was all he could hope for.

Hole and Jones were all right; a squirt of blood was taken from Miller's arm for some reason, and this raised hope in his tough breast that he was ill enough to go to England, where he could get in touch with Mac. He was irritated that Williamson had been promoted over him. He'd got more Huns than Williamson.

'I know Williamson's senior, and all that goddarn stuff,' he groused, 'but they should have given him a flight in another squadron.'

'What does it matter?' said Tom. 'You'll get a flight as soon as you're back at work, sure thing. And why your D.F.C. isn't through beats me.' He knew that Miller wanted to go back to his girl full of glory; but he was glad that he was not himself in the toils of a woman thirsting for German blood.

The amusements of the hospital were bowls, reading, gambling, gramophones, occasional shows in the evening, and flirtations with nurses, who were all supposed to be gentlewomen and out to enjoy the war. During his stay Tom played a few games of bowls: or rather he discovered how difficult it was to get the woods to stop anywhere near the jack, since they were not made to roll straight; and that it was a silly game, anyway.

He went to two shows; the artists providing the first were a major with a fine bass voice who sang 'Shipmates o' Mine' and other stirring sentimentalities; a subaltern who told stories and sang patter songs; and various women who did the usual ballads and musical comedy stuff, of which the most successful item was a concerted one that recommended to everybody to know how to do the tickle toe: and the other show was pictures, to which he went so as to be allowed up till 9.45 instead of the usual 9.30. A film called *Memories That Haunt* was shown, in which a hard-working novelist neglected his pleasure-loving wife, with harrowing results. Tom was chiefly struck by the fact that when the wife wrote a note to her husband ('going to mother') and the husband subsequently wrote a note to his wife ('going to a Foreign Land'), they were both in the same handwriting. The film earned great applause.

Tom borrowed many books from the library, from *Daddy Long Legs* to Wordsworth's *Poetical Works*. But it made him mad to be blared at by a raucous gramophone playing comic songs when he was occupied with Wordsworth's not-too-fine frenzy. 'The sad still music of humanity,' said Wordsworth. 'I'm on the staff, I'm on the staff,' shouted the gramophone.

He had a run of luck at cards and won more than a hundred francs, leaving the hospital before the luck changed; also before he had got beyond mere civility with any of the nurses. There was a great deal of competition for their favours, and it was difficult to make progress in a few days.

Tom found the life pleasant enough except for the lack of sleep. He was not there long enough to get used to the tramping at night, and found night nurses as bad as air raids. And the outing of lights at 9.30 seemed to have the effect of waking him up thoroughly. He was sleepy all day, but as soon as the order to sleep was given thus, all inclination left him. But as there was nothing to do except to eat the plentiful food and await the colonel's dooming, sleepiness did not matter. It was grand to be away from the row of flying and to be able to enjoy fine weather. As he received no letters he did

374

not think it necessary to write any except a line to Williamson, and that was a relief.

The colonel interviewed them on the fourth day. He saw Hole and Jones in the morning, and found them fit to return to duty in three days. As Tom and Miller were not to be seen till the afternoon, Miller formed the theory that they would be sent to England. Then he would get in touch with Mac and perhaps get a flight in his squadron or circus, and come out again in a month or two on Snipes, and get his fifty Huns.

In the afternoon the colonel told Tom that he was still run down, and was to proceed to No. 14 General Hospital for a week's rest in the more bracing air of Wimereux. He would make the journey next day.

Another week's holiday wasn't so bad. He had heard that No. 14 General was a good place; and it all counted as active service. He waited for Miller, who had a longer interview.

'Well, are you going across the Channel?'

'Sure, I'm going right enough.' Miller looked queer.

'You don't seem very pleased. Anything wrong?'

'Tuberculosis.'

'Oh, what's that?' Tom had heard the word before, but had no definite idea associated with it.

'Lungs, I guess.'

'What, consumption?'

'You've said it.'

'Christ almighty, how the hell did *you* get it?' Tom had a vague notion of consumption as something that made pale romantic maidens fade away with a cough when they had been crossed in love for the third or fourth time. And, of course, geniuses: Keats and Mozart. But Miller, who looked as tough as teak!

'Oh, Christ knows. This PUO leaves some fellows with it, the C.O. says.'

'But is it bad? What are they going to do with you?'

'I guess they'll send me back home. The colonel says I'll need six months' or a year's rest, and then I'll be all right as long as I take care of myself.'

'Well, that's not so bad. . . .'

375

'Say, cut out that stuff. I'm going home a ——— consumptive, no durn good for anything, just one shot better'n a leper. Christ, what'll I do? I'll have to tell the girl we can't marry. Oh Christ!'

'Come for a walk, old chap,' said Tom. 'Walk it off a bit.' He took Miller's arm and marched him off seawards, steering him away from people lest they should see the tears that tough Miller could not prevent.

'Christ, I'd rather have been killed. This is what your ——— war does to a man.'

There was nothing that Tom could say. He was horrified at the sudden collapse of Miller, at one moment puffed with ambition and the glory of war; at the next utterly cast down, the present an agony, the future a blank. Here, Tom thought, was one more tiger that found good killing in the jungle of war; he had not met this subtle beast before. God, what war did to men! who were so stupid and quarrelsome that they hunted each other rather than these pad-paw jungle enemies.

But he wondered if Miller was making more fuss than was permissible; if fuss was ever permissible. He didn't seem ill; there was no visible sign that he was other than his old self. Perhaps this was a very subtle tiger, whose first bite was lip-tender with gloating over the sweet flesh of its helpless victim; Tom did not know.

Miller kept silent for some time, and then spoke about other things. They met Jones and Hole, and walked along the sea-front together. Hearing what was the matter with Miller, the horse-faced Jones remarked:

'Oh, sure. I've known of quite a few folk die of that.'

Next morning Tom said see you later to Hole and Jones, and farewell to Miller, and went in a tender up the coast through Boulogne to Wimereux, alone and sad. Poor old Miller! It had seemed to Tom that he was looking worse this morning, probably with worry. He was the sort of fellow that could face sudden death every day and be very little troubled about it, but not the long fear of a broken, diminishing life.

'Forget that damn-fool stuff I talked yesterday,' he had said; 'I'll be O.K.'

'I hope to God you will. Keep a stout heart,' Tom had replied.

Possibly he ought to have used expressions of stronger certainty, but he disliked bedside optimism used by doctors and near relatives to cover up their own inadequacy. Poor Miller!

Tom found that the hospital was the old Splendid Hotel, standing in a dip in the cliffs just above the sand and rocks. A strong west wind was blowing, churning the grey sea into white breakers. He was put into a top-floor room with three beds: one was occupied by a small quiet Canadian Harry Tate pilot named Vickers, and the other was vacant. It was a comfortable place. Tom soon found that the food was really good, better than at Le Touquet. At dinner they were allowed either stout, whisky, red wine, or white wine, but with a little bluff it was possible to have all of them, and the nurse who took temperatures in the morning, having asked him once if he had a headache, only smiled on other mornings. The nurses were not so convinced of their own merits as the ladies of Touquet.

He could not find his shaving brush in the morning. Fortunately Vickers did not mind lending his. Then his strop was missing; he could remember where he had left it hanging at le Touquet. And his bottle of salts. He hated losing things; once he started, he usually had a run of it and lost quite a lot before he stopped; he must not play cards until the spell had worked itself out.

He did not see a doctor, and in the afternoon went out and walked down to Boulogne with one of the other patients. The waves were dashing over the sea-wall, and it was not possible to walk along the front. The tide ebbed in the evening, and after dinner they went on the sands and the rocks, where there was seaweed, red and green and brown, stout whipcord or fine hair; there were mussels and sea-anemones and star-fish and hundreds of crabs. He felt like a boy again, and climbed enthusiastically into the ruined Napoleonic fort on the rocks.

And there were Waacs that came out of a local Waacery in the evening. One could, without great risk, lure them to sit in secluded places on the cliffs, to share enjoyment of the pale sands, the blue sky fading to green in the north where England was hidden in haze, the gentle clouds and the pale gold mists high up. In this pleasant place, with wine in his belly, clean salt air in his lungs, and his arm

377

round a strange red-cheeked girl from Northampton, Tom felt the tide of health flowing in him.

He wrote to Williamson that night, telling him the news, and what a bank-holiday he was having. A young man named Skelton moved into the third bed. He had left Charterhouse less than a year ago and spent a lot of his time reading Aeschylus. Tom could not believe that anyone could read that old bore for pleasure, and accused him secretly of affectation and snobbery, but Skelton seemed genuine enough. Apart from formal school knowledge he was as ignorant as a young man should be, and knew no more than any ex-coalheaver Tommy why there was a war on.

In the morning it rained. Tom was examined by a doctor, who said there was nothing wrong with him. He could blow the mercury in the lung-testing apparatus up to 125, and hold it at 40 for seventy-five seconds. The colonel would see him later.

The rain stopped and the clouds were hackled into ragged flocks by the impellent south-west wind, under whose whip the flagrant sea shone green and grey and blue in the varying sunshine, and roared upon the beach a huge voice of the essential mindlessness of nature.

Tom walked to Boulogne with Skelton after lunch, discussing whether the sea was real and arguing about books, of which Skelton had read a vast quantity for one of his age. He was a literary amateur, full of reverence for great writers of all descriptions.

'What you mean by a great writer,' said Tom, 'is a poor worm who spends all his time thinking of nice ways of putting things. What an occupation!'

'. . . proclaimers of truth,' Skelton ended his speech in reply.

'Truth! It's unreadable. All books that are read are full of exaggeration, prejudice, misrepresentation. An appearance of impartiality is a literary device to increase point. Writing isn't a vocation, like Holy Orders, recruiting, and going to the North Pole, but a trade or profession, and no more honest than the rest.'

'Truth is a spirit,' replied Skelton. 'Genius knows the spirit of truth.'

They had food at a shop in Victor Hugo Road, but the days of cream pastries were over in Boulogne, and ices were made with water. There was even a difficulty about liqueurs, which were served in coffee cups, or sometimes in coffee, to evade a regulation. The French disrespect for regulations was refreshing. Wine, eau de Cologne, and widows were still plentiful.

That evening Tom conversed with a fat pale Waac from Shepherd's Bush. Skelton was above Waacs. Vickers was too sensible to do anything rash. The Huns dropped a lot of bombs on Boulogne during the night, and kept everybody awake. Then it came on to rain. Sunday dawned wet and remained so. There was nothing to do. Tom went with Skelton to a church service. The padre preached at length about miraculous feeding, describing, as a modern parallel, their surprise if a battalion had a good meal from a tin of bully. Tom thought a pair of kippers would have been more apt, and wondered why he had put himself to the penance of being preached to interminably by a well-meaning ignorant bore with a wounding Cockney accent.

He went before the colonel in the afternoon, and heard that he could return to his squadron forthwith, as there was nothing the matter with him; a statement he had heard so often lately that he was beginning to doubt it, especially as he had a cold in his head and felt as though his brain had turned to solid fat. He read through the rest of the dismal, stuffy day, and in the night there was a thunderstorm that awakened him and the others; and when they had got to sleep after it a nurse came round with a lamp, peering to see if they were asleep, and woke them up again.

Monday was fine and still and hot. Tom wandered on the shore and sat on the cliffs and talked and read. He had a letter from Williamson, who hoped to see him again soon. The Huns had been very quiet, but there were 'signs of an increase of activity'. Franklin had got a flight in another squadron and had been dispatched thither drunk and incapable on the floor of a tender.

Tom was glad he would be back very soon. He was tired of hospital life; sick of doing nothing. He felt very fit, his cold having disappeared, and this continued inactivity was no good to him. He wondered if he would remember how to fly. No word came to him as to his departure: 'forthwith' was evidently a relative term; to the colonel it might mean within a month. He got fed up with his blonde after-dinner Waac from Langton Maltravers, and broke away early.

There was another storm in the night. He heard in the morning that he was to leave at two o'clock, so went with Skelton to Mony's and had a farewell lunch with Anjou wine. And then for the squadron. He should be there in plenty of time for a drink and yarn with Bill before dinner. But the tender only took him to a Rest Camp, a desolate group of huts on the heights behind Boulogne, and left him there with no means of escape. There was an adjutant who told him he must pay seven francs for a day's messing, and that he would be handed over to the R.T.O. at Boulogne next morning to be conveyed by train to No. 1 A.S.D. at Marquise.

Tom blew with exasperation. So much for his hope of reaching home that day. It was hot, and the camp was barren of comfort. There were earwigs. Nothing whatever to do. He read a French tale about the universality of human misery, and entered into conversation with a young man with pale blue eyes that seemed too vague ever to behold the hard outline of the world. They talked for two hours, and then the dreamer hurried down to Boulogne to buy Renan's *Vie de Jesus* which he insisted Tom must read at once for its high aesthetic value.

The heat was enervating. Tom felt like a steam-roller going up hill. He had refused to go into Boulogne with his new friend, whose name, according to his baggage, was Porter, as it was almost too hot to move and he had already been there in the morning. Now he wished he had gone. The dusty aridity of the camp was stifling. His blood was irritated. A sudden resolution formed in his body and drove him out of the camp and down the hill into the town.

A girl smiled at him. He stopped. She came up to him. 'You come with me, chéri? I have something nice to show you.'

She was young. It was risky, going with these strays. But she looked healthy. His eyes were held by the maddening lift of her breasts, and his blood became irresistible.

'How much?' he asked harshly, hoping she could not see that he was shaking.

'Twenty francs, and you pay five francs for a room. You come with me and I will make you happy'.

'Ça va. But you will not ask for more; tu ne demanderas plus que ton vingt francs?'

'Mais non, non.'

She took him to a back-street hotel that catered for this sort of thing, and he secured ten minutes' tenancy of a cubicle with a wash bowl and running water for five francs. He paid the girl her twenty francs and felt profoundly unhappy because of the purchase of what ought essentially to be free. She slipped off clothes quickly, until she had on only shoes and stockings and a dark coloured chemise.

'Give me five francs, darling, and I take this off,' she coaxed.

'No. You said you would not ask more.'

'But give me only five francs. Je serai toute nue. You will like it, chéri.' She leant against him. 'Only five francs. You do not mind five francs for me.'

'Oh damn.' He pulled a lot of dirty municipal notes from a pocket and gave her five francs, and she started to pull off her chemise over her head. He hated her. Desire was dead. He gave her a slap on the bare backside that made her yelp, and, full of black rage, crashed open the door and stamped out, the whore's fury breaking about his ears in waves of incomprehensible cursing.

The proprietor appeared, also emitting words.

'Elle est mauvaise fille. Je lui ai frappé l'âne. Voulez-vous ouvrir la porte,' Tom said to him loudly and indignantly.

He opened the front door, shouting over his shoulder at the girl what seemed to be threats. She subsided into grumbling.

Tom was in a rage with himself for being a fool and throwing away thirty francs, and with the world for being a place where such idiotic tragi-comedies could occur. He strode along, very hot. He ought to know by now what those girls were. The air was slightly malodorous. He was sick of Boulogne, but his only refuge was the repulsive rest camp. He would be very glad to get back to the peace and dirty comfort of the squadron, where he wasn't just a bloody unit to be shifted about. When the devil would the world go sane about sex? Or rather, when would women be treated as human beings and not as chattels that had to sell themselves in the disastrous marriage market or that even more pernicious market where he had just spent thirty francs on a bad egg? God, what a world! No wonder there were wars, when men were so hopelessly stupid. And here was he, who hated all their blasted stupidity, loathed it from the bottom of his soul, entangled in their muddle of war and their madness about sex. What was he going to do about it? He had been living from day to day in hospital instead of thinking things out. Perhaps this delay in his return to active service was fortunate; he might have time to make up his mind what he would do.

He reached camp an hour before dinner-time, and disturbed a fatigued and disinclined batman with a request for sufficient water for a sponge down in his canvas bath, which was following him about in his kit and was at length useful, for he felt he needed cleansing.

Porter came in while he was towelling, bringing the Renan and also Anatole France's *Thaïs*. They talked till midnight, but slept in separate huts. They went on talking after breakfast until the adjutant sent for them. They were to report to the R.T.O. at Boulogne and would be able to go together to No. 1 A.S.D. A tender took them to the station, and they left their baggage there and went and had a drink, which lasted till lunch time. A grand final feed before leaving civilization seemed necessary, so they went to Mony's.

After the eloquence of the Chambertin had spent itself, they interviewed the R.T.O., and he told them to entrain not later than four o'clock. From this they judged that their train was likely to start that evening. They went away and drank tea, returning when they had talked themselves out. It was half-past four: their train was nearly full, but they were still able to get seats. Tom opened the *Vie de Jesus*, but it was hot and wine fumes were dulling his mind, so he dozed, just aware of occasional new-comers using up the last inches of seating and standing space. He was wedged against a deep-toned colonel who liked to hold forth. It was infernally hot, and the train as yet lacked an engine.

Tom dozed. The colonel boomed. There was a jolt when the engine arrived. Someone said that French engines had no brakes and could only stop themselves when soli by bumping into something.

Tom dozed. Some time after six there was another jolt, and, looking carefully at the ground, he could see that the train was moving. People who were stretching themselves began to get in.

The train increased speed until it was going at a smart walking pace.

Stimulated by the movement Tom maintained himself awake and read his book. The colonel boomed away. Renan was sweet and reasonable.

'. . . far too much slackness about saluting. How often you see a young subaltern putting a finger to his cap like a cabby who's had a good tip. An officer for his own sake should salute smartly. A good officer is punctilious about every detail. I've seen it over and over again. The type of blub blub blub. . . .'

Damn that hot-airing old bore. Tom remembered someone had told him there was actually no such place as Nazareth in the year one. Was it true? It was impossible to believe anything one way or the other that was connected with an established religion; people were so violent about it. Truth was as nothing in comparison with the clamant need to uphold or destroy.

'Many young officers seem to think that just because there's a war, smartness does not matter. That's not how the British Army became what it is, or how it will maintain its morale. The effect of a really smart officer on his men is astounding.'

Curse him and his smartness. Tom shut the book. What did Jesus matter nowadays? Christianity was dead anyhow: Arnold Bennett had said so quite recently. It was hanging on the old barbed wire, and only church parades remained.

'Shoes!' Thunder was scornful. 'I cannot for the life of me understand how an officer and a gentleman can wear shoes with service dress. Yet how often is authority and tradition defied in this respect by young fops who blub blub blub. . . .'

'Do you know, sir,' Tom asked respectfully, 'that in the Air Force we are officially allowed to wear shoes with slacks?'

'That may be, my boy, but I hope you do not take advantage of it.'

'Well sir, perhaps you will make some allowance for the fact that we are concerned principally with machines rather than men; our most important job is to keep our bus in good shape. Splitarsing about in aerial combat is bound to subject it to abnormal strains.'

Tom had captured attention, and he went on yarning, not from any desire for publicity, but to keep the exasperating old colonel off his hobby-horse. Fortunately all ground people were always interested in flying and willing to hear about it. Tom had a good audience, including the colonel, who perhaps wasn't a bad old stick.

XI

No. 1 A.S.D. was a horrible place; tents, earwigs, machine guns. A sort of purgatory. The mess was war-sick. Food was poor, service slovenly, no one gave a damn. They were expected to practise machine guns all day. Tom loathed machine guns; and firing them on the ground was no practice for firing them in the air; the two things were entirely different. Doubtless some base wallahs had heard that good shooting was the essential thing in the air, and did not know that ground shooting wasn't the same thing. He had hoped that he had left behind for ever those boring-to-death lectures on the long arm of the lock-spring or the multitude of possible stoppages or jams. They were useless, for the only way of clearing a stoppage upstairs was to use the loading handles or pull up the gear handle, and if that didn't do it you might just as well go home and let the armourers see to the trouble.

Tom told the adjutant or whoever he was that took official notice of him when he reported at the office that he wanted to get back to his squadron at once; he was deputy leader of his flight, the squadron was short of pilots, and he had word that they were absolutely pining for his return; so why not put him in a tender and send him there right away? But the adjutant cared for none of these things. As Tom had been in hospital he would have to be passed fit for flying by the A.S.D.'s own doctor before he could be handed over to any squadron. And then he would have to be posted to his squadron in the ordinary way, which might take a few days. The squadron had to supply transport. And he could not be excused machine gunning; there was a regulation.

Tom had arrived at night, and shared a tent with Porter. It appeared that Porter ought not to be there, and would be sent off somewhere else at once. The doctor turned up during the morning

384

and examined Tom and told him there was nothing the matter with him; Tom, tired of hearing this, said that PUO seemed to have left his eyes weak, but the doctor did not believe it and sent him some boracic lotion with instructions to bathe his eyes four times a day.

It was oppressively hot. He did not think it necessary to report at machine guns that day as he had hardly arrived and had to bathe his eyes. Towards evening he went for a stroll with Porter to a near hamlet where they found a pleasant little estaminet. There they settled for the evening and drank wine. Porter had a number of pet subjects that he talked about, such as The Poetry of Experience, Life as the End of Life, Meanness the Only Crime; and another set, The Philosophy of Sin, The Beauty of Evil. Baudelaire was of course the poet of his bosom, but he also leant on Shakespeare's *Sonnets*, in which he found significances new to Tom. He recommended for acceptance what Oscar Wilde had written about them (Tom had not read it), and laughed at Browning's pawky pomposity: 'the less Shakespeare he'.

They drank so much that the talk became deep beyond all fathoming. Madame appeared to find their company fascinating, and sat listening to their conversation, of which she did not understand a word, with an expression of great amenity.

'Vous aimez la poésie?' Tom asked her.

'La poésie? Je l'adore,' she replied fervently.

'Vous connaissez Molière?'

Madame looked blank. They explained Molière to her. Their French was wonderfully fluent with all the wine they had drunk, and madame covered her inability to discover what they were talking about by compliments about their French. They left before dusk, and were led back to the Aircraft Supply Depot and their tent by the benevolent Power which directs the footsteps of good drunkards.

Tom awoke with a headache and no aspirin. Porter was whisked off to the railhead. He ought to have gone the night before. He made a note of Tom's address, borrowing his fountain pen for the purpose, and they parted firmly intending to meet again.

It came on to rain. Tom went and dozed in a machine gun class. The place was infernally boring without Porter. By God, he'd be glad to see Bill again; he longed for his simplicity, clarity, strength.

Then he couldn't find his fountain pen, and remembered that Porter had used it; he must have put it in his pocket absent-mindedly, confound him. The rain was torrential. Tom lay on his bed and read. It was damp in the tent. Even the earwigs must be uncomfortable. A man moved in to occupy the other bed space. He talked a lot, chiefly about abdominal influenza, from which he had been suffering. He said he had gone a week without eating. His eyes and eyebrows slanted downwards, tending to make a curved pattern of his face. When the rain left off, he went out. Tom lay and meditated. A black cat visited him, and sat on his chest and purred. He was glad of its quiet sympathy.

As the next day was Sunday, there was, strangely enough, no machine-gunning. This deference to the Lord's Day Observance Act surprised Tom, but he was glad of it; as long as no one tried to drive him to church. The other man in the tent had not slept in his bed; he had vanished. Tom was glad to be alone; he wanted to think, or to let thought clarify itself in him.

It was a gloriously fine day. He went for solitary walks in the neighbouring country. Near at hand a valley was cut in the plateau by the small river which meandered through it. The valley was flat and green and wooded. The low limestone hills which were its sides were steep and covered with short grass. Miles of caves had been cut in them by some ancient people. Tom found it a delightful contrast with the usual flatness of this part of France. Miles of fields of barley and wheat gleamed in the sun, bright with poppies and cornflowers innumerable, and many other wild flowers whose names he was too urban to know.

In this smiling valley the certainty grew up in his mind that the earth was too pleasant a place to leave yet if he could help it. He had almost completed his third period of danger. In another week or two — surely it could not be longer than a month — he would return to England. During that interim he must primarily look after himself. He was experienced and cunning in the air now, and had a quite good chance of surviving if he was careful. It would take a very good Hun to shoot him down, and very good Huns seemed scarce. He didn't want to shoot down Huns; he was sick of all that. Live and let live would be his motto for the next month. Refusing to go up and all heroics of that sort were quite unnecessary; his time was up, and until they sent him home he would compromise and try to save life; not only his own. He was forced to fight; and he was entitled to meet force with — not fraud, that was a nasty word — with evasion. God, it wasn't his war.

And he would get Williamson to go carefully, and then they would go to England together, and with luck the war would be over before they had to return to active service. There was a chance, anyway. Damn it, they'd done their share of the fighting. Let some of the bloody politicians and contractors and field marshals come and do a bit; the liaison officers and brass hats whose lives were too valuable to be risked, blast their souls, with rooms at the War Office, or at Paris, or in châteaux miles away; the home-front and base-inhabiting nephews of ministers and millionaires, very remote and happy and patriotic, in khaki but out of the war. It was Tom, Dick, and Harry that would win the war with their blood; but he knew who would get the benefit; the generals, the contractors, the cabinet ministers; and probably the bench of bishops hadn't done all its recruiting without seeing something for it; they couldn't run a church on sentiment. Why fight for that crowd, and, as poor old Seddon used to say, in the interests of usury?

He was getting mad about it again. No use. Keep calm. Meet force and fraud with evasion. Watch your tail; safety first. Oh Seddon!

He was all right upstairs, but hoped to God there'd be no more ground-strafing. Glory-hunting Mac and Miller were gone. He could talk to Bill. There was news of a successful push by the French and Americans down south. Evidently the plan was to get rid of the threat to Paris. If there was another push within the next month, it would probably be to free Amiens (Foch being a Frenchman) before the Germans took it into their heads to bring up long range guns to smash the city, and there was no reason why the squadron should be moved so far; there were plenty of squadrons down there already. France was full of British aeroplanes nowadays.

The French people hereabouts all seemed to collect unexploded bombs that German aeroplanes had dropped. Possibly they thought that they might have some value, and anyway they were useful as weights. Apart from this slight deviation from the normal, the life and culture of this happy valley seemed little affected by war. There was a lack of men of military age, but the plentiful crops ripened and doubtless there would be a good price for them if they could be harvested successfully. This was the smiling and rewarding earth that men loved; in river valleys they had first discovered the amenities of life and the possibility of leisure; to them they would return again when war had shattered industrial civilization, and disease and starvation had abolished the strange monster, western man. A new race would dwell in the limestone caves and begin establishing private property, taboos about bodily functions, magic and religion, corn-myths of dying gods; and venture beyond its river valleys and thieve and fight and perish. In the large sweep of time present things were as indiscoverable as a star in the Milky Way. He was outside, and the whole galaxy was his to contemplate. He would not lose the whole for one tiny star lost in the haze. The name of England would be forgotten and unpredictable limbs bathe in Thames. Ice would come, and change, and all the artillery of breastless nature. A black rock would swing in the red solar evening, worthless.

Tom was startled from his meditation by the scream of shells and the noise of rapid gunfire. He retreated from danger at four miles an hour, and soon afterwards met two American officers who told him that their people were trying out a new one-pounder quick-firer. The Yanks evidently had no Lord's Day Observance Act.

He returned to the A.S.D., hoping a tender would come for him. He was posted to his squadron and might possibly go there that evening. But no tender came, and he went to bed at eleven o'clock. Again his co-tenter was not there. Tom was used to sudden dis-appearances, but found this one rather puzzling, and wondered about it as he fell asleep. He might have seized an aeroplane and flown off to Holland; his abdominal influenza might have caused him to return suddenly to hospital; he might have been hit by an American one-pounder; he might have assaulted a brass-hat. . . .

All next day Tom hung about by machine guns waiting to be taken from purgatory. It seemed an age since he had left hospital. What a welter of misorganization war was. Time was as nothing. Probably there was no intention of finishing the war that year, unless the Germans starved. There were rumours that already they were eating dogs, cats, and old boots pending harvest. What would life be without rumours?

Tom chewed inedible beef at dinner, and abandoned hope. Perhaps it was not purgatory. *Lasciate ogni speranza voi ch' entrate.* The punishment of his sins was upon him; to wait eternally at No. 1 A.S.D. doing machine guns; the obverse of the last ride together. He must have been exceptionally wicked.

At nine o'clock the office sent for him. His Crossley tender had come. He recognized the driver and smiled with him. He was Orpheus come to release him from the plutonic regions behind the battle front, where fighting men were cattle and organizers prevailed. Tom soon had his stuff on board, and the tender went homewards through the darkness towards the flashing horizon, arriving at half-past eleven when everybody was asleep. It was too windy and cloudy for night-flying. The nights were darker. The worst part of the year was over and dawn not quite so depressingly early.

Tom crashed into his hut, lighted a candle, and had his baggage brought in.

'What the hell,' said Williamson.

'Sorry to disturb you, Bill. But it's good to hear your voice again.'

'Good God, Tom, have you actually come back? You've swung the lead pretty successfully, haven't you?'

'Pretty well.' It was too late to hail a batman, and he struggled with his blankets alone, telling Williamson briefly about his travels.

'You're a wonderful fellow, Tom. I respect your genius. It was two days you weren't very well, wasn't it? and you wangled a month's holiday, full pay, no mess bills, nurses to tuck you up, free drinks. You ought to be fighting fit now, anyhow.'

'I'm fit enough. But how's things here? Much doing lately? Any casualties?'

'Cable's missing and Watt was shot down by a Fokker. That's two good men gone. In fact, we're very short of experienced pilots, though C flight will be pretty good now you're back. Oh, and a new fellow crashed and broke his neck. I forget his name. But things have been pretty quiet on the whole. Jerry's washing out everything in favour of the new Fokker biplanes. I don't know what to make of them. Some are damned good and some aren't. I suppose it's the pilots. We caught four of them two evenings ago just in front of Nieppe Forest and shot them all down.'

'Who's we?'

'C flight. But other times we haven't been able to get at them. They're fast and climb like hell, or some of them do. You'll soon get to know them. We had another of those damned aerodrome raids. That's when Watt was shot down. Eighteen SEs escorted us and a bunch of Fokkers set about them and a few got down at us, and it was merry hell getting back. However, there wasn't so very much harm done. Huns can't shoot straight, that's about the truth of it.'

They went on yarning late into the night. The major was going home in a few days. There weren't many of the old March push people left, only Williamson, Hudson, Maitland, and Tom. Dubois and Jones were still there. Tom remembered their arrival one day in April. They must have come on a lucky day; everyone else who arrived about that time had gone west. But what a fine crowd the squadron had been in those days! Twenty Huns in a day! They would never do anything like it again. For one thing the Huns wouldn't come and be shot at.

They slept late in the morning, as high wind and low clouds with occasional sputtering rain prevented flying. Tom said hullo to everyone he knew — there were several new faces — and reported to the major. He was rather surprised at the warmth of the major's greeting.

'I'm very glad to see you back, Cundall. We can do with some real pilots. I hope you're feeling fit now.'

The major wasn't at all a bad sort of fellow really, Tom thought. It was probably his own fault if there hadn't been much cordiality in the past. There certainly wasn't any hot air about him, and that was a lot to be thankful for. A pity he was going home. It was nice to be called a real pilot once in his life. It wasn't true, of course. Lucky was the word.

The stormy weather continued for two days, and Tom had nothing to do but talk and answer an accumulation of letters. He wanted to fly, but even a joyride was impossible.

'You'll probably have to borrow an Avro, Bill, and give me some dual. I've forgotten everything.'

'Oh you'll be all right. But I wish you'd forget your humanitarian-ism about earwigs and do your share of slaughter. There's quite twenty thousand taken permanent quarters in this hut.'

Tom made a slaughter. 'I've been thinking while I've been away.'

'I was afraid you had. You ought to remember that you're paid not to think.'

'Yes, but it's not in King's Regs. except between the lines. I know that the side that thinks gets beaten, but my little effort won't make any difference to British invincibility. It's too utterly utter.'

'Well?'

'This business of shooting down Huns is the same thing as if we lost our tempers in the mess and stabbed each other in the back.'

'Is it? You mean, if we split in two parties over some question?'

'I mean that many of the Huns we shoot are probably quite as close to each of us in tastes and character and even race as the people on our own side. Mix us all together and we'd get on very well. Look at the mixtures fighting on the same sides.'

'True. I wish I loathed Huns as much as I do earwigs.'

'Leave off swotting and help me to get straight. The position's intolerable.'

'I can only say again, Tom, do remember you're paid not to think.'

'I was in Spain when the war started. It's a pleasant country if you mind your own business. There's a lot to be said for so-called degeneracy. They have the secret of living. It is *mañana*: never do to-day what you can put off till to-morrow. The Moorish stuff is lovely. All Spaniards have the manners of princes: fairy-tale princes, I mean. Wine is cheap and good, and you dare not drink water. They've kept out of this 'ere war and are probably rolling in money.'

Williamson was puzzled. 'Very interesting. But what's the point, if any?'

'Well, my God, isn't it the very place to go to after the war? Right away from it, but not away from the amenities of civilization. You'd love it, Bill. It's all mountains and medievalism. You sit in the shade and drink slowly and flower girls and boot blacks worry you and cigars are two a penny; the tram conductors smoke them all day. Long grave peasants ride about on small donkeys with their

391

feet dangling to the ground either side, and maintain an air of innate nobility.'

Williamson was interested, and left the earwigs in peace. 'It sounds a good scheme, Tom. But we couldn't stop there for long. How on earth could we earn a living?'

'That's simple. We'd fly. We'd take out a couple of Avros; they'll be giving them away with a pound of tea as soon as the war's over. Then we can hire a field near Madrid and give joy rides to wealthy Spaniards. Five pounds for a quarter of an hour. Fifty per cent extra for a loop. They'd jump at it. Then we might get a fat government contract to start an air force. They're always scrapping with tribes of Moors and darkies across the water; an air force would be the very thing to put the fear of God into them. We might be comic generals with sky-blue and yellow uniforms and clanking sabres and umpteen mistresses before we finish.'

'No damn fear. But that's the hell of a scheme, Tom. D'you think we could raise enough cash? I don't suppose I'll have more than my blood money.'

'We ought to be able to make some sort of start on five or six hundred pounds. There's plenty of time to think it all out. Meanwhile you'd better save up your extra seven bob a day. And — save up yourself. We've got about another month to go out here. We must look after ourselves . . .'

'Hullo, hullo. Is this all a scheme to corrupt my blameless innocence?'

'No, it's not. But there's no point in being heroic at this stage. Take our excellent C.O. as an example. Live and let live. Compromise. The Hun is whacked in the air. So long as we protect our two-seaters and frighten theirs off we're doing our essential job. Let's look after ourselves, and use our painfully learnt cunning for our own protection. And then, for Spain.'

'Tom, you're a villain, a plausible villain. But I like the Spanish scheme. I should feel better with something definite to think about. It takes away the world-without-end feeling. And I dare say the war will end this year.'

'That's settled then,' said Tom, and Williamson did not gainsay, thinking of aeroplanes in Spain.

XII

On the evening of the second day after Tom's return was the binge for Major Barlow's home-going. The occasion was made splendid by the arrival of General Mitchell with his eyeglass, two colonels, and three majors. Veuve Cliquot of Rheims supplied six dozen bottles of her marvellous champagne, which soon loosened everything but the general's eyeglass. Tom was quietly happy talking of past times with his coevals Maitland and Hudson and Chadwick. God, the fellows they'd known who had gone west. The light seemed to change as if the lamps burnt green: Tom imagined other figures than the living sitting at the long table; ribs and spines and grinning skulls showing through a mist of flesh that made them recognizable: Tommy, Beal, Muir, Selby, Taylor, Debenham, Sawyer, Skinner, Smith, Seddon, Grey, Bruce, Watt, Cross and the rest. They lifted glasses and the drink trickled down among their ribs.

Tom drank and abolished the vision, and the yellow light shone on the living. There was Jones, his face luminous and almost expressive with champagne, talking blatant shop, and Baker trying to look as though even Cliquot could not relieve his cosmic weariness. And Fuller, dark and sallow, his black hair flattened and glistening, keeping well on the Christian side of drunkenness. Hole was narrating some scandalous story of concupiscence among the great, his face red and hideous, his eyes brilliant with vitality, his short hair bristling with accumulated lust. Jock, his rival in vitality, was sitting opposite, flushed and leering with infinite knowingness. Hole ended on an arsis amid a gust of laughter and Jock started to cap the story in broad Scots, which impinged on Tom's right tympanum at the same time as Maitland on his left was telling him in his pleasant southern accent about the horses and the comic negro stable lad at home. At the top of the table the major, riotously excited and noisy behind his preponderant nose with the combined intoxication of drink and exalted compliments about his good work, was vociferating about his more active flying in the bad old days of 1916. The general listened to him with that unique air of good breeding which is the glory of

English general officers and possibly, Tom thought, finally determined the Americans to fight on the same side.

But Tom, drinking rapidly even for him, morbidly dilated to Maitland about his mother's death from cancer early in the war and his father's reiterated senile hortations to him to kill more damned Germans; he even seemed to hold them responsible for his wife's death. What a war!

He got so muzzy that he spilt his port and the official eloquence passed by him like an idle noise. There was a rag in the anteroom. Mess waiters kept bringing round trays of yellow bubbling stuff and Tom kept on drinking. He felt ill, and his feet found a way into the night outside. The windy darkness reeled and spun about him. He clung to some part of the unbalanced world, submitting hopelessly and blindly to the agonizing rotation, and spewed.

He went dully and ashamedly to bed. His head was a little clearer. He had been drinking whisky and soda on top of champagne, a mixture he could not stomach in quantity. He loathed that way of ending an evening. He was hot. He reached out in the half-light for his water-bottle. It was glorious, the cold flow through his parched mouth. Cold water was the finest drink on earth. Had he been tight last night? God, yes. And shot his bundle. He sat up in bed. Williamson was dressing.

'Hullo, Tom, so you've come to. How do you feel?'

Tom considered. 'I feel pretty good. Not much of a head.'

'Good. You were as tight as a drum. Never have I seen you look so like a boiled owl.'

'I don't remember anything, except that I thought whisky and soda was champagne. And I remember Forster, but I don't know why.'

'You were trying to dance with him. You couldn't do much, but the way you kept on your feet when you'd lost your balance was a sight for the gods. Then you reeled out of the picture ghastly pale with your eyes sticking out and looking different ways, like an apoplectic cod. I wondered if you'd ever get them straight. You're certainly worth seeing when you're tight.'

The new C.O. arrived during the day and started taking over. He was a slight, quiet, earnest man, and it appeared probable that things would go on as usual.

The weather cleared, and flying started after lunch. C flight had a patrol at 5.30. Tom wanted to have a trial flight before tea, but his machine was not ready. He felt a little nervous about going up for the first time after so long an interval. But once in the cockpit all nervousness went. His engine revved well, and it was fine to see once again the grass changing into a grey-green blur as he accelerated to flying speed, and to feel the lift of wings as he let his Camel leap from the ground after holding it down to a hundred miles an hour; and to watch the heavy world becoming a flat picture as the small blanchet clouds at six thousand feet changed into fogs and then into shining Parian islands below them.

The formation was only four strong. Williamson was leading, Tom flying on his left and Baker on his right, and Fuller in the middle above and behind. Hole should have been with them, but apparently had not got off. Dubois was on leave. There was another active member of the flight, Brindley, but he was not on this job.

Tom thought of the old days when Mac had led and Miller and he completed the spearhead. They seemed in retrospect glorious days. Now Mac had gone on to greater glory, and Miller . . . poor old Miller. That time was past, and now for a month of looking after his own skin before going home.

The business of carrying bombs on every patrol had not been resumed after the squadron's incapacitation by PUO so they had nothing to do but fly up and down the lines. Baker turned back with his engine dud and Fuller took his place. There did not seem to be any Huns about. Tom was enjoying the pure air of the heights. There would be no harm in doing this sort of thing for another month or so. Archie opened fire at them, and made flying more strenuous, but it was like meeting an old friend in the placid waste of sky. He lent the blankness significance, if of the wrong sort: but the negation of blank heaven was itself a kind of evil if one dwelt on it, and Beelzebub cast out Beelzebub.

Then Williamson gave the dud engine signal and turned back, and Tom led Fuller quietly down to Arras. The wind from the west was rather strong, and he was careful not to be blown far over. There were no Huns at all up; no doubt it was too windy for them; but he did not like the sound of his engine. At least one cylinder was not firing properly, and he did not want to have a forced landing near the lines. Then Fuller turned for home. What an epidemic; it was queer how engines caught dudness from one another.

He floated down to a warmer denser level and spent some time frisking idly about, his engine missing occasionally. Then he felt bored and went home twenty minutes early.

He reported at the office that he had been alone, and as there was nothing at all doing he had come home. The new C.O. was there, going into things with James. Tom thought he looked at him disapprovingly about his casual report, though he did not say anything. To put himself definitely in the right Tom added that his engine was missing intermittently. Had he caught a faint whiff of that devil's emanation, hot air? He hoped not, but crossed himself in case he had. Probably the man was normally like that, and intended no harm. He certainly was not a vessel of joy.

The jobs for C flight next day were a dawn patrol and an escort at 10 a.m. Tom and Williamson went to bed early and were called at quarter-past four. Only three machines were serviceable, and only they and Hole ate the hard boiled eggs. Hole had smashed his prop taking off on last evening's job, and a new one had been fitted. The dawn was rosy and promised rain soon. They took off into very clear air, with a breeze getting up, and reached the lines by half-past five, probably too early for Huns. The sun was blaring his red reveille through the eastern mist, and the whole cirque of the horizon echoed his high tumult in falling pitch. Westward there was a thin line of advancing cloud.

Tom's engine began to splutter. He saw that the pressure was down, and he used the hand pump. Pressure came up all right but at once started falling again, and he had to use the hand pump continuously. His arm soon ached, so he switched over to gravity and went home. When he had landed he saw that the little propeller that worked the mechanical pressure pump had come off. That was another job done, and it was very unlikely that the ten o'clock escort would be possible. It was only a little after six, so he went back to bed and snoozed till Williamson returned an hour later, having had a perfectly quiet time.

Nimbus was being driven across the sky by the warm south-west breeze. A few drops of rain were falling when they crossed to the mess for breakfast, and by 9.30 it was a grey wet day. Tom settled in a comfortable looted chair and read in the papers how the war was going officially. There was a photograph of their aerodrome in the *Daily Mirror*.

The war in the air, Tom thought, seemed to have turned quite comic. What with dud weather, dud engines, and dud Huns, it was just a picnic. But, comfortably enough, all this wasted time led no less inevitably to the invisible end than if they were fighting like mad dogs. The blockade went on. Food was getting more and more scarce; there was no need to fight. Starvation and disease were more powerful than the mechanical weapons of war. Why shoot the Huns? They had enemies in their rear that would destroy them soon enough. Let the Yanks get on with the scrapping; they were out for adventure, and were very welcome to all that was going. Tom himself had virtually retired from the war.

The major said good-bye and shook hands all round. 'Thank you for all you've done for me,' was his phrase to the pilots on active service.

'Very sorry you're going, major,' Tom said, and he meant it. Barlow was a good fellow and treated a man decently. He had got a bit nervy in the March push — who hadn't? — but in the ordinary way there was no hot air about him. Well, that was another link with the old fighting days gone. Fighting be damned. He was through.

He yarned a lot with Williamson, slept in the afternoon, and drank moderately in the evening. The weather showed no signs of clearing. He awoke in the morning and the rain was still drumming on the roof. Late breakfast and the pipe of peace; then a quiet rubber of bridge. He had lost interest in card games, but Williamson wanted him to make up a four. In the afternoon he was roused from his nap by a summons to the office.

'Sit down, Cundall,' said the major pleasantly. His voice had a natural or firmly acquired incisiveness. 'I'm making the acquaintance of my pilots, starting with you, as you appear to be next senior to the flight commanders. I've had everybody's record got up to date. I see you've been out here getting on for seven months. I suppose you'll be going home soon.'

'I suppose so, major.' This was a promising start.

'You've quite a good record; somewhere about seven Huns if you add in all the fractions.'

'We did rather a lot of ground-strafing during the March and April push,' said Tom a trifle airily.

'Yes, I know. I allowed for that when I said your record was quite good. But I should like to see you get some more Huns before you go. Are you quite fit after your time in hospital?'

'Quite, thanks.' Tom looked at him. Was this an inquisition? He appeared friendly. Probably he was normally something of a hot air merchant, and was feeling the responsibility of having a squadron on active service to look after. He would settle down.

'A pilot of your ability and experience,' the major went on conversationally, 'should be getting, shall we say, two Huns a week?'

Tom was startled, and probably the major saw it.

'Eight in a month. Surely you don't think that too much to expect?'

Tom said something about opportunity. His mind was far away, visualizing the process of shooting down eight Huns, seeing himself in endless battles, fighting like a mad dog. Killing, always killing or trying to kill; all his vital force subdued to that one purpose; and he felt more than ever the difference between himself and a soldier. He could not, would not do it. The current of his life had set another way.

'Opportunity,' the major was saying; 'you can rely on me to see that you have plenty of opportunity. See if you can't double your score during the next month. You'll show yourself worth a flight if you can do that.'

'Very well, major,' Tom said, as he had to say something; and the interview was over.

He crashed into the hut and woke up Williamson. 'I say Bill,' he said indignantly, 'what the hell do you think that blasted new C.O. has been saying to me?'

'God knows. What's the trouble?'

'Wants me to shoot down two Huns a week regularly. Cundall's Performing Camels, twice weekly.'

'Well, what of it? No harm in wanting. Don't take any notice, he's only hot-airing. That reminds me. Yesterday afternoon he

398

came round the flight with me and wanted to know why so many engines were dud. Talked at large about efficiency. I'd forgotten all about it until now. What's there to be excited about, anyhow?'

'I'd forgotten what hot air smelt like in a big dose.'

The new C.O. was not a great success socially. He worried his flight commanders, chivvied his pilots, and did not relax successfully in the mess. He had sufficient strength of character to make his presence felt. Tom had not been bothered by the win-the-war-quick spirit since the days of Beal. Was he in for such another time? The major would not have so much direct influence over him, but was likely to last longer than Beal.

The rain kept on till the afternoon of the next day. C flight had instructions to attack Estaires as soon as it was at all possible to fly, and their machines were waiting ready loaded with bombs. As soon as the rain stopped engines were run; six of them had been coaxed into giving their revs. The sky brightened quickly and the ceiling lifted to two thousand feet with rifts and transparencies in it, but the weather remained oppressive and storm-threatening. This was the first experience of low work for Hole and Fuller and Brindley. They got off at four o'clock. Williamson took them across the lines at two thousand, going nearly at full throttle. Archie was glad to see them after all the rain, and bombarded heavily. He guessed why they were crossing low down and tried to scare them into dropping their bombs prematurely. Williamson zigzagged up to Neuf Berquin and then south towards Lestrem, and then put his nose down eastwards to surprise anyone who might be in what was left of Estaires. There they got rid of their bombs from three or four hundred feet, and the tracers started flying. Tom dutifully fired a burst at the battered townlet and pulled up and away westwards watching the cloudy sky anxiously for air Huns. But there was nothing moving to be seen above or below except smoke from Estaires drifting away in the wind.

Five of them picked up formation and did an hour's patrol without seeing any Huns. Baker was not with them, but they found him at home badly shot up. He had evidently made a target for a nest of machine guns. No one else was damaged, and they laughed and made funny remarks about the Huns' special dislike for Baker. He must have dropped a bomb in a latrine and plastered some of them. But Hole said they'd just love that.

When they reported at the office, the major warned them for duty in an hour's time. They were to do the escort that had been washed out two days ago; to meet a couple of DH4s at 6.40 over St. Venant and help them to take photographs of the German lines. When this was over they were to continue patrolling till 8.30.

This they did in the heavy storm-pregnant evening among gigantic top-heavy clouds, brazen in the glare of the inimical sun.

The DH4s took photographs from three thousand feet and went home. Archie was bursting all over the sky. The Camels went on and found a Hun two-seater away up by Baileul trying to do a shoot under the black base of a storm cloud in the thunder-murk. They chased it off, and a stray SE joined them, but could not catch it. They were thrown about by the air's invisible turmoil. The excitement of the chase smoothed the bumps, but when they got home Tom's arm ached with pulling his bus about. Two jobs since four o'clock. He was tired and drank a good deal and went to bed. The storm broke; but it was better than bombing. It was fine in the morning, his day off.

XIII

IN the evening he went contour-chasing. He hadn't amused himself in this way for a month, and he caught some of the old joy of frightening groundlings, of jumping over protuberances, watching for telegraph wires, doing turns with a wing-tip on the ground. It was good fun to charge a house, holding down till anyone watching must be crepitant with horror of a crash that would leave a blazing wreck in a pile of bricks and bedsteads; then back would come the stick, and whoosh, you were heading into the blue sky, and there was no house, no earth, no gravitation, only space and the typhoon-roar of the pulling engine. Then gravitation returned, and shook the aeroplane angrily for its defection, and you flattened out and put your nose on the horizon, or where the horizon ought to be.

He crossed over and tried his guns on Merville square. Visibility was too bad for Archie to be accurate. The west was a bright wall with the sun shining on thunder-mist and the east a murk.

He went home and watched a lorry come in with loot from abandoned French houses. The mess was quite luxurious nowadays. It did not matter what was smashed; the furniture van replaced it forthwith.

Williamson was to take next day off, and Tom would be flight leader for two jobs at 10 a.m. and 1.45 p.m.

On the first of these he had a DH4 to escort. It was cloudy. A circus of Fokker biplanes was touring about in the east. Tom counted eighteen of them, and was very unhappy. He kept by his DH4 and waited for trouble; but no trouble came. For an hour he watched the clouds and the region of the sun anxiously, but nothing happened. The DH4 fired a Very light to say good-bye, and he saw it across the lines.

Something came diving out of the eastward sun. Fokkers. But they flattened out without attacking and flew on a parallel course a little above the Camels and to the east. Fuller came diving under the formation waggling his wings. Oh get back, damn you. What the hell were the Fokkers playing at? There were five of them, quite close, perhaps two hundred feet above; good-looking machines with top-plane extensions and lifting surface on the undercarriage, painted all colours of a decorator's paint card.

Five against five would be a hell-fire scrap. He couldn't see any more about. But the Huns did not attack. Tom climbed, but the Huns kept above. Perhaps they were waiting for pals. What ought he to do? Turn eastwards under them and try to get between them and their home? No, damn it, no heroics. Just watch them. He felt cool enough; the usual looseness in the belly. It was up to the Huns to attack; they had all the advantages.

Very suddenly the leader put his nose down and they all dived away. Tom was astonished, but tumbled after them. These Fokkers could dive. He fired a burst going vertically, then caught a sideways glimpse of a big formation coming among the clouds from the east. He pulled out into a zoom at once. The Fokkers were decoying him under a bunch of their friends. But then he saw it was a squadron of SEs. He waggled his wings at them and dived away. The SEs did not follow down, so he pulled out and waggled again. Still they held on their way home. He cursed them and dived

By now the Fokkers were nowhere to be seen. They might be miles away. He searched about, but could not find them. Well, that was all right. There was no harm done; he had protected his two-seater, the Fokkers had cleared off, and it was past time to go home. But he was puzzled by the whole business. The Huns evidently did not want to fight, yet they had nerve to dive under him like that. Was it that they knew that they could out-dive Camels but weren't so confident about fighting them? Then why hadn't they done the dive and zoom stunt? And why had they gone under those SEs? That certainly was rash. They couldn't have seen them, just as the SEs hadn't seen the Fokkers. What a lot it was possible to miss on a cloudy day. But why had they dived at all? They were quite safe where they were; or had they seen some high Dolphins? Tom gave it up, and reported a successful escort and an indecisive combat with five Fokker biplanes that dived away; and that a squadron of SEs had refused to assist.

It wasn't a good show. He ought not to have pulled out to waggle to the SEs a second time. But he didn't give a damn, anyway. It had been an exciting job with no bloodshed, and that was all right. The Huns were just loopy, half-witted, irresponsible, irrational, like so many air Huns.

Then, after lunch, he took his men for a pleasant follow-my-leader among multitudes of delightful clouds. There did not seem to be any Huns about and he did not search for them rigorously. It was summer in cloudland, golden summer, and the sun spilt the opulent colour of ripening corn on the bright hills of his kingdom. The earth was very remote and dim and unimportant; so that Tom thought that this was the mechanical likeness of great emotion; a physical symbol of love, or salvation, or martyrdom, or whatever might make men so ecstatic that the earth was remote, dim, unimportant, and the cloudy manor of skiey paradise immediate. But the mechanical had this advantage over the spiritual: that it was fun, and need not be paid for with death or disillusionment.

But after an hour the earth began to resume importance, and the joys of heaven to fade; Tom became bored with glory that was intangible; he could not remain exhilarated for two hours together. If he had been alone he would have flown against the deceptive surface of a cloud to get the mechanical counterpart of disillusionment. Obviously it was too cloudy for Huns to be flying, so he turned for home after ninety minutes. He went alone to the office to give a negative report.

'Not a sign of a Hun,' he said to the major. 'Too cloudy for them.'

'Are you sure you looked for them?'

'Quite sure, major.' He felt as people who say 'I've never been spoken to like that in my life before' must feel. Then he reacted to the major's point of view. After all, he had given very little effort to Hun-finding that afternoon. He thought of Mac; how persistently he would have hunted among those clouds, and have started, perhaps, a lurking two-seater. But what could the major know? Even if he was right, it must be pure guessing. He came back to what the major was saying.

'After your show this morning I haven't much confidence in you. I suppose you don't know that I was over the lines then?'

'No.'

'I was; and those Fokkers you let go came down on me. I was at about four thousand; you were at eight thousand, weren't you?'

'About that, major.'

'They dived four thousand feet on to me, and you let them. They must have seen that you were no good, or they wouldn't have risked it. My guns jammed, but I splitarsed about and put the wind up them, and they cleared off. But it's little thanks to you I wasn't shot down. You didn't even see me.'

Tom was embarrassed by the unexpected weight of this attack. He had to say something, and the topic that occurred to him was the SEs that would not heed him.

'I've reported them,' the major replied, 'but you shouldn't have bothered about them. Your job was to catch the Fokkers. And if you really can't tell the difference between SEs and Huns after all this time, you must be blind or extraordinarily stupid.'

Nothing worth saying occurred to Tom. Yes, he must be extraordinarily stupid.

The major perorated. 'It won't do, Cundall. You're not doing your job. You've got to pull yourself together. I shall be watching you, and if I don't see a big improvement, you may depend upon it I shall take action. Now you let me see what you can do. You seem to have got it into your head that you've done your time and can slack off. No one of us has done his time or can ease up for a moment till the war's over and won. Think this over and remember I must see results.'

Tom suffered from feelings of guilt and shame for the next half hour. He had been slacking and he had been found out. Then the shock of the attack wore off and bias in his own favour began to tell. Even from the major's point of view his only error was mistaking the SEs for Huns; which was understandable in a steep dive on a cloudy day when all the circumstances had pointed to their being Huns; moreover the Fokkers hadn't seen the SEs at all, and the SEs hadn't seen the Fokkers; there were other blind men about. And of course he hadn't seen the major; he had to be watching the Fokkers above him. And he was quite right to pull out and make sure that the SEs weren't Huns: it was his job as leader not to walk into any decoy traps. Perhaps it was wrong to have pulled out the second time, but, come to think of it, what difference had it made? Fokkers could outdive Camels, and he would never have caught them; but the SEs might have. As for the major's tale of fighting five Fokkers without guns, if there had been any fight it would still have been on when he went down after only a few seconds' delay. Probably what actually happened was that the major had seen the Fokkers diving and cleared off out of the way, and the Fokkers, having perhaps seen the SEs by then, had gone east at two hundred miles an hour. That was about it; the Huns had seen the major's solitary Camel but not the SEs, and had gone down on it, loving, as all Huns did, to catch a stray. They knew that they could outdive and outspeed the top Camels and anyhow weren't likely to be hit in a vertical dive. They would be able to get in a burst at the solitary Camel and go east along the floor at an almighty lick that a Camel couldn't touch.

After this reasonable reconstruction Tom's self-respect was repaired, and he took the offensive. He found Chadwick in the mess and said to him:

'Are the major's guns all right now?'

'I didn't know they were wrong.'

'I understand from him they jammed this morning.'

As Chadwick took an interest in keeping his cushy job, he was a little agitated to think that the C.O.'s guns had jammed and he knew nothing about it. He went out all set for a strafe. Tom accompanied him.

But none of the armourers knew about the jam, and Chadwick inspected the guns and found them in good order.

'Is this some sort of joke, Tom?'

'No. I'll explain later. Perhaps he just had a stoppage that he cleared.'

When they were alone, Tom said: 'The major's been trying to impress me by telling me how he scared off five Fokkers this morning by sheer splitarsing when his guns were jammed.'

'By Jove, did he really?'

'Fact. He said five Fokkers dived on him, and he splitarsed about and put the wind up them so much that they cleared off, although he couldn't fire a shot because his guns were jammed.'

'Good God,' said Chadwick disgustedly, 'is he like that?'

Tom shrugged his shoulders, feeling pleased with himself. His self-respect was in fine condition now. He had revenged himself; the story would soon be round the mess, probably with exaggerations. But he must be careful of the major, who might try to make life unpleasant for him. 'Take action' was the threat. Very vague. After all, what could the man do so long as he didn't obviously shirk? He could give Baker his streamer: and that would be damnable. But Williamson would never agree, and the major would make himself very unpopular if he forced it against the flight commander, and would have to think twice about upsetting morale. Could he send him back to the infantry in disgrace? Not without a court martial probably, and there were no grounds for that. If he became really unpleasant Tom would take the matter to Wing, to Brigade, to Army. He'd find out just what he could do. He'd . . . oh hell, why bother? Probably he'd never hear any more about it; the major had had a scare and had taken it out of him, that was all. And, by God, he had hit back hard. The man was a bloody fool. He wouldn't heed him.

Next day, the last of July, C flight was on wireless. Tom was standing by from 6 a.m., but did not have a job till 8.50. His partner was Brindley, a likeable man, oldish for flying, very conscientious: he took the war in professional spirit and tried to suppress all personal feelings while on duty. They did not find their two-seater, which was supposed to be in the neighbourhood of Calonne, and returned after an hour, but went up again immediately as the other two pairs were out.

This time they found a DFW east of Locon, but it made off at their approach and they only got a long range shot at it. It was too fine and clear a day for surprisings. During the afternoon there were two more calls for them, but no Huns, and another at 6.25 in the evening, when again there was no Hun where one ought to have been, by Vieux Berquin, but Tom saw a burst of white Archie up towards Bailleul, and went to investigate, and saw a two-seater going east and took a dive at it. The Hun put his nose down and went home at a hell of a lick.

Altogether there were fourteen calls that day and Tom went up five times: a record. Jerry was busy, according to wireless indications, but elusive. Only four two-seaters had been seen and they had all got away. There had been some scouts about, and A flight had made contact with six Fokker biplanes and Forster and Maitland had shot one down between them. But it wasn't possible to massacre Fokkers like Pfalz or Albatri. They were very fast, splitarse, and marvellous climbers. In the hands of confident pilots they would be dangerous, but the Huns were too scared to take advantage of what Fokker had done for them and generally avoided formations of Camels, SEs, Dolphins, and Bristols. Nevertheless, the general adoption of Fokkers in place of other scouts was bound to make the war more dangerous.

In the evening, tired and aching after six and a half hours' flying, Tom was alarmed to hear that the major had arranged to lead a two-squadron show of thirty Camels at ten o'clock in the morning with the idea of countering the menace of Fokker circuses. It would be Williamson's day off, so Tom attended the major at the office, with Large and Forster, for instructions.

The major's idea was to lead C flight himself in Williamson's place, with Tom next to him as deputy flight leader. They'd be able to share a few Huns, he said. And if there were any Huns about they were going to get them. They'd got to knock the stuffing out of the Fokkers at once. A flight would be above and behind on the right and B above and behind A. They would meet over Merville two flights he had borrowed from another squadron, and these would fly on the left, and they would all go away east *en echelon*.

How these win-the-war-quick merchants liked to have him near them, Tom thought. Beal had been the same. They sniffed his Laodicean smell at once and were indignant and wanted him where they could see him. Well, his tail would be well looked after and if he must do a patrol twenty miles over, that was the safest way. But sooner or later Major Yorke's attentions were bound to make things difficult.

'The major's properly after my blood,' he said to Williamson. 'Like Beal used to be. He's something the same type, without Beal's genuine heroic quality, in fact without everything that made me admire Beal more than I hated him — if I did hate him.'

'I imagine you didn't. He was the central figure in your particular nightmare, that's all.'

'Anyway, he damn near succeeded in getting me killed, and now this fellow's on the same tack. What a life. But what Beal couldn't quite do, I hope Yorke can't either. Beal was worth a dozen of him. I've followed Mac often enough, and I know what a real Hun-getter is like; but, believe me, Mac's not half the man that Beal was, and Yorke isn't a tenth of either.'

'Prejudice,' said Williamson. 'Wait and see. We don't know the major yet. But don't bother your head about him. He'll calm down.'

'That's what I used to hope about Beal. I haven't much hope that a megalomaniac who must lead enormous formations will calm down.'

XIV

THE thirty Camels climbed to fifteen thousand feet going east over Estaires, Fleurbaix, Bois-Grenier, beyond the dark blotch of Armentières, and patrolled over Quesnoy and Harbourdin, with Lille huge and near in the east; no place for Camels. There were some Fokkers about, but they did not care to go near so large a fleet, and remained distant watchers, while Archie tried to split up the formation.

This sort of thing went on for a long time. It was no use trying to catch wary Fokkers. They were fast and could outclimb Camels two to one. Half a dozen of them came and sat in the sun overhead and looked as if they might be going to attack some part of the unwieldly armada. The major turned sharply to the right. A flight could not turn inside, and so got in front. The major was looking at the Huns. His left wing hit Smith's tailplane, and tore his rudder adrift. Smith did a sort of flat spin to the right, and then his nose dropped and down he went.

Tom saw him spinning down to death, beyond help. Quite a youngster; just come from school and England. He had hardly exchanged two words with him; this was only his second time over. The major seemed to have got away with it, and was heading west. Tom followed. A long way to go if he was badly damaged. Why the devil should be get away with it? The collision was mainly his fault, not poor young Smith's. But oh, by Christ, he hadn't got away with it. His wing disintegrated into a flop of wreckage. Tom saw his arm go up in a futile protective gesture as some of it crashed against the fuselage and he fell into a jerking dive and grew smaller and smaller into the earthward mirk.

Tom found himself leading the great formation westwards; it had reformed with him at the apex in the dead man's place. He looked for Fokkers. At the moment there was none near. He was profoundly convinced of the futility of large formations for aggressive fighting, and did not know what to do with the force suddenly placed, if not in his command, at least under his leadership. He hardly liked to retreat westwards, so turned gently north over Houplines towards Ploegsteert Wood and Messines Ridge.

Archie had been troublesome owing to the stiffness of the formation, but the thickening weather below was hindering him. It would soon be too bad for them to stop out, and probably it would rain. They were near Ploegsteert; he'd better sweep round over Neuve Eglise and go south-west towards Nieppe Forest so as to be getting near home.

He did this, and as it happened, caught a couple of Hun two-seaters east of Bailleul. They had no chance at all with twenty-eight Camels between them and home, and went down. The action broke up the formation, and people collected round their flight leaders and returned home as separate units. Tom had not fired at the two-seaters. He had seen one of them crash, but thought the other might have contour-chased home. He had not been very near the ground to investigate.

It came on to rain, but cleared up again in the afternoon. No further jobs arrived, and Wing did not bother them, but set about finding a new C.O. for them. Tom was the authority on the collision, having been nearest. No one was very distressed at Major Yorke's demise. What the devil had he wanted to go over at the head of a huge formation for, instead of letting his flight commanders get on with their jobs? Swelled head was his trouble. Damned hard lines on poor young Smith.

'You see what happens to your enemies,' said Williamson to Tom that night, amid the air raid. The Huns were over in great force, and the crashing was continuous of bombs near and distant. All lights had been extinguished. It seemed a very serious effort on the part of the Huns.

'Don't be a b.f.,' Tom replied. 'It's what happens to damn near everyone.' They were so used to uproar at night that they gave it little attention, but talked above the din of bombs, the crumping of shells, the blast of heavies, the barking of Archie, the buzz of engines of various throats, Gothas, FEs, night-flying Camels that never seemed able to find Enemy Aircraft; and sometimes a machine gun rattle. The flashes, bright or dim, red or yellow or white, oval, rapierlike, and bulbous, were not related to the noise, for a huge flash might occur at the same time as a tiny bark, and then a growl like thunder overhead accompany a remote field-gun flicker; usually it was a confusion and compound of lights and noises, unsortable and unarranged and chaotic. But the turmoil was dominated by a huge leap of fire in the southern sky that might be of interplanetary scope; as though the earth were warning across the abyss. This was a dump going up; masterpiece of war's fireworks; most showy plume in man's soaring wings of futility.

Cloud came over the Western Front and rain fell and washed away most of the uproar; watchers over no-man's-land swore at it. The burning dump glowed on the low sky. Bodies were pulled out of bomb-shattered huts and buildings, and the wounded removed to hospital and treated with iodine, potassium permanganate, and morphia. Columns of transport serpented along dark roads, carrying food and munitions and troops. Strings of silent men moved up communication trenches to take over. Combatants far back in base towns slept between sheets. Men died: the object of it all was that men should die.

The rain went on for thirty hours. A new C.O. arrived surprisingly soon. He was Major Ling, an Australian, with a row of decorations, including a plain white ribbon which had something to do with antarctic adventures. It was guest night, and the new C.O. had a set of yarns and a laugh for other people's that made everyone happy. He was obviously a great fellow. There was a sing-song after dinner and some acrobatics by Forster and his imitators, and a mild rag. Everyone went to bed sober, agreeing that Ling was a damned fine fellow.

The rain left off in the morning of the third of August, but C flight had no job till six o'clock in the evening. Then they went out on patrol, and at seven o'clock were at twelve thousand feet over Lens. Williamson waggled his wings. There was a Hun formation flying west below them towards Fouquières. They dived down, down, down to meet the Huns. They were six Fokkers, at about four thousand feet. Presumably they were looking for two-seaters doing shoots and had not seen the Camels above in the sun.

Tom dived and fired and zoomed, not getting his Hun. He dived and fired again, and, pulling out, saw a red Fokker coming towards him, climbing. Tom was moving at wire-screaming speed and was able to zoom above the Fokker before they got to effective range. He went down again at once, getting the Hun in his sights at too high an angle for him to reply. Rattle of guns and flash of tracers and the Fokker in a vertical turn, red, with extensions to the top planes. Tom hated those extensions. He was doing a very splitarse turn for a Hun, but tracers seemed to be finding him. Got him, oh got him: over, flopping over, nose dropping, spinning. Tom followed down. Another Fokker on someone's tail underneath. The bastard. Rudder him into the Aldis. Again the flicking of tracers, rattle of a long burst. The Hun dived, Tom after him, going vertically at the hell of a lick. Almost on the ground. He eased out and the Fokker went on down to hell. Tom zoomed up, opening full out, gaining all the height he could in case there were any more.

There was no one at all in sight. He went away westwards in a cloud of Archie, but he was too low for good shooting. Must have been a good show for the fellows in the trenches; seldom had a dogfight so low. Two he'd got. Not so bad. Hardly felt nervous except a bit at first when that red fellow had come towards him. Not a shot fired at him though, as far as he knew. Remarkable thing that. But where was everyone?

He circled about and then went back to where the fighting had been, feeling good and not giving a damn if they shot at him from the ground, and made a reconnaissance and saw the wreckage of three Fokkers there in the evening sun. He climbed away. Archie went for him and he threw a few stunts just to tell him what he thought of him. He was feeling the hell of a fellow.

A Camel appeared from nowhere. Hole. Then they met Williamson and Baker, but not Dubois. He was at home when they got there, shot up, very melancholy about it all. Poor Dubois was too unhappy even to play his violin nowadays. He had just been on leave in Paris and hadn't enjoyed it at all. He was almost ill with nostalgia. Williamson claimed a Hun and so did Baker. Tom reported that he had made a reconnaissance and seen three new crashes that appeared to be the debris of their fight. They rang up Archie who was able to confirm three, but did not think any more had gone. Anyway, it was a good show. Tom received the C.O.'s congratulations.

'Very fine effort, Cundall. Stout fellow,' he said.

Tom felt elevated. He was the man of the moment, quite rehabilitated. Yet he was the same man whom Yorke had seen through. What was the truth about himself? A lucky coward, probably. Luck was a great maker of five-minute heroes.

'We seem to have got these Fokker biplanes beat as well,' he said to Williamson.

'I don't know. We certainly caught that lot on the hop. They seemed duds; there was only one pilot among them: the bloke that shot up Dubois and that you knocked off his tail. The rest didn't know their backsides from their elbows. At least, that's how it seemed to me.'

'Their leader must have been blind.'

'Yes . . . but I thought you'd given up murdering the gentle Hun?'

'I said so, but what does it matter what you say? You get in a dog-fight and things happen: pious resolutions, or impious, matter sweet Fanny Adams. What about a quick 'un before dinner?'

Tom got comfortably tight that evening, there being no job for C flight till five o'clock next afternoon. He was a stout fellow; no need to bother about himself any more; he could take himself for granted and not worry his head; his was not to reason why; he had no personal responsibility amid the vast irresponsibility of war; it was kill or be killed; he must protect himself, his way of life, against alien assault; that was the way of things. And anyhow, what was the use of reasoning? It was just shadow-play; it meant nothing vital. A man acted according to the influence of circumstances on his true nature; reasoning was just an effort to disguise the true nature of action, to bring it into line with prejudices and moral oughts. Far better to have none, get rid of them, and act as one must, a sentient automaton.

It was a balance of fears that kept him going, fear of his friends balancing fear of the enemy, and reasoning was only the accompanying shadow-play. And practically everyone was a coward: very few seemed to lack fear, and they were dolts without imagination or decent feelings; heroes. Cowards were the salt of the earth if they could fight their cowardice and poise themselves on — what the hell! More whisky. But the fight against cowardice was the only thing worth while — and drinking whisky. But he drank whisky because nothing was worth while. Life and death were just blasted nonsense, and all the blokes that had talked big about it, bloody fools. Their mouths were stopped with dust. They hadn't known what a real Christian-nationalist-industrial war was like.

Well, it was fine, really it was fine to get shot of all the artificial flowers and musty old ground sheets and get down to the mud. No nonsense about mud. Life was fighting, fornication, feeding; driven by lust, regulated by fear. All the rest had been shot away like Ypres and Delville Wood, and they were down in the mud, the safest place. Here's to the good old mud — no, whisky: drink it down.

It was all right while he kept to whisky; he could go on drinking as long as he knew where his mouth was, and he always came to in bed or on the bed afterwards, with drinking water within reach and aspirin. His sober time in hospital had cleared him of alcoholism and left him a clear liver that should last his time in France.

It was necessary for him to be tight to endure the eternal shop that everyone talked. Drunk he could discuss enthusiastically Fokkers and Snipes and Bentley Camels. Sober, he was sick of them.

A Fokker, a Snipe, and Bentley Camel
Met for a scrap at Beaumont Hamel.

Hadn't been near Beaumont Hamel, or any of those ghastly Somme places for a long time. War had been a picnic lately. What names they were: Fricourt, Mametz, Contalmaison, Martinpuich, High Wood, Delville Wood, Thiepval, Longueval, and the rest: all other words were trivial to these. Well, Jerry had all those places now and the soil was well manured if he wanted to grow cabbages. And Villers-Bretonneux: the memory of that last stand in front of Amiens gave him the creeps.

Why the hell was he worrying himself about all that? Far away and long ago. He'd finished with that part of the world. Dogs were getting scarce in Germany; they were eating wallpaper and rats and nettles. War would be over in a few months. Then he was going away out of it. Going away; to Spain. Where he was when it started. Wished to Christ he'd stopped there. Couldn't have stopped there four years. Yes, by God, four years ago to-morrow it started. Ought to have a binge in celebration. Worth getting tight about.

But every day a bloke lived through was worth getting tight about, seeing how much was being spent on killing him. He did his best, but it took longer to get tight than it used to. And he could often stop the mess when it was starting to spin by looking fixedly at the piano. It was a good idea to go to bed then.

He woke up in the morning full of headache and reaction. It was a rotten life this; he was becoming a damned dipsomaniac. Soon be seeing things. Ruin his liver and stomach. Hell, what did it matter? There was precious little to live for. He'd never be able to come to terms with the world. But that there was little to live for meant that there was still less to die for; and now that his reputation was at height he could play the skin-saving game as much as he liked; the new C.O. wouldn't see it for some time. A good thing Yorke had gone west; he was a nuisance. No, damn it, he mustn't think that, especially as young Smith had gone with him. But why not? It was the truth. Who was it said that any sort of truth is better than make-believe? There was no escaping the fact that he was glad, profoundly glad, that Yorke had gone. He was a swine to be glad, but there it was. It was the old Beal business over again; though without the racking element of hero worship.

Then he remembered that Williamson had said on that occasion: that it wasn't Beal's death, but his removal that he had been glad of. And that was true. Thank God for Bill and the straw of comfort he had thrown him; for drowning self-respect could keep afloat miraculously with a straw.

And for aspirin.

C flight went up after tea and chased a couple of two-seaters and a solitary Fokker biplane. It was windy and cloudy, and rain came on during the night, and it was too dud for jobs next day. The war had gone to sleep again. Tom went up among the low clouds for a joy ride in the evening, and he was right down by Arras when it came on to rain. He had to go all the way home through rain-mist just over house tops, and he opened full out to a hundred and ten miles an hour, keeping his head well in the office. A mountain suddenly loomed up in front of him. The Camel shot up the side of it and staggered over the top. Christ, a slag heap. He felt shaky after the menacing instant. If he hadn't been going all out he'd never have zoomed it. The things he got away with.

He found the aerodrome and made a good landing, very glad to be home out of the rain and safe. It was quite a long time (pulling off gloves to touch a strut) since he had crashed anything. He really was quite a pilot nowadays.

414

Then he had a day off, and it was dud; not too dud for any jobs, but for any Huns. It was irritating to have a dud day off: one didn't miss anything. A tender went to Boulogne, but he was fed up with Boulogne, and stopped at home and talked to Williamson. They went for a walk in the evening among barley fields. The Huns were gradually retiring from the salient on their front. Perhaps this was the beginning of the end.

Tom kept sober as he was to be in charge of the flight at five o'clock in the morning: standing by for wireless. There was a lot of noise during the night, and when he was called at 4 a.m. it was difficult to wake up. Then he hung about all day, waiting, waiting, waiting; tired and bad tempered; and when at last a call came through at seven in the evening he was quite glad of the opportunity to shoot at something, but he could not find the Hun. He stood by, growling with irritation, till half-past nine.

Then the bombing started, and there was a dawn patrol which meant being called at 3.30. He didn't get to sleep till it was within an hour or two of getting up time; but a mist came up and procured him a little sleep. Nevertheless they had to get up at five o'clock and stand by for low bombing in case of a clearance. Possibly something was happening in the mist; but the guns were not unusually noisy.

It was irritating and absurd to have to stand by on such a morning. Everyone was bad tempered. After an hour the stand-by was washed out, and they all went back to bed. Tom slept like a mummy till nine o'clock.

In the afternoon two strange girls came from Estrée-Blanche selling vile French chocolate, but it was better than nothing, and the girls themselves were fleshly fire. One of them had black moon-light eyes that made Tom gelid with lust. He and Williamson were in imperfect but pleasant conversation with them outside the hut. They wanted to see what the hut was like inside, so they walked in. Williamson and Tom glanced at each other and followed; but James had seen this law-breaking from the squadron office opposite and hurried from it calling out:

'Hi, Williamson and Cundall! You must get them out.'

Tom went in and grabbed his girl for a second before James

reached the door and said in his most formal manner: 'Mademoiselles, il ne faut pas absolument entrer dans les maisonettes des officiers.'

The girls obediently went out.

'Sorry,' he added for Tom and Williamson, 'but it's absolutely forbidden,' and went.

'Que voulez-vous? C'est la guerre à l'anglais,' said Tom, and tried to make arrangements for a rendezvous in some secluded place. This was not easy, as they were good girls and had to be careful. They talked incomprehensible patois together; they thought something might be arranged; they would visit them to-morrow or the next day in the ordinary way of business.

Tom and Williamson bought up all their chocolate at great expense to encourage them and to make it unnecessary for them to talk to anyone else. 'A demain,' they said, 'à la même heure.'

'My God, what eyes,' Tom exclaimed. 'I feel as though my arteries were full of hot whisky. Something's got to happen.'

'You've certainly got a scorcher. Mine isn't so flashy, but she has points.' They talked anatomy.

There was a job for C flight after tea, and an epidemic of dud engines. Only four machines got off, and Williamson and Baker went back soon, leaving Tom to do a patrol with Dubois. The air was populous with all sorts of British aeroplanes. Occasionally two clusters of dots were visible in the eastern sky twenty miles over. On the ground a good deal of shelling was going on and Jerry was retreating.

People were cheery in the mess that evening. The news was good: Jerry falling back all along the line. In front of Amiens a really deep advance had been made; a division smashed and its general captured. At last they were winning the war on the ground, having won it already in the air, in spite of all the new machines the Huns brought out; they were too demoralized and whacked to do any good with them, or rather, any harm.

Wing was late with the next day's jobs. At ten o'clock instructions came through: pack, proceed to Vignacourt near Amiens in the morning, to another Wing and Army. Fifty miles south for the big push. The Somme again.

THE aerodrome at Vignacourt was an uncomfortable and dusty place. The accommodation was tents; they did not look rainproof and were full of earwigs, flies, mosquitoes, wasps, and all kinds of beetles and bugs. Among the tents young fruit trees were attempting to establish themselvs. It was hot. Amiens lay some twelve miles to the south-east, a dead city.

After a scrappy breakfast and the fatigue of packing, the squadron had done a farewell patrol in layers on their usual front and then worked southwards past Arras and Bapaume and Albert, and then back to Vignacourt, which was about twenty miles behind Albert. There were a few Huns about far over and a lot of shrapnel bursting on the floor.

They had to go begging round the neighbourhood for lunch. There were Bristols and Big Aks on the same aerodrome. Tom got in a tender and visited a Camel squadron at Havernas, and heard all about the war. Bombing, ground-strafing, low reconnaissance; plenty of casualties. No. 1 Pursuit Flight, Richthofen's old circus, was on this front. They were pretty good with their new Fokkers that would climb like lifts, dive like bricks, zoom to the moon, and were as splitarse as Camels on a left hand turn.

Tom didn't mind Richthofen's gang so much; it would be interesting to see what a real Hun pilot was like. But he hated to hear about all the ground-strafing. Camels were being shot down in dozens. The only bright spot was that a lot of them got down on their own side, the pilots wounded. Well, the low work had to be done. He had a rudder.

The big advance was still going on. In places it had reached a depth of about twelve miles; it was the best British show of the war so far. Maps were issued in the afternoon, and the latest position of the front line red-pencilled. Work started. Tom took Brindley to explore the region between Albert and the Somme. Brindley would be conscientious and go peering into every trench to find out who was there; he would do a good professional job and not bother about bullets any more than a doctor was supposed to bother about infection. Tom would look out for danger; he had no desire to be set on by a gang of Fokkers while he was nosing through a battle looking for the line; he had had enough of that.

They flew at two thousand feet towards the Ancre, with the vast grey smudge of Amiens to the south. Amiens had been saved by the spilling of fifty thousand gallons of British blood. The cathedral was still standing; Tom could just see it; and no doubt the big lunatic asylum on the other side of the city was still intact. Perhaps the French would give him free quarters there one day for his share in the defence.

Over the Albert-Amiens road and the Ancre to the familiar country between Albert and Morlancourt. He drifted downwards unhappily to where tanks were creeping about in advance of the infantry. Some of them were dead and smoking. The German front line must be hereabouts. He saw some Huns on the move towards Bray and dropped his bombs, glad to get rid of them.

He nosed around and made out that the Huns were fighting a rearguard action about half way between Morlancourt and Bray. He had unhappy memories of Morlancourt. Bullets seemed to be flying. He used his rudder and worked up to a thousand feet out of the battle din. In the cemetery outside the reddish square of Bray he saw guns firing and dipped and let off a burst at the flashes. His engine was missing on one cylinder. Brindley went past him in a dive, firing. Then he pulled up sharply in a zoom and turned west. Tom followed. He crossed the lines and seemed to be going home. Tom kept with him: having a dud engine he might as well go home too, though they had only been out forty minutes. But why hadn't Brindley given the dud engine signal?

They crossed the Ancre. Tom was at a thousand feet, watching Brindley a little below him. Brindley's prop became visible as a circular blur, and he put his nose down to glide. Either his engine had cut out or he wanted to land because he was wounded. Tom watched him anxiously; saw his nose come up; he hung in the air stalling, and flopped into a spin. He must have fainted. It was horrible to see him going down; to be able to do nothing.

Then, thank God, he seemed to regain control. The spin stopped, but he came out in a vertical dive and crashed without attempting to pull out. No doubt he was killed.

Tom pinpointed the crash and went home to report.

Dinner was a wretched meal of bully beef and dog biscuits, and some of the fellows scrounged invitations to other messes. Tom didn't feel sociable, and he and Williamson had a lot of chocolate to eat up. They would never see those girls again. Tom's lamp glass was smashed and Williamson's lamp had vanished, so the tent they shared had to be lighted with candles. The hut appeared palatial in retrospect. They carpeted the tent floor, but there was no room for furniture. A bar had been established in the big tent which was the ante-room, and one could get gloomily tight, or rather half tight, for there was a squadron patrol at seven in the morning.

Then the night-flying started. First the FEs went out and then the Huns arrived, some of them making a tremendous row. These must be their new long distance bombers, with five engines and a small army on board. They were on their way to bomb base towns. Tom wished them luck.

'God, man, they aren't all scoundrels at the base,' Williamson remonstrated.

The noise went on half the night. They got up in the morning tired and went out to patrol the front between Albert and Roye. The squadron was in layers; C flight on top at sixteen thousand feet. There were other Camels about, patrolling and ground-strafing, and SEs and Dolphins high up. In the east there were many Hun scouts in layers; forty or fifty of them. They were difficult to see with the strong morning sun behind them, and when you thought you had located the whole lot there would be a wing flash in blue emptiness.

A good deal of manœuvring and threatening went on, but not much fighting. It was difficult for Camels to attack with their inferiority of speed and climb. Williamson got in position to dive on a formation of six, but they were very splitarse and climbed so fast that soon the advantage of height was likely to be lost. Moreover there were others about on top that ought to attack. The only thing to do was dive, zoom, and away; and keep together.

The Huns played the same sort of game, trying to pick off rear men by diving out of the sun. The formation leaders seemed to do most of the shooting, and their followers to be chiefly for moral effect.

Nothing notable happened as the result of several brushes; on both sides defence was better than attack. The Huns used their speed to avoid dogfighting and to secure the attacking position, but when they had it they did little but loom threateningly. Then some SEs or Dolphins would come up and the Huns would go away. It was the uncomfortable paralysis of large units. The sky had a way of becoming suddenly full of dots and flashes, and it was very difficult for a careful flight leader to know what to do about it. It was no use making a target of his followers on chance that the Huns would come down and dogfight on level terms.

Williamson was worried about it all. This was a new variety of war, and he didn't know the tactics; if there were any tactics for fighting against machines that climbed past you like a swift past a house-martin.

'They can't always go about in the huge gangs,' Tom argued, 'or most of the day they'd have no patrols out at all. As for tactics, you seem to have the right idea. Don't go underneath them. Unless you offer yourself to them they don't seem to do much. They're too many; no initiative. God, it's hot.'

'That's all very well, but I can't always be just keeping out of danger.'

'Why not? There's no sense in danger for danger's sake. We're through with that sort of thing. And anyway, if they want us to chase Fokkers, they must give us Snipes to do it with. We've been hearing about them for the past year, and still they don't come. Why does it take a year to turn out a few hundred aeroplanes. Is it just bloody incompetence?'

'Strikes, I expect. For higher pay or to end the war.'

In the afternoon C flight carried bombs and went to look for suitable ground targets while the other flights patrolled above. They worked south of the Somme, searching along towards the north-south bend of the river beyond Peronne, bombarded incessantly by Archie. They found prey near Barleux; dark specks on the yellow road, a transport column. They went down on it. Bombs rained down. Lorries were smashed, blocking the road. The front lorry dashed off alone, but crashed in a hole. Huns were running for shelter. They fired at them and some rolled over. Tom saw a fellow

420

scramble out of a lorry he was firing at and run for his life. But they were not having it all their own way. Tracers from ground machine guns were flying about. Hunland was full of machine guns.

The instructions were to split up after bombing and do individual reconnaissances. Tom saw some specks high up that looked like Huns, and he went across the lines until they had gone. Then he had a look round, finding British tanks and troops as far east as Chuignes and Herleville. He saw two clusters of dots in the sky make contact, and one of them detach itself and go spinning down, wings glinting in the sun at each turn.

He climbed away out of range of the ground, wandered up and down for a while, watching the sky more carefully than the ground, and went home to count bullet holes.

They all got back. Dubois had been chased by Huns and had over-revved his engine till something melted, and he staggered on to the aerodrome making a remarkable clatter. He wasn't feeling any too good after it. Everyone had bullet holes. Tom had five. Baker's petrol tank had been missed by half an inch. Hole was pleased with himself for having killed at least three Huns. Williamson shepherded them into the office and they constructed quite a well-sounding report. The position of the front line had to be telephoned at once to Wing.

They heard that evening that there probably would not be any more low work for the present as the advance had gone far enough on their front. Tom and Williamson walked over to the village of Vignacourt after dinner, but it was too dark to see much of it when they got there. It seemed singularly uninteresting. The days were over for flying by half-past eight; the worst of the year was past. But night-flying was getting more and more intense, and the racket began before ten o'clock. The big Hun bombers going over made a terrific din, but kept their bombs for remoter regions.

There was a clatter of distant machine guns, and a sudden red moon appeared in the northern sky. It dropped earthwards, a streamer of flame shooting from it as it disappeared; and there was a glow like moonrise for five minutes where it had gone down. A night-flying Camel had found a target.

Tom slept late in the morning as there was no job for C flight till midday. It was Sunday; distinguished from ordinary days by an open-air service which very few officers attended. Tom heard that Brindley's body had been examined and, as he had expected, there was a bullet in it. The Hun shot down in the night had five engines and a crew of eight if all had been found; some of them were burnt, some had preferred to jump. It had a load of bombs that did not explode.

They crossed the lines at 12.30 and almost at once found Huns in abundance. Williamson went down on a bunch and got one in a spin. Tom fired at several, diving and zooming, but they were very splitarse and he did no damage. They went away east and more came up overhead, and the Camels were in a difficult position. Tom was a little apart from the others and he watched the zenith anxiously. 'One, two, three, four, five, six, seven, eight . . .' he was Hun-counting and was interrupted by a loud pop-pop-pop-pop-pop behind him. Earth and sky whirled round, round, round, and the machine-gun noise went. He came out in a dive westwards with full engine. A wonder he hadn't pulled the wings off. His hand eased the throttle as he looked up back at the Hun-filled sky. Westward the march of empire . . . there was a noise of several machine guns and flashing of tracers: he was for it this time. He trod on the rudder. Westwards the — he pulled himself back into his seat, having been thrown out by the violent sideslip. There was a persistent and too definite pop-pop-pop: a Hun on his tail. Bloody hell. Only one. The others had pulled out and gone aloft like Tom Bowling, so it wasn't so bad. He zoomed, sideslipping, and the Hun pulled up away above him and came down on him firing. Tom splitarsed round and the Hun followed after his tail. They went chasing round and round. Round and round the mulberry bush. The Hun could fly. This must be one of Richthofen's young men. Round and round. A rhythm went round in Tom's head: *quorum quorum quorum quibus quibus quibus, quorum quorum quorum quibus quibus quibus* . . . To the right. Camel might turn inside Fokker to the right. Nose down losing height. He couldn't get a shot at the Hun, who occasionally pulled up and climbed above and then dived at him; but he edged away westwards whenever the Hun went up. He had met his match this time; an ugly yellow Fokker biplane with red stripes; and some more might come down on him any moment. His mouth was chalk-dry; if ever he got home he would get some chewing gum. Hame, hame, hame — hame fain wad I be. The Hun hadn't fired for some time. He was wobbling about. God, he must be trying to clear a stoppage. They were at five thousand feet over Chaulnes. Tom throttled back and pulled his nose up and the busy Hun went past overhead. Tom dived away, and saw no more of him.

His luck was holding. He went for a joy ride to recover from the excitement and landed at the correct time. Williamson landed soon afterwards, and they were glad to see each other safe. B flight was out and returned an hour later. Jones was bashful with achievement. He had got himself mixed up with a large formation of Fokkers and ought to have been shot down easily, but instead, scared to death, he had fired at a Hun that got in his way, dived westwards and somehow got across the lines safely. He was not at all clear about anything except that the Hun he fired at went down in flames, and this was confirmed by others. His horse-face was red with remembered fright turned to laughter.

C flight's evening patrol was uneventful. They met no Huns at all. It was interesting to fly home in close formation at tree-top height and see all the movement on the ground; the big guns being hauled up, the big tanks and little tanks in companies and nests, the horses, the lorries and ambulances, the khaki going forwards and the grey prisoners flowing back; everything prosperous and orderly; how different, Tom thought, from the chaos and despair of March and April. This was victory. And there were plenty of targets for the Huns if they felt like a little ground-strafing.

Almost the entire population of Vignacourt was assembled on the aerodrome, and had to be dived on and scared. They were, however, used to this sort of thing, for it was the local custom to flock to the aerodrome on fine Sunday evenings to watch the wonderful *aviateurs*. Tom exchanged civilities with some of them when he had climbed out of his aeroplane and found himself regarded as a sort of superman by the innocent villagers.

The mess was out of drink except for French vermouth and Grand Marnier. Wing telephoned the surprising information that thirty-four Huns had been shot down by it that day. James was posted

423

away and would be leaving for England in the morning. His successor, named Hollis, who was rather a living scar than a man, but had been sewn and bolted together so successfully that only a half finger and a fragment of his right ear were missing, arrived during the evening. The major remarked to Tom that he was due for leave in about three weeks if he hadn't gone home before then. Or west, Tom added.

They were kept awake as usual by night-flyers and Archie, and there was to be a dawn show. It was a tiring life.

'What are we going to do about these Fokkers, Bill? It's no use trying to dogfight them when they're real pilots. The Fokker biplane's too good. I've tried it.'

'Dive and zoom seems indicated.'

'But we have to catch an isolated bunch, or else they just go east and their pals on top come down on us. What about big formations in layers?'

'Theoretically, I don't see what on earth we can do except get shot down. But actually we haven't done so badly; two for no casualties to-day. I know we ought to have had a lot of casualties, but we haven't. Circus or no circus, most of these Huns seem to have a great deal too much respect for us and their own skins to do much damage. And they're quite mad. After you'd gone for a run with your red and yellow pal there were four of us with about eighteen Huns sitting nicely over us. What did they do? Nine of them cleared off, and of the rest five dived at us out of the sun, and when we splitarsed round they just climbed away again without firing a shot and sat there looking at us. What are you to make of it? It's my belief that only one Hun in two dozen is any good nowadays. With this improved Fokker biplane they ought to be cleaning us up: Camels especially; and yet there's thirty-four Huns down to-day, and I bet there weren't more than half a dozen casualties on our side. These enormous formations are in themselves signs of wind-up.'

'And I bet a lot of that thirty-four was faith-kills,' Tom replied. 'Anyhow, if they want me to scrap with Fokkers they must give me Snipe to do it with. I'm not playing Jack the Giant Killer at this time of day. Don't forget we've still got three weeks to get through.'

XVI

A HUN dropped a solitary bomb on the aerodrome during the night and woke everybody up. The only damage was a hole in the tent occupied by Hudson and Maitland. Mist came up and prevented the dawn patrol. Maitland said it was fine to have extra ventilation on a hot night. Prisoners arrived to dig them in; they were to make circular pits three feet deep for each tent so that the occupants would sleep below ground level and be protected from flying bomb splinters.

The owner of the land somehow got wind of these operations, and she arrived full of fury to defend her young fruit trees which she feared would be damaged by the digging. She was a terrific virago and threw herself upon the Huns and routed them, and had no respect for the guard and his bayonet. A delighted crowd assembled; work was at a standstill; the major himself attempted to reason with her, but was overwhelmed by a spate of patois and threat of assault. A tender was sent to Vignacourt to the *mairie* and soon returned with the village gendarme, very small and wizened. This hero walked nonchalantly up to the fury, not attending to the speech that flowed from her so rapidly as to form a single web of sound. He was only a third of her size and seemed, like a male spider, in danger of being devoured. He warned her off. They talked at each other vigorously for a time, waving their hands about, either voice in crescendo trying to talk the other down, until the gendarme lost his temper and drew his sword and drove her off at the point of it.

When the major had finished laughing he told Tom to take up a practice patrol of new fellows, give them some formating, and show them the lines. This was a pleasant hour's occupation, wandering about on the safe side of the lines in the cool heights, throwing occasionally a half-roll for the confusion of his followers, returning when he was becoming bored.

In the afternoon there was more serious work: individual reconnaissance. People went out alone, each with a load of bombs, to make personal war on the Huns and observe their movements. Tom took off at 2.30 and flew over the Somme. He followed the St. Quentin road, and as the sky was clear, crossed the lines and dropped his bombs on Estrées, as that looked the sort of place that ought to be bombed. Then he spiralled up to four thousand feet. Archie put up a few bursts. Something seemed to be moving on the road to Peronne, by the north-south bend of the river. He ought to see what it was. He opened the throttle full and went north-east at a hundred and five miles an hour. After a minute Archie put up two bursts not very near him. Immediately he did a half-roll, for these were certainly pointing out bursts. He eased out of the dive and pulled back the throttle to thirteen hundred revs and then looked back to see what was happening.

Three Fokkers were coming down the sky after him, getting larger and larger. They could catch him easily. There were others above, difficult to see against the bright sky, but they seemed to be staying up. Again that dry mouth and thudding heart. He was certainly cold meat this time.

His pitot showed a hundred and fifty. Two minutes to safety, for they wouldn't chase him far over. The firing started. Tracers flashed like streaks of light. He kicked the rudder. The first bursts had missed him. Fear stunned him. He sat outside his body watching its efforts of self-preservation. It was calm, and had the nerve to keep engine revs down to thirteen hundred to avoid the fatal risk of a seize up.

Feet kicked the rudder bar this way and that, and hands pulled the joystick from side to side. The aeroplane was swaying and side-slipping wildly about the sky, but always moving towards home. Tracers streaked past, the enormous speed of bullets made visible. A formula came into his mind: $KE = \frac{1}{2}mv^2$.

One of the Huns had got into position on his tail, not more than twenty yards away. He could see the pilot's head behind the sights and the spurts of flame from the two guns. It was marvellous that he was not hit yet: fourteen bullets a second at twenty yards range.

Body was flying chiefly by ear. As the pop-pop-pop-pop of guns grew louder it kicked the rudder and bore harder on the stick. The machine was standing the strain, but the Hun's bullets only had to cut a few wires and it would collapse. This was not flying, it was lurching through the sky; but the Hun's sights did not allow for movement sideways.

The machine-gun noise got dangerously loud. Left stick and right rudder. Falling sideways downwards. He was thrown hard against the side and safety-belt. The noise was fainter. A thousand feet, almost over the lines. What would it feel like to be hit? Total eclipse, or else increasing faintness and incapacity to fly. Or flames: O God, not flames.

Mustn't get wind up. Kick the rudder. Why the hell wasn't there a patrol to rescue him? He was over the lines. Make for the earth; earth seemed to offer shelter. He saw khaki. A soldier raised his rifle to fire at the Huns. The machine guns had ceased firing. He looked round. One of the Huns was still there. Must have used up all his ammunition. As he looked, the Hun turned away east. Why the devil wasn't there anyone about to strafe him?

Well, that was over. He took an inventory, and there was no visible damage. He felt anything but heroic; he must have had at least five hundred rounds fired at him and had made no reply. But he would live to fight another day.

He went home and reported what he had seen. But it was difficult to get people to believe that a Hun had fired all his ammunition at him from twenty yards range, for the only damage was two bullet holes, one in each wing-tip. He was certainly a marvellous pilot when it came to escaping.

'Bill,' he said, 'I solemnly swear by God's holy trousers that that Hun sat on my tail for nearly two minutes at twenty yards firing bursts all the while.'

'I believe you. I'm only surprised the Hun didn't pull his wings off or meet some other shocking end for daring to shoot at you.'

Some of them went in a tender to the Somme at La Chaussée for a swim. The current was strong, and Maitland nearly got drowned. One of A flight failed to return from his reconnaissance. The evening was misty, and B flight did a patrol without finding any Huns. Mist prevented the dawn show again. It was a heat mist. C flight went up at eleven o'clock, and Williamson worked up to eighteen thousand feet, and was able to dive on a formation of eight Fokker biplanes behind Chaulnes, all brightly painted in red and very splitarse. They played the dive and zoom game but only made the Huns contort and then go away east at high speed. Later the Huns came back at about nineteen thousand, but were driven off this time by Dolphins, and apparently went home.

This was all C flight's work for the day, as their dawn job had been washed out. Dubois had something wrong with his right arm, a sort of paralysis, and the Wing doctor washed him out. Tom and Williamson went to the river again in the hot afternoon. A flight met a Hun circus and Gibbon went down in flames. Maitland got a Hun in a spin and had a very narrow escape when another dived on him out of the sun and made a tight group of eight holes in his centre section. It was the closest thing possible, and the best group anybody had ever seen. A new fellow named Tully, who had a contraband camera, took a photograph of it.

At dinner news went round that the first Snipes had been allotted to Major Miles' crowd, lucky blighters. They would have a fortnight or three weeks for practising flying them, and then the slaughter would commence. Mac was also coming out with a new and very choice squadron of Snipes in a few weeks. The rumour was that his squadron would form a sort of nucleus, and other squadrons would be affiliated to it, thus forming a large circus. No doubt Mac would have his old squadron in it, and he would be a colonel, and the Huns would be exterminated. There would be no air Huns on the Western Front in 1919, if the war went on.

But in the meantime. . . .

In the meanwhile the Richthofen Circus was above Chaulnes. Every day the sky between ten and twenty thousand feet over the Somme was infested with three or four layers of multi-coloured, barred, streaked, slashed, checked, and zig-zagged Fokker biplanes (but that was not what the eye saw — they were dots or colourless aeroplane-shapes and only one or two that came very near showed colour or markings), thirty to fifty in all. This great circus was not collectively aggressive; it kept on its own side of the lines and waited to be attacked. If it could split up a hostile formation its more enterprising members would chase the scattered individuals. As a rule it waited to be attacked; but Camels could not outclimb the Fokkers to attack the top layer: and when they dived on a lower formation, they put themselves in a dangerous position.

Every day the large Hun formations sat above, diving occasionally and firing or not firing. The only thing to do was to watch carefully, dodge at the right moment, and keep determinedly with one's formation. The strain was tremendous. The weather was fine and very hot. There were patrols twice a day. Rarely a Hun was shot down. Williamson got one, Baker got two. Fuller went down in flames. Hole was killed: he was split off from the flight and chased down. Apparently he was wounded but got across the lines before he crashed. A Hun followed him right down and put a final burst into the crash in case he wasn't dead. Everyone in sight on the ground shot at the Hun, but he got away.

Williamson and Tom and Baker remained as the strength of the flight. Dubois went away to hospital, pale and quiet. He had hardly spoken for days, but moved about the mess pale and drawn. The other flights suffered. Hudson was wounded. Vick went in a spin from fifteen thousand feet. Several new fellows were killed or missing on their first, second or third patrols. Tully went up to practise flying around the aerodrome; he went up and vanished; nothing was heard of him. Another Smith arrived. As he was practising diving on the aerodrome an Ak-W flew across below him at about two hundred feet. He hit it amidships, cutting it in two. The Camel crumpled and burst into flames. They could not get near the crash for the heat and he was burnt to nothing. Smith was an unlucky name in that squadron. The two pieces of the Ak-W floated down, and the pilot was not quite killed; the back seat, where it was struck, was not occupied. The mess was drunk dry except for French vermouth; for twenty-four hours there was nothing but that. Bottle after bottle after bottle was emptied; it was no good. The afternoon heat was scorching. A blue lustrous dragon-fly flew into the mess and settled on the tent wall; clung there sheening metallically, hour after hour. Fellows went up to it and stared. It did not move till night, but in the morning it was gone.

Enormous red-copper clouds formed after every noon, resting on a dingy stratum of mist. The air was full of invisible precipices and rocks near the ground. The clouds towered higher than Camels flew; they were the authentic Himalayas of heavy summer, strange harvest of the sun-tilled air. The Fokkers showed up against their brazen sides, and the black smoke of Archie was not alien to their sultry fires.

For millions of years had summer heat burdened the skies with this empty grandeur, nature's dream-world, only significant by its utter non-significance. At length human purpose had penetrated these eagle-baffling heights, the purpose of murder. Dominant, triumphant, intelligent murderousness had driven man to scale these airy precipices and rend grandeur's garment of silence with the terrible staccato voices of his machine guns and the idiot bark of exploding shells. The maniac clangour of war echoed through the blue halls of the winds; terror and brutality ranged the inviolable heavens; iron laughter shook the vault of sky and obscured the pathways of the stars.

The contagion of man's evil vilified the clean high air; fear drove its invisible chariot among the clouds, leaving a spiritual miasma that choked the mind: fear, most anti-human of passions. It yellowed the sky's clarity and magnified the stridor of war into a mind-dinning yell of malice. There was a harsh rhythm of iron wheels in the stultified brain, echoing and clanging among metallic clouds; the sky had turned to brass.

XVII

THEN the weather broke with thunder in the night and in the morning rain was plashing on the taut canvas, running down it inside as well as out, drip-dripping on to beds and chattels. The smell of dust was washed away.

'Thank God for rain,' said Tom when he was sufficiently awake for conversation. 'If it lasts all day it will just about save my life.'

'And mine,' said Williamson.

It had been impossible lately with all the casualties to have days off; to take a lot of raw pilots among the Fokkers would be murder; the experienced men had to stick it. The squadron would have to be rested soon, or go back north, else the experienced men would be dead or gibbering. Yet they had been only ten days on the Somme front. The horrors of ground-strafing, of continually fighting machines by which they were altogether outclassed had made this time as wearing as the previous three months. Where were the Snipes? Surely to God they could be supplied as easily as Camels: why weren't they? It was one of those grisly mysteries whose solution would never come to light; eminent people were probably interested that it should not; it was not in the public interest. The Germans seemed to suffer from the same sort of thing; they had fiddled about with their Fokker biplane for a long time before really using it; perhaps they were being cautious after their not very satisfactory experience with the triplane. But the Snipe was a Sopwith.

'God, what a war,' Williamson remarked. He was duller nowadays; his lustre thickened, Tom thought, and no doubt he himself seemed so to Williamson.

The rain held all day. They began to cheer up towards evening. Food and drink were obtained and one or two guests invited to dinner. Noise increased from a buzz to a roar. There was a dawn show for C flight in the morning, but it was raining steadily and there was almost a certainty that rain or mist would prevent it. Tom staggered about the mess asking people their names. Besides guests, there were several new pilots he had not bothered to know and he had a dim feeling that this was wrong in him.

'How d'you do. My name's Cundall.'

'Yes, I know. Mine's Lucas.'

'North country?'

'Blyth, Northumberland, 's my home, but . . .'

'Hail to thee Blyth spirit.' He laughed drunkenly at his own wit. 'Have a drink. Hancock!'

'Thanks very much, but I don't drink.'

'Ho!' The whites of the boy's eyes had a bluish tinge. His own must be yellow and bloodshot. He was a ruin. He saw Williamson.

'Hi, Bill, Willi-am-son, this is Lucas of Blyth, Northumb'land. He doesn't drink.'

'Quite right too. B flight, aren't you?'

'Hancock, two whisky'n-sodas and a squash. Of course he's right. No good to anyone. And all the more for me.'

Williamson was chatting with Lucas. 'No, I've never been north of York.'

Yorke! Tom started. Something bumped him. He turned and saw it was the marquee pole. He cursed it and shook it in sudden blind rage. But Yorke was a mess of bones in aspic away in Hunland. Curly yellow hair and smiling pink-and-white face that were Lucas had slipped away and Hollis was grinning at him, that living scar, with purple congealed cheeks, bony nose, part hairless head.

'Christ, Holly, you look as blotto as I am.'

'Blotto? Of course I'm blotto. Sometimes I'm more blotto than others, but I've been blotto for two years continuously, and shall be. 'S quite all right, I've got two livers, and when one gets red hot the other takes over.'

Bloody good fellow, Holly. He said he was two people that were blown up together. About enough pieces to make one man were collected. They were sewn together and the memory that survived happened to be that of Hollis. Even so, he occasionally remembered things he hadn't done, or at least he hoped to God he hadn't.

But Tom was not happy-drunk. For him there was no release but insensibility.

'Shut up snoring, Bill,' he said when he had floated up through successive stages of less-than-consciousness into the wretched reality of a tent in France. But it was not Williamson. This was not his bed on which he was lying fully dressed. It was light and raining. He had a raging thirst, and went to his own tent for a drink. Jones, with his boots off, was on his bed, and he gave him a drink and got rid of him. Williamson had found the right bed; he woke up for a drink and went to sleep again. There was a general stir of people sorting themselves out and gulping water: under canvas you could hear everything your neighbours did.

There was very little demand for breakfast that day: tea and coffee at nine o'clock, and a hair of the dog at eleven; and with the rain still falling, lunch was quite a good meal. It looked as though it would go on raining for a month, but after tea it cleared up sufficiently for B flight to do a job, and Tom took up a practice patrol of new pilots. He had a new red-nosed Camel — the engine cowling and propeller boss painted red — and it was one of the best he had ever flown.

After a morning mist the heat returned, clear white heat, and the war went on. For Tom flying had become a weary business that happened almost automatically; his limbs did what was necessary in a sort of somnambulism. The engine roared and the aeroplane went into the air; it was no stranger than walking. Ten thousand feet was low, almost on the ground. Height made no difference except that it was cool at sixteen or seventeen thousand feet, and above that controls began to get floppy. There was nothing else; the map-like earth was so familiar that it was real. The aeroplane flew itself. He thought of everything and nothing. If there were Huns close his guts weakened with cold excitement.

They caught a two-seater, a DFW, and drove it down so that it crashed near Fresnes. A formation of nine Fokkers climbed above them, but it was chased off by a squadron of SEs that shot down one of them. This was in the afternoon; as the dawn show had been prevented by mist, it was C flight's only job. In the evening the major gave everyone detailed instructions about next morning's work. There was to be a push north of the Somme, to release Albert and Bray.

'This is the general scheme. The squadron will co-operate with the advance and also act for Intelligence as usual. Pilots will go out in pairs at intervals of twenty minutes, the first pair leaving the ground at six ak emma. Each pair will remain over the lines for an hour, looking for any checks, or strong points holding up the advance. Pilots must particularly watch over the tanks, spotting anti-tank guns and attacking them. Of course there will be the usual ground-strafing. Now for details. I'll read them out, and then give you each a copy of these orders and the time-table by which you will see exactly what objectives should be reached during your time over the lines.'

Afterwards the major, who had come to be known as The Digger, set them going in a sing-song, and got them to bed sober and cheerful.

Just before six in the morning, Tom was awakened by the roar of guns. His tooth brush in the mug was chittering to itself. The tent walls were vibrating. He turned over and tried to sleep.

At eight o'clock he took off. The first objectives had been reached, and all seemed well. He saw some queer insects scurrying along the Albert-Bray road and went down to investigate. Cavalry! There

433

had been nothing about them in orders. Dozens of tanks were lumbering about; he must look for anti-tank guns; any sort of flash near the front trenches might be one; but the tanks seemed to be all right: the Huns had probably retreated and left their heavier stuff. The infantry ran about and skirmished in the wake of the tanks and disappeared into the earth away from the shrapnel that was bursting all along the line in white puffs. Big high explosive shells were sending up columns and phantoms of smoke and debris; he saw one that stood for a second just like a topiary peacock, and then faded into ragged smoke and drifted and vanished. There was an atmosphere over it all sinister and brazen and filthy. The sunshine was brilliant. It must be infernally hot fighting down there.

The push was going on as planned. The Huns were falling back everywhere, and occasionally some would become visible. He saw a straggle of retiring grey soldiers and bombed them. They vanished. He dived and fired at others, and they scattered and disappeared. The air was crowded with British aeroplanes, bombing, firing, observing, spotting for artillery; and patrols above were busy keeping off a large formation of Fokkers glinting within the outer solar haze, looking for opportunities to pounce on stragglers. They were of little military value, being unable to interfere with British low fliers. Tom avoided their neighbourhood; bullets enough were coming up from the ground. He wasn't quite so scared of these as he used to be, or the sense of fear was less active, though he had even less will to overcome fear.

His follower was Major Bob, a Canadian, a likely new member of C flight, becoming bald, seeming solid and permanent, keen enough to give up majoring and act as a miserable second lieut. Leading this stalwart, Tom had to put up a reasonably good show. He bombed and shot and observed and collected bullet holes with less than his usual lackadaisicalness until it was time to go home and report progress.

They flew home low over the supply columns, nests of tanks, Red Cross ambulances, dumps of shells and trench mortars and white boxes of small arms ammunition, long files and concentrations of thousands of grey prisoners, field guns flashing away in the midst of it all, lorries, GS wagons, cars, limbers, cavalry troops, motor cycles. Occasional shells from German heavies burst in red-gold instant flashes from which tall grey-yellow columns erupted: and immediately following the nearer explosions an air-shaking crump lifted and dropped them.

The push died out. Only one pilot failed to return. Lucas came back with blood dripping from a leg of his flying suit, and fainted when he had climbed from his bus. He was rushed off to hospital. Wing telephoned that the show had been completely successful and conveyed Brigade's congratulations on the fullness and accuracy of their reports. Wing did not give them any more jobs that day.

It was exhaustingly hot. Chocolate left in the tent melted and flowed. They went down to the Somme to bathe. He bought chewing gum from an American Y.M.C.A. In the evening The Digger took Williamson and Tom and Maitland to Abbeville and stood them dinner.

They found some infantry having a particularly noisy binge. It appeared that two of them had been recommended by the colonel for decoration after a recent show; but when four decorations were rationed to the brigade, the brigadier snaffled one for himself, and handed the others out to his brigade major, staff captain, and transport officer. The colonel, blowing with rage, had paraded his battalion that day and told them the facts. The colonel was twenty-three years old, with six wound stripes, a double D.S.O. and an M.C., a bank clerk before the war, and by his appearance, a bank-robber after the war, if he survived.

It was a cheery evening. There were some damned good fellows not yet killed. It was a good drive back over the bumpy roads and track. The night was cooler. A fragment of shell made a hole in the tent and stuck in the carpet. Williamson felt queer in the morning and Tom led the nine o'clock patrol: Baker and Bob and two new fellows. The squadron was all new fellows nowadays. The great days were over. But they had whacked the Huns. The younger Richthofen's Circus might make a stand over Chaulnes, but they knew their armies were beaten.

Tom hated to go near Chaulnes, so he made straight for it and found empty skies. They wandered up and down the lines, over the seams and dribbles and pock-marks in the chalk. About thirty Huns in three layers came up from the south, skirmishing with some SEs.

435

He had no excuse for not attacking the bottom layer, as the others were busy, so he went down on them: they splitarsed about, doing climbing turns, and were very difficult to hit. The only thing was to stay down among them and dogfight.

When they did this the Fokkers kept on climbing and were soon on top, but not before Baker had got one in a flopping dive. The Fokkers in turn dived and zoomed at the impotent Camels; but a flight from another squadron came up on top and the Huns moved eastwards.

The upper layers were being chivvied by a crowd of SEs and Dolphins; one or two of them were shot down, and an SE. This sort of thing was not in accord with Hun tactics, and they cleared off south-east. Dolphins were awkward for them, being as good as themselves at twenty thousand feet, and they had to go up there to get on top of the SEs.

But it was extraordinary that so many British machines were at the same place at the same time. There must be a great concentration of squadrons on this front. Even No. 1 Pursuit Flight could not deal with this sort of thing, and when Mac with his Snipe circus came the Huns would be smashed. At present, although the Huns were out-numbered in the air, the concentrating of their best pilots on the Somme front enabled them to make a stand there with the help of the Dutchman Fokker and his 185 h.p. biplane.

In the afternoon Williamson and Tom, fast asleep, were roused with urgent haste to do a low patrol around Bray. The Australians, making a local attack, were being fired at by low-flying Fokkers. Williamson, who was feeling better, led. It seemed as though every Camel squadron in France had been called upon, and the air got thick with them. There were no Huns. Things quietened on the ground and they went home.

Clouds were forming, and it rained in the evening and looked set dud, so Tom, dead tired, filled up with whisky and went to bed tight. Rain came splashing in through the slit in the tent. Who cared what rain did as long as it came? God, he was tired, could sleep in a pond. His pillow was sinking, sinking.

Thirst penetrated through dreams in which he was searching in some deep place for — he did not know what. He reached for his water-bottle and drank. It was still dark, and not raining. Not raining—oh hell, there would be jobs. It was impossible for him to go on any longer and not be killed. He couldn't be missed by bullets for ever. A Fokker would get him or a machine gun on the ground. He would certainly be killed if he went on; he could feel death in his bones. He would be shot down in flames. O Christ. He sweated at the thought of it and groaned and turned over, and lay listening to the rumble of guns.

Then it was light: a grey morning of low clouds and humid air; not fit for flying. He lay talking to Williamson for a time, and had to bolt to the latrines suddenly. After breakfast there was nothing to do but mope. God, what a state he was in! He must stick it for another week. Another dozen jobs. A dozen jobs was a lifetime. There was no end to it.

He had one or two drinks to keep himself alive till lunch. But it wasn't so bad as March; they would have been out ground-strafing on a day like this for certain: the ceiling was at about two thousand. He felt less numb with whisky in him. He would have to give up the idea of not drinking during the day. He wouldn't get tight, but just kill the ache.

After lunch he settled down to sleep. It was cold and damp. Always it was cold and damp or hot and dusty. The hole in the tent had been patched. He was dozing when the major sent for him. Hell, what now?

A solitary reconnaissance at Bray. The Huns, outflanked, had evacuated the town, and Tom was to see where they had retired to. He took Baker and Bob for top protection and went nosing among the tracers till he spotted the Hun line half a mile beyond Bray. He returned with his information and several bullet holes. God, that low work!

And the next day's jobs were all to be low. More pushing on both sides of the Somme.

He had agreed with Williamson that they would keep together on these low jobs. On the morning one they were to go down and drop their bombs and then patrol. Williamson arranged rendezvous over Morlancourt.

It took quite a long time to reach the lines nowadays. When

437

they got there, a hell of a war was going on. Explosions, shrapnel, tanks, fires. It was a filthy mess to go down into. The Huns were being driven back everywhere, but there were few to be seen. Probably they remained in their trenches and surrendered. Most of them were half-starved boys of seventeen and eighteen years. It was necessary to go farther over to find anything to bomb, retreating troops and transport; but there the Fokkers were, and ground machine guns with nothing to do but fire at aeroplanes.

Tom followed Williamson, and they made a dash east when the sky was clear. He dropped his bombs near some troops and climbed away west. Hanging over the side, he thought his bombs did some damage. He was low and getting shot up and shaking like hell. God, he was no good for this game. Near the ground he felt sick, clammy, empty. He made for Morlancourt. Bill was coming along behind. He came up and gave the dud engine signal and continued homewards. Tom picked up Baker and Bob over Morlancourt. The other man did not turn up, so Tom led a patrol of three. He was damned if he was going near a bunch of Fokkers if he could help it, three strong. They would get eaten up. What was the good of trying to fight Fokkers, anyway?

Luckily there were none about, and the rest of the job was peaceful except for Archie. Williamson had reached home all right; he was all shot up and his pressure gone. The fifth man had vanished. No one minded that much; new youngsters came and vanished or killed themselves before anyone got to know them. Not one in ten settled down.

Then at four o'clock in the afternoon they went out to do it again; but this time they were to split up for individual reconnaissances and ground-strafing. It was cloudy, and it was certain there would be Fokkers hanging around the clouds to catch solitary low fliers.

Tom somehow lost Williamson on this job, and went cruising over the old Somme battlefield by himself, keeping a watch on the low clouds as much as on the ground.

He could see a good deal of movement on the floor; Huns moving back; and he worked eastwards watching, keeping close to convenient clouds for hiding in. At Flers he nearly ran into a Hun two-seater. He hated to tackle a two-seater alone, but he couldn't very well avoid

438

it. He fired immediately in the direction of the Hun, and it proceeded to show him how splitarse it was. The Huns had some very nice two-seaters nowadays, and they seemed to bring out a new kind every few weeks. Luckily it made off east all out, and Tom followed at a cautious distance, sideslipping away from the observer's tracer No guts, those Hun two-seater merchants. But their job was not fighting.

Well, that was another victorious combat: enemy driven off. There was a lot of transport on the roads towards Le Transloy. He ought to go and shoot it up, but it was rather a long way over for a solitary; was it safe? No, it certainly wasn't safe. There was a bunch of Fokkers in the eastern sky, and Archie was calling them. He hurried into a near cloud and flew west, and came out in the hell of a sideslip over the ghastly square of High Wood. The Huns were away in the north-east, eight of them. There was hardly ever a patrol in the right place at the right time. He put his nose down towards Bazentin, but had to zig-zag because of Archie. The Fokkers disappeared among the clouds; probably they had gone back to protect their transport from other raiders.

But it was too dangerous to go nosing round there alone any more. A two-seater would see the transport and send down a zone call about it; that was what two-seaters were for. He wandered around the lines for a while, watching the shells bursting, and thinking how marvellous it would be to get away from all this. It would be like toothache suddenly leaving off, when for a while the very absence of pain was bliss. And it might well be all over before his time to come out again. How would life feel unmenaced? Imagination could not reach so far.

Then he returned home, and flopped. He had felt all right up, but his legs were like lead on the ground. It was difficult to walk.

'My God, what a washout I am,' he said to Williamson. 'Worn out with fright.'

'Don't worry. Drink up and keep yourself going a few more days. Then home. Think what a hell of a blind we'll have when we get to London.'

'I'm not so sure I'll be posted in a few days.'

'Ask to be. You're entitled.'

439

'I can't bloody-well say to the major, "I'm sick of this 'ere war and I want to go home".'

'You're coming home with me. Don't forget I'm your bloody flight commander and I've got to look after you and I tell you it's time for you to go home. I'll see the major.'

'You will hell. Flight commander, you said, not nurse.'

'Oh, shut up man, for Christ's sake. Come and drink.'

XVIII

Tom slept heavily through a thunderstorm, but woke up before dawn feeling like death. The morning turned out dud, but the weather cleared enough in the afternoon for them to go out ground-strafing under clouds at twelve hundred feet. Every day the war was getting less funny. The advance was going well everywhere; a steady push forwards across the old Somme battlefield was flattening the Arras salient, and south of the Somme there was continual nibbling. But that meant little to Tom, sitting for an hour to be shot at while he looked for the front line, for invisible anti-tank guns, for troops to bomb. His immediate problem was to keep cool, to resist the temptation to clear off for a joy-ride, and to obtain the maximum amount of side-slip without falling into a spin. He would see tracers flash, and scuttle away across the lines like a frightened rabbit, get his breath back, and go to it again. His mouth was dry; he had bought some chewing gum, but seemed to have lost the blasted stuff. Every time he put his nose down to loose off a burst at the ground he was terrified he might be giving a sitting target.

But nothing happened to him. Probably he killed, maimed, or enraged a few Huns; certainly he sweated with mindless fear. Then Williamson went home, and he followed, doing a leisurely cross-country, breathing deeply.

Williamson's D.F.C. was through, and there would be a binge about it. After tea Tom went with Chadwick in a tender to Abbeville to buy champagne and lobsters; and the first thing they did was to split a bottle of champagne by way of sampling, and the girl who served them was such a nice little thing that Chadwick's eyes went

440

fishy and they would never have got any lobsters if Tom hadn't dragged him away.

Chadwick was annoyed, and wanted to know why Tom couldn't have gone after the lobsters alone and left him to it; and Tom said why the bloody hell should he, and there was a coolness, but they got back to time.

The Wing Colonel came to dinner and shook Williamson's hand, and most people got tight. The Digger stood up and said that Williamson was a stout fellow, always cool, and of unerring judgment, and he was mighty glad to have the chance to congratulate him, the oldest member of the squadron, on his hard-earned distinction, and of proposing that they should drink his health.

Tom, sozzled with Pol Roger, stood up to second the proposal. They probably expected him to be funny. God, there wasn't much to be funny about. But his owlish look and difficulty of articulation made people laugh more than wit. 'Good old Tom,' he was encouraged.

He'd known Bill, he'd known Captain Williamson, hell of a long time. Since he was born almost; anyway, since the beginning of the year, and that was a lifetime. They'd shared a hut all the while, and now a tent, and were leaked on by the same leaks, so he knew Bill well, very well. But he wasn't going to give him away. A bloke who'd been ground-strafing through Cambrai, the March retreat, and was still at it in the present little show was entitled to every consideration. (This must be the worst speech ever made; if the fellows weren't tight they'd hoot; and if he wasn't tight he'd shut up and sit down.) And if you had to do all that for a D.F.C., he hoped to God no one would ever expect him to try to earn a V.C. (Idiotic. Why the hell couldn't he say something worth saying?) Of course, Bill's career had not been entirely blameless. Some of them would remember the time when he crashed somewhere far away and met pals there who made him so blotto that he couldn't remember in the morning where the crash was; and as far as he knew that crash never had been found. His own belief was that Bill hadn't crashed at all, but had pawned his bus and got tight on the proceeds, and he called on him to tell for the common benefit how much you could raise on one perfectly good Camel. (God, the fellows were laughing at that.)

What was there to say? They all knew Williamson was a damn good fellow and a stout pilot; perhaps he knew it rather better than most of them; and he could assure them from long personal experience it was so. And he would remind them that Williamson had worthily filled Mac's place, the hell of a place to take. (Better not say too much about that though. Bill was damn good but he wasn't a Mac, thank God.) Probably there never was a better earned decoration, and it made him very very happy to be able to say that about a bloke whom he liked personally as much as he liked Bill, and he begged them all to drink most heartily as he knew they would, the health of one of the best and stoutest blokes above ground.

Tom sat down and got on with some drinking. He hardly knew what he'd been talking about. He'd blown Bill's trumpet for him; apart from that the speech had felt perfectly futile; but they were all cheering because they were tight; cheering Bill really.

Large made some remarks, the toast was drunk, 'For He's a Jolly Good Fellow' sung, and Williamson was shouted up to reply. He told them all how nice they were and what a fine squadron it had always been. He didn't deserve a D.F.C. any more than all the rest; everyone was earning one every day now. The squadron as a whole had earned it, and he was just a fellow who had been there so long that they thought he ought to have something to take home; a sort of leaving prize.

He was glad that the worst charge brought against him was that of pawning his bus. You couldn't raise more than five francs on a Camel anywhere, and he thought it had dropped to two-fifty now that the Fokker biplane had arrived in force. So it obviously wasn't worth it. In fact he was surprised that so distinguished a pilot as Tom Cundall had made the charge; distinguished, that was, for having crashed more aeroplanes without hurting himself than any man flying. And after all, that was the art of flying. When he first knew him he used to write off a Camel regularly every week; it was his only recreation besides elbow lifting; but he had given it up entirely for some months now because, after a crash when they had found him sitting in the midst of the fragments of a brand new machine strewn far around, he had discovered a small scratch on his arm when he was changing for dinner that evening.

Williamson spoke some conventional stuff, and the dinner broke up for noise and drinks in the ante-room. There was still champagne going, and Tom kept to that, only twice drinking whisky and soda by mistake. He woke in the night with belly-ache, probably from the lobster salad, and dozed uneasily, dreaming and dreaming, and felt rotten in the morning. He had his usual matutinal diarrhoea that had been troubling him for the past week or so, further depleting his small store of energy.

They went up at eleven o'clock to do some ground-strafing and a patrol, and Wing thought it would be nice if they got a balloon. Tom shuddered at this addition to their toil. Things were quite bad enough for them already.

They dropped bombs on some troops retreating from Maricourt. Tom was sick of dropping bombs on people, but he was merely an automatic machine; authority put the penny in and he did his tricks; not usually at all well, for his machinery was clogged with fear.

Then they ascended and looked for balloons: but others had been out before them on the same quest, and the balloon people were waiting for them. Whenever they went within two miles of one Archie put up a barrage and nearly blew them out of the sky; he was wonderful. Tom had never known anything quite like it. A dozen batteries at once seemed to open up and to have them ranged to an inch, putting bursts on their wing-tips, bumping them about. And then a bunch of Fokkers came and sat over them. Williamson turned away. The Fokkers sat and watched. 'Oh come down and sink us while you can, you bloody idiots,' Tom yelled at them. But they sat and let them go. Why? What were they afraid of? There was no particular danger in diving and zooming. Was this bunch sick of a war that seemed nearly over?

They crossed the Somme and climbed towards the south, meeting no other Huns except a couple of two-seaters over Estrées. They dived on one of these; it went down in a spin and they lost it in a cloud; the other escaped. They did not know if the spinner had crashed, but learned afterwards that Archie had seen something spin into the ground at that time and place, so it was a kill.

After tea they had to go out and do it all over again. This time they

443

met the Circus cruising about in layers in the neighbourhood of Chaulnes. They could do nothing with them, and Williamson kept at a distance; it was no use being dumb targets. Nevertheless there were so many formations above them that they were dived on twice, and the bullets flew without doing fatal damage. But Tom found the noise of machine guns more than ever terrifying, and he feared that fear was gaining on him; that it was becoming morbid.

On the ground it was even worse. Memory of the iron staccato was more horrible than its actuality. A primitive ego of unreason in him screamed and screamed with terror, and he had to dope it with alcohol. He was drinking so much that semi-drunkenness was normal in him, and he despised himself for it. He was weak; he had no guts; other fellows stuck it. He was bad-tempered, afraid of talking to people lest he should give himself away; but in the evening, tight and secure from fear, he fooled and yelled and smashed, but remembered very little of it afterwards.

He woke up as usual between two and three o'clock. He felt as if broken glass was in his blood-stream. The darkness was terrible with visions of Fokkers in formations towering to terrible heights over the Somme and Chaulnes. He flew infinite dream-distances over nightmare battlefields; telling himself all the while that this was merely the early morning ebb of vitality. But the knowledge did not help him; his blood carried the broken glass into his brain; he lay impotent against the forces of night. He must endure. Death seemed waiting in the darkness. He must endure. He dozed and dreamed that he was wandering and searching, always wandering and searching.

The batman woke them up for the dawn patrol. Williamson put his head out of the tent to look at the weather.

'Don't call anyone else,' he said to the batman; and to Tom: 'It's a complete washout. Clouds at a thousand.'

Sometime afterwards they were re-awakened by the C.O. himself.

'Sorry Williamson, but Wing insists that a patrol must go up.'

Williamson sat up in bed. 'Good Christ, what for? There's a thick layer of cloud at a thousand feet.'

'And a strong wind and occasional showers,' said the major. 'But I'm afraid you'll have to go up.'

444

So the flight ate hard-boiled eggs indignantly. A patrol when you couldn't get above a thousand feet! Wing must have gone bloody-well batchy. It was an ideal morning for not flying.

'Look here, troops,' Williamson said to them confidentially. 'I'm not crossing the lines below a thousand feet. It's bloody ridiculous. We'll keep on our own side and do some contour-chasing and see how many crashes we can count.'

These instructions were applauded, and a cheerful patrol went up into the westerly half-gale that was blowing. They reached the battle-fields very quickly and spent an hour looking at the hundreds of burnt and crumpled wrecks of British and German aeroplanes that were strewn about in the battle area. Tom looked without success for the remains of a red Fokker triplane at Sailly-le-Sec where Manfred von Richthofen had been shot down. They crept home against the wind under lowering clouds and through rain mist, and reported that there was nothing to report.

The rest of the day was too dud for patrolling. A and B flights went out ground-strafing under the low clouds and had a frightful time of it: C flight had been lucky. B had a man wounded. Jock was very annoyed because a bullet had hit the flask he carried and wasted half a pint of whisky. The advance was now nearly across the old Somme battlefield. They had to fill up forms about their private lives: someone had invented a scheme for educating the troops in France against their return to civilian life. Evidently there was a serious intention in high places of finishing the war some day.

'Our war is almost over,' said Williamson to Tom. 'The major says my successor will probably be here in two days' time. I asked him about you, and he said if you weren't posted to Home Establishment by then he'd use his weight about it. Anyhow, you can have leave then.'

'What exactly did you say about me?'

'I said, "Do you think Cundall will be posted by then?" and he answered, "He may be, but if he isn't I'll do something about it". He spoke about your working hard and needing a rest, and then mentioned leave. Satisfied?'

'Yes. That's good. Thank you, Bill. By God he's right. I could

445

rest for a year. I'm all to hell. Had an argument with Chadwick yesterday. He challenged me to a duel.'

'His trouble is too much rest. Did you accept?'

'Of course. And as I had choice of weapons I said Camels. He wears wings.'

'Comedians. But that's a nice idea of yours. Meet me at two thousand over Charing Cross with a hundred rounds.'

'And the villain is shot down and crashes on the heroine's rich uncle, who marries the hero on the proceeds.'

'I believe you're feeling better.'

'God knows. I feel all right talking to you. Somehow you keep me just sane.'

'I don't do anything. I owe a lot to you. . . .'

'Oh, for God's sake don't let's start throwing bouquets at each other. We've stuck it together somehow, and that's plenty.'

'All right, you bad tempered bastard.'

C flight's first job was at ten o'clock in the morning. They were to do a low patrol to protect the ground-strafing people. It was further than ever to the lines. North of the Somme there was a battle for Bapaume going on. South of the Somme, Estrées, Chaulnes and even Nesle were captured. In front of Chaulnes there was a bulge touching almost to the north-south reach of the river. There would be no more Fokkers over Chaulnes.

It was a fine day, but clouds were fairly frequent at about four thousand feet. Williamson climbed above these to have a look round. The sky was clear except for a few Dolphins. Tom, watching his tail assiduously, suddenly became aware of something diving out of the sun at him. His nerves leapt, he jerked into a skidding turn; the thing after him loomed; it was a Dolphin. What the bloody hell was the fool up to? It pulled out and zoomed away. He shouted curses after it. His heart was bumping; he was shaky. No doubt the idiot thought he was mighty clever, diving out of the sun like that. Why the hell didn't he keep his cleverness for the Huns?

But, good God, what a state he was in to get such complete wind-up because a stray Dolphin dived at him. Dolphins looked so confoundedly Hunnish and moved about so quickly. They had back-stagger and their props went round the wrong way; beastly things.

They ought to stay up above twenty thousand where they belonged; they had enough gadgets for making them comfortable there.

In the afternoon they had to go out and do their share of low work. The front line was changing so rapidly that a constant flow of reports was wanted. The flight went out as individuals, but Tom kept by Williamson. They flew along the Somme to Peronne and dropped bombs on Mont St. Quentin whence a swarm of tracers came up at them. They turned south with the river, and nearly got blown up when a column of smoke shot up in front of them; a bridge going up. The Germans had retired across the river.

They pried into Brie and Le Mesnil. The enemy seemed to be taking up his position along the east bank of the Somme. They followed the line north by Peronne and Mont St. Quentin along the road to Bapaume. Bapaume was taken once again. Tom kept saying to himself 'only a few more jobs'. Bullets were flying. He was watching the cloudy sky as much as the floor, circling and splitarsing all the time.

They made a dash for the lines when some Fokkers appeared, and got across in time, and kept over until the Huns were well out of the way.

Williamson went home early. They had dropped their bombs and done their reconnaissance, and he considered it better to go home and report than to hang about doing nothing particular. Tom agreed with him entirely. He was tired and after tea lay on his bed for an hour. Another day's work over, thank God. Only two more days in August. Could he endure them? Then Home Establishment or leave; if it was leave he would only have to return to France for a week afterwards and then go home again.

His eyes ached. The glass was moving again in his veins. He daren't open his eyes in case the tent was floating and dissolving in brazen sunshine and he was alone in some vacancy beyond the world where he must see the very figure of hideous death that was awaiting him. Seddon had gone, and that queer fellow, what was his name? Grey. And Beal. And how many others. Absorbed into the deathly nihilism of the battlefields. Something seemed drawing him to the same fate. He must open his eyes. Thank God the tent was normal. But he was tired — very tired, numb, insensible. He could not think

447

nor remember. Events sank at once beneath the quicksand surface of things and left no memory. There was no basis to the spinning earth, and death was the only reality.

Then Williamson came in, steadying the round world by his presence.

XIX

HE lay still, breathing slowly, deliberately. Two more days. Only two more days. Then they would go to London, celebrate briefly, and go away into the West Country and stay as long as they could on a farm where food might be comparatively plentiful, and they would not have to eat tripe and margarine. They would drink beer and cider, lend a hand with the harvesting, sport with village maidens, climb hills and lie in the sun. They would do no shooting. They would have bicycles and wander carefree from village to remote village, curse dud weather instead of blessing it, swim in the sea, explore old churches, peer into streams. Bill knew well the East Anglian Perpendicular, and the fine beer and cider of Norfolk and Suffolk; the West Country, variation on the same English theme, but hilly, would delight him.

Only two more days; there was infinite relief in the thought. If only it would be dud for those last hours. But the night was fair when they went to bed, sober, talking of what they would do. In the morning there was an open sky above the heat haze.

And on that penultimate day they took off from the dusty aerodrome at 11.15 o'clock and flew unhurryingly to the lines, a journey of thirty miles now. In front of Albert he saw a formation of strange machines above them. Snipes, by God. They were having a look at the lines, and very soon would be taking part in the war. And Mac was coming, and the Fokkers would be driven out of the air. He went alongside Bill, pointed upwards, and waved his fist in an orbit of cheering. Bill nodded and did a thumbs up in reply. Tom dropped back into place.

They split up before Peronne and went to look for targets individually. Tom, as usual, kept near Bill. Only three more jobs at the most after this one. The war was going splendidly. The Huns were on the run, and it was hardly possible they would ever be able to stand against all the tanks that were crawling after them. For a moment his heart was lighter, but then they went down.

Williamson had taken a good look round before crossing the line between Bapaume and St. Pierre-Vaast Wood, and there seemed to be no Fokkers about. A patrol of SEs was protecting low fliers. They went east beyond Sailly-Saillisel and zig-zagged southwards behind St. Pierre-Vaast Wood. Files and straggles of Huns were retreating out of the wood. A wonderful target. They let their bombs go. Most of the Huns vanished at once, but the bombs must have done damage. Bill was diving and firing. Tom followed him. He supposed he'd better loose off a few rounds, and wished he wasn't shaking so much. Bill did a roll. He did not come out. A double roll. What the devil. He was spinning. Christ, oh Christ. 'Come out, Bill!' he shouted. It couldn't be happening to Bill. He followed him down. Oh God, Bill was hit, he would never get out.

'Bill, Bill, for Christ's sake, Bill,' he screamed. The Camel spun on. Full engine. It crashed behind the wood. It hit the ground and burst to fragments. It was like a shell exploding. A cloud of dust and smoke flew up. It did not burn, but Bill was smashed to bits.

He flew right down on the crash. Bullets were holing his planes. He saw flashes of machine guns. There were two in an open pit. They had killed Bill. Damn and blast them. God, he would get them. He was grinding his teeth and drawing back his lips with rage and hatred. God, he'd get them.

He climbed and sideslipped away, watching. They were firing at him. He must be cunning. It would be no use diving straight at a pair of machine guns; he would give them a sitting shot, and they would probably get him first; get him as well as Bill. There seemed to be three men in the pit. He circled about sideslipping and wondering what to do. He dived away from them and fired a short burst at nothing in particular to warm his guns and to make them think he had not seen them.

He could dive vertically on them; they would be unable to reply effectively, but he could not go right down on them vertically. No, he must attack them at an angle that would let him dive right into the pit so that they wouldn't have a chance. He would shoot them from a dozen feet.

What cover had they? There seemed to be a darker patch on the north side that might be a scoop or shallow dugout. He must attack from the south so as to fire into it in case they ran in.

He got in position just in time. One of the guns was not firing. They were doing something to it. It would be out of action some seconds at least. He would take a chance of outshooting one gun with his two.

He dived steeply, pressing his trigger, and eased slowly out, bringing his sights on to his target with his guns already firing. The Huns should not have the advantage of getting in the first burst.

The pit came into the centre of the Aldis. He held it there expertly. Tracers flashed inches away. Chips flew from struts. The engine was hit.

Then it was over. He pulled up out of the pit. There were two dead men in it. He must have riddled them. One man seemed to have got away.

Rage was gone. There was no feeling left in him. He was shaking. Bill was killed. He had avenged him: what was the good? Bill was gone. He did not even know for certain that it was his killers he had killed.

He made for home, engine missing. He was being shot at. They would not get him. He crossed the lines, and flew dazedly westwards, homing by instinct. He landed and walked to the office.

The major and Hollis were both there. 'Williamson is killed.' Hollis ejaculated 'Christ.' The major did not at once speak. Tom walked out. His instinctive feeling was to be alone.

'Cundall.' It was the major calling him. He turned back. The major came up to him and put his hand on his shoulder.

'I know how you feel. But come and make your report.'

Tom went back to the office and told them about it in flat phrases. When he had finished, the major said:

'That was a wonderful effort of yours getting those machine guns.'

Tom had nothing to reply.

450

'You're not to fly any more to-day. You're not fit.'

He went to the tent and took off his gear. There was Bill's stuff that he wouldn't want any more. He was dead. Bill of all people; that rock. Ground-strafing, ah! He was not coming back: Bill of all people. Smashed up. Utterly gone.

In the mess people asked him about Bill. Drinking neat whisky, he told them. He had never known the squadron so troubled by a death.

Then lunch. He sat down to it, but found eating impossible, so drank. Hollis told about his avenging of Bill, and people asked Tom details, eyebrows slightly up, solemn before this exploit.

They gave him drink. He went to his tent. He slept, but it was hell to wake up in the desolate tent.

He drank tea. The thing was gaining on him; the glass in his belly was beginning to move and pierce. He couldn't face the night alone. He said to Chadwick, who was P.M.C.:

'Can the mess sell me two bottles of whisky?'

'I'll see you get it, Tom,' he replied: and later: 'I've put them in your tent. The corks are drawn.'

The major said to him: 'The wing doctor will be here in the morning, and he'll just run over you.'

By dinner he was able to eat something and stop the light-headed feeling produced by alcohol in an empty stomach. He sat about in the mess for a time, but it was impossible to inflict his gloomy presence on fellows trying to make themselves cheery amid all the war.

So he went to his tent, and mourned alone. There was no chance now, that, as once before, Bill would come back. He was gone for ever and for ever. The whisky was on the grassy ledge where the tent overlapped the hole. He filled his tooth mug and drank. God, the way he could swallow whisky nowadays. He could never recover physically or mentally. Body and brain were dull and rotting. He ought to have been killed, not Bill. Better get into bed while he was able. Damned difficult clothes were. 'Bill,' he was saying, 'Bill, old dear.' Talking away, tears streaming down his face. Bloody fool. Somehow he got into bed and poured out more whisky, spilling it. He sank into whirling oblivion and then woke up again to the wrongness of the world. The candle had burnt out. Wrongness turned into physical pain. It precipitated out of the darkness and became definite, localizing in his guts. He drank whisky from the neck of the bottle; then he knew he was going to be sick. He groped under the bed for his pot, and spewed into it. He had little to bring up, but went on retching for hours. He lay dully intent on his guts-ache, which at least shut out mental agony.

He heard the pilots for the dawn patrol being called, engines being run, talk in the mess, the take off. He dozed. The batman came in at eight o'clock to see if he wanted anything. He had a cup of tea. Soon afterwards the M.O. arrived.

'Well, how do you feel this morning?' He opened wide the tent flap for more light.

'Rotten. Trying to vomit all night.'

'What d'you put that down to?'

'Lobster salad.'

'H'm.' The M.O. paused for a moment, and then said: 'Drinking much?'

'Soaking.'

The doctor considered him. 'Try to cut down the drink when you get home, or you'll spoil your stomach permanently. You must give up war-flying for a bit. The prescription is a month's leave and Home Establishment. But don't binge. Just go easy for a time. All right?'

'All right, doctor.'

'I should think you'd get away to-morrow. Good luck.'

Tom got up and wandered about the countryside. The peasants had done most of their reaping. He stood in a stubble field watching a pair of swallows circling, admiring their skill and swiftness. It was marvellous that they could get so much speed with so little effort. He started a hare, and it fled like the spirit of fear. He felt remote from the war. The advance went on; it might have been in a campaign of Marlborough. The squadron was to move forward to Allonville next morning. He would not have to go, as transport from Wing would be ready at eight o'clock to take him to Boulogne. He wrote up his log book finally, and found that he had done altogether one hundred and sixty-three jobs, totalling two hundred and forty-eight flying hours.

In the afternoon he packed Bill's stuff, destroying dozens of letters which he thought he would not have wanted his next of kin to possess. He found a photograph of him which he kept. They had been friends, and this eternal parting was bitter. He had become used to thinking of the future as theirs. Now the future was nothing. The desire for life, which had always flowed in him like a strong tide, had ebbed. His life, it seemed, was saved, but the gods that gave back his life into his hands had taken away the value of the gift. They were true gods.

Baker shot down a Fokker on the British side of the lines near Bapaume, and he went in a tender with some others to see the wreck. Tom went to the hangars to have a last look at his red-nosed Camel. It was patched and serviceable. Its streamer of deputy leader was taken from its tail and some new pilot would fly it down to Allonville in the morning. It had been the best machine he had ever flown: and he had treated it well, not strained a wire of it. Now it was just anybody's Camel. If he had been able to feel any more sadness, this farewell would have saddened him.

Probably he would never look down on the lines again, never hear the woof of Archie, never search the sky for Huns, never fire his guns at a living target, never hear the infernal staccato behind him, never see tracers come up from the ground; all that was over and past. Never more the dawn patrol and the hard-boiled egg; never more the terrific binges and the inimitable comradeship; never more the frantic excitement and the ghastly fear; all that was over, and life was empty.

The tender came back from the battlefields laden with loot; equipment the Huns had left behind in their retreat. Pistols and bayonets were handed out as mementos. Baker had even got a machine gun off his Fokker.

The last evening passed. Tom had few people to say good-bye to; nearly all his friends were gone; it was a squadron of ghosts. Maitland was his only coeval; a tired, quiet Maitland. There were Forster, Large, Chadwick, Baker, and the unwithering horselike Jones. Some of the newer people he knew, as Major Ling, Major Bob, Hollis, Jock; but many of the squadron he had scarcely perceived as individuals.

453

He drank and made an effort to put away grief. Afterwards it did not matter what happened to him, but he must spend this last evening worthily. Soon he was tight, shouting the old songs, ragging, playing the fool, drinking till the place spun. He staggered to his tent, fell on his bed, and was sick.

He lay a long time half-conscious, then took off some of his clothes and got under his blankets. There was a raider dropping bombs near. He had spoilt his stomach. Burnt his guts. That didn't matter. Everything was over now.

He dozed between sleeping and waking. The night seemed unending. He floated through infinite reaches of pale time.

The whole squadron was astir early for the move. Tom got up at six and drank tea, then packed. God, this was not the home-going he had expected. Then he had an hour to wait; an hour of blank desolation.

His tender arrived. He shook hands with everybody. The major gave him sealed credentials. He got on board. The tender started. He waved farewell and heard the parting cheer.

It took four hours to Wimereux; then he was back on the top floor of No. 14 General Hospital; a world of unfamiliar amenities: a bath to lie down in, electric light, clean sheets, a plastered room, unmilitary food, cleanliness. He had escaped from the wilderness of dirt, chaos, death. He shared a room with a north country man who talked, O God, for ever.

A doctor would examine him on the morrow. When he had eaten and settled in and written to warn his sister of his imminent arrival, there was nothing to do. It was always like that, nothing to do. Once he had been able to read all day. Now he did not want to read. He wanted some steady, monotonous work that must be done. He took out a pencil and note-book and started to sketch the old fort on the rocks. But the effort lapsed and he sat brooding. Several times he resumed, and relapsed into endless gloomy meditation on the past.

He was glad to go to bed at nine o'clock. Lights were put out at 9.30 because an air raid was expected. The man from the north talked for half an hour and then abruptly fell asleep, and snored. Tom was dead tired but remained awake. The scene of Bill's death went on and on repeating itself to his mind's eye; and the two dead

Germans in the machine-gun pit. The hours were black monarchs that ruled by torture. Again and again he saw the double-roll and the full-engined spin. And then a ghost of the red rage that had driven him on to vengeance arose in his heart, and then horror of it all, and of war and bloody-mindedness. He saw the dead Germans as a symbol of all vengeance that in turn would be avenged. The blood shed in the machine-gun pit demanded retaliation no less than the bloody crash a few hundred yards away. And so the blood feud of the nations would go on from war to war, from horror to horror till the world was one great shambles. They called this the war to end war; so men were encouraged to fight on. Somehow it was understood to mean that the final victory of the Allies would end war for ever. But the blood of the German dead would remain unavenged; it would go on calling and calling through future years. War could never be ended by victorious war.

He had killed those two Germans in rage and hatred; he had raised a devil that would not die. This was the frightful thing he had done for his own dead, whom nothing could benefit. This it was to fight for one's country. He had opened a rift in the boundary of the human world, and beyond it there was lightless chaos. Himself was drifting out into blind blackness. Nothing could save him from it. He could not move or cry out. He was rigid with horror. He was floating in the air high above a red snake. It was the bloody Somme amidst a land of fiery desolation and inexpressible evil.

Someone was supporting him. It was Seddon. His face was puckered, there was a gash on his forehead, his eyes were dead. It was Beal; he was gigantic, he was terrible, he would cast him down. He shrieked and fell and fell.

There was a blinding light. Someone was saying, 'You're all right. You're all right'. A nurse was there, shading the light from his eyes. But the other, not this, was reality. He was sitting up in bed. The horror slowly diminished, and he said, 'I'm all right now'.

The northern voice complained. The nurse brought him some hot milk to drink. He was still awake when she came back an hour later, but he pretended to be asleep. Then dawn came, and he dozed until temperatures were taken.

He was examined during the morning. He could only blow the

mercury up to 105, and could only hold it at 40 for fifty seconds: his revs had dropped.

'How do you feel?' asked the doctor.

This was not an easy question.

'Tired?' the doctor prompted.

'Yes, tired. Not sleeping.'

'I see. Lost enthusiam for war-flying?'

The doctor made a note that he felt tired and had lost enthusiasm for war-flying. Then he sounded and tapped him, and finally wrote down F.S.D.

'Flying Sickness D.,' he said.

'D. for drink?' asked Tom.

'No. Debility. It's the usual phrase applicable to people in your state. Too much war-flying. You'll soon get over it.'

'That's good.'

'Of course you will. A month's sick leave and H.E. You'll be evacuated to-morrow morning. And while you're on leave, relax. Forget about the war and flying.'

'Forget?'

'So far as you can. Have a good time. Take your girl out — or girls, is it? Enjoy yourself. Finest thing for you so long as you don't overdo it.'

That night they gave him veronal, and he slept.

The morning was hazy, and the English coast did not become visible till the boat was within a few miles of it. The white cliffs. Then Folkestone, desolate in the sunshine. He remembered it crowded at this time of year.

After enormous delay the train started and rattled inland among the chalk hills. The warm autumnal afternoon was delicious. Green hedgerows again between green meadows and cornfields where reapers were busy. Beyond Ashford, the Weald. This was England. Wandering lanes, hedged and ditched; casual, opulent beauty, trees heavy with fulfilment. This was his native land. He did not care.